THE
EXES' REVENGE

THE
EXES' REVENGE

Jo Jakeman

BERKLEY / NEW YORK

BERKLEY
An imprint of Penguin Random House LLC
375 Hudson Street, New York, New York 10014

Copyright © 2018 by Jo Jakeman
Penguin Random House supports copyright. Copyright fuels creativity,
encourages diverse voices, promotes free speech, and creates a vibrant culture. Thank you for
buying an authorized edition of this book and for complying with copyright laws by not reproducing,
scanning, or distributing any part of it in any form without permission. You are supporting writers
and allowing Penguin Random House to continue to publish books for every reader.

BERKLEY is a registered trademark and the B colophon is a trademark
of Penguin Random House LLC.

Previously published in a Harvill Secker (Penguin Random House UK) hardcover edition as
Sticks and Stones.

Library of Congress Cataloging-in-Publication Data

Names: Jakeman, Jo, author.
Title: The Exes' Revenge/Jo Jakeman.
Description: Berkley hardcover edition. | New York: Berkley, 2018. |
Also published as a Harvill Secker (Penguin Random House UK) hardcover edition/July 2018. |
Identifiers: LCCN 2017058796 | ISBN 9780440000341 (hardback) |
ISBN 9780440000358 (ebook)
Subjects: LCSH: Abused wives—Fiction. | Abused women—Fiction. |
Abusive men—Fiction. | Revenge—Fiction. | Psychological fiction. |
BISAC: FICTION/Suspense. | FICTION/Contemporary Women. |
GSAFD: Suspense fiction.
Classification: LCC PR6110.A39 S75 2018 | DDC 823/.92—dc23
LC record available at https://lccn.loc.gov/2017058796

Harvill Secker (Penguin Random House UK) hardcover edition / July 2018
Berkley hardcover edition / September 2018

Printed in the United States of America
1   3   5   7   9   10   8   6   4   2

Jacket art: image of stairs by Tim Daniels/Arcangel; woman (left) by Elisabeth Ansley/Arcangel;
woman (center) by Peppersmint/Shutterstock; woman (right) by Taveesuk/Shutterstock
Jacket design by Emily Osborne
Book design by Laura K. Corless

For James

THE
EXES' REVENGE

CHAPTER 1

The day of Phillip's funeral

I expected to feel free, unburdened, but when the curtains close around Phillip Rochester's satin-lined coffin all I feel is indigestion.

Naomi perches in the front row, shifting uncomfortably as the congregation whispers at her back. There are creases under her eyes where cried-out mascara threads its way through the cracked veneer. I wonder what she's crying for because, after all he's done, I am certain that it is not for *him*.

The vicar talked of a man who bore so little resemblance to the Phillip that I knew that I almost shed a tear. It is a time for lies and cover-ups, not truthful observations.

I twist my wedding band with my left thumb. No engagement ring. *Too flashy, Immie. You're not that kind of girl.* Five hundred and forty-eight days have passed since Phillip left me. I know I should take the ring off, but no amount of soap can free me from the snare. Years of marital misuse have thickened my hands, my waist, and my heart.

I am sitting five rows back, in the seat closest to the wall, as befits the ex-wife. Though, in reality, am I his widow? We didn't finalize the divorce. The paperwork is still on the sideboard along with the unpaid bills and the condolence cards. Fancy that. Me. A widow.

Some might say I shouldn't be here at all. Friends from my old life try not to stare at me, but they can't help themselves. When our eyes bump into each other, there is a timid acknowledgment, an apology of sorts, before a gosh-look-at-the-time glance at wrists and a scurrying for the chapel door. Nobody called when Phillip traded me in. They went with him into his new life along with the Bruce Springsteen CDs and the coffee machine.

Mother sits by my side alternately tutting and sighing, unsure whether to be angry or sad. She promised not to speak during the service, and though the effort is nearly crippling her, she has kept her word. Her eyes burn holes into my temples. I know that her nostrils will be flaring like they always do when she is displeased. Mother tends to convey more through her eyes than her mouth, and I regret not telling her to keep those shut too.

We disagreed on whether Alistair should attend his father's funeral. She says that, at six years old, he is too young. I say that he should be here to say good-bye, to keep up the pretense that Phillip will be missed. Mother won. Some battles aren't worth fighting. We wrote notes attached to helium balloons instead. Up, up, and away. Bye-bye, Daddy. Rot in hell, Phillip.

There are simple flowers at the front of the crematorium and Pachelbel's Canon is piped in from an invisible source. Everything has been carefully orchestrated to whitewash the darkness of death and to disinfect the walls against the smell of decay. A palate cleanser, if you like, between death and the wake. Naomi has booked the function room at the Old Bell, but I won't go in case the sherry loosens my lips and I smile a smile that shouldn't be seen at a funeral.

As the mournful parade passes us by, we file out of our rows with the order of service in hand. Phillip's photograph on the front is a grotesque, grinning specter. It was taken before he was promoted to CID. A decade ago at least. I used to think he looked so handsome in that uniform.

Mother stands in line to pay her respects to Naomi. It will be a brief conversation as high opinion is in short supply. My best friend, Rachel, is talking to DC Chris Miller with a red shawl fastened about her shoulders. She refused to wear black. As she rightly pointed out, black is a sign of respect. Both she and Chris held Phillip in the same regard. I'd hoped it would be Chris leading the inquest into Phillip's death, but they've brought in someone from further afield. Neutral.

I'm aware of Ruby behind me, though I am careful not to make eye contact with her. She is wearing a diaphanous frock of fresh-bruise purple, the most somber outfit she owns. It's the first time I've seen her wearing shoes. Usually barefoot, sometimes in flimsy flip-flops. It's anyone's guess whether this is a nod to conformity or she has simply come equipped to dance on Phillip's grave. She sits at the back row, as far away from the coffin as she can get, and commensurate with her ex-*ex*-wife status. The first Mrs. Rochester, the woman that Naomi and I have been measured against, holds an icy-white tissue under her nose, a pomander against the contagion of grief.

I stand and edge my way past the eye-dabbers and the head-shakers until I feel the sun on my face and smell the freshly mown grass. I squint against the sudden glare and a treacherous tear escapes my eye.

A stranger touches his cold hand to my elbow in a shared moment of I-know-how-it-feels, but how could he? There are only three of us here—Naomi, Ruby, and I—who know how satisfying it feels to know that Phillip Rochester got the death he deserved.

3

CHAPTER 2

22 days before the funeral

The Barn was one of those new-old houses. Only one story, but never to be referred to as a bungalow. Large sand-colored bricks and small dark windows with their frames painted National Trust green show history has been given the once-over with a bleach wipe. Everything is reclaimed, sourced with the utmost integrity from salvage yards and auction houses. Old made to look new and new made to look old.

I'd never set foot inside of The Barn. It was laughable that barns were desirable residences rather than shacks for animals. Farmers made a fortune selling dilapidated sheds with planning permission, and I could think of no better habitat for Phillip and his heifer.

I rang the doorbell and waited as the echo of the bell chime ran off down the hallway. I adjusted my armor: handbag across my chest, leather gloves pulled tightly over my wrists, scarf wound about my neck like ribbons on a maypole.

It wasn't easy for me to see Phillip in his new life, in his new house, with his new girlfriend, but this wasn't about me. This was about Alistair.

We had agreed to be grown-up about the whole situation. Civil. For the sake of our son. But there was still the small matter of finalizing the divorce, and it wasn't bringing out the best in either of us.

On paper, we would split everything amicably down the middle.

For better, for worse.
For richer, for poorer.
In sickness and in health.

If it were left up to Phillip, I would be awarded worse, poorer, and sickness while he got the rest. My solicitor said no one won by going through the courts. I told her, where Phillip was concerned, I couldn't win anyway.

Alistair hadn't suffered when his father left us. In fact, he might have felt life was considerably better. I know I did. Alternate weekends were conducted through clenched teeth and false smiles. Lately, however, Phillip wanted more than I was willing to give. More family time with Alistair and a woman who wasn't family, more sleepovers where sleep was never had. The more he wanted to take, the less I wanted to give.

With calls going unanswered and solicitor's letters ignored, I'd agreed to have "a word" with Phillip, but, standing in front of The Barn as day tipped into night, I still hadn't made up my mind which word it would be.

I'd stretched out a gloved finger to press the bell again when I heard a door open. Footsteps getting louder.

The girlfriend answered the door wearing next to nothing. She was attempting to pass off a sash of denim across her hips as a skirt, and I wondered how high their heating bills must be. She folded her thin arms under her chest and leaned against the doorframe with a faint smirk tickling the corners of her mouth.

Her long red hair was out of a bottle, but I suppose it suited her pale skin and brown eyes. I was transfixed by her eyelashes, so thick and long. Real? False? Questions that could as easily have been about the woman. And the breasts.

"Imogen. What a nice surprise," she said.

She should've given her face fair warning before she spoke, because it betrayed her in her lie.

"Hello, Naomi. Is he in?" I asked.

"Not back yet."

"Can I come in and wait?"

"Does he know you're comin'?"

We looked at each other expectantly, she expecting me to go away and *I* expecting her to find some manners, though *my* manners stopped me from saying so.

"Come on in, then, but you'll have to tek off yer shoes."

She spoke with an unfamiliar, difficult-to-place twang that suggested north of Derbyshire and sheep farming. Perhaps that's why she felt at home in The Barn.

Out of politeness, I told her she had a lovely home and I wasn't even lying. The house smelled white—of vanilla, and lilies, and bedsheets drying in the sun. Everything was cream or soft gray, giving the impression of moving through low-lying clouds. *Beware of turbulence*, I thought. Her head snapped to look at me and I wondered whether I'd spoken out loud and out of turn.

"It's beautiful," I said. "Just beautiful."

She waited while I unzipped my boots. I saw her take in my odd socks and she seemed to grow two inches taller at the sight. I bristled, feeling shabby and unkempt beside her painted nails and stenciled eyebrows.

"Renovations have been a chuffing nightmare. The beams"—she pointed above our heads to the exposed rafters—"are the original beams of the local abbey. They reckon they used them to build the farm after the abbey burned down. There's a conservation order on 'em. We had to get special permission to open all this up, and even then we had to be dead careful what we did."

She'd adopted an air of false irritation that belied her pride in her home.

"Really?" I said. "Fancy all that fuss for secondhand wood."

I took off my gloves and scarf, folding and pushing them into my Mary Poppins bag to get lost among the used tissues, old receipts, and Pokémon cards.

Even without her being a weekend stepmum to my son, and only half my age, and weight, I still wouldn't have liked Naomi. People who didn't know what Phillip was like assumed I was jealous. If I complained about him, they thought I was bitter at being thrown over for a younger woman, and if the tables were turned, I might have thought the same. I didn't know Naomi, nor did I care to spend the time getting to know her. She'd be gone before long. From where I stood, she was shallow and self-obsessed. She was far too pretty to be a nice person, because the universe just didn't work that way.

Naomi made Phillip look good. She was the lover, the coconspirator, the neon sign that proclaimed his dick still worked. To the outside world, Phillip had found love again after the breakdown of our marriage. Or slightly before, if you read his text messages when he left the room. I was a single mother gripping onto the final years of her thirties. Left behind. A solitary battered suitcase, doing another lap on the airport carousel.

"Coffee or tea?" she asked.

"Is it filter coffee?"

"Instant."

"I'll have tea, thanks."

She held my gaze and blinked rapidly, eyelids tapping out Morse code for *cow*, then disappeared into the kitchen. I simply couldn't help myself. I found it impossible to make life easy for her.

The only drink I wanted was clear and served over ice, but how else would we survive awkward situations if we didn't *make* tea to fill our time, *hold* tea to busy our hands, and *drink* tea to stop our mouths from running away?

I looked around the sparsely decorated room, my hands playing with the strap on my handbag. Phillip hated clutter. He was too em-barrassed to bring people to our home, because I could never elevate it to his standards. I wondered whether he had made me fearful of mess or whether I'd always had the tendency. Of course, he was *Phil* nowadays. A reinvention. I wondered who he was trying to convince.

On the beech table beneath the window were thirteen mis-matched photo frames. Thirteen. I tensed. Good God, why were there thirteen? I picked up the picture of Phillip wearing a snorkel-ing mask and slid it into my bag between the folds of my scarf. Twelve. Far better. A curved, round, gentle number. My shoulders loosened and the flow of anxiety in my chest reduced to a mere trickle.

I smiled to myself, pleased I had defused a potentially difficult situation. The therapist had taught me some breathing exercises, but sometimes it was easier to remove the problem entirely. The last thing I needed was to have a panic attack in front of The Girlfriend.

I looked at the remaining, even-numbered photos. Phillip and Naomi on a beach, at a wedding, kissing dolphins. Naomi as Catwoman and Phillip as a plump Batman. It had been his standard party outfit through the years. His crime-fighting persona had always been important to him. Phillip had what I liked to call a hero complex. He failed the tests to become a firefighter and his poor attendance at school, and even poorer grades, barred him from the RAF, and though the uniform wasn't as seductive, the police force was good enough.

His job had even brought the lovely Naomi to his door. He told me about the woman who laughed uncontrollably when he caught her speeding. He'd implied that she was a dotty old dear who shouldn't be driving rather than an attractive adolescent who shouldn't be making sheep's eyes at another woman's husband.

Traffic violations usually went one of two ways. Either the drivers came up with excuses: being late, not seeing the signs, wife in labor, dying parent. Or they accused him of being a jobsworth; of conning innocent people out of their hard-earned money, asking why he wasn't out arresting real criminals.

But the woman at the wheel simply threw her head back and laughed.

"Do you know why I stopped you?" Phillip had asked.

"Because I'm an idiot?"

"This is a thirty-mile-an-hour zone."

"I weren't doing thirty," she said.

"What's so funny?"

"There's no point denying it, is there? That's the end of me license too. I've been collecting points like there's no tomorrow. If I don't laugh I'd cry."

I didn't find out until much later that he'd let her off the hook by suggesting he might have accidently captured the speed of the car traveling behind her. Of course, she couldn't wait to thank him, and there was only one thing that Phillip found as satisfying as getting the bad guy, and that was getting the girl.

Naomi slithered into the room, her footsteps absorbed by the plush carpet.

"Tea," she said, placing the cups on the pristine mirrored table. No grubby fingerprints from a small child or ring marks from cups and glasses.

"Thanks. I was just admiring your photos." I placed my body between her and the table so she wouldn't notice one was missing.

"Why?"

The question threw me. Why? Because I'm nosy? Because I want to know if your life is better than mine?

"I don't really know," I said. "They're nice, aren't they?"

She shrugged and sat heavily on the sofa. I perched opposite her and smiled.

It was the first time Naomi and I had been in the same room without Phillip circling us like a lion around his pride. I could have got some things off my chest. I could have launched into the wronged-wife routine. It would have been a good time for Naomi to apologize to me. Not that I minded her having Phillip—he was *her* problem now—but common decency should have pricked her conscience into addressing the tension between us.

Phillip and I should have brought our relationship to an end years before, but I clung to the dream of the childhood that had been denied to me. I'd grown up without a father and I didn't want Alistair to do the same. Some people call me stubborn; I prefer "determined." It wasn't the breakdown of our marriage that bothered me. I didn't look upon it as losing a husband but as gaining a nemesis. One more person to consider when I was hardly a people person at the best of times.

"Phil should've been back from work by now," she said, looking at the clock.

"Right," I said, and looked at the clock too. "Is he working today? Only I went by the station and they said he wasn't in work this week."

She didn't meet my eye. There was surprise behind the painted eyebrows but her voice was low and calm when she said, "I forgot. He's at the doctor's."

"Nothing serious, I hope?"

"What?"

"The reason Phillip's gone to the doctor?"

"Oh." She looked out the window, her thoughts somewhere else, a slight frown bringing her brows together. "No."

"That's a shame."

I reached for my drink, realizing I was sounding bitter and hating that Phillip brought out this side of me. My hand trembled at the effort of remaining calm and I spilled tea over the table. The milky pool dripped twice onto the cream carpet before I could get my hand underneath it.

Naomi flinched. A sharp intake of breath.

"Whoops!" I said. "Sorry about that."

Her body was rigid. Years of living with Phillip had made me an expert on body language and reading signals, like imperceptible vibrations in the air. I expected to feel her anger—another remnant of living with Phillip—but instead I saw something that unsettled me more.

Fear flashed across her face like a shooting star. It was instantaneous and I might have dismissed it had I not seen her hands. She rubbed the soft skin between her thumb and forefinger. I knew that fleshy spot. I remembered what it felt like. For a moment, neither of us moved. I stared at her.

A prickle of sweat coated my forehead, though I was suddenly cold. A door to the past had opened and memories blew in on a cold draft. Phillip used to bend my thumb back until I fell to my knees. Always the left hand too, just where Naomi was rubbing. That way it wouldn't get in the way of the housework, the ironing, the cooking of his dinner. He'd got the most from his police training. Maximum pain, minimum effort. It was barely more than a playground scuffle, nothing that would stand up in court, but I knew what it meant.

Naomi caught me looking and there was a jolt of recognition. Her eyes, wide with fear a moment earlier, narrowed and hardened. I opened my mouth to speak. So much to say and yet, as the words jostled to find the right order, Naomi stalked into the kitchen. My words of comfort floated up beyond the conserved beams and hung there like cobwebs.

I stood and looked back at the photos. The picture of Phillip with his arm around Naomi now looked like he was holding her a little too tightly. Her smile forced. No wonder there had been thirteen frames. Thirteen. Unlucky for some. Unlucky for her.

Naomi bustled back with a cloth and cleaning spray. She began dabbing at the beige spots on the carpet. She'd suddenly become fragile, as if light would pass through her and leave no shadow. I wanted to reach out, touch her shoulder, but the abrupt switch from scorn to sympathy had wrong-footed me.

"I am *so* sorry. Is there anything I can help you with?" I asked.

The question was ambiguous enough that it could have been about spilled tea or much, much more. Unspoken words cowered in corners.

"No. I'm fine."

"I never can remember which things are good for stains. Can you? There's salt, isn't there? But I think that's for red wine. I'm more likely to spill wine than tea in my house. Not that I drink more wine than tea . . . just, well, it's easier to spill, isn't it? Must be the glasses. Perhaps I should drink wine out of a mug."

I ventured a small laugh that was lost in the vast room.

She ignored me.

"Would you like me to go?"

The urge to flee was causing beads of sweat to gather on my top lip. The fight-or-flight response was making my heart pound quicker and I was in no mood for a battle.

She had wiped the table and most of the tea from the floor, but a faint mark remained on the carpet.

"Or I could stay if you want to talk to me about anything? You know, before Phillip gets home?"

She sat back on her heels and wiped a strand of hair off her heart-shaped face. I clutched my bag tightly and slowly lowered myself onto the arm of the sofa.

"Don't sit there! He don't like it if people sit on the arms."

I stood up quickly.

"Sorry. You were going to say?"

"Nothing. You should go."

"Are you sure?"

I glanced at the clock. *Phil should've been back by now,* she'd said.

He would be home at any minute. Ready for me to confront him about the divorce.

Or about bullying Naomi.

Or he would confront *me* about spilling tea on his impractical carpets. Confrontation suddenly didn't seem as important as self-preservation, so I rooted around in my bag, pushing the purloined picture to one side and retrieving a fat white envelope.

"Righty-ho. If you're sure there's nothing I can do?"

She sprayed the carpet and worried the mark in circular motions.

"Perhaps you could ask Phillip to call me? About the divorce papers. I mean, I'm sure you're as keen as I am to get this all . . . well, put behind us. Here, could I leave these with you in case his solicitor hasn't been forwarding them?"

I placed the envelope on the table as Naomi dabbed at the stain.

"I think a formal arrangement would benefit us all, don't you? Make sure that certain . . . responsibilities are met."

"You've got some nerve," she said, getting to her feet.

"Sorry?"

"You've been poisoning that boy against Phil since the day he left you."

"Me?"

"You're letting your bitterness at a loveless marriage—"

"That's really not what this is about!"

"—ruin Alistair's relationship with his dad and he'll grow up hating you!"

There was a silent second, a frozen instant where all I could hear was my own breathing. With our faces inches apart, I could see the anger in her eyes. She was embarrassed and lashing out. It was all too familiar.

This was my moment to tell her that I understood, that I knew what Phillip was capable of. But I breathed out and let the words disperse like dandelion seed heads on the breeze. Any sense of solidarity disappeared when she brought Alistair into this.

"Well, if that's how you feel . . ."

I walked from the room, pausing only to slip into my boots. Naomi shouted something about me sucking the joy out of life and about being jealous because I was left all alone. "A bitter old crone," she called me. I consoled myself with something like satisfaction. Well, I'd tried. What more could I do?

Naomi was still shouting as I closed the door softly behind me. Her outburst had given me the excuse I needed to walk away from her, and the life that used to be mine. Perhaps I should've been smiling as I started the engine and rejoined the high street. Maybe I should have been content that she wasn't living the picture-perfect life she portrayed.

But she was no different from me.

My shoulders hunched and an uneven percussion of tears fell into my lap. I was kidding myself if I thought I could ever be free of Phillip. Almost two years since he'd laid a finger on me, and yet, after five minutes with his girlfriend, it was as if the bruises were still fresh. I could feel his fingers digging into my upper arm, see his sneer as he called me useless.

I had been naive to think that the past would ever let me go.

CHAPTER 3

21 days before the funeral

Rachel caught my eye and nodded toward the lift. The phone on my desk was ringing and I put my hand up, fingers stretched, to show I'd be with her in five.

"Imogen speaking. How can I help?"

I took off my glasses and picked up my pen. Despite the smooth silence in my ear, someone was there. Their reticence to speak was disturbing. I shifted in my seat and watched the display on the telephone tick through the seconds. All I could hear was the *clack-clack-clack* of Claire's nails on her keyboard at the opposite desk.

"Hello?" I said, uncertain and tentative.

"Don't come to my house again," the voice said.

"Phillip?" I leaned back in my chair. "For a minute there—"

"If you've got something to say to me, use the phone like a normal person."

"I did try calling. Perhaps you didn't get my messages?"

"Did it occur to you that I might be busy?" His voice was terse.

"Well, yes, but—"

"I'll call back when I'm good and ready."

"Sorry, I—" As soon as the apology left my mouth, I wanted it back again.

I worked in an open-plan office where everyone pretended not to listen to each other's conversations. As little as a raised voice or a low whisper, and gossip-hungry ears would prick up. Wolves sensing prey. Eyes following ears, they would read humiliation in the pink spots on my cheeks. I kept my voice calm.

"I only wanted to . . . to . . ."

I lost the ability to speak in front of Phillip. Always quick to jump on my mistakes, laugh at my stutters and hesitations, he made it difficult for me to form coherent sentences.

". . . chase up on the paperwork. I was passing anyway, thought it might speed things up if I dropped the papers off. Have you looked at them yet?"

I waited for a response that didn't come. The silence on the telephone became dense.

"Phillip?" I said. "What do you think? Is there any chance you could get it signed and back to my solicitor by the end of the week?"

Still nothing.

I sat forward in my seat and looked at the display on the phone. It showed the date and time. Nothing else. The call had ended.

I kept the receiver to my ear, pressed it into me so that the back of my earring came close to puncturing the soft skin on my neck. There was sudden laughter from across the office. Opposite me, Claire looked up and tut-tutted.

"Right," I said to the hollow mouthpiece. "That would be perfect. Thank you."

Claire glanced at me and I cast my eyes skyward. *Husbands, eh?*

17

I counted to three.

"Don't be silly. There's no need to apologize. No. Really, I wouldn't use the word 'tosser' as such."

Count to four.

"You're too kind. Stop it—you're embarrassing me."

One. Two.

"You too. Take care. Bye."

I put down the phone, put on my glasses, and added a note to my to-do list. It now read:

1. Call school re: parents' evening.
2. Cash for child-minder.
3. Submit expense form.
4. Type up notes from meeting.
5. Kill Phillip in most painful way possible.

It took longer than it should have to compose myself. Claire declined my offer to bring her "something back," by waving a Tupperware box of home-prepared salad at me.

I took the lift to the café on the top floor. Windows reached from floor to ceiling, offering views of office blocks and cat's-cradle roads to the assembled caffeine-hunters who sniffed out coffee like a heat-seeking missile. The irresistible smell of midmorning muffins pulled us all in. Cardboard-cuffed paper cups taken to go identified Dominics and Sarahs in black Sharpie.

Rachel waved when she saw me, as if I wouldn't notice a six-foot blond with sunglasses on her head as soon as the lift doors opened. Rachel and I didn't go to the same places nor move in the same circles. In fact, I didn't move in circles at all. I zigzagged between work and home. Our paths would never have crossed if it hadn't been for a drunken Christmas party. She was the drunken one and I was the one holding back her hair.

She was younger than me, lived for the weekend, and was adamant that she would never get married. Her money was spent on spray tans, manicures, and Jäger bombs, while mine was spent on school uniforms, toilet roll, and milk shakes. And yet, she was the only person who knew how Phillip treated me.

I didn't have many friends. Phillip hadn't expressly forbade them, but he made it difficult for me to meet people and had discouraged me from inviting anyone to the house. The women I used to mix with were mostly the wives of his friends, and I could never confide in them in case it got back to Phillip.

Rachel had been a breath of fresh air. I'd first told her about Phillip's treatment of me when she was drunk and I was sure she'd forget, but Rachel was one of those drunks who, though she couldn't remember how to walk, would recall every confidence you'd whispered. She hadn't met Phillip, so hadn't been blinded by his charm. Phillip had been away on a golfing weekend—otherwise I wouldn't have been able to go to the party. Mother had babysat and I'd had my first night out without Phillip in five years.

Rachel had tracked me down in the office the following Monday and said she wanted to buy me lunch to say thank you for looking after her. In reality, she wanted to tell me to leave Phillip. It was an unlikely friendship but one I was grateful for. For months she urged me to leave him, and then, when he was the one who did the leaving, she threw me a party.

"I'd assumed the usual," Rachel said, pushing my coffee toward me.

"What? They do Merlot now?"

She laughed once, and loudly, so it was more bark than laughter.

"So," she said, "I've been reading . . ."

"Steady . . ."

"It's okay—there were pictures. Anyway, this article said the end of a marriage—even a crap one like yours—is huge, right? Even if you wanted it to end, you still need to, like, process it. And it's natural to be angry about it. You need to let it out of you."

"It's been eighteen months . . ."

"Yeah, and you still haven't moved on. You need to, like, hit something. And hard. So, I think we should join a boxing class."

"Rachel . . ."

"No, hear me out. It's for women only. It's called Rum Punch or something. What do you think?"

"I've decided to practice the ancient and long-forgotten art of forgiveness. I'm doing okay, Rach, trust me. Anyway," I said, "back to what I wasn't saying . . ."

"Passive-aggressive. That's what you are. You'd be better off smacking her. Or him. Or both. Get it out of your system. And you really need to start dating again."

"I can't. Not while Alistair is still so young. Anyway, will you listen? I have news."

She sat back and took a sip of foamy coffee, ignoring me.

"I *know* people," she said. "I could have Phillip . . . *neutralized.* There was this guy I was dating at Christmas and he—"

"Your loyalty is appreciated, even if it is the tiniest bit scary, but I read that the best revenge you can take is to live your life to the fullest."

"And how is that working out for you?" she asked.

"Listen," I said. "Phillip is acting strangely."

Rachel sucked at the froth on the top of her coffee and raised an eyebrow.

"I went to see him yesterday about signing the divorce papers and guess what?"

"What?"

"He wasn't there. And then this morning he phoned me and told me to stay away from the house."

"And this is strange because . . . ?" Rachel asked.

"Because Naomi said he was at work. But I'd already been to his work and *they* said he wasn't in and he wasn't expected back anytime soon. Then Naomi said he must be at the doctor's, but when I went by the surgery his car wasn't there."

I looked at her triumphantly. She leaned in closer with her elbows on the table.

"So," she said, "putting aside the fact that you're stalking your ex and are two, maybe three steps away from boiling his bunny . . . I still don't get it."

"I think he's having another affair."

Rachel shook her head but she wasn't surprised.

"Did you tell Naomi?"

"God, no. I spilled my tea and then she went all . . . well, peculiar. She freaked out and I had to leave. Besides, it's not really my place."

"Of course it is. Don't you wish someone had told you when Phillip started knobbing Naomi?"

"If I recall clearly, someone did, and that someone was you."

"You're welcome."

A secret was no longer a secret once it was shared. Rachel reminded me of that fact almost daily. She was the person I confided in when I wanted to have confirmation of how terrible my life was, or have her rip Phillip to shreds, but if I wanted sympathy, or my innermost thoughts kept between the two of us, then Rachel was not top of the list. But then, as lists go, it was a short one.

Rachel was an advocate of honesty being the best policy. She'd yet to come across any thought that would remain better off unsaid. Perhaps that was why I didn't tell her the whole story.

I didn't want to believe my own eyes. If Phillip really was abusing Naomi, how could I sit by and watch? Once I admitted it to Rachel, I would have to intervene. Until I was sure what was happening, I would keep it to myself. It was a cowardly way to behave, but I still wasn't a match for Phillip even with Rachel by my side.

"I don't like to gossip," I said.

"Oh, bless you, but it's not gossip when it's in the other person's best interest. Think of it as 'information dissemination.' Imagine telling the tart that Phillip is doing the hokey-pokey at someone else's shindig." Her eyes sparkled at the thought and she held up her index finger.

"*Numero uno*, he gets his balls sliced off as he sleeps because, as we know, she is a psycho bitch."

"Do we know that? Because—"

"*Numero duo*"—she held up two fingers—"she gets that smug look knocked off her Botoxed face . . ."

"I don't think she's had Botox. That's just how skin looks when you're in your twenties."

"And *numero* trio—"

"I don't think that's Italian—"

"—you get to sleep soundly at night, knowing that you have saved another woman, albeit a cheating witch, from going through the same bollocks that you did."

I smiled. "You have a fair point."

"Indeed I do."

She inclined her head graciously.

"And if it was that simple, maybe I would. But he's Alistair's dad.

What affects Phillip affects us all. I just want things to be . . . I don't know . . . *normal* between us. We'll be coparents for the rest of our lives and I want to enjoy Alistair's graduation, and wedding, and the birth of his children without feeling awkward every time I'm in a room with Phillip. I never want Alistair to feel he has to choose which parent to invite to important events. I never want him to worry about hurting our feelings."

"He's six, babe. There's still time for Phillip to get run over by a bus."

I laughed.

Rachel took my hand and stared hard into my face until I returned her gaze. "Stop worrying about stuff that might never happen. Alistair won't thank you for being a doormat."

I felt myself color. I didn't want to be a pushover, but it wasn't in anyone's interest for me to cause a scene.

"Anyhoo," she said, dropping my hand and picking up her coffee. "How are you fixed for Friday night? I'm thinking double date . . ."

CHAPTER 4

20 days before the funeral

There had been love between Phillip and me once. Difficult to believe it now, I know, but there was a time when he doted on me and I would have done anything for him. I hadn't needed anyone else but Phillip and our baby.

The baby *before* Alistair.

As late-afternoon sun bled into the fields I stood and brushed the dirt from my knees. Crocus spears covered the ground early thanks to a mild winter. New green leaves unfolded around me while soft white clouds brushed over the horizon, lit golden from beneath, as they hurried after the setting sun. The first butterflies of the season swooped and fell like streamers in the breeze. I didn't believe in reincarnation—didn't believe in anything really—but I often looked out for signs that *she* was still with me.

I would have called her Iris, if she had lived. The messenger of the gods, the personification of the rainbow, the symbol of hope. When she was taken from me, I mislaid the little bit of hope I had set aside for a rainy day. I was yet to find its hiding place. Every time I saw a rainbow I thought of her reaching out to me and telling me she was okay. That *I* would be okay.

It was the anniversary of the day she should have been born. I could not, would not remember the date of her death, but every spring I would go to the place where I had lost her and say sorry. As far as the world was concerned, she had never existed. She was a note on my medical file and a scar on my heart.

Grief, when it comes, takes many forms. I had lost enough people from my life to have experienced them all. But the tears shed following the death of someone close to you were nearly always the tears of the future. People cry for what will never be, the days they won't spend together, the celebrations they will miss, the conversations they will never have. They are the tears of absence.

This year she would have been eight glorious years old. I wrote a card and bought a gift, just as I would have done if she had lived, and spent the afternoon thinking of what might have been. I spoke to her as if she were in my arms and I told her stories of her little brother and how much I missed her.

Rachel sat in the car. She didn't have children, said she never would, but she knew what Iris meant to me. She would drive me to pick up Alistair from the child-minder and order pizza for our supper. Hot and spicy for me, cheese and tomato for Alistair. She wouldn't ask me how I felt nor shed tears of her own. She was there to pick me up when I fell, and top up my wineglass when it was empty.

Phillip never spoke about that night anymore. Didn't wonder out loud, *What if?* Her death didn't alter his course, yet it had knocked me off my axis and spun me out of control. That's not to say it didn't affect him. He was different after that night. We both were. Phillip became crueler, angry at the world. It was his way of coping, I guess. But it seemed, after that night, he always kept me at arm's length.

Sometimes I'd look at Phillip and see him, as he should be, twenty years from now, gray haired, in a morning suit, walking Iris down the aisle. She'd look beautiful and he'd look proud. A significant event wiped out in the turn of a wheel. A future, a dream destroyed.

Our marriage became a minefield to be navigated with caution. I used to wish that I had died in the accident rather than live with the pain of loss. Most people were scared of death. I was afraid of life.

When I think about it now, it unfolds as if it were happening to someone else. The car had appeared from nowhere and retreated to the same place. Hit and run, the police called it, but that sounded like a game of cricket. End of the over. All out.

In those first months, the only thing I lived for was to find out who'd done this to me and who had killed my unborn child. How could I forgive them if I didn't know who had been behind the wheel of that car? How could I put it all behind me if I never heard them apologize? The only reason I had to get out of my hospital bed was so that I could stand and look them in the eye. I'd sworn the car that hit me had been black, dark green maybe, but when they retrieved paint samples from the bushes they said they were looking for a blue car. I scanned every blue car I saw in the following weeks for signs of damage or repair, fancying myself an amateur sleuth who would find the person who was eluding the police.

Months passed and no one was charged. I swore at Phillip, and he swore back. He worked late following up leads, checking with more and more garages out of town. They were called and visited, especially those known to the police for operating on the wrong side

26

of the law, but no one had brought in a car with damage that was consistent with having mown a pregnant woman down in the street.

Phillip wasn't officially allowed to be on the investigating team, but those who were working on the case were his friends and they told him they'd keep him in the loop and that they'd "catch the bastard." I drew up my own shortlist, of people he'd arrested, those who might hold a grudge, but he wouldn't listen. He was hurt that I'd dream of suggesting it was something to do with the job that he loved, as if by "doing the right thing" he had brought grief to our door.

When his ex-wife, Ruby, sent me a letter suggesting that "these things happen for a reason," I accused her too. I knew she hated me and wanted Phillip back. Had he checked Ruby out? Where was she that night? What car was she driving nowadays? But he threw his plate against the wall and shouted, *"Enough is enough!"* I never trusted her after that—though, in fairness, I'd never trusted her, period.

Phillip visited me at the unit, where they talked in hushed tones and gave me tablets to make me float over the pain. Not that I minded the solitude. The quietness. The kindness. Phillip was considerate in understated ways. He didn't talk about his feelings, or ask about mine, but while I was in the hospital he did his best to dispose of things that would remind us of what we'd lost. He replaced the nearly new car with an extra roomy trunk for a baby carriage, had taken the stair gate and bassinet to the charity shop, and given away all the books on pregnancy and contented babies.

It wasn't my first encounter with depression, but it was my most significant. When I was sent home with a pocket full of Prozac, it was there. Its clothes hung in the wardrobe, its toothbrush still in the bathroom like it had just popped out, door on the latch, and coming back at any minute. Even now I sometimes caught its scent when I walked into the room.

Phillip would tell you I started to lose my mind about that time. His affairs, his brutality—they were my fault. The first affair, and the second, I forgave him for. I accepted their inevitability. He was searching for attention that I was reticent to give. There was no point dwelling on the past, he'd say. With the third affair and the fourth, I stopped pretending to care. He was hurting too, he said, but I would drive a saint to distraction with my constant weeping. Chin up. Life goes on.

Except for the baby's. Hers was forever suspended somewhere between my heart and my mind.

I locked my grief away. I took it out when I was alone at night, when Phillip was working, and when I was sure that no one would catch me crying. I didn't tell him when I fell pregnant with Alistair. I waited and waited, fearing the worst, not letting myself hope. But then it was real. A pulsing heartbeat and a grainy image. A second chance. I barely left the house after that. I wasn't going to let it happen again. No one was going to take my baby this time.

For one day each year I would think about Iris and then I would spend the evening being thankful for Alistair. There was no point in worrying about what I didn't have when what I *did* have was so precious.

I was tired but calm after a day thinking about my daughter as Rachel and I pulled up outside the child-minder's house. I couldn't wait to collect Alistair and hear all about his day at school, whom he'd played with and what he'd learned. I loved him with a power that hurt. And that was why I was slow to get out of the car and why

I was measured in each step I took toward the neat semidetached house with the miniature windmill in the front yard. Self-reproach trumps joy. I hated that someone else knew more about his day than I did.

Another woman would tell me whether he'd done his homework, and how he'd been when she picked him up from school, and what he'd had for his dinner, and I felt each of her words as a sharpened arrow of judgment to my conscience.

Alistair was younger than six in all the ways that counted. He slipped into his sixth year while the labels in his clothes still read "4." He was in a "big-boy" bed when he was anything but. Six candles. Six friends to tea. Six bumps. Six years of making the world a sweeter place through cuddles, sticky kisses, and smiles. Alistair. A cinnamon-scented stretch of a boy yet to find control of his limbs and emotions. Holding on to his infant ways like a favorite pair of threadbare pajamas.

I could see him at the window. He had his coat on and I knew he would have been wearing it for the past twenty minutes asking, "Is it time yet?"

I rang the doorbell even though I could see his blue duffle coat through the little window and knew he was reaching for the lock that he was still too short to reach. I wriggled my fingers at him and his face creased to show dimples so deep that you could lose kisses in them.

Ella opened the door, smiling, in her apologetic way, from beneath her fringe, and ushered me through to the warm hip-high cuddle of my boy. She was skinny with a mass of curls and an oversized mouth like a child's drawing of a stick woman. The school lunch smell of gravy and mash lingered in the hallway. Finger paintings and photos on wood-chipped walls led upstairs, where toys and books were neatly stacked. Music played in the kitchen, a kid's television program keeping Ella's youngest child rooted in her high chair and Mummy's hands free to deal with the paying guest.

"Mummy, Mummy, Mummy!"

"Hey there, buster." I pulled him onto my hip and kissed his hair.

"Everything okay?" I asked Ella.

Ella's rubber mouth twisted to one side and then drooped at the corners.

"Well . . ."

"Go get your schoolbag, Alistair. And find your shoes." I plopped him down and he scurried away.

"It's fine *really*, but we did have a little accident. And then we tried to cover it up. Said he didn't know he'd wet himself. These things do happen to little ones from time to time. We've dealt with it now."

"That's not like him." I watched him down the corridor, concerned that something had upset him, and embarrassed that Ella had dealt with it instead of me.

"And it's probably nothing, but . . ."

Alistair came running back into the hallway and barreled into my knees.

"Where are your shoes?"

He dropped his bag and ran back to the kitchen.

"We did use a naughty word today. He called me a *b-i-t-c-h*."

The word was spelled out in crisp syllables, her lips enunciating each letter so that I would be in little doubt as to what she was saying, or to the gravity of the situation. She closed her eyes and shook her curls as if the very act of spelling such a word caused her a great deal of personal anguish.

"No. Really? I don't know where he's heard that kind of—"

"Says he heard it from you."

"Did he?"

"Along with a poem about beans being good for your heart?"

"God! Sorry. That probably *was* me. Funny at the time but in hindsight . . . Have you got those shoes, Al? We need to move. Rachel's waiting in the car."

"Obviously, we don't like to encourage that kind of language. But given your situation, poor lamb . . ."

"Situation?"

"Broken home." She overenunciated again, and I rushed into the kitchen to find Alistair transfixed by the television as vegetables sang a song to a ginger-haired man in a hat.

"Shoes on? Good. What do you say to Ella?"

"Beans, beans, good for your heart—"

"Okay, thanks, then."

I took Alistair's warm hand in mine and pulled him out of the house.

"We'll see you next week," I said.

"Beans, beans, they make you—"

"Bye!"

I slammed the door. Ella always made me feel like a fraud, like she was the perfect mother. Or was that my own insecurity leaching into the evening air? I took Alistair's bag from him and walked to the car idling at the curb. Rachel was uncharacteristically immobile in the driver's seat. Usually she would hang out the window or blast inappropriate music from the stereo to make Alistair laugh. But something had changed in the five minutes since I had left the car. I could see, sitting by her side in the passenger seat of the car, the unmistakable outline of Phillip Rochester.

CHAPTER 5

16 days before the funeral

I t was gray out. Cold too. I squinted through the kitchen window but the raindrops were too fine to see. They were polishing the patio with their touch and darkening the soil, but they landed so lightly you wouldn't have known they were falling. I pulled my jumper down past my wrist. Three bruises, the size of grapes, on the top of my wrist, one slightly larger, oval underneath. A thumbprint. They would fade, and until they did, I would hide them. And not because I was protecting Phillip either, but because I was excusing myself from the questions and the pitying looks. I was sick of being Imogen Rochester the victim.

Mother was on her way, but our Sunday lunches weren't a time for honesty and soul-searching. They were another box to be ticked on the long list of Things Normal People Do. She got to spend time with her grandson and I got to be made to feel like I couldn't cope.

Phillip had been all smiles when he had turned up unexpectedly outside of Ella's house on Wednesday. The way he always was when there were witnesses. Hair tousling for Alistair, and "Have you grown again?" Ignoring the fact that Alistair was jumping up and down like an overexcited dog wanting to be picked up. And for me, "Might I have a quick word?"

At first, I'd thought he'd remembered. I let myself believe that Iris was on his mind too, and that he'd come to share a moment with me. But then I saw the look in his eyes.

We walked a few steps away from the trunk of the car while Alistair climbed into the backseat. Phillip's hand was on my wrist, viselike, as tight as his smile.

He stood so close to me I had to tilt my head back to look up at his face. He was an inch below six feet, though he was prone to round up if asked.

"I read those papers," he said. "Who's your solicitor? Mickey Mouse?"

I tried to pull my arm from him, but he tightened his grip.

"I said you wouldn't like it, Phillip, but unreasonable behavior can cover a whole host of things. If it's a problem, we could always divorce on the grounds of your adultery?"

He shook his head as he looked me up and down. It was written all over his face: what had he ever seen in me?

"You'll get your divorce," he said, "but not because of your lies."

He dug his thumbnail into my wrist as he dropped it. Reputation was everything to Phillip, though he was yet to work out that it was easier to manage if you didn't sleep with other women behind your wife's back.

He reached inside his pocket and pushed a slim envelope into my hand. It was bent at the edges, where it had curved around his body.

"Change of plan," he said. "I'm divorcing *you*."

"I don't care whose name's on it, Phillip. I just want it done."

I should have known it wouldn't be acceptable for someone like Phillip to be the passive party in this. It was the principle of the thing. Phillip Rochester divorced on the grounds of his unreasonable behavior? Unthinkable.

He stepped closer to me and lowered his voice. "And if you're not out of my house by the end of the month . . . you don't get your divorce."

"What?"

"You heard," he said.

"Don't be so ridiculous. It's our home. Where are we meant to go?"

"Not. My. Problem. But if you don't leave that house when I say, I'll fight you every step of the way. Do you think you're cleverer than me? Because you're not. I'll see to it that you don't get a single thing. I'll blow the lot and declare myself bankrupt before I let you take a penny. What will you do then, without me paying your bills? No maintenance, no child support. Do you think your pathetic salary will put food on the table? Get out of my house and then, when I sell it, you'll get a fair share of the profits."

"Why can't we put it on the market while we're still living in it?"

"End of the month, Imogen. Or else."

At home, Rachel looked at the papers Phillip had handed me and swore. She told me to burn them, to stuff them down his throat, to make copies of them and show everyone what a bastard he really was. Then, when her anger began to subside, she told me to make an appointment with my solicitor and take Phillip for all he was worth.

"Come on," she said. "You can't be considering this? He's bluffing. Phillip declare himself bankrupt? He'd rather die. He's got this place and he's got The Barn. Between them, they must be worth a fair bit."

"He remortgaged this place to get the deposit for the new place, and from what he says, he's taken on a hefty mortgage over there."

"You let him take money from here to buy a place with that tart?"

"I didn't let him; I just didn't stop him. He owns half this house—it seemed reasonable at the time."

As we talked it over, it seemed ridiculous that I would simply pack up and go. I was still getting used to this new reality where Phillip didn't have any say in what I did. But just in case, I asked Rachel if we could move in with her until the financial settlement was agreed and I could get Alistair and me somewhere small. Safe.

She said no.

"Babe, you know I love you, but I will not let you roll over and play dead every time he confronts you. He can't kick you out of the house. Any sane-minded court will let you stay. It's the way it goes when kids are involved. Phillip doesn't have a leg to stand on. He's got no leverage."

And for a moment, I almost believed her.

The back door opened as I pulled the pot roast out of the oven in a cloud of spectacle-fogging steam. A glass of wine in the pan. Two in the chef.

"Hello, darling."

"Mother."

I pressed my cheek upon hers and she shook out her umbrella. She patted down her hair, a sleek silver bob, never a strand out of place.

"Ghastly weather out," she said, affronted by the incessant drizzle.

"Good for the garden," I said.

We had a strained relationship. Stretched to the point of no flexibility. Perhaps we had a better relationship before my father died, though I hardly remembered that time at all. Funny how death becomes a milestone for life, a before and an after.

She often banished me from her presence, as if the sight of me could bring on "one of her heads." Mother said I reminded her too much of *him.* The same wavy light brown hair, wide blue eyes, and whirlpool dimples that had been passed from Father to me, and from me to Alistair. A genetic baton in life's relay race. I liked to think that I was a lot like my father in temperament as well as looks. He loved books as much as I did, whereas Mother said reading was the favorite hobby of the bone-idle.

"When I think of the hours," she said, "the *hours* you could spend doing something useful instead of being away with the fairies. Your once-upon-a-time and your happily-ever-after is only setting you up for a lifetime of misery. And besides, it's getting in the way of you washing the pots."

I used to hide books from her the way that other teenagers would hide booze and cigarettes. Wilkie Collins beneath my mattress; Daphne du Maurier under the rug; Louisa May Alcott secreted between layers of winter jumpers. I dreamed of owning a bookshop that served cakes and tea, where books would be read out loud and no one would judge. I'd have a system for matching books to readers based on their mood and their need, with comfy chairs and blankets. And then Phillip Rochester breezed into my life like Darcy and Heathcliff rolled into one and I was lost.

"No Yorkshire puddings?" Mother asked, looking to the oven.

"No."

"Probably for the best."

I put the kettle on to boil and pretended I didn't see her shake her head in disgust as I fetched gravy granules from the cupboard. She picked the cutlery off the kitchen table, sighed, and gave it a polish.

We sat opposite each other, Mother and I, while Alistair sat to my right. I sipped my Malbec and Mother frowned over her roasties. Conversation flowed smoothly, and by "smoothly" I mean that Mother talked and I listened. The floozy upstairs had a gentleman caller again. The milkman forgot her eggs again. The country was going to the dogs again.

Inevitably the conversation turned to Phillip and I shot Mother a look that, I hoped, warned her about what she said in front of Alistair.

"Divorce is nothing to be proud of, Imogen."

"Never said it was."

"Do you know what would make *me* proud?"

"Not a clue."

"Learning to stand on your own two feet." She lined up her cutlery and folded her napkin.

"Let me tell you one thing," she continued. "If you're waiting for another man to come along and sweep you off your feet, you've got another think coming. No man wants to raise someone else's child. And if I were you, if someone said he *was* interested, I would be suspicious. You'd probably find his name on the sex offenders list."

"Mother!"

"What's a six offender?" Alistair asked.

"Ice cream, Ali?" I asked. "We've got chocolate."

I scraped the plates as Alistair licked his bowl and Mother

looked through the mugs for one that met her standards. I was desperate for them to leave so that I could let my thoughts off the leash. I had resigned myself to the fact that I wouldn't meet anyone else to share my life, my bed.

Alistair had to come first. And yes, I was scared that I might never be loved again. But worse still was the realization that I had never been loved at all—not by Father, who chose to leave me at the end of a rope; not by Mother, who wished she'd never had me; not by my husband, who was off as soon as he found a better offer. Perhaps I was loved by my son, though he had little choice in the matter. I was doing my best to make myself worthy of his love.

"Swimming in half an hour," I said. "You don't want to be late."

She was a better grandmother than mother, though that wasn't saying much. Alistair was easy to love and she'd always wanted a son. I'd known this from an early age, and in case I forgot, she still reminded me from time to time. That's when she wasn't picking holes in my parenting techniques or my dress sense, my cooking, the cleanliness of my house, my weight . . .

I took my tea into the yard. Though the sky was still somber, the rain had let up. I sat on the tree swing, which was a present I'd bought myself last summer.

I looked back to the house that had been my home since before Alistair was born. A light glowed from deep within where he was getting ready. He lived with a simple innocence that came from believing that everything would be all right with the world. He knew only love and security; he was not old enough to know the ways in which life could cut him down. If Phillip got his way, this time next month we'd be living in a home that didn't have Alistair's height marked on a wall in black marker pen. If I gave in, we would no longer live in a house where he'd taken his first steps, said his first words, nor be able to sit in the backyard where he'd learned to ride his bike. I knew the memories were portable, but they would lose their strength, fade, if I had to recall them out of context.

It began to rain again, and I felt cold specks on the top of my head. If Phillip was having an affair—and all the signs pointed to the fact that he was, *again*—was she the reason he wanted us out of the house? It made sense that he would need somewhere else to live if he was leaving Naomi, but I wouldn't let him take our family home because of the poor decisions he'd made.

Since he was seventeen, Phillip had never been single. Not even for a day. Most of his relationships overlapped. He thought it proved how irresistible he was, but I knew that he was insecure and needed constant validation. At the risk of sounding like his first wife, Ruby, he needed the love of other people because he hadn't learned how to love himself. Not that I ever wanted to agree with the woman, but she had a point. He took offense too easily; he lashed out when he was hurt. He was a child who needed constant soothing. The fact that he was being so difficult at the moment showed that someone, or something, had upset him. From what I'd seen at The Barn, my money was on Naomi. She didn't look bright enough to have worked out that you don't poke a wasps' nest.

CHAPTER 6

16 days before the funeral

I'd drunk too much—a common side effect of Sundays with Mother. But instead of the warm glow of a bottle of 12.5 percent in my stomach, it had turned to acid, causing my insides to squirm, my mouth to dry, and my eyes to be slow to focus.

"Since when have you had a Mercedes?" I asked Rachel as the traffic light turned to green.

The orange streetlights lit her face. *On. Off. On. Off.* She squinted at the road signs and looked over her shoulder.

"Not mine. I'm in the wrong bloody lane. Yes, thank you, asshole. No need to flash. What a surprise . . . an Audi driver. Do you think car dealerships make them take, like, a Myers-Briggs personality test and say, 'Yes, sir, you are a complete wanker. You should drive an Audi'?"

"What do you mean, not yours?"

"It's Mario's. I accidently swiped right and ended up on a date with him."

"God, sorry! You were on a date?"

"No. That was Friday."

"But you've still got his car?" I asked.

"He's not gone home yet. If you'd let me set you up, you could've had a nice ride for the weekend. And I'm not talking about the car either."

We were on our way to the hospital. They hadn't given out much information on the telephone, only that Mother had passed out at the swimming pool and they would like to keep her in for observation. I was halfway out the door with car keys in hand before I realized I'd drunk the best part of a bottle of wine. Rachel would take Alistair home for me and put him to bed while I stayed with Mother at the hospital. Perhaps I should have called Phillip. Perhaps if he had been a better father, I would have. I was still reeling from our confrontation on Wednesday and was in no mind to forgive him.

"Is he Italian?" I asked.

"Who? Mario?" She shook her head. "Why d'you ask?"

"The name?"

"No. At least, I don't think so. It's probably not his real name anyway. He's probably called Stuart or Colin or something sensible. No one tells the truth in the world of online dating, do they?"

"Don't they?"

"Jesus, no. As far as Mario is concerned, my name is Amber Conway. You know, your porn star name?"

Sensing my confusion, she elaborated. "It's the name of your first pet and then the street you grew up on."

"In that case," I said, "I'm Poker Paddocks."

"Ha! That's a more specialist industry, that is."

She came into the hospital with me only to wish Mother a speedy recovery and whisk Alistair away. I tried to leave with them, saying,

41

"You probably need some rest, Mother." But something about Mother's limp arms and slack face kept pulling me back to her bedside.

She was frail. Her eyes were open, but she looked through me as if she could see something that I couldn't. She'd used all her charm on Rachel, and now that I was the only person there, there was no need to raise a smile. I didn't understand why she liked Rachel so much. I knew why *I* liked her, but she was so different, so removed from how Mother thought a woman should behave, that it amazed me that she smiled whenever she saw Rachel. She would wag her finger at Rachel as she described her escapades, but then call her a "firecracker."

I moved my chair to let a nurse get by. He checked the time and looked at the bag of clear liquid suspended above Mother, dripping via a needle into the back of her hand.

"What's this for again?" I asked.

"Fluids," he said. "Her blood pressure's a little low, which might be due to dehydration."

"And apart from her shoulder"—I pointed to the freshly slung arm—"there's no other damage?"

He shook his head and wrote in a folder before putting it in the sleeve at the end of the bed.

Mother drifted off to sleep with her mouth open, but she didn't look peaceful. The lines on her face were battle scars from fighting sleep and tackling unsavory dreams. I took her hand in mine and looked at the bruise surrounding the cannula. There were callused purple walnuts where her knuckles should have been. Her thin wedding band was loose about her skeletal fingers but would never slip over engorged finger joints swollen with time. I wondered why she still wore it but then looked to my own wedding band and almost laughed aloud. Both of us, a pair of idiots. Still pretending we were anchored to men who had drifted long ago.

There were many reasons why I'd kept my wedding ring, but none of them told the whole picture. I had meant every word of my wedding vows, and in my mind I was still Phillip's wife "until death do us part." The thin platinum band also kept away any chancers who thought they could chat me up, and it hid the truth that I was a single woman when all around me were married. It hinted that I was loved and lovable, instead of discarded and disgraced. It was my comfort blanket. And it was also stuck there until I lost ten pounds.

I stroked Mother's hand with my thumb. The hands that had peeled a thousand potatoes, knitted hundreds of jumpers, and wiped noses and knees were weakening with age. Those hands would be my hands one day. Skin thinning with use and veins bulging with the effort of keeping my heart beating.

Visiting hours had finished and the patients were shuffling to and from the bathroom with wash bags and towels. The hospital took on a cotton-wool sound. Padded to the point of no echo. Clocks ticked slower, voices were lower, the ward was bedding down for the night. I stood carefully so as not to wake Mother, and slipped past her to the nurses' station.

"Do you think she'll be home tomorrow?"

"We've not found a reason for her collapse yet. Call after the ward rounds in the morning and we should know more."

"Okay. Will you tell her I'll be back in the morning?"

I staggered through the windowless corridors, weary with worry and strain. I wanted to get home to Alistair and leave the quiet and aged imposter wearing my mother's face far behind me. Night air slapped my face as I stepped from the stuffy, airless building into the star-pimpled night. Patients in gowns huddled outside the hospital door under a cloud of cigarette smoke. I skirted around them over the open square to where taxis glowed like fireflies. I didn't notice the small woman scurrying in the dark until I collided with her. She faltered in her step as she looked to check if I was all right. She held a dark cloth to the side of her head, and her long red hair was matted down one side of her face.

"Naomi?"

"Shit. What're you doing here?" she said.

"Visiting. What are *you* doing here?"

She looked at the illuminated lights of the ER and then back at me. She hadn't wanted anybody to see her—least of all me—but knowing that some things can't be undone, she asked, "I don't s'pose you've got a minute, have you?"

We sat in awkward silence as the chairs in the waiting room emptied. Broken wrists, cut fingers, dizzy spells were acceptable maladies that were nothing to be ashamed of. And then there was Naomi. And me. An unlikely pairing.

"Is there someone I could call?" I asked. "A parent? A friend?"

"Haven't really got any. Foster kid," she added by way of explanation. "Don't know where half me family are and the other half are dead."

She stared ahead, careful not to meet my eyes, which tripped from her cut face to her wet hair and her stained clothes.

"I'm not saying it were my fault," she said. "I'm not daft. But I should know better than to say them things to him when he's in a mood and I'm backed into a corner with nowhere to run. Nan always said I didn't have the sense I were born with."

The shoulder of her gray sweatshirt was black with blood spots and there were rusty smears across her jeans. She was scraping at the stains with her thumbnail. Blood had dried around her eye and caked in her eyebrow.

Now that we were in the light I could see that she had a gash across her forehead that led up into her hairline. Her bottom lip was swollen and cracked.

"What happened?" I asked.

"He pushed me over and I split my head open. That's about all there is to it."

"But why?"

"Doreen Maclaren?" a nurse called.

An elderly woman got gingerly to her feet, helped by a younger man, her son maybe. She was cradling her arm as if it would fall off if she let it go. Naomi and I watched as she went by.

"You know," I said, "if it helps, I *will* believe you. Whatever it is that you tell me about him . . . I've probably experienced something similar. I doubt anything you could say would shock me."

"When you know stuff you can't unknow it."

"Hit me with it."

As soon as the sentence left my mouth, I cringed at my choice of words, but if she was offended, she didn't show it. She moved in her seat until our shoulders were touching and spoke quietly, barely moving her lips.

"He were complaining about work. I said to him, 'You're full of shit. Imogen's told me you've not been in work for ages.'"

I cringed. Had I caused this?

Naomi picked at the skin around her thumbnail.

"And then what?" I asked, though I wasn't sure I wanted to hear the answer.

"He did his nut. Went full-on psycho. 'Who do you think you are, checking up on me?' Then he kicked over the coffee table and it broke in half. The mirror bit? Just clean in two. Then he pushed me and I s'pose I hit my head but I didn't feel anything at first. And he were screaming at me, 'Look what you made me do! Couldn't keep your nose out, could you?' But he weren't worried about me—it were the table he were upset about. And I was like, 'You know what? I've had enough. We're done.'

"Anyway, he slammed out of the house and were gone. Just like that. Pissed off in, like, two minutes. He went from mad and scream-ing to . . . *gone.* And I reckon I've got, like, a couple of hours to pack my stuff before he comes back. So I'm thinking about, you know, where to go and I'm in the kitchen running the tap into the bowl and trying to stop my head from bleeding and I don't hear him come back.

"He . . . he grabbed the back of me head and pushed me face into the washing-up bowl. Didn't say a word. I weren't even sure it were him at first. Scared the shit out of me. I kicked, like kicked his knees or something, 'cause he went down and pulled me out of the water as he went."

"Naomi Green?" called the nurse.

We both started, dragged back from our minds, Naomi seeing it as it happened, I imagining every moment.

"That's me," Naomi said. "You coming?"

"No, I'll wait for you here."

Her narrow back disappeared behind the white door. I released the tension from my shoulders and rubbed my eyes. The buzz from the afternoon's wine had worn off, but it would take more than a couple of drinks to get my head around what I'd just heard.

Phillip was mean, controlling, would chip away at your self-esteem until you were sculpted into a pitiful imitation of the person you used to be. In the beginning, he'd use pressure points, threats, words sharper than a blade to secure your submission. Occasionally he'd snap, push, and send me flying down the stairs, but it always seemed to be in the heat of the moment, an eruption of anger that he couldn't contain. I'd never known him to walk purposefully back into a fight and never thought him capable of . . . what? Murder? Because if Naomi hadn't kicked out at him, who knew how long he would have held her head underwater? Just long enough to teach her a lesson? Or too long?

I wondered if Naomi could be lying. Almost hoped she was. But she had no reason to mislead me. The blood smeared about her face was further proof, if any were needed, that Phillip had a new way to ensure obedience.

I took the phone out of my bag and kept muttering "Christ almighty" under my breath as Naomi's words sunk in. Twice I keyed in the wrong code on my phone before it sprang to life. Rachel picked up on the second ring just as I reached the automatic doors that were a second slower than I was. I had to pull up short to save my head from making contact with the glass. Just one preoccupied moment and I could have been joining Naomi for matching stitches, though mine would have been for trusting the doors would magically open, hers for trusting the man she loved wouldn't try to kill her.

"How is the old bird?" Rachel asked.

"Sleeping. I'm sure I heard one of the nurses say 'mini stroke,' but no one's said that to me yet. They'll keep her in overnight to see if they can find a reason for her fainting."

"Bless her."

The night had changed in the brief time I had been inside. I could no longer see the stars beyond the thick cloud that hovered above me like a water balloon waiting to burst.

"Look, I've run into a bit of a problem," I said.

"Everything all right?"

"Well, *I'm* fine but on my way to the taxi I bumped into Naomi."

"*Naomi* Naomi?"

"Yep, they're cleaning her up. Phillip's done a number on her. She's in the ER having stitches right now."

"Shit!"

"You should see her, Rach. She's covered in blood."

"Where's Phillip now? Has she called the police?"

"I don't know where he's gone but I don't think Naomi's spoken to the police yet."

"Is she going to?"

"Doubt it. You know how it is. Who are they going to believe? The police officer with the perfect record or some girl who would look more at home in one of their cells?"

"She can't let him get away with it!"

Rachel was indignant, and I loved her for it, but she had no idea how much the police liked to look after their own.

When Phillip pushed me down the stairs, I told him I'd report him. I wouldn't let our son grow up seeing me treated like that. He laughed in my face and wished me luck. Without witnesses, it would be my word against his—the man who had received a commendation for bravery. The officer who put his body on the line to protect others every single day.

I called his bluff. I still believed in a fair world back then.

The officers who turned up were friends of Phillip's. I knew one of them from a wedding or christening. They didn't take notebooks out of pockets, didn't ask me any questions. Phillip spoke in hushed voices, told them he was so embarrassed I'd wasted their time. An argument, that's all, tempers frayed. You know how it is. Teething baby . . . He shouldn't have lost his temper, but it happens to the best of us, right?

They said he wasn't to worry. It wasn't the first domestic they'd been called to and wouldn't be the last. They were joking as they left, trying to make him feel better about his wife who called wolf.

Rachel's voice in my ear brought me back to the present.

"What did they fight about? Was it the affair?"

"Sort of. She knows he's hiding something and they had a big row. Look, I have to get back inside. She'll be out in a minute. Don't answer the door if Phillip comes round and don't answer the phone either."

"Why can't I answer my phone?"

"You can answer *your* phone. Just don't answer *my* phone, okay?"

"You think Phillip'll come here? I hope he does. I've got some things I'd like to say."

"He won't. It's just in case, you know. Judging by the state of Naomi, he's in a foul mood. God knows what he might do. Look, I'll explain everything when I get home, okay? How's Alistair?"

"Tip-top. We're having a great time. He's drinking hot chocolate and I've finished off that nice bottle of Bordyux."

"It's pronounced *Bord-oh*," I said.

"Whatevs. I mean the half bottle of red stuff that goes nice with lemonade."

"Rach, you didn't! That's a twenty-pound bottle of—"

"Keep your Spanx on! I'm kidding. You wine snobs are easy to wind up. Listen—" She paused while she gathered her thoughts. "Are you really okay? This must be weird for you, being with Naomi."

"I'm okay. You don't need to worry about me. I won't be here for a minute more than is strictly necessary. I'll get rid of Naomi and be back within the hour."

I was shaking my head as I clicked off my phone.

"Get rid of me?"

I spun round to find her standing in front of me with her arms folded and her shoulders hunched under her ears.

"Naomi! Hello. You're finished, then? I wasn't—" I couldn't find the words to explain what she'd heard.

Naomi put her head down against the cold and stormed off. I almost let her leave, but, as tempted as I was to bury my head in the sand, I couldn't let her walk straight back into his arms. I ran after her and grabbed her shoulder. She turned to face me with narrowed eyes and a curling top lip.

"What?" she spat.

"Don't do that. Don't just walk away."

"Why not?"

"Because we haven't finished. I meant what I said; you can tell me anything. I'm sorry you heard what I said on the phone but . . ."

I cast about for a suitable excuse but only had enough energy to come up with the truth.

"You know what? I *was* hoping to get rid of you as soon as possible."

She laughed unkindly and looked away.

"I don't want to spend my Sunday evening with *you* any more than you want to spend it with me. I don't want anything to do with Phillip. And you making me see . . . *this*"—I gestured to her head—"is a lot to take in. So yeah, when I said I wanted to get rid of you, part of me meant it, because I'm scared of being sucked back into Phillip's world. I'm scared of what he's capable of, and my first instinct is to protect me and my son.

"If you were anyone else apart from my ex's girlfriend, I wouldn't hesitate to run to your aid. I'd tell you to leave him and help you pack your bags. I'd give you a bed to sleep in and protect you from him, but the man who attacked you is the father of my son. I still have to see him every week and if I don't keep him on my side he could make things difficult for me and—"

I paused. Did I really believe he would hurt Alistair? I knew he loved him, but then, he used to say he loved me too.

"Listen," I said, shaking the fear from my head. "It was a shitty thing for me to say and I truly am sorry. Can we start again?"

An ambulance pulled up at our side and the doors opened slowly. We stepped backward to let green-suited men pass, pushing an old man on a stretcher. He was emaciated and his body hardly made an impact under a pale blanket. He had an oxygen mask over his face and we could hear the hiss of air as he passed. It brushed away some of Naomi's anger as it wheeled on by and she took a step closer to me. She kept glancing over her shoulder like she expected Phillip to appear.

"You know," I said, "you could leave him. He shouldn't treat you like this. There are places you can go that—"

"You say it like it's a choice. Why didn't *you* leave him?"

I looked at the pavement. It was a good question. Why had I put up with him for years? The affairs. The mental abuse. Perhaps I thought I could change him? I had enough reasons to walk away and only one to stay: I hadn't believed I deserved better.

Funny how people assume that you have a choice, that you choose to stay, to be treated like dirt, to live in fear. And they also forget that the man you once loved is in there somewhere and you're still holding out hope that he'll come back to you one day if only you can love him more and annoy him less.

"You don't need to make the same mistake I did," I said. "I'll never be completely free of him because of Alistair, but you can start again. You can leave and never look back."

I placed a hand on her arm and she flinched.

"It's not that simple," she said. "Don't you ever wonder what his hold is over Ruby? They've been split up for years and yet she still hangs around. You know as well as I do that once he has you, he'll never let go. We're marked by him now. Face it. He thinks we're his until the day he dies. And as far as I'm concerned, that day can't come soon enough."

CHAPTER 7

12 days before the funeral

It had been four days since I'd seen Naomi at the hospital. Four days of picking up the phone and placing it down again. I was scared of making it worse for her and scared it was already too late. She'd gone back to Phillip, saying she'd work something out, and if he went for her again, she'd be ready.

I was loading the dishwasher after dinner. Disposing of the leftovers via forkfuls and glassfuls, rinsing plates before stacking them in the machine. My mind was wandering, the kettle was boiling, and Alistair was having "five more minutes" on the trampoline before bed. The evening had retained none of the day's warmth, yet he was out there in a T-shirt and shorts making me feel cold just looking at him.

I rubbed at my eyes, feeling the mascara come off on my fingers and not caring that my makeup was smudged. Since I'd seen Naomi, my racing mind had made sleep impossible to catch. It felt like all I had to do was take one long blink and I would fall asleep where I stood, yet once I was in bed with the lights off, my mind would switch on and assault me with visions of Phillip pushing me down the stairs, pulling my hair, bending my fingers back.

Was loneliness ever felt more keenly than at four a.m.? The silent slumber of those around you dampening the night so that no sound can travel. And you, all alone, in a bed too big for one. After Phillip left, I tried sleeping on the left, the right, and even in the middle. Sideways, upside down, star shaped. Who was to stop me now? But I returned to the right, where I was closest to the door in case Alistair needed me. And through my sleepless nights I never ventured onto the other side. The morning light would show a neatly tucked-in sheet and an undented pillow reminding me—as if I needed it to— that I was all alone.

I yawned. I only had to hold it together for another twenty minutes and then Alistair would be in bed and I would be acquainting myself with a nice fruity red that was on special offer in the Co-op, hoping it would lead me to sleep.

The kettle clicked as it reached the boiling point. The sound appeared to echo in the kitchen. Except it didn't. The noise behind me was slight, but purposefully so—separate, uninvited, and out of place. I turned around slowly.

"Jesus Christ!" I fell backward against the sink, knocking the washing-up liquid into the bowl.

Phillip was standing by the door to the hallway with his hands in his pockets.

He smiled out of one side of his mouth but didn't say anything. His eyes crinkled with pleasure at having startled me. Fear had always been his greatest bargaining chip.

"How did you get in?"

"Still my house, isn't it?" he said.

"You can't do that, Phillip. You can't just let yourself in."

I stepped away from the sink, mindful of what he'd done to Naomi.

"I think I've proved that I can, and I will. Did you sign the paperwork?"

I put my hand to my chest and waited for my heart to calm down. I shook my head in annoyance.

"I've got an appointment with my solicitor on Monday. She said I shouldn't sign anything without her seeing it first."

Phillip looked past me to where Alistair was bouncing, bouncing, dropping, bouncing on the trampoline.

"The clock's ticking. Sign the papers, Imogen, or you'll end up with nothing."

I didn't like the way he was looking at our son when he spoke.

"The thing is . . ." I began.

I had always feared Phillip, but mostly his disapproval. Now that I'd seen what he'd done to Naomi, it was a different fear that caused my voice to come out higher than I'd intended.

"The thing is . . . that there is no way Alistair and I can find somewhere else to live by the end of the month. You're being unreasonable. I'm happy for us to go forward with the divorce, but I think we need to come to a fairer arrangement about the house. If we could sit down and discuss it, perhaps we could come to a compromise."

I started the dishwasher. Keeping busy. All the while my eyes were trained on him.

"Compromise? How about living rent-free in my house for two bloody years?"

"If we have to sell the house, then why can't we do that with Alistair and me still in it? Let's put the house on the market this week. We'll split the profits fifty-fifty. That's fair, right?"

"Fair? How much money have you contributed to the mortgage?"

"What's this really about?" I asked. I knew that look on his face. It went deeper than anger. He was worried about something, and to cover it, he was lashing out.

"End of the month, Imogen. Or else."

He was good at misleading me. Or I was terrible at spotting lies. Perhaps a little bit of both. I was more prone to suspicion now, a gift given to me by my cheating ex along with the crippling self-doubt and the chlamydia.

Changing the subject to deliberately knock him off-balance, I asked, "How's Naomi?"

Phillip's icy blue eyes narrowed slightly, no doubt wondering if I knew what had happened.

"I feel awful that I upset her by turning up at the house last week. I'd like to talk to her. Apologize."

"She's asleep," he said. "Migraine."

"Oh."

I supposed splitting your head open on the side of a table would give anyone a headache, but I knew he was lying.

He was more closed off than usual. Difficult to read. I hoped that all he was covering up was that Naomi had left him, rather than the fact that she had a black eye to go with her stitches. But if she was out of their house, I didn't know why he would be so desperate to have mine.

The back door swung open. "Daddy!"

"Hey there, kiddo," Phillip said.

Alistair wrapped his arms around his father's hips, but Phillip made no attempt to pick him up or return the hug.

"Just hearing your exciting news," he said with an exaggerated smile. "Mummy tells me you're moving house."

56

Alistair looked at me, but I didn't take my eyes off Phillip.

"Silly Daddy's got confused. I said that we would move one day. Not for a long time yet."

"Really? I could have sworn you said you would be out of here in a couple of weeks. Goodness! Would you look at the time?" he said without looking at his watch. "Shouldn't you be heading off to bed, kiddo? You go get in your pj's and I'll be up in five minutes to tuck you in."

Alistair ran through the kitchen toward the stairs before I could call him back.

"Don't involve him in this," I said.

"You involved him as soon as you chose to go back on our deal."

"What deal?" I hissed. "There is no deal. I'm more than happy to finalize the divorce, but I won't give our home over to you. I'll take this to court if I have to and I will fight you for it." I was feeling braver now. I'd had enough of his controlling behavior and I wouldn't let it carry on anymore. He would only get the better of me if I let him.

"What a good idea." He took a step toward me and lowered his head to mine until we were almost touching. I turned my face away, recoiling from his stale breath.

"Yes, let's do that," he said. "I can bring up my concerns over whether you're a fit mother. In fact, come to think of it, it might be a good time for me to make my case"—he took a slow breath—"for sole custody."

I fought the urge to move away from him, to take my son and run from the house. I stood my ground, stood up straighter, and glared at him. He took a small step backward. Whatever he read on my face unsettled him. I wasn't scared of him in that moment; I was furious. He could threaten me, he could hit me, he could call me names, but threatening to take away the one thing that mattered to me was a blow too low to bear.

"Don't think for a second that I'd let you take my son. There is no way a court would—"

"Are you sure? Given your mental health problems . . ." He sniffed, just inches from my face, matching my defiance with his own.

"Do you really want to talk about mental health problems? If anyone has problems, it's you. How about I tell the courts about your behavior? Your temper, and your violence? You'd be lucky to even see Alistair at visiting times in prison."

"I'm not on medication for my little problems," he said. "I've not been crying to the doctors that I've considered killing myself . . ."

"That was just after the accident. It has no—Urgh!" I stopped midsentence, not wanting to be drawn into explaining myself to him. Yes, I was on antidepressants and tablets for my anxiety, but so were many people nowadays. Could it be held against me?

I breathed heavily through my nose against the rising sickness. To the outside world, Phillip was the doting father. A court might be fooled into thinking that Phillip was all he appeared to be: a police officer, a family man, a man with his child's best interests at heart. I couldn't run the risk of losing Alistair. I'd lost too much already.

I'd need to expose Phillip for who he really was and I couldn't do that on my own. I thought about Naomi and her anger at the hospital. If I could convince her to press charges, I might have a better case against him. I wished now that I had gone to the police with each incident of cruelty, but what could they do when there were no bruises as evidence and Phillip was one of their own?

I could hear everything like it was coming through loudspeakers. The rush of water in the pipes as Alistair flushed the toilet. The *whoosh* of the dishwasher. The *tap-tap-tap* of the radiators coming to life. Laughter from people walking on the street. The initial adrenaline from my anger had subsided as quickly as it had come. A familiar tightness gripped my chest, a threat of an anxiety attack. I couldn't let it overcome me and play into his hands. I needed time to think, time to plan, but for now I wanted him to leave me alone.

"Fine," I said. "Fine. Leave Alistair out of it, okay? It's just a house. It would mean nothing if I didn't have my son." I turned toward him and tried to look beaten. It wasn't hard. I wanted him to underestimate me. I lowered my eyes, which he would take as a sign of submission, so that he wouldn't see the fire in them.

"Good. No more messing about. Sign those bloody papers while I get some of my things from the cinema room." He slid his hands into his pockets and whistled through his teeth as he walked out of the kitchen and into the hallway.

What Phillip called a cinema room I called a cellar. He used some of the money inherited after his mother's death to lower the floor, soundproof the room, and install a projector. It had been his sanctuary for when he could no longer stand the sound of my voice. The leather sofa pulled out into a bed and there were nights when he had slept down there.

I hated the low ceilings, the lack of natural light, and the smell of the leather. Call it whatever you liked, but it was still a cellar, a dungeon of sorts, somewhere to be shackled, a place of nightmares and creepy-crawlies. Watching back-to-back rom coms wouldn't lighten the association to an acceptable level, and I had rarely been down there since Phillip had left.

He opened the door and sighed loudly.

"What have I told you," he shouted, "about dumping stuff at the top of the stairs? It's an accident waiting to happen, all because you're too lazy to put things away properly." His voice wasn't angry; he was almost conversational.

I walked into the hallway in time to see him toss my yellow coat on the floor.

"And throw that thing away. You look ridiculous in it."

I bent down and picked it up. I'd treated myself in the sale, loved it because it was the very opposite of everything I wore when Phillip and I were together. He used to choose my clothes for me, and at the time I hadn't thought there was anything wrong with that. He seemed to know what suited me better than I did. When I'd attempted to have a night out with colleagues or other mums, he'd look me up and down and pass judgment on my outfit. Too short, too tight, too much like I was going out to scare children. It was safer to let him dress me. I put the coat hood over the end of the banister and stroked its arms. I wondered whether I would wear it again without asking myself if Phillip was right.

I could hear him huffing his way down the cellar steps, sidestepping the vacuum cleaner, and his pantomime exhalation when he saw the bags of clothes I'd dumped down there waiting for a lift to the charity shop. Clothes that Alistair had grown out of and clothes that I had grown away from.

I hovered at the cellar door, waiting for his criticism.

"I just don't understand you, Imogen."

He never had. He was referring to the bags of clothes and boxes of items with no natural home, but, for a moment, I thought he showed rare insight.

"How can you live in a pigsty? Have some pride. You know you're a laughingstock, don't you?"

I closed my eyes and breathed deeply. I hated the way he made me feel and act. I'd had enough of him talking to me as if I were worthless. In my head I was shouting, *Shut up, shut up, shut up!* but in reality my lips remained tightly closed. I wanted to blot out the sound of his voice and make him listen to me for once.

I'm not sure I knew what was truly in my mind as I stepped back into the hallway and took the heavy wooden door in my hand. I had no single, distinct thought as I slowly pushed the door closed until it clicked. The hands that turned the key hardly looked like my own, but there they were, sliding the bolt across the top of the door. Safe as houses.

Phillip was still searching through the DVDs he'd left behind, thinking he was in control, thinking he could walk all over me.

My hand lingered at the door. He would discover what I'd done in the next few minutes unless I unlocked it now.

"Mummy?" Alistair shouted from his bedroom.

"Yes, darling?"

"I brushed my teeth."

"I'm on my way," I called back.

Now or never. I could open the door and walk away and Phillip would never know, or I could show him who was really in control. It was crazy that I was even considering it. I placed my fingers around the key, and even though a voice in my head was telling me not to make Phillip angry, I slid it out of the lock and put it in the back pocket of my jeans.

CHAPTER 8

12 days before the funeral

"If you don't let me out right this second, I'll—"

"Shush! Calm down, Phillip. You'll wake Alistair."

It was a little past nine and Alistair was fast asleep. He'd needed two bedtime stories to make up for the fact that Daddy had left without saying good-bye.

I bent my knees, sank to the floor, and leaned back against the wall with my feet on the door. Though it juddered with every punch and kick, I knew it wouldn't break. Everything beyond that door was state-of-the-art but the old door itself was over a hundred years old, and solid. The knowledge blew air into the embers of my confidence. There was an old black bolt across the top of the door and a lock and key at hip height. It was a long, narrow key, heavy and strong. It was long enough to stretch the depth of the door and had been touched by many hands before me. Phillip used to keep the key on the other side of the door so he could lock it from the inside. He used to want to keep me out. He never considered that I would want to keep him in. With no windows in the cellar and no door other than the one my feet were against, there was no way he was getting out of the cellar unless I decided he was free to go.

"When you've *quite* finished," I said.

I held the key to his freedom, and it was a warm velvet feeling across my chest. If I didn't think too far ahead, if I didn't consider the consequences, I was almost happy.

"Naomi'll be wondering where I am," he said.

"Ah, but will she *care*?" I spoke quietly, doubted he heard me, then raised my voice.

"Did she tell you I bumped into her at the hospital?"

He remained silent, but I knew he could hear me.

"Nasty cut, that. I was with her when she went for stitches. Do you think the nurse believed she walked into a door? I bet they're used to seeing those sorts of injuries. Classic case of domestic violence, I'd say. You're getting daring, aren't you? You never used to do things to me that would leave a mark. Or 'evidence,' as you'd call it."

I liked the new me, the one who could say what she wanted to Phillip without fear of retaliation or abuse. He couldn't lay a finger on me anymore, and when I set him free, which I would have to do eventually, he'd know that I wasn't to be messed with. It felt good to finally stand up to him, and I wondered why I hadn't done it years earlier.

I had a peculiar, elated feeling of not quite being myself, but I liked who I'd been replaced with. She was stronger than me, a wicked cape-free crusader righting marital wrongs and slaying domestic demons.

"Work will notice when I don't turn up for my shift tomorrow," he said.

"Actually, that's how I know you're hiding something. I went into the station and they said they didn't know when you'd be back. It was a new guy, didn't recognize me. He said that all your cases had been reassigned. He wouldn't tell me why. Clammed up when I pushed. Why is that? Phillip? What's going on?"

I heard him move on the other side of the door but he didn't reply.

"I know you're hiding something. Naomi thinks that you're going in to work each day. At least, she *did* until I turned up on your doorstep telling her you weren't at the station. That's why you attacked her, isn't it? Because she confronted you about it. Is it another woman? I tell you, women will be the death of you, Phillip."

"I'm going to count to three . . ." he said.

"I'd think you could do better than that at your age," I said. "What I can't work out is why you're off work. She'd have to be one hell of a woman to keep you away from that job. Phillip? Can you hear me in there?"

"Yes, I can bloody hear you. I wish you'd shut the fuck up."

I smiled to myself. I was getting to him. I might not know what his secret was, but at least I knew he had one.

"You don't want to tell me what's going on, then? Fine. I'm sure it won't take me long to find out. I still know people at the station. All it would take is one phone call to find out what reason you've given for being off work. Oh, and while I've got your undivided attention, can we agree on a couple of things? Firstly, there's no way I'll let you take Alistair away from me. For what it's worth, I don't think any sane judge would let you have custody. Which brings me to my second point: as I'm the one looking after him day in, day out, there's no chance a court would agree to you kicking me out of the house. This is our family home but—Are you still listening?"

"I'm listening."

"Well, as a gesture of goodwill, I'll agree to sell up and start again somewhere new. And I won't slow down the divorce either. How does that sound?"

"What about Alistair?" he asked.

I sighed. "I don't know. Do you really want to spend time with him or is that just your way of getting back at me?"

"He's my son! It's . . . it's not the big things like school plays and sports days; it's being there when he wakes up and seeing his face when he loses a tooth. It's the simple things."

I moved closer to the door. It would destroy me if I was denied those moments with Alistair, but Phillip hadn't given any indication that these things mattered to him. Perhaps he found it easier to talk with a closed door between us—I know I did. I wished I knew which of his words were truthful.

"I suppose we could work up to you spending more time with Alistair, but only if it makes him happy. If he ever tells me you've hurt him or that he's scared of you . . ."

We sat in silence.

I didn't want Alistair to spend more time with Phillip, but he *was* his father. Perhaps I had been unreasonable. I told myself that the moment Phillip put a foot wrong I would cut all contact with him.

"If I agree to let you spend more time with Alistair, will you agree to let us stay in the house until it's sold?"

He didn't say anything, but at least it wasn't a no.

"And that thing with work? I won't call anyone. I'll stay out of it, okay? It's your business, and as long as it doesn't affect Alistair, I promise to keep my nose out. What do you say?"

I put one hand over my eyes, trying to stop thoughts of Naomi, trying to pretend that it didn't matter what he was hiding, and clinging on to blind hope that somehow we could work this out.

"And if I say no?" His voice was muffled.

I sighed and looked up at the ceiling, hoping to find strength there.

"Then I'll refuse to leave the house, stop you from seeing Alistair, and report your attack on Naomi."

"You wouldn't dare."

"There'll be doctors' reports to back me up. Even if it doesn't stick . . . Well, no smoke without fire, eh?"

Phillip's reputation was his Achilles' heel. Always worried what everyone else would think about him, though this didn't appear to extend to me. Even though he had committed adultery, he'd managed to escape with his image intact.

He didn't say anything, but I heard him moving around. He knocked into the vacuum cleaner and swore.

"Are you going to let me out or not?"

I knew I had to let him go before Alistair woke up, but I was nervous about how angry he would be when I finally opened the door.

"Do we have an agreement?" I asked, touching my fingertips to the wood.

"What? Yes! Just bloody well let me out of here," he said.

"How do I know I can trust you?"

"Godsake, Imogen. What do you want from me? A letter signed in blood? I've said yes, haven't I? Despite what you might think, I don't want to argue with you. I only want what's fair."

I nodded to myself. I smoothed my hair behind my ears and got to my feet. I'd got what I'd wanted, yet somehow I wasn't satisfied. Had he given in too easily? Should I have asked for more?

I hesitated with my hand on the bolt. He was still hiding something. Perhaps I should have kept him there while I checked in with Naomi. If I could have bought an extra couple of hours, I would have, but I couldn't keep him there any longer without being unreasonable in the eyes of Phillip and the law.

I unbolted the door first and then rattled the key in the lock, hoping it sounded like I'd unlocked it. If he was planning to rush at me, I wanted him to attempt it while the door was still locked. But there was no movement from behind the heavy wooden door. I placed my hand on my chest as if I could physically steady the beating of my heart. I was expecting the worst, which wasn't entirely unreasonable, but for once it appeared I was being paranoid.

I turned the key and the *click* echoed about the hallway. I deflated as I began to turn the doorknob. Once I let him out, I would no longer have the upper hand, but it was nice while it lasted.

I saw Phillip's hands dart out at me before I'd even noticed he was standing up. I yelped with surprise and fell. His hand scraped my face, fingernails connecting with my ear and ripping my earring out. I banged my head against the wall and he used the doorframe to steady himself. His eyes were cold and his teeth clenched. I brought my knees up to my chest and kicked out at him. My heels struck his stomach and he folded in half. His clawed hand slid off the wooden frame. There was a brief, gravity-defying moment where he fluttered at the top of the steps. Arms flapping, circling, and then he stumbled. His shoulder brushed against the wall and spun him round. Phillip doubled over himself, contorting his body into shapes that didn't seem possible. He fell step by step by step with a force that couldn't be stopped.

"Shit. Shit. Shit, shit, shit."

"Mummy?"

Alistair's sleep-heavy voice came from upstairs.

I slammed the door and pulled the bolt home. I backed away until I was against the wall. My ear throbbed, but I felt no pain, only the aftermath of fear and confrontation. My limbs fizzed with fatigue and my chest was raw. My fingertips were bloodied where they'd stroked my damaged earlobe.

"Back to bed, sweetie. Mummy just knocked the vacuum cleaner down the stairs. I'll be up to check on you in a minute, okay?" My voice was high and panicked.

"Night-night," Alistair murmured.

"Night, sweetie."

I waited for the sound of his soft steps to cross the landing and then turned the key in the lock.

I walked into the kitchen and back out again, wondering about calling Rachel, an ambulance, the police. *It was an accident, Officer. I only meant to lock him up. I never meant to . . .* What? Kill him? Dear God, what had I done? I pictured him lying at the bottom of the stairs in a heap, his neck broken. I leaned on the back of a kitchen chair working on slowing my breathing. *People fall downstairs all the time,* I told myself. *He'll be hurt but not dead.*

"Idiot," I said aloud.

I shouldn't have trusted him, shouldn't have opened the door. But the police wouldn't see it that way. I shouldn't have locked him up in the first place. Panic crushed the air from my lungs. I picked up the phone but hung up before I could decide whom to call. I drained a glass of wine without remembering pouring it. I closed curtains and locked doors. I prayed and I swore. I moved swiftly and silently up the stairs and looked in on Alistair's sleeping form. I closed the door behind me and found myself back outside the cellar.

The moment of truth.

I had to see what I'd done but didn't know—couldn't know—if

Phillip would be lying in wait for me behind the door. I pressed my good ear to the wood and leaned on it but couldn't hear anything. I counted in twos all the way to eighty and unlocked the door. I listened. I counted again to eighty and slid back the bolt. I opened it in a rush, my body shielded by the door.

Nothing.

I glanced around the corner quickly and pulled my head back again.

Still nothing.

I cautiously peered around the corner. The steps, the cellar, being exposed inch by inch. I could see the bottom of Phillip's shoe. Then his leg. In the weak-tea-colored light, I saw that he was lying on his back with his arms out to his sides like he had been crucified. One leg was folded underneath him and his face was turned away from me.

I couldn't tell if he was breathing, couldn't tell if it was a trap, but I had to know if he was still alive. I entered the cellar one silent step at a time, sliding my back against the smooth, cold wall to steady myself. Phillip's rib cage didn't appear to be moving; there was no sign that he was still breathing, that I hadn't done the unthinkable. Suddenly, he exhaled loudly and I froze. I reversed two steps and sat down. I was relieved that he was still alive. And then I was scared that he wasn't dead.

I hadn't meant to hurt him. Not like that. When he came around, he would be furious with me and I would have more than a torn earlobe and barbed comments to worry about. I had to buy time. I had to keep us safe until he'd calmed down, until I knew he could be trusted, until I knew he couldn't go back on his promises.

I rushed back up the stairs and out to the shed. I didn't know how long he would be unconscious for. I found a climbing rope, an old set of Phillip's handcuffs with the key taped to the cuff, and a bike lock. I ran back to the cellar.

His outstretched leg reached up the bottom three steps. I clicked one cuff around his ankle. It wasn't long enough for me to attach his leg to the radiator without me lifting or dragging all thirteen unresponsive stones of him. I uncoiled the bike lock. It was heavy in my hand and long enough to chain all three of our bikes together on the few times we'd been out as a family. I threaded it through the cuff that wasn't on Phillip's ankle and strained to make it click shut behind the radiator. I rattled the radiator to check it wasn't going to come off the wall. Solid. I was beginning to be thankful that Phillip had spent so much on remodeling the cinema room.

I tied Phillip's wrists together using the blue climbing rope and covered him with a blanket from the sofa. When he woke up, he would see that I wasn't being cruel, just practical. I nudged him with my foot and he groaned lightly. I walked around him and pushed him with a bit more force.

"Phillip?"

His breathing was steady but he still wasn't conscious. I patted him down as if in an American cop film. I found his mobile, wallet, and the keys to my house and held them to my chest.

"Can you hear me? I didn't plan this. You were meant to stick to your end of the bargain and then leave. But now look what's happened. You wouldn't have fallen if you hadn't attacked me, and I wouldn't have shut you in here in the first place if you hadn't attacked Naomi. I hope you can hear me, Phillip—" I crouched over his body and touched his face where the slightest hint of stubble grazed his chin.

"Because you are about to find out that your actions have consequences."

CHAPTER 9

11 days before the funeral

Panic, like an arrow in my chest, woke me before Alistair stirred. I couldn't remember falling asleep. I was on the sofa and the early-morning light was pushing its way between wooden shutters, casting piano keys across the floor. I could see the cellar door from where I lay. Still closed. Still locked.

Still silent.

The clock ticked loudly, providing the beat for the day. Hands jerked past five a.m. Scant sounds of life from outside: a door slamming, an engine starting, a dog barking. Someone dragging bins out to the side of the road. Ordinary people just starting their ordinary day. But no sound came from the cellar.

My neck ached and my cheek was wet with drool. I was wearing yesterday's clothes and could smell my own breath. I sat up and reached for the wineglass on the table, which still held an inch of ruby liquid. There was a small black fly floating on the surface. I prodded at it until it stuck to my finger. I flicked the black body away and downed the wine in one gulp. Waste not, want not.

I called work early so that I would have the benefit of only lying to an answering machine. I borrowed Naomi's migraine for the day and it fit me perfectly. I pulled on a clean pair of jeans that were hanging on to their knees by a thread, and a baggy black jumper which I'd always hated. I fussed Alistair into his uniform and out of the house without even passing the cellar door.

"But, Mummy, I haven't had any breakfast."

"Just do as I say for once," I snapped.

His eyes watered, the hurt pooling into thick tears, and I pulled him into me and kissed his messed-up hair.

"Sorry, sweetie. Mummy's tired. We're having a special treat, okay?"

With over an hour to fill, we took the long route through the park. Rowers were already out on the river, slicing the water and making us feel cumbersome in comparison. We nodded to the runners and the dog walkers while the cathedral bells rolled over the morning to softly cuff our ears. Trees clung to the last of their blossoms, sprinkling confetti as we walked by.

We stopped at Bakin' and Eggs for beans, sausage, and toast. It was too early in the year to brave an outdoor table, but we did it anyway. I buttoned up my yellow jacket and sipped my extra-large coffee with the extra shot of caffeine and the extra sugar hit of caramel syrup. Alistair drank milky sweet tea and swung his legs in time to a song in his head.

I scanned the park for anyone looking at me like I was a crazy woman who had a man tied up in her cellar, but everyone was all intent on stirring their teas and eating their breakfast or power walking and petting their dogs.

Alistair talked about the everythings of life, the when-I-grow-ups and the big picture he was yet to paint. It was up to me to make sure that the future was as open to him as any dream had a right to be. Pave the way. Remove obstacles. Suddenly school seemed trivial, play much more important.

This new version of me, the one who locked her ex in the cellar, considered letting Alistair stay off school and have a day of building dens and telling stories, but the *old* me gave us one of her looks and I returned our plates to the café and skipped him off to school. I hugged and held him until he wriggled free of me and left me with nothing else to do except return home.

The sun, which had dominated the sky not an hour before, was smothered by a smooth cloud blanket. I had to tighten my eyes against the gray glare to look toward home. My house was the same shade of noncolor as the sky, but the front door was dangerous red. There were no swirling storm clouds gathering overhead, nor a murder of crows screeching out, *He's here, he's here!* It still looked like an ordinary house on an ordinary street owned by a subordinary woman, and a passerby would be forgiven for not noticing the dungeonlike qualities of the lower floor.

I pretended to fumble in my bag for my keys, listening for a sound from within. Through the glass panel I peered into the hallway. As far as I could tell, the cellar door was still closed. I glanced behind me and saw Mary, my neighbor, with her hand on the net curtain. I waved my keys at her and unlocked the door, closing it softly behind me.

The morning sun hadn't penetrated the cool hallway, so I kept my hated-by-Phillip jacket on as I shuffled to the cellar door.

I leaned my forehead and palm against it, trying to picture Phillip. There was still no sound. He was breathing when I left him. I knew he was.

It was self-defense, I swear.

I opened the cellar door, slowly took a deep breath, and stepped inside. I thought I heard a rustling like someone scratching their head.

"Phillip?"

He grunted.

Thank God.

My shoulders relaxed and my breathing slowed.

"Would you like a drink?"

His voice, when it came, was calm and quiet, but his words leaned against each other lazily.

"Ifsnot too much trouble, I'd like a cupperty."

I found the polite self-control more alarming than if he had shouted and sworn.

"Sure. One minute."

I made him coffee instead.

I took it down on a tray with aspirin, a bottle of water laced with sleeping tablets, and two slices of toast topped with his least favorite spread.

He was lying on the sofa with his head on the cushions and his cuffed leg on the arm closest to me. The handcuffs were still on his ankle with the other end threaded through a bike lock, which in turn was attached to the radiator, but his wrists were untied and the rope was coiled at the floor by his side.

"Oh," I said.

"You never could tie knots."

His voice was still calm, as if this were a normal situation.

I put the tray on the small white table, just out of his reach. It was colder in the cellar than upstairs. The small radiator hadn't been used in months. I could do something about that if I wanted to, but I didn't. Phillip had spent thousands turning our small dank cellar into the cinema room of his dreams. A projector was trained against one smooth white wall, and there was a sofa and one armchair. The walls were white, the furniture tan leather with blue cushions. Minimalist and male. At one time, he'd had shelves lined with action figures, though he told me these were limited-edition collector's items, not toys. They'd gone with him to The Barn along with some of his films and the rest of his paraphernalia that I could never get excited about.

"Is that Marmite?" he asked, sitting up and shuffling to the edge of his seat.

"Yep."

"I hate Marmite."

"Do you? I must've forgotten."

He was sleepy, eyes still half closed, hair sticking up on one side, the shadow of a bruise on the left side of his face. It was fresh, a few hours old, and must have happened when he fell down the stairs. His stubble came high up on his cheeks, dark and thick, out of place on his usually smooth face.

"How're you feeling?" I asked.

"Like I drank a bottle of cheap wine and fell down the stairs."

He lurched at me without warning, but I stepped backward and his fingers only brushed my hip. I was on my guard.

"Now, then . . ." I said.

I gave a quiet nasal laugh that betrayed my nerves, but Phillip didn't smile.

"You do remember, don't you, that there's the camping toilet be-hind the wall? The bike lock should be long enough to—"

"Jesus, Imogen. I can't believe you've chained me up."

"I know. No one's more surprised than me," I said. "I didn't know what else to do."

I sat down in the armchair and crossed my legs, forcing myself to loosen up.

"You could have *not* chained me up," he said, and then added, "Like a normal person."

"Normal," I said. "Not a word I'd apply to either of us. Sometimes you have to think outside the box."

"There's a difference between outside the box and outside the boundaries of sanity."

He grimaced as he reached for the aspirin and swallowed two down without water. I looked at the water bottle, wondering whether he knew what I'd done to it, whether he could tell.

"You should drink the water," I said. "Keep hydrated."

"I'm touched that you should care," he said with a sneer.

The overhead light was unflattering, casting his face into shadows as dark as the look in his eyes.

"Why the hell have you cuffed me?"

"I didn't fancy being attacked again. I'll let you go as soon as you agree to my terms."

"Assault," he said. "Unlawful imprisonment."

"What are you doing?"

"Attempted murder, kidnap."

"Phillip . . ."

"Just thinking about what they'll charge you with."

"You're not making me want to let you go," I said.

His bonds were only physical. I knew he could still reach me with his words if he wanted to. He used them as others would use a knife. A thousand small surface cuts to weaken you, an unbearably painful lattice hidden beneath an outfit of normality, chafing when you moved.

"You've made your point," he said. "Unchain me and I'll give you an extra month in the house."

"It's not about the house, Phillip."

He rolled his eyes at me.

"And you can keep custody of Alistair, of course," he said.

"I'll need that in writing."

"You can take my word," he said.

"I won't fall for that again."

Creased puffy bags hung beneath husky-blue eyes. They were dusted gray and purple. The whites of his eyes reminded me of the beige paint on the walls of the hallway. Something was eating away at him and I didn't think it was just because he was locked in the cellar.

I clenched and unclenched my toes. Concentrated on the rug beneath my feet. Made myself calm.

Breathe in.

Breathe out.

"Why do you want me out of the house?" I asked.

He shook his head and looked away.

"Fine," I said as I stood up. "I know you're up to something, Phillip. I'm not letting you go until you agree to my terms. And if I'm going to let you see more of Alistair, I'm going to need assurances that you won't hurt him."

"I've never laid a finger on that boy, and you know it."

"The things you say wound as much as the things you do. You've hurt him in ways that he will never recover from. Remember that time you shouted at him until he wet himself?"

"Bloody delusional, you are."

Phillip had a way of making me doubt myself, but I knew the truth.

Alistair had been four years old. He had done something. A something that may as well have been a nothing. Crayoned on the wall maybe, or—I don't know—forgotten to wash his hands before dinner. It didn't warrant the strength of the reaction from his father. Phillip was furious. Shouting so much that spittle formed at the sides of his mouth and his cheeks were rage reddened. He stood Alistair on the table so that they were eye to eye and he bellowed. He yelled at him until Alistair cried and called out for me. I stood on the fringes, wanting to go to him, but Phillip stretched out his arm and kept me back. He roared and shouted vile things about disappointment and embarrassment, told him how everyone laughed at him for his baby-ish ways and his pathetic attempts to join in with the grown-ups.

I watched a dark line thicken Alistair's trouser leg. Phillip curled his lip and told him he was a disgusting little baby, a pathetic little boy, he was ashamed to call him his son. I shouldered him aside, scooped Alistair up, and ran with him to the toilet. I felt warm liquid on my side and I loathed my husband at that moment. I remember the rush of earnest, handcrafted hatred and the liberation of being able to feel anything at all. I had been so unhappy for so long that it had been preferable to feel nothing at all than to be wounded anew every day. This new brand of hatred demolished the wall and I could see a light shining some way off. Little did I know that light was called Naomi.

No amount of *shush-shush*es and *there-there*s would calm my baby, and I slept in his bed with him that night for my benefit more than his.

It was the first time I had openly disobeyed Phillip.

"Come to bed."

"No."

"I mean it, Imogen."

"Screw you!"

Two weeks later he moved in with Naomi. My only regret was that I hadn't kicked him out sooner.

O nce, Phillip had been my savior. He'd promised freedom from my pedestrian life, but he rescued me from one tower just to lock me up in another. He had appeared before me smelling of cigarettes and pay packets and talking of the police force and "protecting people." He talked about his vision for the future. He'd been married before but it had been a mistake, a young and foolish accident. The wife was a cold fish, an old fish, and she liked dogs more than kids, and all he wanted was a big family someday and a wife he could "take care of."

He told me about his wife, Ruby, how he hadn't laid eyes on her in years but he was trying to track her down and ask for a divorce. The girlfriends he'd had since the breakdown of his marriage had meant nothing, until he met me.

He understood what it was like to lose a parent. He'd experienced the same. His father died when he was only eleven. *Snap.* He had no siblings. *Snap.* He was alone. *Snap.* But not anymore. We marveled at fate for bringing together two such damaged people who deserved happiness and love.

My father, Andrew Stanley Neville Winston Joyce, exited my life when I was nine years old. He had been named after a series of Conservative prime ministers. The first, Andrew Bonar Law, was prime minister for just 209 days. Andrew Joyce was my father for just 3,413 days.

After he died, I misplaced a part of me. One day I was happy and whole, a confident child who no more thought about death than walking on the moon. But the next, I grew silent and scared. Phillip became that missing piece. With him in my life, everything started to work again, make sense.

I could trace my triskaidekaphobia back to Father's death. He died on the thirteenth; there were thirteen white roses blooming over the love seat, thirteen stones in the duck pond, thirteen ripe tomatoes on the plants in the greenhouse. Only thirteen people attended his funeral, and that included Mother, Aunty Margaret, and me. I cried for him thirteen times a day, the exact number of times a day that Mother cursed him.

I counted the olives into a Greek salad, twelve or fourteen but never in between. The volume on the car stereo was never at thirteen. I knew that logically there was no reason for this. But what if there *was* something in it? A slight chance? The smallest of chances? Would it hurt anyone if there were only twelve olives in the salad?

The thirteenth of August was the last day that my father had witnessed both sunrise and sunset. It had been a gloriously hot one that melted pavements and tricked eyes into believing that the world above the road was shimmering. The sun stung the backs of legs and the music from the ice cream truck had children streaming onto the street like ants onto a dropped lollipop. I knew it was a scorcher when Dad stripped to his vest in the garden and rolled up his trouser legs. He clucked over the tomato plants and said they'd need watering more than once this day, but the hosepipe ban was in force and he'd have to trek backward and forward with his green watering can. We had one bottle of elderflower cordial left over from the previous year's bounty and I sucked it delicately through a striped straw like it was nectar.

The twins from across the road came over to play that day. They were two years younger than me but seemed to know much more than I ever would. Our hands were sticky with melted popsicle and our summer skirts were tucked into our knickers as we lay on the picnic blanket, talked about music, and read Nicola's copy of *Are You There God? It's Me, Margaret.* Mother thought it was good for young girls to be reading books about religion. She'd not heard of the book's author, nor that the local library had banned her books. Mother's ignorance was my bliss.

Father busied himself with watering the plants and the cracked ground drank it thirstily. He stopped by us every now and again to splash us with water and laugh at our squeals. He was a quiet man, my father, kind and playful. He was never too busy for hide-and-seek or too tired for bedtime stories. He was everything to me, and my friends loved him too. How could I have known, back then, that he was battling his own demons?

After the twins went home, Mother and Father argued. I heard her shout, "I don't care what you're thinking—it only matters how it *looks.*" My mother was from a stiff-upper-lip generation where appearance was everything. She was as furious as I'd ever seen her. By the look on Father's face, he was as confused as I was about what he'd done wrong.

The light was on in the garage well into the night. It must have been late because I remember the sun never wanting to set that summer. The days ruled the evenings, barely letting the stars get a word in edgewise. I waited for him to leave the garage so I could lean out of my open window and wave to him, so he'd know that I was on his side. But he only came out of the garage one more time. And by then I was asleep, and he was covered in a sheet from head to toe.

Girls—especially naive, flimsy girls like me—grew up looking for the fairy tale, waiting for those three magical words: *I love you.*

My mother's love included slaps to the back of the legs and go-to-your-room-without-any-supper because she *loved* me. No, I was waiting for *five* magical words: *I'll take care of you.*

The years following my father's death, and Mother's subsequent, and perhaps understandable, breakdown, were flat cold years, stark in comparison with the warm rounded days of my childhood, when our unit had felt unbound by limitless love. Before my father died, I could have sworn it was always summer. But afterward, it rained. A lot.

I could have gone off the rails, smoked or drank, but I sought Mother's attention in the only way I knew. I never put a foot wrong, never came home from school with a grade any lower than an A. Never stayed out late nor had boyfriends. Never sought a life away from Mother's Parma violet scent.

But then I met Phillip.

I gave myself to him before I knew what I was giving away. I had mistakenly thought myself lucky to be shaped by him. I let him chip away at me until he found something that he liked. And when there was nothing else to work with, he moved on to a more pliable subject.

Though Naomi was effectively my liberator, she was still the woman who stole my husband. Prettier, younger, firmer, with a stomach unstretched by pregnancy. I knew what he saw in her, and it wasn't brains.

I left Phillip in the cellar with his food, his bad mood, and his belief that nothing was ever his fault. I made my way back up toward the hallway with a promise that we would talk again soon.

Naomi was in my mind, a vision at the tail end of a memory as I closed the cellar door. I recalled her floral scent that failed to mask the fact that she'd been smoking, so vividly that I thought I could smell it in the air. It had been hard to get her out of my mind since I'd seen her at the hospital.

I saw the outline of a woman walking up the driveway, and rushed to open the door before she rang the bell. I squeezed outside to cut her off at the doorstep and send her on her way.

I stopped with a jolt as my memory was made manifest. There she was, Naomi, with a crooked smile on her face.

"Y'all right, duck?" she said. "You look like you've seen a ghost."

CHAPTER 10

11 days before the funeral

I shepherded Naomi through to the kitchen, closed the door to the hallway, and mumbled something about "keeping the heat in" and "chilly today." I crossed quickly to the cupboard in the corner, where the boiler was neatly hidden, and switched the heating on. Gurgling and tapping filled the kitchen for a moment and would have drowned out any sounds from the basement. Naomi took off her thin denim jacket and laid it across the back of the chair, in defiance of my lie.

She was wearing a shirt thin enough for me to see the shape of a tattoo on her shoulder blade. The cut on her forehead was stuck together with graying butterfly stitches, and in the light of the day I could see she'd done her best to conceal the bruising with makeup.

"Not working today?" she asked me.

"No. Not feeling too great."

"You look like crap." Her eyes dared me to contradict her.

Naomi was obviously in the mood for an argument. I wasn't.

"I wouldn't say no to a brew, seeing as I've driven all this way," she said.

I rearranged my features into an apology, but inherent politeness wouldn't let me find the words to ask her to leave. Old, compliant me was still in there somewhere. I was skating on thin ice and it felt like she was pushing me toward the middle of the lake. I wanted her to leave without making a fuss. I needed her to keep her voice quiet and her movements limited. I had to keep her from discovering her boyfriend in my cellar.

"I'll pop the kettle on."

I warmed the pot, offering Naomi a biscuit by saying, "Elevenses?" like Gran used to say, and felt the age gap between us widen some more.

"No, thanks."

She was looking at her mobile, checking messages and refreshing screens.

"How's the, er . . . head?" I asked.

"Sore, but you know . . ."

"I'm glad you came around," I lied. "I wanted to call to see if you were okay but thought I'd make things worse if Phillip knew I'd phoned. Anyway, I wasn't sure you'd still be there."

"Told you," she said, putting her phone facedown on the table and fixing her attention on me. "I got nowhere else to go. I wasn't thinking straight on Sunday."

"I'm sure there are—" I began, but she cut across me.

"Seen Phil lately?"

My scalp tingled and there was a sensation of cold water trickling down my spine. I paused before answering, taking a moment to peer into the fridge.

"Skim milk okay?"

She nodded.

"As a matter of fact," I continued, "I saw him yesterday. He wanted me to sign some paperwork."

"And?"

"And that's it, really. I didn't sign it because he wants me out of the house by the end of the month."

Naomi folded her arms and leaned back on the wooden chair, causing the front two legs to lift off the floor.

"You didn't sign? Last week you couldn't wait to get everything done. What changed?"

"I . . . We need to come to a better arrangement about the house."

And Alistair, I thought.

"Why'd he want you out of the house so quick?"

"Don't know. You'd have to ask him," I said.

"I would," she said. "But he didn't come home last night."

Blame it on lack of sleep or blame it on stupidity, but I hadn't considered that Naomi would notice his absence and come to my door. Self-preservation has a way of dealing with guilt. I needed her to stop looking for him.

"Perhaps," I said, as if a thought had just occurred to me, "he's realized that the two of you can't go on like this. Is it possible that he's left *you*?"

The day was darkening even though the morning was not yet spent. Nature was colluding with me to explain my door-closing, heat-switching behavior.

She didn't take her eyes off me. "Maybe. You think he's found someone better, do you? Maybe an *old* flame?"

She looked far too smug. She wasn't buying my explanation. And worse than that, she was looking at me like I might be the old flame.

"Listen, Naomi. I wasn't going to say anything, but a friend of mine said I owed you the truth. I can't keep it from you any longer."

She raised an eyebrow. I'd got her attention. She looked almost eager, like this was what she had come for.

"At your house the other day, you didn't seem to know that Phillip hadn't been at work. He wasn't at the doctor's either, but I think you already knew that, didn't you? There's no easy way to say this, Naomi, but Phillip's been lying to you. And if you put that together with the fact that he wants us out of the house by the end of the month . . . well, isn't it obvious? Phillip's having an affair."

I let the news sink in for a moment. If she wanted to storm out now, I wouldn't stop her, but she kept her eyes on my face, wanting more.

"It wouldn't be the first time, would it?" I continued. "So, if I were you, I'd go home and pack my things. Perhaps go to a hotel while you work out what you want to do?"

I knew she would eventually find out that her partner had spent the night in my cellar, but hopefully not until he'd signed the papers.

I expected shock, or denial, possibly a tear, but I didn't expect the laughter that came.

It was my turn to fold my arms. Still she laughed. It was the dry, rasping laugh of a smoker. Breathless and coarse. She shook her head and looked about her.

I glanced at the door, wondering whether we'd hear Phillip if he began to shout. Just how good was that soundproofing he'd paid a fortune for?

"I tell you what," she said. "You almost had me fooled."

"Sorry?" She couldn't possibly know. Could she?

"I mean, God, is it even true?"

"I don't know what you're talking about. Is what true?"

"Fine. Whatever." She stood up and shrugged her shoulders into her jacket. "One thing, though—if you don't want me to know he's here, he shouldn't leave his car on the drive."

"I can explain," I said, following Naomi outside. "It isn't what you think."

"You're still in love with him, aren't you?"

"No, I—"

"Did you think I wouldn't notice you'd taken a photo of Phil from my house?"

I grimaced with embarrassment.

"If you'd just let me explain."

I'd switched from wanting her away from the house to not being able to bear the thought of her leaving. I couldn't let her believe I was having an affair with Phillip. The idea was ludicrous, but then, so was the fact that I'd taken a picture from her house just so there wouldn't be thirteen photos.

"When you said he were having an affair, did you think I wouldn't know it was you? Well, the joke's on you 'cause I don't want him anyway. The shit I've put up with . . . You've done me a favor and I hope the both of you rot in hell. Is it even true? Does he even have cancer?"

Cancer.

I tilted my head to one side, hoping I'd misheard.

"What?"

"Or were that another lie? Hard to tell anymore."

Phillip with cancer? Naomi was angry and her voice was raised and shrill.

"Well, if it *is* true, you're welcome to wipe his arse and feed him

88

through a tube as he gets sick. You can be the one who sits by the side of his bed as he wheezes away. I hope you enjoy the time you've got left. You'll be lucky to get a couple of months with him. You'd better make the most of it."

I put both my hands upon the hood of Naomi's car and bent over to wait for my head to stop spinning.

"He's got cancer?" I asked quietly.

"I'nt that the reason you've taken him back?"

"I haven't taken him back."

Naomi put her hands on her hips and glared at me, but some of her defiance was gone.

"Then what's going on?" she asked.

I looked back at the house. Who knew? Phillip was a master manipulator and I couldn't trust anything that came out of his mouth. But . . . the erratic behavior, the time off work, the desperation to get more time with Alistair . . . If he'd told me he had cancer, I would have called him a liar, but the deceit, and the fact that he was obviously hiding something, had a ring of truth to it.

"If . . ." I stammered, not sure what to ask first. "If . . . he does have cancer, why is he in such a hurry to get me out of the house and to finalize the divorce? He could just . . . wait."

Naomi threw her hands up to the skies as if it was anyone's guess.

"All I can tell you is, he *said* it was so that we could get married before he died. Said he wanted to make sure that loose ends were tied up and that I were entitled to his pension. But now, here he is, shacked up with you."

"He's not shacked up with . . . Oh, shit."

I concentrated on my feet, my breathing. Now wouldn't be a good time for a panic attack. I studied the pebbles beneath my feet. I counted to ten and then ten again. This didn't sound like the Phillip I knew. But then, did I really know him anymore? Had I ever? If Phillip had been trying to do right by Naomi for a change, then I'd misjudged his motives. Surely I could be forgiven for that.

"No," I said. "That still doesn't explain everything. He could sell the house and finalize the divorce without me moving out."

"He thinks you'd put any buyers off."

I shook my head, but he had a point. I certainly wouldn't have made things easy for him. Naomi unlocked the car and the side lights flashed.

"What kind of cancer is it?" I asked. I needed facts, something tangible. I didn't want to believe that I had locked up a terminally ill man.

"Lung. But it's spread."

The same as his father had. *No, no, no.* I still didn't trust him, but Naomi, who wasn't given to blind faith, did. I mentally gave him the once-over. He'd lost a little weight, hadn't he? His skin looked slacker and duller than usual. He might—just might—be telling the truth.

"If that's true, how long's he got?"

"No one knows but he reckons he's got weeks, not months."

"Why didn't he say something?"

Naomi raised her voice again. "Look, I came here to give you the chance to be honest wi' me. I'm not gonna stand here to be made a fool of."

"It's not how it looks, Naomi."

"Really? So tell me what's going on, then."

I wondered about letting her drive away; perhaps I should have. If she washed her hands of him, my rashness might not be discovered for a while longer. It would give me time to work out what I was going to do. Tempting, but I knew how it felt to be betrayed and I couldn't let her leave believing that I would do that to her.

"You're right—I do have something to tell you," I said. "First, though, just so I understand—you'd agreed to stay with him until the end? Marry him?"

She nodded.

"And is that . . . I'm sorry to ask, but is that because you love him or because you want financial security?"

"What's that got to do with—"

"Humor me."

She screwed up her face. We both knew that the honest answer wouldn't paint her in a good light or let her maintain the moral high ground.

"Right," I said. "In that case, this situation can still be salvaged."

I stepped closer to her and lowered my voice.

"I can promise you, on Alistair's life, that Phillip and I are not having an affair."

She nodded, a little unsure, but willing to listen.

"You see, it's far, far worse than that," I said.

I knew a fall was coming, felt the climb to the top of the roller coaster—once I told her, there was no going back.

"The thing is, Naomi—" I looked about me and listened for the sounds of neighbors. I didn't want anyone else hearing what I had to say. I'd not even intended Naomi to hear it, but here we were and I was left with little choice.

I lowered my voice to a whisper. "You see, the thing is, Naomi, I've locked Phillip in my cellar."

CHAPTER 11

11 days before the funeral

Naomi and I sat in her blue Fiesta facing the house. I had a grave mistrust of blue cars since the night of the accident, but Naomi hadn't even been old enough to drive when I'd lost the baby. The front door was slightly ajar. The house was waiting expectantly for us to go back in, as it knew we must.

Soft spots of rain appeared like teardrops on the windscreen. Naomi was silent as I told her about Phillip's ultimatums and the threats. I explained how he went into the cellar of his own free will and all I did was close the door. The fight, and subsequent fall, was his fault, and really, did I have any choice but to subdue him?

If I'd known about the cancer, I might have done things differently. But I might not.

"He's in the cellar right now. You can go and look if you like. If we were having an affair, would I lock him down there? Think about it. I've got no reason to lie about something like this."

She didn't take her eyes off the house and I didn't take my eyes off her. I was trying to read her face, but it was emotionless. I was shaking with nerves. I couldn't tell how she was going to react. Would she tell me I was crazy? Call the police? Demand I let him go?

"I didn't plan it," I continued desperately. "It's not like I want him here. What am I going to do about Alistair?" I held my hands up. "It's rash and stupid, but there's no easy way to fix what I've done. If I let him go now, two things are likely to happen. One, he's going to beat the shit out of me, and two, he's going to report me to the police. If I'm charged, I could lose custody of my son.

"Best-case scenario is that he does neither of these things, and instead he holds it over me to make sure I'm out of the house by the end of the month. Which means me and my son will be homeless."

She shifted in her seat to look at me and sneered.

"No, you won't. You'll live with your mum or your aunt or your next-door neighbor or whatever. You don't know what it's like to be homeless—like, actually living on the street, sleeping under a bridge. You haven't the first idea."

The way she spoke made me think that she had more than a theoretical grasp of homelessness.

"Okay," I said warily. "Okay. You're right, but a home is important, yeah? A place where you can feel safe?"

I was beginning to see how I could win Naomi over.

"This is the only home Alistair has ever known. Wouldn't it be great if he never had to worry about having a roof over his head? To know that he always had his mum? You know what it feels like to be separated from your family and to be taken from your home. And I don't think you'd want that for Alistair."

She was nodding gently. I had to keep pushing, though I could hardly believe I was doing this.

"I'd like to stay in this house, Naomi. And if Phillip really is dy-

93

ing, I can't see how kicking us out would benefit you. I know that it seems harsh for us to be considering our financial security while there's a dying man locked in my cellar, but me leaving the house isn't going to help him. And yes, you might feel a little more secure if he married you before he died, but I don't think we can guarantee he'd live long enough to make that a reality, or that he'd even go ahead with it once he's got what he wants from me. Besides, you're too young to be a widow."

I cleared my throat. She was staring at the house, but her face didn't betray her emotions.

"I know we don't have any reason to trust each other, but we both have reasons to distrust him. Am I right?"

She shrugged. At least I knew she was listening.

"You've worked hard on The Barn. It's more than a house; it's a home, isn't it? That must be nice. But . . ."

I turned in my seat to face her, leaning back against the car door. I needed a different way to get through to her.

"Do you know what's in Phillip's will?"

She shook her head briskly and took a deep breath. "Don't know if he even has one."

"Right. Which means he could screw you over, leave you with nothing. If he *is* dying, he might not have long left. And as he's still legally married to me, it's me who'll get The Barn, Naomi. And his pension. Work with me and I'll make sure that we both benefit from his death. We can get paperwork drawn up to make sure that everything is divided equally between us. I won't go after your home if you don't go after mine. Have you . . . have you any idea how big your mortgage is?"

"Dunno. Big, I think. He's always moaning that the deposit took all of his inheritance and the repayments are killing him."

"His life insurance will help, then, won't it? There might be enough to pay off both our mortgages. As long as we work together."

Her lips grew thin and hard.

"You've got nothing to fall back on, Naomi. No job. No family. And he knows that. How much power are you willing to give him? Are you going to let him ruin your future too? After everything he's done to you?"

She shifted uncomfortably in her seat, looked down at her hands. I was starting to get through to her. The heat from our bodies had begun to steam the car windows, and the house was an indistinct shape now.

"You know what we should do?" I continued. "We should take back control. We could use this to our advantage, Naomi. And you don't have to do anything except leave him where he is."

I let that sink in for a minute.

"You deserve better. We both do. All I'm suggesting is we take this opportunity to build a better life for ourselves, to make sure that his will benefits us all."

She laid her head back against the headrest. I gave one last push.

"All we have to do is make him see things our way. There's a bed and a fridge and a telly down there; I've stayed in worse hotels. I'll keep this house and my son, and you get to keep The Barn. We'll split any money that's left over after the debts are settled."

"And what will we do with *him*?" she asked, nodding toward the house.

Good question.

"We could look after him until he dies. If what you're telling me is right, it shouldn't be long. What could be more innocent than the two of us taking care of him?"

"Are you serious?"

"I don't know." I groaned. "Are you sure he's got cancer?"

"Makes sense, doesn't it? I mean, he's always been a bit of a shit, but lately he's taken it to a new level, you know? And you were right that he's not been in work for weeks. I went into the station and they could barely look me in the eye. Said they couldn't talk to me about Phillip without his express permission or something. I knew something were on his mind but I never guessed it were this."

"What about treatment?" I asked.

"Doesn't want it. Says it wouldn't cure him, so what's the point?"

A woman walked by pushing a stroller. The wheels rumbled over the sidewalk. I glanced over my shoulder at her, but she didn't seem to notice us sitting in the car scheming to keep someone in handcuffs.

I wasn't the type of person to plot someone's incarceration. I didn't break laws—I didn't even break the simplest of rules. And yet here I was, calmly talking about how to use a man's death to my advantage. I could hardly believe I was in this situation, but unless I talked Naomi into joining me, the whole world would know what I'd done and I would lose the only thing that mattered to me. Alistair.

"He really is dying, then," I said.

"Looks like it. I mean, I thought he were talking rubbish at first. Just a way to get off the hook for trying to drown me. But for a while now he's been hiding something. His mind's always somewhere else. He said I could go with him for his next oncology appointment. He'd already canceled it, said he didn't want to know how far it's spread, but he'd rearrange it just for me so I could hear it for myself."

"And are you going to?"

"No. Hate hospitals. I can see why he doesn't want to go. It won't make a blind bit of difference."

Perhaps I should have felt sad, but none of what Naomi was telling me felt real. I found myself pleased that he was dying, relieved that he wouldn't be a problem for much longer, and then my stomach lurched as I was stung by guilt.

"Well, it's up to you, Naomi. What will it be? Are we going to leave him where he is, or are we going to walk back in there and set him free so you can take him home with you to die?"

Naomi's fingers touched her hairline, where the cut was still raw, and slowly followed the line toward her eye. She took a deep breath and sat up straight.

"But if we're not going to let him go, why would he sign anything we ask him to?"

"Because," I said, "he's not the only one who can keep a secret."

Naomi drove Phillip's car home and returned in a taxi with a large suitcase, a bottle of brandy, and a second pair of handcuffs. She was unpacking Phillip's bag when I walked into the kitchen.

"Who else are you expecting to cuff?" I asked.

"You never know."

I picked up a box of tablets and turned them over. Naomi pointed to the middle of her chest. "For his acid reflux."

I nodded and put them down, surprised by her simple act of tending to his needs despite what he'd done to her.

"If we've got to convince people we're looking after him proper," she said, "I thought we should at least pretend we care."

I smiled.

"Shall we get this done?" I asked.

Naomi held the cheese sandwich and a glass of red wine. I picked up an armful of clothes and the second pair of cuffs. We'd need to cuff his wrists to the radiator before we undid the ones for his ankle if he were to get changed. Though I was in no mood to dress him, it was important that he thought we were looking after him.

I opened the cellar door and stood back to let Naomi descend to the cool, dimly lit room.

There was a faint musty smell in the cellar that I hadn't noticed before.

We rounded the corner cautiously and Phillip laughed unkindly when he saw Naomi.

"I should have bloody known," he said.

"Missed me?"

"Like the fucking plague."

She held the sandwich out to him.

"Not hungry," he said.

"Then starve," she said.

He took the wine when offered. He made it swirl up the sides and settle, then swirled again. He looked like he was in a fine restaurant. He sniffed it.

"Not that I'm complaining," he said, "but isn't it a bit *odd* to tie a fella up, then bring him wine?"

"Forgive us," I said curtly. "We're new to this."

I placed the folded-up bundle of clothes on the sofa next to him. Brown cord trousers, crisp white T-shirt, and a navy blue round-necked jumper, over socks and boxer shorts. That was new. He'd always worn briefs when he was with me.

"This isn't the way to go about kidnapping," he said.

"Don't be so melodramatic," I said. "You've not been kidnapped. We're bringing you wine, for God's sake. We want to talk to you about some important things without you threatening us or walking away. For now, though, we've got some sorting out of our own to do, so we'll all sit down and have a good talk tomorrow, okay?"

Naomi and I left the cellar without waiting for an answer.

"Will you be all right?" I asked Naomi quietly. "I need to dash if I'm going to see Mother before I get Alistair."

She let out a low whistle. "Yeah. Think so. That went better than I expected."

"He's not as calm as he looks," I said. "He'll be seething about being locked down there. Don't get too close to him, don't undo his cuffs, no matter what he says."

"What should I do if he kicks off?" she asked.

"Don't worry—he won't. Perhaps I should have said, I put a couple of sleeping tablets in his wine. He'll be pretty docile for the rest of the afternoon. We'll keep him drugged until I can get Alistair out of the house tomorrow, and then we can go to work. I'll make sure we get everything we want from Phillip. He doesn't need money where he's going."

CHAPTER 12

11 days before the funeral

Mother refused to stay at my house when she was discharged from the hospital. It was just as well.

She sat, cocooned by cushions, on a sagging dark green leather sofa facing the French doors that opened onto the garden. The sofa didn't suit her. Too soft, too inviting, too likely to have you stay a while—the exact opposite of her personality.

Her ground-floor apartment had a shared garden, which she never lifted a finger to weed. The residents paid Bill to come around and coax life into the garden, though he appeared to spend most of the winter weeks in Mother's kitchen inspecting the biscuit tin and talking of longer, sunnier days when the lasses would flock to him. Better days, long-gone days, the likes of which he'd never see again. He talked of the residents as "old folk," but he was as timeworn as any of them—he just hadn't realized it yet.

The flower beds were peppered with daffodils. They struggled to remain upright against the wind that sideswiped the space beyond the patio. Spring, like summer, and any hint of warmth, arrived later at Mother's than anywhere else in the county. It would be unkind to suggest that it was her glacial temperament that caused buds to seek solace underground.

Small birds wove and plaited their paths around the bird table in search of nuts, and discarded their unwanted seeds over the scarce grass. "Food for the squirrels," Bill would say.

For each of the three days since she'd come out of the hospital I'd visited her after the morning school run, helped her get dressed, and wiped a duster over the figurines. Today I was late. Lunchtime had come and gone—and so, it seemed, had her patience.

"Would it have hurt you to call?" she snapped.

"You look nice," I said, sidestepping her barb. "Is that a new blouse?"

"Do I look like I'm in any fit state to go shopping? It took me an age to do up the buttons."

"It's a shame you didn't take advantage of that care package they offered, isn't it? Someone could have come in to help you."

"The next time I let someone else dress me, I'll be in a wooden box."

"But it's okay for me to do it?"

"You don't count."

"Nope. I never have."

"Stop the self-pity, Imogen. It's not your best look."

I looked about the room for something to tidy or put away. Trying to find a way to make myself useful before I had to leave. Fringed lamps sat atop dark wood tables. A magazine rack, like a Venus flytrap by her side, was stuffed with old copies of *Derbyshire Life*. There were no personal touches, no photographs of Alistair or me, and none of my father. I knew that she bought herself flowers on their wedding anniversary every year, but my father's name was never mentioned.

"Can I ask you something?" I said.

She shrugged.

"When Father died—"

Her head snapped back to look at me.

"—was there anything you wish you'd have done differently? For *me*, that is?"

I couldn't stop thinking about Phillip having cancer. When *my* dad had died, it had come as a shock. But with Phillip we knew the end was coming, and I wondered how it could be managed to cause as little hurt to Alistair as possible.

"Do you do this just to hurt me, Imogen?"

"No, Mother." I sighed. "There are other reasons too."

Since my run-in with Phillip, it was as if I couldn't stop speaking my mind, but I decided to let the subject of my father's death drop. Mother never liked to talk about him, and seeing as I couldn't explain to her why I was asking, I thought it safer to move on.

Whether I kept Phillip locked up or let him go, there was no denying that this time next year there would be little trace of Phillip Rochester. How would I recall him when I talked to Alistair about him? Would I give Phillip the same treatment as most of the deceased got? A eulogy fit for a saint? Or an honest account of a man who destroyed anyone who was stupid enough to love him?

"I've put your milk and eggs in the fridge. You've got a couple of those M&S meals in there too. Are you going to be all right on your own? I need to dash to get Alistair."

"The eggs don't need to be in the fridge."

"Still, that's where they are, in case you were wondering."

Mother shifted in her seat to look at me. She was no longer wearing her sling.

"I am not an invalid, Imogen. It's been nearly a week since I had a fall. They said I only had to rest for a few days."

Older people always *had* a fall, they never fell. I wondered at what age falling became something that happened to you rather than something you did.

"Still, best not to rush things, eh?" I said.

"That's become your motto in life, hasn't it?"

Mother was adept at the verbal slap. And I was skillful in turning the other cheek. Until today.

"Yep, getting it tattooed on my arse. Anyway, have you thought any more about going to Aunt Margaret's?"

Aunt Margaret was the younger, prettier sister and the apparent reason that I was spared any siblings. They had never seen eye to eye. Ever since she'd retired to Spain and picked lemons off her own tree for her presupper G and T, she was to be actively despised. They bickered constantly yet seemed to enjoy the sport.

"I suppose it might be nice to get away a while. Maybe next week."

"Let me know and I'll make sure I'm around to take you to the airport."

"It's okay. Bill will take me."

"Bill? I didn't realize you were close."

She looked at me, affronted. "He's the handyman."

"Yes, but how *handy* is he?" I aimed a theatrical wink in her direction and she batted it away with a look that said I was deluded.

I kissed the top of her head, but she sat rigid. I breathed her in.

She smelled of Dove soap and washing day. All things clean and scrubbed. I associated Mother with cleanliness. Never a speck of dirt under her fingernails, never a hair out of place, and never a stray emotion muddying the waters. If what they say is true—that cleanliness is next to godliness—then Mother was a shoo-in for heaven.

"I won't be able to pop round tomorrow. I've got this . . . this *thing*. Well, lots of things. I'm really busy. I'll bring you over your lunch on Sunday, though. Yeah? Is that okay? And you'll call if you need anything?" I was already halfway to the door with car keys in my hand. She didn't reply.

I drove to the school scrolling through radio stations for something to occupy my mind but ended up switching the radio off and letting my thoughts roam. By the time I'd parked the car, an informal group stood by the gates waiting for them to be unlocked. I hung back, not wanting to be pulled into conversations about homework and holiday plans.

Tristan was in front of me. His suit jacket was crumpled at the back, suggesting a long car journey or hours stuck in meetings. I imagined his tie rolled into a ball in his pocket and the top button of his blue-striped shirt open. His neck was tanned except for half an inch below the hairline, which suggested a recent haircut. He was tall and slender, built like a cyclist but with pianist's hands.

He was good-looking with the right amount of stubble on his chin and enough flecks of gray at his temples to make him seem human. His glasses made him look intelligent and vulnerable at the same time. He had a gentle smile and kind eyes, but it was his broad shoulders that caught my eye a split second before he caught me staring.

I blushed like I had been caught doing something wrong.

"Hi," he said, and stepped back a couple of paces so we were level.

"Hi."

I smoothed my hair and combed it a little with my fingers at the same time.

"Busy day?" he asked.

"Yeah. Family stuff, errands, and you know . . . I've been off today, so . . ."

"All right for some," he said.

"Yep. Life of Riley."

He tilted his head on one side but didn't say anything. His hazel eyes were shining behind his thin-rimmed glasses. I wondered who Riley was, bemused that I had chosen this precise moment to use the phrase for the first time in my life.

Tristan had the PTA hearts aflutter since he'd become chief carer for his two children. It was only rumor, but there were whispers on the playground grapevine that Sally had left Tristan for her female gym instructor. Tristan didn't court the sympathy bestowed on him. He challenged the stereotype that children should stay with their mothers after a breakup and won countless hearts in the process. He was the opposite of Phillip in looks and temperament, but still, the fact that he had sole custody of his children had made me fearful that Phillip's threats of taking Alistair away from me could be realized. Was it wrong to be thankful that Phillip was dying and would never get his hands on my son?

"Anything planned this weekend?" Tristan asked.

"Me? I've got . . . people staying."

"Sounds nice."

"In that case, I've oversold it. You?"

"What's that?"

"Anything planned?"

"Oh. No. Sally's turn to have Ethan and Freya, so I'm home alone. I'll probably catch up on some reading, maybe paint the kitchen, watch a bit of telly."

I nodded. I knew the emptiness of a child-free weekend. There'd been days I would have given anything for some alone time, yet when Alistair was at his dad's, I couldn't remember how I used to fill my hours. Without him, I lost my purpose. I tried taking up hobbies, but the half-finished watercolors ended up in the bin, the knitted scarf never reached longer than four inches, and the new trainers I'd purchased for early-morning runs in the park still hadn't made it out of the box. My mind elsewhere, it took me a moment to realize that Tristan was saying something.

"Sorry?" I said. "Didn't catch that."

"I said, I can't remember what I did before the kids came along."

"I was just thinking the same thing."

The gates clanged open and we filed across the hopscotch and the painted snakes.

"Well, if you're ever at a loose end one weekend, if your ex has the kids at the same time as Sally, then we'll have to grab a coffee or something."

"Phillip doesn't really have Alistair much. Well, not anymore."

"Okay. Never mind, then."

"Sorry."

"Not a problem. Have a good weekend."

"You too."

We filed round to our different doors to await our children and I cursed myself for passing up the opportunity to spend time with an attractive single dad. Rachel would have known what to do.

When Alistair noticed me, he pulled on the sleeve of Miss Hambly. She looked up and searched the crowd until she caught my eyes and nodded. Alistair ran to me with his shirt untucked and his tie at an angle.

"Hey, buddy!"

I picked up his schoolbag, sports bag, lunch box, and artwork.

"So, guess who wants to take you to the movies tomorrow?" I asked.

"Daddy?" His eyes shone with excitement. Even though—or perhaps *because*—Phillip treated him with indifference, Alistair craved his dad's attention. I couldn't blame him. It wasn't that long since I'd been the same.

"No, not Daddy. Rachel has invited you for a sleepover and she's going to take you to see a film. How cool is that?"

He nodded. He loved Rachel. She was the closest thing he had to an aunty and the closest thing I had to a sister, but, try as she might, she was no substitute for a father's love.

CHAPTER 13

10 days before the funeral

Saturday rumbled in on the back of whip-crack lightning that split the sky in two and illuminated the room as if setting the scene for a film noir.

My bedroom door sprang open and Alistair tumbled on top of me as reverberations of thunder shook the house. We lay in bed counting the seconds that kept the flashes and the rumbles apart like a referee at a boxing match. Alistair's heart hammered beneath my hand and he shrank into the crook of my arm. He still believed in that special kind of magic—a parent's touch that could keep fear at bay, kisses that could heal a scraped knee, hugs that would mend a broken heart.

I'd let Alistair watch telly in bed with a tray of treats in order to keep him as far away from Phillip as possible. Once he was asleep, Naomi and I checked on Phillip from time to time, but otherwise we sat staring into space, drinking vodka, and waiting for Phillip to wake up. By eleven, we gave up waiting and went to bed. I agreed to stop giving him any more sleeping tablets.

Another flash lit up the corners of my room but disappeared before I could identify the shadows and dark shapes that had been illuminated. The cracks were beginning to show, but the storm was yet to break.

Naomi was sleeping, or at least lying, in the spare room with its rosebud curtains and matching bedspread. I'd decorated it with Mother in mind, thinking she'd be the only one to sleep there. Each Sunday after swimming she would retire to the rosebud room so she could help with the Monday morning school run while I dashed to the early-morning team meeting.

Phillip hadn't encouraged visitors and we hadn't any friends who would visit from afar or come around for a dinner party and stay the night after one too many. We weren't *those* kind of people.

Like everyone who had secrets to hide, we kept ourselves to ourselves. Barriers up. Distances kept. Mr. and Mrs. Rochester, friendly folk who always asked after your ailing father and remembered your birthday but had to dash off the moment the conversation turned to them.

I wasn't comfortable with Naomi sleeping under my roof, and less so with Phillip under my floor. I didn't sleep. Sleeping tablets wouldn't help, because I didn't want to lengthen the distance between me and consciousness. With Phillip in my house, home was no longer a place of safety. His presence made me desperate to stay alert. It was the beginning of an earthquake. He was the tremor beneath me that unsettled my foundations and promised more disruption to come. There was a tsunami coming and it was only made possible by my rashness. I had put us all in danger by taking on someone I couldn't beat. He was only a man, but he was the only man who knew how to destroy me. One smirk, one look, one comment. That was all it took. He might be dying, but he was showing no signs of weakness.

As long as Phillip was locked up, then I was in control. I got to say when he ate, what he ate, *if* he ate at all. I might be deluding myself, but for once it felt good to have the upper hand.

Alistair flopped into sleep and I moved my arm, flexing my fingers against pins and needles. A house alarm was whining down the road. I knew it would be number 27. Their alarm went off every time the wind blew. I looked at the clock to note, with indignation, the time that my peaceless night of nonslumber had been interrupted, but the radio alarm was in complete darkness. I glanced at the door where the orange glow of the bathroom acted as a night-light for Alistair, but there was only the solid immovable certainty of darkness. Phillip.

I snatched my arm from underneath Alistair's neck, and he murmured and turned over. The fuse box was in the cellar, but Phillip's chain shouldn't be long enough for him to reach it. Unless he'd ripped the radiator off the wall. Unless he'd picked the lock. Unless someone had freed him.

I slid out of bed and picked up the bedside lamp, holding it like a baseball bat. The door was still open from when Alistair had flung it open. A flash of lightning bleached the landing and I saw an empty staircase. I struggled to hear any sound above my own beating heart.

Thunder boomed overhead and I ducked, pulling the lamp with me and yanking the plug from the wall. I stayed crouched on the floor, less of a target to hit. I mentally scrolled through our escape routes. We could lock ourselves in the master bathroom and wait for help to come. Which was fine, as long as Phillip hadn't already slipped past me and was waiting for me there.

A floorboard creaked on the landing. I could picture stealthy footsteps edging toward my door. Even if we could get past him on the stairs and get to the front door, the chain, the bolt, and the lock would delay our escape. I stayed crouched but slid toward the door, waiting for the next flash and rumble so I could dart out and surprise him. I got to one knee and held the lamp firmly in both hands. The flash came quicker this time and flickered for two, maybe three seconds. I sprang up and rounded the door. The landing was empty. I let the lamp fall by my side and gripped the doorframe.

I glanced to the bedroom window, which was little more than a faint gray shape on an already gray wall. The bay window of the living room was beneath us. Where it jutted out, there was a small sloping roof, a parapet, but the drop was still a long one. Without taking my eyes off the door, I edged around the bed to the window to see for myself whether this was our best escape option.

I looked cautiously around the curtain, measuring the drop to the driveway beneath. I almost didn't notice what was wrong about the night. The colors were wrong. I couldn't see the bottom of the driveway. The bushes and shrubs of my front yard were smudged.

I could see that some of my neighbors were at their windows too. A few had wrapped themselves in curtains; others had opened their windows and were leaning brazenly over the ledges in their pajamas. There was only the slimmest of moons and the whole street was without electricity. Starved of glowing orange streetlights, my once familiar road had become alien and frightening.

Darkness. The whole street was without power. After first wondering how Phillip could have caused such a thing, I realized that this power cut was nature flexing its muscles, not man. Phillip was still where I had left him and he was not coming for me. I laughed aloud, some of the tension leaving my body. I was shaking as I sat down on the end of the bed and knotted my fingers in the duvet cover.

Lack of sleep was to blame for my sudden jump to an extreme conclusion. Phillip was cruel, but he wasn't superhuman. He was probably still groggy with sleeping tablets, if he was awake at all. His old handcuffs that served as his restraints had been used on stronger men than him. I didn't need to worry.

If it hadn't been for Alistair, I would have curled up under the duvet and waited for morning, but the dark scared him. Landing lights had to be left on, night-lights positioned in his room. More than once, Phillip had made him walk up the stairs in the blackness in order, he said, to prove that there was nothing to be afraid of. It didn't work. Any mother could have told him that, but not me. I was too scared of him to disagree; Phillip was *my* darkness.

I didn't believe Alistair would wake until the first shafts of sunlight hammered gold leaf over the room, but, just in case, I fumbled into my robe and brushed my way downstairs to get emergency lighting. I gripped the banister as a lifeline. I felt the stairs beneath my toes, and when the carpet turned to tile I knew I was at the bottom. I groped my way into the kitchen, eyes wide, though there was no light to be had. Though the cellar door was locked and bolted, I pushed myself against the opposite wall as I went past, fearing that Phillip's malevolence would hook me from beneath the door. The distress of thinking he was free in the house was yet to leave me. I was skittish and confused. I quickened my pace and knocked into a chair, which screeched my presence and caused me to swear.

I fumbled for tea lights, matches, and a flashlight under the sink in an old ice cream tub. I clicked on the flashlight and put everything else in my pocket. I had to take a moment to calm myself before I left the kitchen. I opened the vodka bottle, poured myself two inches of composure, and knocked it back. I left the glass on the table and stopped by the cellar door to listen.

Just as I knew he would, Phillip called my name.

I wondered about walking on by, ignoring him. I didn't have to answer to him anymore. What was the worst he could do if I didn't answer?

I opened the door.

"Yes?"

"What's happened?" He sounded sleepy. His voice was soft and warm.

"Power cut. The whole street's out."

"I can't see a bloody thing. Bring me a candle." There was a moment's pause, just long enough for it to be noticeable before he added, "Please."

"You'll have to wait a minute."

I walked, without haste, back to my bedroom. The ceilings looked higher lit up by flashlight, and the corners sharper. The light didn't go far enough to illuminate my path and only succeeded in making the darkness blacker. I lit a tea light on the top of the dresser and kissed Alistair's downy head. I sat on the side of the bed watching him sleep, the firelight glow stroking his face each time a breeze pushed through the rotting window frames. I knew I wouldn't be able to protect him from everything, but I would do my best.

I brushed my hair into a ponytail and pulled on some leggings. I listened outside Naomi's room but there was no sound. Enough time had passed to make Phillip think he was way down on my list of priorities, so I made my way to the cellar. The flashlight's orb bounced ahead of me down the stairs and cut across the cellar steps.

When it alighted on Phillip, he blinked and sat up. He was wearing his jumper in bed and rubbed his hands together to bring warmth to his fingers.

"Bloody cold," he said. "You got another blanket anywhere?"

Naomi had helped him turn the sofa into a bed and he looked almost comfortable. I coaxed the tea light into a small cream tea glow and went behind the partition to where we kept the camping equipment. I found a flashlight, clicked it on, and handed it to him. Then I pulled a sleeping bag out of its cocoon and unzipped it so it lay flat. I placed it over him. It smelled fusty, but beggars can't be choosers.

"Cheers," he said. "You forget how dark it gets down here. And cold."

"You're welcome."

"How long till the power's back up?"

"Don't know. Soon, I hope."

I sat on the bottom step so I wasn't quite in the same room as him. I watched as he put the flashlight on the arm of the sofa bed and tucked the sleeping bag around and under his legs. He shivered and coughed twice. I wondered whether the cancer was announcing its presence.

"Naomi and I have been talking," I said.

"And?"

"I know about the cancer. Why didn't you tell me?"

There was a moment's hesitation, a pause as he carefully chose his words.

"I'm not sure it's any of your business."

"Not my business? What about Alistair? When were you going to tell him?"

"When it became difficult for me to hide it anymore."

The weak light from the flashlights and tea light highlighted his heavy brow and the bags under his eyes. Shadows crept between the creases on his forehead. The light tricked his face into looking older than it would ever be.

"Naomi says you've refused all treatment."

His mouth drooped at the sides, bottom lip slightly protruding. He cocked his head from side to side as if he were weighing up the validity of the statement.

"'Refused' is a bit strong." He pushed himself up the bed. He raised his chin and peered down his nose at me, a sad smile lifting one side of his mouth.

"They caught it too late. Doesn't matter that I've not smoked in twenty years. The damage is already done. Any treatment at this point would just make me sick for the time I've got left. You know me, Immie—if I'm gonna go, I've got to do it on my terms." He waved his hand in a flourish, like a magician announcing his final trick.

I stared at his chest as if I could see through his rib cage to the dark mass that was killing him from the inside out. Incurable. Terminal.

"Tell me about it."

He sighed. I thought he wasn't going to speak, but then he took a deep breath and told me everything, or at least everything he wanted me to know. He told me about the routine checkup that led to nonroutine scans and the discovery of masses and lesions. He told me about ignoring the signs, putting it down to old age and discovering that he wasn't immortal after all. He told me he was beyond the point of recovery. He used words like "metastasized" and "stage four" and he dismissed my replies of "chemotherapy" and "hospice." In forty years he'd never gone to the doctor's for anything more serious than tennis elbow brought on by a dodgy golf swing. It had taken him by surprise that his body had let him down.

"How long do you have left?" I asked.

"How long's a piece of string? And what does it matter anyway? The best days of my life are finished. Over the next few weeks my lungs'll shut down and I'll choke to death. That's it, Immie. That's it. It's over."

"I'm sorry to hear that, Phillip."

"Save it," he said. "We both know you're not. Couldn't have come at a better time for you, could it?"

"No, I really am sorry. I know what it's like to lose your father at a young age, and I wouldn't wish that on Alistair."

He coughed out a laugh. "At least that's honest. I'd not want you to pretend that you were sorry for me anyway. Just Alistair. Always Alistair."

"No, it's not that," I muttered. "It's just that I . . ." My words dried up.

"So now you know," he said, "why I've been trying to tie everything up as quickly as possible. I didn't want you to find out like this, but now that you have, you're surely going to let me go. Right?"

I studied my knees, picking at the pilled material. It was impossible to explain my thoughts when I didn't understand them myself. I wondered whether I was a monster for locking him up. Did this make me as bad as him? Faced with Phillip at his most reasonable, I began to wonder about my own motivation for keeping him down here. I had to keep reminding myself that this had only happened because of him. Because he'd tried to kick us out of the only home Alistair had ever known, because he'd threatened to take my son away, because he'd attacked me. None of this was my fault, but I was so used to being made to feel guilty that I was finding it difficult to remember that.

"I don't trust you," I said quietly. "Naomi and I have agreed to get one of those do-it-yourself wills. I don't mean to be insensitive, but you don't exactly need money or property where you're going. This way we can make sure that we have some security."

He shrugged and looked at the ceiling.

"Let me go and I'll make an appointment with my solicitor first thing on Monday. Get that will and divorce sorted at the same time."

The candle fluttered and went out.

The light from the flashlight was harsh and cold.

"It's not just about what I want. It's what's best for all of us," I said.

He clicked off his flashlight. On again. Off again. The only light came from the flashlight I was holding, which was trained on the floor at my feet.

"Are you not sick of trying to save me yet?"

And that was half the problem. I used to think that if I walked away from him, no one else would care enough to help him become a better version of himself. If I gave up on him, who would stand by him? How would he ever change? He would never show love if he didn't *know* love. Funny how we all think that we have the power to save.

It was difficult to be angry with someone who was terminally ill. I felt guilty for hating him when his life was due to be cut short.

I could hear running water outside; the rain had come and it was hitting the ground hard. I lay my head against the cold wall. Phillip was silent. We both were. We watched the shadows dance across the walls. There wasn't enough light to reach into the corners, and it was getting colder.

"I should go in case Alistair wakes up. It's late. Can we talk about this later?"

"I'd like to see him."

"I know you would. I'll see what I can do tomorrow."

"Sure. Whatever you think is best."

He was being so reasonable that I further doubted my own motives for having him there. I'd made him out to be a monster, and yet all I had to do was sit down and talk to him. A person can't get the news that he is terminally ill without changing on a fundamental level. His cancer could be the best thing that had ever happened to us.

I raised my hand good night and left the cellar. This time, though I shut the door, I didn't lock it. What danger could he possibly be to us now?

I went up to the bedroom, opened the window, and leaned out into the dark night. The rain had slowed to a steady patter and the air smelled like freshly dug earth. It smelled like the grave.

CHAPTER 14

10 days before the funeral

Rachel's three-story house clung to the side of a hill so steep that I had to check, and double-check, my handbrake before Alistair and I got out of the car. There were black iron railings out front and a glossy black door. The stern facade was more like a solicitor's office than a home. It was in a nice neighborhood and in walking distance from some swanky bars. There was no yard to tend to, just a courtyard; there was no driveway, just a parking permit. In what was largely a child-free suburb such as this one, bedroom curtains were still drawn at nine thirty in the morning. I both envied and pitied them.

I'd never left Alistair overnight at Rachel's before. He'd only rarely slept at The Barn. If he wasn't under the same roof as me, I couldn't sleep.

Rachel answered the door with oven gloves over her shoulder. Her hair was pinned in a messy bun that would have taken me hours to re-create. Even in shorts and a hoodie, she looked stylish.

"Bloody hell. What time do you call this? When you said mid-morning, I thought you meant elevenish."

"Since when is eleven 'midmorning'?"

"When you don't get out of bed until ten, eleven is very much midmorning. You're lucky I'm even bloody dressed."

She swore more in an hour than I did in a year. Motherhood had placed a permanent hold on my tongue. Aggressive drivers had become "wallies" instead of "wankers" and I had been known to mutter such rich obscenities as "flip off" to the judgmental "balatard" who worked in my office.

When my son was only two and in the process of expanding his vocabulary, I managed to enrich it further by reversing into a lamp-post and saying "bugger." Every time he dropped a toy or the wooden blocks tumbled down, he would use his newfound word. It took weeks for toddlers to recognize the difference between a cat and a dog, but only a split second to remember the only time Mummy had sworn in front of them. If anything, I was to be congratulated. If there was a role that invited profanity more than motherhood, I was yet to find it.

Rachel gave me a brief squeeze and high-fived Alistair. With a wave of her hand, she signaled that Alistair should go through to the kitchen and she proffered a parking permit for the dashboard of my car.

"I'm not staying."

"Bollocks you're not. I'm not letting you leave until I hear every last drop of gossip. Our film doesn't start until two. Bags of time."

I did as she said, then joined them in the kitchen.

"I'm making cupcakes," she said.

"You bake?"

"I do now."

The kitchen looked more like a Jackson Pollock canvas than the high-gloss minimalist gallery it had previously been. Alistair ran straight outside to the courtyard and jumped on Rachel's mini trampoline.

"Do you really use that thing?"

"Abso-bloody-lutely. Best exercise you can get, apart from the obvious."

She moved closer to me and spoke quietly so that Alistair couldn't hear.

"So Naomi's at the house? *Your* house? Shit. Forget the cinema. Give me a bag of popcorn and I'm there. So the two of you are going to . . . what? I don't understand why the hell either of you care what happens to Phillip anyway."

"I don't. Well, I do, for Alistair's sake."

"Does Alistair know about the cancer?" asked Rachel.

"Not yet. We need to decide how to break it to him. But first we have to agree on who gets what when Phillip dies. If he was left to his own devices, I wouldn't put it past him to spend the last weeks of his life spending every penny he's got or leaving it all to the dogs' home. It's best that Alistair's here in case it gets . . . heated."

"D'you think that's why he wanted you out of the house? So he could take the money and scarper?"

"I don't know. Something still doesn't feel right about all this. Naomi says it's so they can get married. Easier to sort the financial side if we're dealing with actual cash rather than assets and policies."

"And you don't believe her?"

"It's not *her* I doubt—it's him. I can't imagine him wanting to get married again, or caring whether Naomi is financially comfortable after he's dead. He's not mentioned how this will affect Alistair at all, so why would he provide for Naomi and not his son? I don't know. Do you think I'm being paranoid?"

"Yes, but for once, it's justified. If he's thinking about anyone, it's himself. If it didn't benefit him, he wouldn't do it. Whatever's behind it, though, I can't see why he'd listen to you and Naomi about the will."

"Oh, I don't know," I said carefully. "I think we've got him in a position where he can't really walk away."

I wanted to tell her what I'd done, but I dreaded how she would look at me. I was scared that her eyes would tell me that I had finally lost the plot. She wouldn't hold back on her judgment—it was one of the reasons I loved her. I was more than aware of the legal ramifications of locking someone up. If Rachel knew the truth about why I needed Alistair out of the house, she could be an accomplice to a crime, and I could never do that to her.

"Thanks for this, Rach."

"No probs. We're going to eat our body weight in popcorn while watching animals sing and dance. It's how I always spend my Saturday afternoons. Actually, it's a while since I've been to the movies, and for once I won't have to worry about my date trying to touch my breasts. Besides, I told you, it's a pleasure having Alistair around."

"His pj's, teddy, change of clothes, and toothbrush are in the rucksack."

"Right."

"He needs to be in bed by seven thirty at the latest, so I'd start the bedtime routine at six thirty?"

"You know I've done this before, right?"

"Sorry. I'm a bit—"

"You're being a bit of a mum."

"Yes, I am. I'll be round at ten tomorrow to pick him up. Alistair? Kisses!" He held on to me until Rachel told him about the planned trip to the movies, and then he couldn't wait to usher me out of the house.

Once outside Rachel's, I didn't drive away immediately. I looked at her house and wondered what I was becoming. Was I a bad mother for leaving my son, or a good one for making sacrifices to ensure we had a safe future?

As I drove slowly away from Rachel's house, I wondered about going to the police. I toyed with the idea that justice would be done, but there was no getting around the fact that Phillip was a popular and valuable member of CID. There was only one man in that station who saw past Phillip's facade, and that was Chris Miller, who'd caught his wife in bed with my husband.

Did I have any choice but to get Phillip to agree to our demands and nurse him until his dying day? I couldn't compete on a physical level with him, and I was an amateur in comparison when it came to being deceitful and devious. I knew he couldn't make a case for full custody of Alistair now, but I wasn't so convinced that he couldn't get me arrested for locking him up, and who would look after Alistair then?

The petrol gauge on my car was showing I was cutting it fine. The amber light was blinking. I would never usually let the level fall under a quarter of a tank, but today I almost wished for the car to break down so I wouldn't have to go home and face what was in my cellar. I had enough petrol to get home, but I would have to fill the car up before I went to get Alistair.

I pulled onto my drive to find Naomi waiting at the front door, smoking a cigarette. I turned off the engine and pretended to be looking for something in my handbag. Toy dinosaur, wet wipes, migraine tablets, lipstick, unposted birthday card, receipts. Whatever I was looking for, it wasn't there.

I sank back against the headrest with one hand on the door, not quite ready to face the music.

Naomi dropped her cigarette butt on the ground and leaned against the doorframe, looking past me into the far distance, where the unknown was loitering and our futures were yet to be set.

Naomi looked ready for a night out. Her long hair had been curled about her shoulders, and her lipstick was bright pink to match her nails. She was wearing a white vest top, with purple bra straps showing, over jeans that looked like they'd been painted on.

"You took your time," she said as I got out of the car.

"Have you heard much from him?"

"He gave me some agro when I took him his breakfast, but apart from that, not a peep."

I turned sideways to pass her and she didn't try to move out of my way. Before I'd kicked off my shoes, she called, "Hello, you expecting someone?"

A rattling old red Volkswagen Beetle pulled onto the drive next to mine, but seeing as there wasn't enough room, it bumped over my sparse flower bed. Music was shaking the rust-dipped car. The sound of Simon and Garfunkel singing over panpipes was abruptly cut and a heavyset woman flung the car door open.

When she got out of the car, I could see that she was barefoot under a long blue dress that was edged with mud and the skeletons of crushed leaves. A long cream chiffon scarf hung over her shoulders and the fringe shook as she slammed the door behind her.

Bangles rang and clanged all the way past her wrists and spun in the light as she adjusted her scarf. Her hair curled past her ears in softly graying waves.

"Shit," Naomi said.

The woman waved. I remembered that smile, all crooked teeth and thin lips. It was Phillip's first wife, Ruby.

It had been two years since I'd last seen her, but apart from a few more gray hairs, she hadn't changed. Since Phillip and I had separated, she'd become Naomi's problem, not mine. I'd been able to drop the pretense that I could stand her.

"How lovely to see you," I lied without a smile. "What are you doing here?"

Ruby was the ex-wife who had become the perpetual friend. It had caused arguments between us, but I never understood why Phillip kept seeing her. They shared jokes and remember-whens that I couldn't be part of. I wondered whether she just hung around so that she could pick up on my faults and show him what a mistake he'd made by leaving her. As for Phillip, he would never say no to someone hanging on his every word and looking at him like he could walk on water, and perhaps it suited him to remind me that nothing was forever.

I stepped out to greet her so she wouldn't come any closer to the house.

For so long, she had been the woman who infuriated me more than anyone else, the one who I was compared to, the first love. She had been my Rebecca: the outgoing, vivacious, mystery ex who I could never live up to. The perfect hostess and cook, the generous lover and friend. *You could learn a thing or two from her, Imogen.* The only difference being this one wasn't dead. She was a living specter in my life. And now she was stepping on my geraniums.

The first year after Alistair was born, she had come for Christmas dinner. Phillip didn't tell me he'd invited her until the morning. Ruby had been generous with gifts for Alistair, and was "only trying to be helpful" by buying me cream for my stretch marks. She was effusive over my burned offerings and my mediocre puddings, like she was praising a difficult child. She was all smiles and overflowing compliments, jam-packed with all the superlatives to describe my awesome, amazing, and—"quite frankly"—astounding parenting skills and my striking, stunning, and stylish house, and, oh, that dress, where *did* I get it? Yet nothing about it was genuine. The more she praised my attempt at making my own Christmas pudding—"I prefer them on the dry side, as it happens"—the more I wanted to ram it down her throat.

Ruby's heavy-lidded bovine eyes were too big for her face and were half closed as if she was just coming out of a particularly pleasant dream, one where she made coats out of puppies no doubt. She had dark eyes and skin and could have had ancestry anywhere from Italy to India.

Nothing touched Ruby. She was oblivious to the way other people looked at her. No joke could ever be at her expense because she wouldn't feel the barb. She floated along on a cloud of incense, looking at the joy and beauty of the world. She would stop her car in the middle of the road to look at a particularly beautiful sunset and be entirely unaware of the honking of the car behind her as the traffic built up. She was a vet, a vegetarian, her food was organic, and she gave a third of her income away to charity each month.

I disliked her intensely.

Two of her three dogs jumped and wagged at her knees. One was a standard medium-sized, rough-haired mutt with intelligent eyes. The smaller one was a dirty white color and had a back end that was indistinguishable from the front. The larger of the two immediately went to the small circular lawn, crouched, and relieved itself.

"There's no one at The Barn," she said. "Which is strange because Pip knew I was coming and his car is in the drive."

"Really?" I said, trying not to give anything away.

I used to hate her calling him Pip. She only did it to remind me they had pet names for each other.

"I was starting to need the bathroom and I knew you never went anywhere at the weekend, so here I am and what luck to find Naomi here too!"

Naomi's face dropped. "Was that this weekend?"

"Was what this weekend?" I asked through a tightened smile.

Ruby's third dog—an old black-and-white border collie with seen-it-all-before eyes and a wag kept for special occasions—unfolded from the car with some stiffness and walked past me into the house.

"Don't mind the dogs," Ruby said. "Soft as candy floss and twice as sweet, they are."

"Naomi? What's Ruby talking about?" I asked.

Ruby answered for her.

"Dinner, darling. Of course, I should have been here last night, but the weather! I tried calling, but there was no answer, which was odd because you were expecting me." She chided Naomi gently with a wagging finger.

Ruby batted her hair out of her eyes, put her hands on my shoulder, and looked me up and down. Seemingly satisfied, she folded me into her arms.

"So good to see you. *So* good. It has absolutely been too long, darling." Turning to face Naomi, she said, "Naomi, my sweet. What have you done to your head? Don't tell me—fallen over when you were drinking again? What did I tell you after last time?"

She put her open palm on Naomi's cheek and smiled. "Come here!"

Naomi was pulled into an embrace that she didn't return. She extracted herself and we stood side by side, like bouncers at an exclusive nightclub.

"Did you get storms here too? Bertie's wipers gave up the ghost long ago, so there was no way I could drive last night. Okay if I use your lav? I'm bursting."

I wanted to say no, to send her on her way, but I was struck dumb as she walked past me and into the house, leaving Naomi and me to look on in horror.

CHAPTER 15

18 years, 6 months, and 11 days before the funeral

R uby kicked off her sandals and hung her scarf over the sofa. The house was in darkness, but she could feel that Pip was home. It was a small cottage. Homey. From the front door you could see straight through the lounge and kitchen and into the downstairs bathroom. The only bathroom. The stairs ran up the space between the table that they never ate at and the corner with the sofa and the television. It was cozy, characterful, and big enough for her, Pip, and the dog. They would need to move to somewhere bigger when they had a family.

"Pip?" she called.

Ruby dropped her clutch onto the ottoman and went through to the kitchen. The party had been fun even though she hadn't touched a drop of alcohol all night. She was on a health kick that no one knew about. When people asked why she wasn't drinking, she told them that she was the designated driver.

What they didn't know was that she had joined the fancy new

gym in the converted mills by the park and was on the treadmill by six a.m. four mornings a week. The doctor said it wouldn't hurt to lose a bit of weight and look after herself a bit better. There was no reason why she couldn't conceive. These things would take time. All the best things did.

She opened the fridge to see how solace was dressed tonight. A mantle of cold meats or a robe of rich cheese? But with her resolve stronger than her greed, she closed it again. The remnants of today's dinner lay in the dish on the stove. She scraped at the edges of the fish pie with a fork. Just cleaning up the ends, not worth counting those calories.

The night air pushed its way into the kitchen through the open back door and the curtains swayed gracefully. The scent of warmed rosemary bushes and the lingering of a neighborhood barbecue reminded her that this was summer's last fling. She took a glass of water and flipped the switch for the outdoor light before she stepped outside.

Pip was on the low wall that separated the patio from the flat piece of ground that could be a lawn if they paid it some attention. He held a tumbler in one hand and a cigar in the other. He blew smoke rings into the air as she neared him, ever the kid playing at being a grown-up, trying to look cool.

"There you are. Didn't you hear me calling?"

Pip didn't answer. He was giving her the silent treatment, though Ruby didn't believe *she* needed treating.

Pip could be the most charming person you were ever likely to meet. His smile was the dawning of the sun. Ruby felt loved and important when it touched her, but when he turned away, the contrast was so marked she thought she might freeze in his shadow.

Ruby had given Pip two hours to calm down before she drove

home to face him. She had learned that no amount of talking could change Pip's mood. He dug in his heels if you tried to push, but if you waited long enough, he would come around. It was a good job that Ruby was patient.

Pip was still wearing his tie, though it was loose now around his unbuttoned collar. His jacket had been discarded somewhere between the party and the yard, but the rings of sweat still darkened his armpits and radiated toward his shirt pocket.

"Missed you at the party, darling," Ruby said in her singsong voice. She didn't want to antagonize him.

Pip took a swig from the tumbler and bared his teeth as if the liquid had stung his gums. Ruby let her head fall backward and she rotated the tension out of her shoulders. She sat on the wall a few feet away from her husband. As in the presence of a wild animal, it would be unwise to get too close too soon.

"I was worried about you. You didn't say good-bye."

He sucked on his cigar. "Huh."

"Come on, Pip. I hate it when we fight. Especially when I don't know what we're fighting about." She lowered her head and looked up at him through heavy eyelashes, but he didn't acknowledge her attempts to win him over.

"You were having a good enough time without me."

"Come on, Pip. That's just—"

"What? Stupid? I'm stupid now, am I?"

"That's not what I was going to say. You're one of the cleverest people I know." She edged closer to him.

"Not as clever as your vet friends, though."

"Pip, they're lovely people, if you'd take the time to get to know them. And they loved you."

He shrugged and emptied his drink.

"I don't want you working there anymore. You're embarrassing yourself. Everyone says it's not right how you put animals before people."

Ruby's smile faded and her eyes hardened.

"You don't mean that," Ruby said, still trying to keep her voice light. "I've worked hard for this. And think about the extra money. We can have nice holidays and—"

"Now you're saying that I don't make enough money, is that it?"

"No, I—"

"Are you doing this to humiliate me?"

Ruby undid the top button on her skirt. It wasn't made for sitting down in, even if she had lost nine pounds. She pulled her long hair into a knot on the top of her head, held it there for a moment to let the cooler air kiss her neck, and then let it drop again.

"This isn't any old job. This is my career, Pip. I've wanted to be a vet my whole life, and thanks to you"—she looked at him as she said this so he would acknowledge her gratitude—"it's thanks to you that it has become a reality. I never thought I could do a degree at my age."

"You should have warned me."

"About what?"

"That he was gay."

She looked away to hide her annoyance. *So that's why he was in such a foul mood.*

"Do you mean Jason? Until he turned up with his boyfriend, I didn't know, and even if I did, I wouldn't have thought to mention it."

Pip snorted and upended his glass over his open mouth even though there was nothing left but a drip.

"Pip, you're not really this angry about him, are you?"

"He touched me."

"Inappropriately?"

"He rubbed my arm."

"How? In a sexual way?"

"I don't know. In a fucking gay way, that's how."

Ruby knotted her fingers together and pursed her lips for a moment before she allowed herself to speak. Pip was important to her, but so was her job, and she wouldn't let him ruin it for her.

"Let's talk about this tomorrow. Now I'm going to bed. Coming?"

Ruby walked into the kitchen and poured the last of her water into the dog's bowl.

"Is Rufus out there?" she shouted into the darkness. "He didn't come to see me when I came back."

"The front door was open."

"It was *what*?" She stepped outside and looked at Pip with her hands clenched in front of her mouth.

"You forgot to shut the door. He must've legged it," said Pip.

"No, I didn't. He wouldn't." Ruby's eyes were wide with fear.

"You were the last one out of the house."

Ruby looked at the floor, trying to remember. Sweet lord, Phillip was right. She had run back into the house to use the loo. But she was certain she'd felt the latch catch behind her as she dashed to the car. Hadn't she?

"Pip, help me. Quick!" She ran into the house and looked for her car keys.

"Where to?" Pip called.

"I need to drive around, see if I can spot him. He'll be so scared. Pip, please—help me."

Ruby went back into the yard, her eyes beseeching Pip to help her.

"There's no need," he said.

"Please, Pip. I need another pair of eyes."

"I know exactly where he is. I saw him when I was walking back from the party."

"Where? Where was he? Why didn't you get him?"

"Because," he said, "my wife, the animal lover, left the door open and let him run straight out into the path of an oncoming car. Well done. You've killed your own dog. He's dead."

Ruby felt the blood drain from her face. Her hand was trembling. Pip put his hands in his pockets and she thought she saw him suppress a smile. The night was suddenly colder and the air brittle. Ruby heard a buzzing in her ears and had to swallow hard to clear them.

"What did you say?" Her voice was barely audible to her own ears, yet Pip heard her.

"Hit by a car. He's dead."

She shook her head so the words couldn't take root.

"I need to get to him!"

Pip said nothing.

"Where is he, Pip?"

"Told you, he's dead. Your expensive degree can't help you now, can it?" He stood up and looked her squarely in the eye.

"It's about time you realized that your husband is more important than a stupid animal."

"Please, you know what he means to me. I have to see him."

Pip walked past her on his way into the house. She grabbed his arm. He looked at her hand with narrow eyes and a twitching jaw. She let go and asked softly, "Will you show me where he is, Pip, please?"

"I'm going to bed. Why don't you get *Jason* to help?"

Ruby ran from the house. The pain was physical and she kept stopping to double up with gripes in her stomach and her heart. She lurched from streetlight to streetlight, pausing to steady herself on walls and hedges. Late-night revelers slipped off curbsides and laughed into the night as she rushed by.

"Have you seen a dog? A dog? Have you seen him? He's a red setter. About *this* big. His name's Rufus."

There was still the smallest germ of hope in her heart. Another dog, perhaps? One that looked like Rufus? Pip might have been wrong. Might have been lying. Yes, that was it. Lying to hurt her. She retraced the route that Pip would have taken from the party, but she couldn't see a body. Her hopes lifted. Perhaps he had got up, walked away. He could be looking for her somewhere.

"Rufus!" she called. "Rufus, where are you?"

There were tears on her face. She spun about, looking everywhere.

An accident? Or a punishment for refusing to put Pip first?

Ruby wiped her face. Whatever the truth was, Pip was on his last warning. He wasn't the only one who knew how to hurt people.

CHAPTER 16

10 days before the funeral

Naomi, Ruby, and I sat in the living room facing each other. Ruby looked from Naomi to me and back to Naomi, and then smiled. We were waiting for someone to say something of significance, but all I could do was smile and scratch a pretend itch on my shoulder. My smile was to hide my nerves, awkwardness, and the truth. Ruby's might have been genuine. Or medicated.

"How long did the journey take you?" I asked out of politeness.

"Wouldn't have a clue, darling. I don't believe in clocks," she said. "The one in Bertie broke years ago. It's better for your mind to be free of the constraints of hours and minutes, don't you find? In the morning, we set the alarm because of all the things we have to do instead of waking when our body tells us to. We'd be so much more productive on a full night's sleep. All this watching the clock and 'I'm going to be late' or 'too early' . . . Imagine how much calmer we'd be if we all left the house when we were ready."

"Imagine," I said, though I couldn't think of anything worse.

I picked up my mobile phone from the arm of the chair and waved it in Ruby's direction.

"It's a shame you didn't phone. Could have saved yourself a journey."

"I don't have a phone—not a mobile one anyway. I had to get a landline when they turned our phone box into a defibrillator, but I don't see the need to be contactable at all hours of the day."

She smiled, but it still felt like an insult, and I placed my mobile back on the chair arm. The image of Alistair on a swing flashed across the screen and I turned it facedown.

"A pity Naomi didn't remember you were due for dinner," I said with a pointed look at Naomi. "She could have met you at The Barn."

I kept rubbing at the back of my neck as if I could feel someone's eyes on me. I didn't know how to ask Ruby to leave without arousing suspicion, but couldn't tell her the truth without sounding crazy.

"Where *is* Pip anyway?" she asked.

Naomi and I shared a look. Passed it between us like a silent game of pass-the-parcel waiting for the music to stop.

"I'm not sure," I said. "Work, I suppose. Naomi? Phillip's at work, isn't he?"

"What?" she said. "Phil? Sure, if that's what we're going with."

I pretended to find it funny. Funny Naomi, making it sound like we were hiding something!

"Naomi loses track of Phillip's shifts, don't you, Naomi? But I'm pretty sure that he's on days this weekend. Why don't we get him to call you when he's free? Perhaps you should drive home while there's a break in the weather. I'd hate for you to be stranded."

"Has something happened?" Ruby asked. She was alert. Gone was her hazy look.

"No, nothing's happened. Not really," I said.

"What's he done?" she asked with a sigh, like she was talking about an errant child rather than an irate adult.

I wanted to tell her everything. I wanted to tell her about the threats to take my son away, the assaults, the cancer, the cellar, but I didn't know where to start. Ruby and I didn't have the sort of relationship where we would wait to hear the full story without passing judgment on each other, and if I knew anything about Ruby, she would side with Phillip before a word left my mouth.

"It's nothing," I said. "Things are a bit strained while Phillip and I sort the divorce out. You know how difficult these things can be."

"Not really," she said. "Our divorce was perfectly amicable because we both still cared about each other."

It took all my restraint to point out that Phillip wasn't so amicable toward her when he was declaring his love for me before he'd even asked her for a divorce. She seemed to view me as a phase that Phillip was going through, and he would return to her eventually. In her eyes, Alistair was an unwelcome anchor that tied Phillip to me. She was undoubtedly thrilled when he left me, but she hadn't counted on there being a Naomi.

I saw an opportunity to deflect attention from the secret in my cellar and said in a rush, "Naomi's been a great help. Haven't you, Naomi?"

Naomi raised an eyebrow in response and I continued. "Yes, she's helping me move the divorce along so that she and Phillip can get married. Isn't that great news?"

Ruby's eyes lost some of their shine, but the smile was fixed.

"Congratulations, darling," Ruby said to Naomi. "I had no idea."

"Hasn't Phillip told you?" I asked with wide-eyed surprise. "I bet he was waiting to tell you in person this weekend. Funny how he forgot you were coming, though—he must have so much on his mind with the wedding."

"And when will the happy day be?" Ruby squeezed out her words through a clenched jaw.

"Never," said Naomi.

I laughed again.

"What Naomi means is—"

"He'll be dead soon anyway," Naomi said. "Cancer."

I watched Ruby's expression change from false smile to confusion to horror.

"Naomi!" I snapped. I put my head in my hands and rested my elbows on my knees.

"Why are we covering for him anyway?" she said.

"We're not. We're covering for *us*."

"She knows summat's up. Look at her! She's not an idiot."

I looked up and saw Naomi pointing at Ruby, who was watching first one, then the other of us with her mouth slightly open.

Naomi and I glared at each other. She wasn't backing down and neither was I. I felt panic rising and blood pulse in my ears. Ruby's voice broke the silence.

"I don't understand," she said.

"You and me both, duck," said Naomi.

Ruby tilted her head in confusion.

I was on my feet, pacing, unsure how to explain it. It was important that I found the right words, but before I could open my mouth, Naomi spoke again.

"Jeez," said Naomi. "Thing is, Ruby, Phil's got lung cancer. He says he's got weeks to live."

Ruby gasped as her hand flew to her mouth, but Naomi batted

away her concern. "Yeah, yeah, bloody shame and all that. But that's no excuse for him attacking the pair of us in the space of a week." She pointed at the butterfly stitches on her forehead and then at the side of my face.

I tucked my hair behind my ear so that Ruby could see the red scabs where he'd ripped my earring out.

"Imogen knows what happened to me because she saw me at the ER. I reckon Phil only told me about the cancer so I wouldn't report him. He told Imogen that she had to be out of the house by the end of the month or he'd go after custody of Alistair."

Naomi barely took a breath. She delivered this news like she was reeling off items on a shopping list.

"He said we should get married before the end and that we'd have to be quick about it. He didn't want Imogen to know, in case she slowed down the house sale or whatever, and he didn't want any delays in sorting out the money side of things. He weren't serious about the custody—I mean, how could he? He'll be dead by Christmas. But Imogen didn't know that, obviously. And she didn't know about the cancer neither. She thought he were for real, so she flipped out and shut him down in the cellar. Put him in handcuffs and everything."

Ruby's hands were clamped over her mouth. A sound somewhere between a wail and a scream slipped between her fingertips. The dirty white dog yapped.

"I . . . I don't quite . . . He's got cancer?"

Naomi nodded.

"And he did *that* to your face?" Ruby pointed at Naomi's head.

Ruby stared at the carpet, her eyes darting about, as if she were working out a difficult puzzle. It was a lot for her to take in, and if I hadn't been so annoyed with Naomi, I might have felt sorry for her.

"I think that's everything?" Naomi looked at me for confirmation. I closed my eyes, feeling the blood drain from my face.

"That's the simplified version but . . ." I said.

Ruby cleared her throat. "He's in the cellar?"

"Well, it's the cinema room really," I said. "There's a bed and a—"

"In handcuffs?" she asked. Her words were clipped. Sharp.

"I know it doesn't sound good, but if you could have heard how he was threatening me . . . I was going to let him go, but when I opened the door he attacked me and I reacted just as any sane person would. I pushed back and he fell down the steps. I've cuffed him for my own safety."

Ruby got to her feet and the older dog barked.

"I need to see him. I can't believe Pip would attack you like you say he did. And I need to hear about the cancer from his own lips." She folded her hands in front of her and pulled herself up straight. "I can't believe you'd do something like this, Imogen."

Her voice was shrill with disapproval.

"Exactly," I said, my voice rising. "That about sums you up, Ruby. You can't believe what *I've* done, but you're not angry with Phillip for what *he's* done. Stop being so bloody blinkered, Ruby. Why can't you understand that I had no choice?"

She had the decency to look away. When she spoke again, her voice was so quiet and calm, for a moment I thought I'd managed to get through to her.

"If you don't let him go this minute," she said, "I will call the police."

"I can't," I said.

I sank to the sofa with my head in my hands. I was more frustrated than upset, but still the tears came.

God knows what I was crying for, but once I started, I couldn't stop. Neither Naomi nor Ruby moved to comfort me. Ruby was still smarting from my outburst and Naomi didn't look like she knew where to start. I was grateful. It would be better for us all if we didn't acknowledge my unraveling.

Least said, soonest mended.

I tried to hold it in, to make it go away, but the tears coursed down my face. My breaths juddered inward, and squeezed out again through clenched teeth with a whine. The tears were bitter and stung the back of my throat. My stomach muscles ached from gripping on to the vestigial flicker of my self-esteem. I looked up and saw that Naomi was studying her hands with the concentration of a palm reader, and Ruby was patting the rounded belly of the larger of the dogs.

Least said.

I pulled my sleeve over my hand, past the bruises that had almost disappeared, and wiped my nose on it. Still without looking up, Naomi passed me a box of tissues. I took a deep breath and let it out slowly. Pulled myself upright and swallowed hard.

Mended.

"Sorry," I said. "I've not been sleeping. This has been hard for me."

I pressed the tissue into the corners of my eyes.

"I understand why you feel I should let him go, Ruby. But Naomi and I have discussed this at length. I did try to let him go and he attacked me. If we do it again, he'll hurt us. I know it. And if he goes to the police, I'll be arrested, and then when Phillip dies—well, my mother's getting on a bit and there's no one else to look after Alistair. I can't lose him, Ruby."

Ruby came over and sat next to me, taking my hand in hers.

"You're scared," she said. "And that's okay. But it won't be as bad as you think it'll be. I'll talk to Pip. I'll make him see that he was partly responsible for what has happened to him and tell him—"

"You can't reason with him," I interrupted.

"I'll tell him that if he doesn't go to the police, neither will you. Pip'll listen to me," she said with absolute confidence. "I know him better than anyone. He's done stupid and rash things in the past, but only ever because he's been hurting. It's a defense mechanism, that's all."

Out of all of us, she was the only person he came close to respecting. She'd been a constant support in Phillip's life. There was something about Ruby, when she spoke with such authority, that made you believe every word she said, and, for a moment, I thought she might be right.

It was so simple. If *he* didn't go to the police, *we* wouldn't.

It wouldn't solve the problem of keeping the house or arranging the will, but my biggest fear—that he would get custody of Alistair—was irrelevant if he was terminally ill.

"You might be right," I said. "But, while it was fear that had me lock him up in the first place, it's practicalities that make me want to keep him there. This is an . . . opportunity, if you like, to make sure he does right by us. We're not ill-treating him, Ruby. I wonder . . . I wonder if you'd let us get him to sign a few things before we let him go."

"You can't take someone's freedom away," Ruby said. "People fight and die for liberty. It's no coincidence that the biggest punishment that we have in our society is the removal of freedom. Imogen, I'm sure your heart is in the right place—"

"Yes, and you've convinced me to let him go. I agree. All I'm asking is that we get his signature first."

She took her hand off mine and leaned away from me slightly.

"We'll talk to him," she said. "But I won't let him sign anything under duress."

I sighed and went to get the keys from the kitchen.

Ruby wanted to see Phillip on her own. She said she'd get him to agree that he wouldn't go to the police. I asked her to get assurances that he wouldn't hurt us either, but she shook her head gently as if I were deluded. She only believed what she wanted to believe and, at that moment, she wanted to believe the best of Phillip, not me.

"Oh, Pip! You poor, poor thing. Look at you, my darling!"

Her voice rang up the stairs from the cellar.

Phillip coughed.

I'd barely noticed his cough before, but now I couldn't ignore it. The signs of his deteriorating health were there if I cared to look. I didn't.

Perhaps I should have been more sympathetic. Surely someone other than me—dare I say *better* than me—would have spoken of him in gentler words? Most people revered the dead and the dying. No one was better than Death at propaganda. It made saints out of sinners and those who had been so easily overlooked in life into people we couldn't live without.

Ruby spent thirty minutes with Phillip, and when she came out she went straight into the kitchen. Naomi and I waited. Lunch had passed us by without being marked with food. It had left us lethargic. Empty in stomach, head, and heart.

There were noises from the kitchen. A cupboard opening and closing. Drawers doing the same. I went to see what Ruby was looking for.

"Can I help?"

"There's something a bit off about him. He's slow," Ruby said. "I'm worried about concussion, but I'm going to start with getting him a nice cup of sweet tea. He's refusing to drink the water. Says he thinks you're drugging him. I told him that—"

"I am."

Ruby froze with a teaspoon in her hand. Forgetting, for a moment, what she was doing.

"Run that one by me again?" Her smile almost slipped, but she grabbed it at the last moment and pulled it back into line.

Her eyes, I noticed, were red rimmed and puffy. Pained, no doubt, by the thought of Phillip dying. She was still in love with him. I failed to see how anyone who had spent years as his wife could still love a man like that, but Ruby was baffling in so many ways.

"I put sleeping tablets in the water to slow him down," I said. "Not today, though. We need him to be lucid while he hears what we want from him. I've made a list of things to discuss."

"You mean demands?" she said haughtily. Smile still in place.

"Yes, if it's not too demanding to ask him to ensure the safety of me and my son and not kick us out of our home. What did he say when you told him?"

"He said he'd been nothing but fair and that you got completely the wrong end of the stick."

"He would say that, wouldn't he?"

Ruby made him tea with two sugars, poured a glass of water straight from the tap.

"Yes," she agreed. "Just as you *would* say that he was treating you badly and deserved to be locked up. I'm not taking sides but—"

"Yes, you are."

"*But* there's always two sides to a story. If I was a suspicious person, I might say that you and Naomi have ganged up on a sick man in order to strip him of his assets. If I were unkind, I might say that you planned all of this together, and you're planning to kill him."

I almost laughed out loud at the absurdity of her statement, but if Phillip could convince her, then he might be able to convince the police too.

"So, you suggest we let him go and then what? He'll stick to his word and not take his anger out on me and Naomi? Can you put your hand on your heart and guarantee that he will walk away from this quietly?"

"What exactly do you expect him to do?" Ruby asked, her voice rising with uncharacteristic anger. "He's got cancer, bruised ribs, and is suffering from concussion."

"Something that living with Phillip taught me, Ruby, is to never underestimate your enemy."

I couldn't pretend that I wasn't angry. Phillip was manipulating people again, though I didn't think that Ruby needed much persuasion, and he was about to get away without facing the consequences again. This was the first, last, and only time in my life that I would have some control over Phillip, and it was an advantage I was reluctant to give up.

The three of us filed down the stairs, I at the back carrying the small silver keys that would release him from any chance of doing what I asked.

"Here, have some water, darling." Ruby sat by Phillip's side while Naomi and I hung back and watched.

With one hand, Ruby held a glass to Phillip's lips. The other rubbed his back in small circular motions. She was reveling in her Florence Nightingale role. Naomi stood over them with arms folded and head shaking. She wasn't buying the poor, helpless invalid act any more than I was. There was no compassion in her eyes, but there was no hatred either. She caught my eye and both of us raised our eyebrows in a can-you-believe-it? arch.

We all wanted different things *for* and *from* Phillip. Ruby loved him regardless of any actions he took. She was blind to his faults and, in that way, was more mother than wife to him. She looked at him with such tenderness that it was painful to watch. As far as I knew, she hadn't had another relationship since Phillip had left her. He kept throwing her just enough crumbs to keep her at his feet. Naomi wanted Phillip out of her life. It was written all over her face. The impatience, the feigned boredom, the pursed lips holding back the many things she wanted to say. More than anything, though, she wanted this to be over. She wanted to put the pain and the fear behind her. In some ways, he'd been a father figure to her. He'd rescued her from a life of foster families and care homes and promised a brighter future. But he'd disappointed her in that crushing way that only someone you love could do.

Phillip had always been better than me, cleverer than me. Always holding love at arm's length, there for the taking if I could jump a little bit higher. He was nothing to me now, other than the father of my child, and it did me no credit to admit I couldn't wait for him to die.

He would not be at Alistair's graduation or wedding. We would never again pose for photographs as a family or argue about how best to raise our son. A part of my life, a part that had held such promise once upon a time, was about to end. I was sad for the past, but glad of a future without him.

But still, I felt guilty. For my part in it, for thinking I could change the future, for doing to him what he had done to me for years. For thinking that I knew better than he did. For believing that I could be the one to save us all.

"I gather Ruby's spoken to you about what we want to do?" I said.

He coughed and nodded. "I was only trying to get things sorted financially so that I would know what the house was worth and make sure that Naomi was well looked after too when I . . . when I go." He looked at Naomi and smiled. She looked away.

"You threatened us," I said. "You hurt us."

"I've done some things I've regretted. Can we put it behind us now and move on? Ruby's going to help me draw up the will, aren't you, Ruby?"

"Yes, Pip."

"I don't want us to fight . . . in the little time I've got left."

Ruby pulled him closer and kissed the top of his head.

My hands were shaking, though it was hard to tell whether it was because of anger or fear. Phillip was being reasonable, there were two witnesses, so why was I still scared?

A sudden bang from the top of the stairs made us all jump. I wasn't the only one on edge.

"One of the dogs," said Ruby. "Must have brushed against the door and closed it."

I could hear the *clack-clack* of dog paws on the tiled hallway floor and relaxed a little.

"Okay, then," I said. "I'll unlock your cuffs, but I'm not going to lie to you, Phillip—I'm scared that you're going to do something to *punish* me for doing this when you know that I didn't feel I had any choice and—"

He put up his hand to stop me. "I get it. Really. I don't know what I can do to convince you—any of you—that I'm not as bad as you think I am."

There was a flicker of humanity behind his eyes. I wanted to believe that the cancer had changed his outlook, that the last day and a half had convinced him not to mess with us, but I wasn't as trusting as I used to be.

He rubbed his hands together and his dry skin hissed like a snake passing over dried leaves.

I crouched by the side of the bed and Phillip sat so that his shoes touched the floor.

I fumbled with the key a little, on purpose, and then I felt the click of the lock springing free. I let the chain and cuffs drop onto the floor without taking my eyes off them. It was difficult to back down before Phillip.

I waited for him to get up, but I couldn't look him in the face.

And that's where I was, crouched on the floor, when Phillip cracked the bridge of my nose with his heel.

CHAPTER 17

10 days before the funeral

I fell to the floor, with my hands over my face. The pain was instantaneous and blinding. I blinked rapidly against blurred vision and touched my hands to my nose. It was tacky with blood. Warm, salty liquid coated my lips. My head was spinning.

"Pip, no! What are you doing?" Ruby's voice came from far away.

Even through my pain I wanted to say, *I told you so.*

I was right. We couldn't trust him.

I squinted up at Phillip, who was now standing taller than I'd ever seen him. His foot smashed into my ribs and I skidded sideways. If I hadn't been sprawled across the floor, I would have laughed. How could I have let Ruby talk me into thinking that he would go quietly? Which one of us was more stupid?

Naomi screamed and I looked up to see her on Phillip's back with her arms clamped around his shoulders. She was stronger than she looked, but it didn't count for much. It took Phillip little effort to pry her off him. He turned, held her arm, and slapped her around the side of the face. The sound bounced off the walls. It sounded like a Christmas cracker being pulled, but there would be no party hats.

Naomi fell on Ruby and both toppled onto the bed. Naomi scrambled to get up but kept falling. I pulled myself backward across the floor, away from the nightmare. Phillip was on a rampage, beating anyone in his path, and all I could do was watch.

My breath was catching in my chest. The familiar feeling of panic-tightened lungs causing me to wheeze. Phillip had Ruby's hair in one hand and Naomi's in the other. He dragged them off the bed, taking sheets and pillows with them. Ruby's hands were on his forearms, trying to get free. Her bangles were jangling again. Naomi was swearing and kicking out, but the impact made no difference to him and he pushed her to her knees.

Ruby began shouting, "Pip, no! Think about what you're doing!" She was alarmed, her eyes wider than I thought possible. *Now do you see?* I thought. *Do you?*

He threw Ruby at my feet, where she cowered into a ball. It was one thing for Phillip to be the person you always knew him to be, but to Ruby this must have been a shock. Phillip pivoted and kicked Naomi hard in the stomach. She groaned as the air left her body and she doubled over, leaning her forehead on the floor. I felt like I was watching something too ludicrous to be true, a bout of theatrical wrestling.

Phillip turned in my direction, but it was Ruby he was looking at. He picked the cuffs up and smacked one side over Ruby's wrist and squeezed it tight. The other end he attached to the radiator.

"See how *you* like it!" he said.

Ruby's mouth fell open, and she stared at her wrist.

Naomi was on her feet again with a hand on her stomach. She

circled the bed, not blinking. Before she could reach him, Phillip pushed out with two hands into her chest. She flew backward, tripping over the arm of the chair, and fell with a thump. Phillip laughed as he went to straddle her, pinning her arms with his knees.

He tightened his hands around her smooth throat. His shoulders tensed and his head vibrated with the pressure he was exerting. Naomi's legs bucked as she tried to kick him off her, but he was too heavy. Too strong.

Ruby was screaming over and over, "Pip. No! Stop it! Pip! For God's sake, no!" She was straining at the cuffs and trying to reach them.

I could taste my own blood in my mouth as I pushed myself up against the wall. I was at the bottom of the stairs trying to think in a straight line. To run and get help or to stay and *be* help. I didn't know anything other than that I couldn't leave Naomi and Ruby alone with this monster.

I looked around the room for something to use on him, but I'd been careful to take away anything that he could use as a weapon. Quickly but quietly I ran behind him, scared that he would turn around, but he couldn't hear anything over the sound of Naomi's gasps.

Her face was deep red and her eyes were bulging. I picked up the side table, holding a table leg in each shaking hand, took a deep breath, and smashed it across the side of his head. The noise shot through the cellar. Ruby stopped screaming and Naomi sucked in deep breaths.

I let go of the table and covered my mouth with the back of my hand. Phillip had let go of Naomi but was only momentarily stunned. He turned to face me slowly. He was angry but not surprised. At that moment, I was as scared of Phillip as I had ever been. His eyes were hard disks and his mouth was curled into a sneer. Before he could move, I grabbed a handful of his hair and smashed my knee into his face. I missed his nose, but his eye socket cracked under my knee. I called out in shock even though the cry should have come from him.

He should have stopped. He should have gone down, hurt, realizing that he was outnumbered, overpowered, that we weren't to be messed with, but he grabbed my arm as he fell. We tumbled together in slow motion. I smacked my head on the side of the bed and was jerked out of his grasp. He rolled away and sprang to his feet in one easy movement. He wouldn't be caught off guard again.

Naomi was coughing and sucking in shallow breaths. Ruby sobbed. The dogs barked in distress behind the closed door.

Phillip pulled me to my feet by my hair and smashed my head on the wall. I spun away from him too stunned to feel pain, too disoriented to do any more than stagger toward the bed.

He took the second set of cuffs from the radiator, rolled Naomi onto her front, and fastened her right wrist to her left ankle. I fought to stay alert. The ground swayed. I blinked my eyes open as Phillip's face swam in front of me. My head was throbbing and the pain from my nose was radiating across my cheeks.

"Immie, Immie, Immie."

He shook his head.

"Look what you've made me do."

He sat on the bed and pulled me up beside him. My neck hurt and my ribs stabbed me with every deep breath. Tears were already on my cheeks. He put his arm around my shoulders and squeezed. I audibly sucked in air through clenched teeth against the pain.

"Take a look," he said, gesturing at the scene around us.

"Poor Ruby. Did she deserve this? And Naomi—she's just a kid, and now look at her. Lucky to be alive, I'd say. And that's all because you thought you could get the better of me. You did this, Imogen."

"It's not my fault."

"No? Then who was it who shut me down here? Eh? Who made me angry? Was it Ruby? Was it Naomi?"

I shook my head. I wouldn't let him lay the blame for this on me. I couldn't let him get in my head.

"I've known you for a long time, Immie, and yet your stupidity still astounds me. When will you learn that you can never out-smart me?"

"Let them go." I was surprised at how calm my voice sounded.

"Why would I do that?"

"You said it yourself. It was all me. They didn't agree to this. Both of them told me to let you go," I said. "It's me who locked you down here. It's me you're angry with."

I couldn't breathe through my nose. Phillip noticed; keeping one hand around my shoulder, he put the other over my mouth and pushed hard. I knocked his hand away and he laughed.

"Too easy," he said. "I could end your life if I wanted to, silly bitch. Now tell me, where's Alistair?"

"What?"

"My son. Where is he?"

I thought I'd misheard him, couldn't understand why he'd want him. We both knew that his illness meant he wouldn't get custody. My mind was in turmoil, I could hardly think straight, but I still knew that I wouldn't let him near Alistair. Not in this state. Not ever.

"He's out. A friend's house."

My heart was racing.

"What friend?"

I said the first lie that came to mind. "A friend from school. Thomas."

In my head, over and over again, ran the words *Stay away from my son*. Would he take him just to hurt me? Did he hate me enough to hurt Alistair? I wouldn't put anything past him.

"And where does this Thomas live?"

"They're . . . they're out . . . bowling."

"What time will he be back?"

"He's staying overnight."

"What's their address?"

Naomi had gone quiet and there was no noise from Ruby. No sounds from the outside world could reach us down here.

"I don't have their address," I said evenly.

"Lies!"

He took a handful of my hair and pulled it back so that my chin pointed upward.

"You expect me to believe that you don't know where they live? *You*, who never lets the boy out of your sight? No wonder he's such a bloody wimp. Time to cut the apron strings, Imogen. Now where the fuck is he?"

His voice was getting louder, and I'd already seen what he was capable of. I'd always known that he could be cruel and had recently seen his anger boil over, but the man next to me was unhinged. I'd fallen for his lies too many times and now it was time to make him fall for mine.

"I don't know his address, I swear. I dropped Alistair off at the bowling place this morning and Thomas's mum said she'd bring him back here tomorrow. They've got my number if there's any problems. Yes, it's out of character for me to let him out of my sight, but so is having my husband in a cellar. I was desperate, Phillip. I wanted him out of the house while we spoke to you, and when Thomas invited Alistair over it seemed like the perfect opportunity."

Phillip let go of my hair and said, "Why isn't he with your mother?"

At last something I could give an honest answer to.

"She blacked out and dislocated her shoulder. Naomi'll tell you—I bumped into her at the hospital after I'd seen Mother. That's how I knew about the stiches. I swear it's the truth."

"If I find out that you're lying . . ." He left the threat hanging in the air.

"Is all this about Alistair?" I asked. "Because if you really want the best for him, Phillip, you have to let us go. The more reasonable you are now, the more likely you are to be able to see him more often."

"I can feel him pulling away from me, no doubt because of the rubbish you fill his head with. You're not fit to be a mother," he spat. "I'd been thinking that there's nothing more important than family, that it was time I had more of a hand in Alistair's upbringing, but I've had some time to think, thanks to you, about what I really want. And do you know what I've decided? That there's only one thing more important than family. Can you guess what it is?"

I shook my head.

He slapped my face. "Guess!"

My hair fell over my eyes and I looked up at him through strands of knotted brown.

"The only thing you care about is yourself," I said.

"Try again."

He grabbed me by the back of my neck and pulled my face to his.

"I don't know. Please, Phillip, you're hurting me."

"Try again."

"Money? I don't know . . . Love, maybe?"

He leaned into me and smoothed my hair off my face so that I could feel his breath in my ear. He said one word.

"Revenge."

His eyes held mine and I felt my breath start to quicken. The adrenaline was starting to leave my body and now my overriding emotion was fear.

Naomi wasn't moving. She had rolled onto her side but was facing away from us, and I couldn't tell whether she had her eyes open or closed. Phillip blocked my view of Ruby, but I could hear her sniffles and knew she was okay. I lowered my head.

"If I were you, I'd leave while I could."

"What would you do," he asked, "if I took Alistair away so you never saw him again? We could go anywhere in the world. We might be in Saint Lucia or Stoke. You'd never know."

"I won't let you take him."

"It's time to toughen him up," he said. "Make him a man."

"If you touch him, I'll kill you." I meant it. I shook his arm off me and sat as straight as my throbbing ribs would let me.

"I'd like to see you try," Phillip said.

"It's a matter of time. If I don't kill you, the cancer will, and . . ." My words died in my mouth as I saw his slowly spreading smile.

"You bastard!" I said.

I saw it then, the truth. "You don't have cancer, do you? I should have known it was another one of your lies." Even as I said it, I hoped I was wrong, but I knew by the look on his face that I wasn't.

"Ah, yes," he said. "The cancer." He gave a false little cough.

"I've got to thank Naomi for that one. That little story was only meant for her ears. I intended to buy some time and to stop her from reporting me. I knew that not even Naomi would leave a sick man to fend for himself. I had no idea that it would play so nicely into my hands. Admit it, Imogen. You felt sorry for me after our little heart-to-heart the other night, didn't you?"

He was smug, and I was stunned. Lately, I'd held Phillip in low regard, but this seemed beneath even him.

"You let us think you were going to die just so that you could . . . what? Find somewhere else to live? Is that why you wanted me out of the house? Because you want to live *here*?"

He held his hands up like it couldn't be helped.

"Don't you think Naomi would've noticed when you didn't bloody die?" I said, my voice rising.

"But by that time, I'd have made sure she couldn't get her hands on my money and I'd have made plans to leave *her*. You should know by now that you only get to leave if I say so. Hands behind your back!"

I did as I was told, still too shocked to do much more. I kept my face turned to his. I wanted him to read in my eyes how much I hated him.

"So, you asking Naomi to marry you . . . ?"

"A distraction. Girls and white dresses, eh?"

Ruby sniffed loudly. I'd almost forgotten she was there. By the look on Phillip's face, he had too.

"Pip?" she said. "Pip? You don't have cancer?"

"Thought you'd be pleased," he said gruffly as he used her scarf to tie my wrists.

"What a rotten thing to tell people. I understand why you lied to Naomi, but why didn't you tell *me* the truth? I could have helped you."

"Nothing personal," he said, not looking at her.

"You should leave," I said.

"But we're only just starting to have fun, you and me. Remember fun, Immie? It was something we used to have before Alistair came along. Back before you became a miserable bitch. We used to have a laugh, you and me. Didn't we? Eh? Oi! I'm bloody talking to you!"

"Yes," I said. "Yes."

"Tell me what was fun," he said.

"Erm . . ." I studied my feet, trying to remember something, anything, but struggled to recall memories that had been formed outside of this room. He lied to me. He was after my son. I couldn't let him leave.

"'Erm'?" he mocked. "Cat got your tongue? Go on, Imms, we had lots of fun times. You said so yourself. Come on! Good times. Tell me!"

"The . . . thing. The bike rides?"

"The Suzuki? Now you're talking. Your mother's face when I turned up with my bike. Remember? I thought she was going to have a coronary. Where did we go that day? Was it Scarborough or somewhere? It was the beach anyhow. The weather was shit. You said you may as well be grounded for staying out all night as for getting on a bike. What else? I bet you can do better than that."

"Holidays?"

"Which one?"

I closed my eyes, conjuring up sunshine and suitcases.

"The time we went to Italy," I said. I began moving my wrists against the fabric of Ruby's scarf. The more I wriggled, the tighter it got, but I thought I might be able to tear the whole thing apart if I could make a hole in the material.

"Nah, I didn't like Italy. It was full of bloody mopeds and ponces. Didn't I get my wallet stolen in Pompeii? It was an absolute shithole. Try again."

"The, um . . ."

"Yes?"

My mind was blank but I needed more time.

"I don't know. You're putting me under pressure. There's too many things. I can't think of just one."

"You do disappoint me, Immie. What d'you want to go and do that for?"

He shook his head and pushed a strand of hair behind my ear.

"I—I don't want to disappoint you. There's too much to choose from. Remember Tunisia? And the hotel entertainment with those dancers and—"

"Pathetic," he said. "It seems my memory is better than yours. We got food poisoning, didn't leave the room for three days, and when we did, I got stung by a jellyfish. Remember now?"

I did. It was ten days of torture where everything was my fault for booking such a terrible place, even though he'd chosen the resort.

He leaned his chin on my shoulder. I could feel his breath on my cheek. I looked at the table, four feet away from me, and wondered whether I could use it on him again. I could grab it, swing it, run for help. He seemed to sense my thoughts, because he tightened his grip around my shoulder and with his free hand he stroked my cheek.

There was a shift in the atmosphere, as if talking of times we'd shared brought back memories of physical intimacy I'd rather forget.

"You really need to go," I said. "People will be here soon. They'll find you. They'll call the police."

"What people? You said yourself that Alistair won't be back until tomorrow. And who else is there to care where you are? And as for the police . . . it was you that locked me up, remember? I'm sure the police would love to hear all about that."

"Fine. *You* call them," I said.

His hand moved to my neck and he stroked one finger down to my collarbone.

"There's three of us who will all testify to the fact that you attacked us and chained us up," I said, arching my body away from him. "Witnesses. They'll believe us, not you. You don't have a leg to stand on. I'm sure you'd be really popular in prison. Lots of old friends."

His hand continued snaking down my body, over my breast and down to my waist, where he rested it on my hip.

"And why," he began, "would they believe a bunch of bitter exes?"

"You'd back me up, right, Ruby?" I called over my shoulder.

"Pip, this isn't like you. You need help. What's going on with you? They told me you'd attacked them and I didn't believe them. I didn't believe them, Pip, because I thought I knew you. And I do. So tell me what this is really about," she said.

He sighed, as if dissatisfied with us for ruining his fun. Then he stood up. He frowned at Ruby, and I wondered whether he was considering what she'd said.

I relaxed a little now that his hands weren't on me, and my breathing slowed. I looked at the floor, making myself small so he wouldn't think of me as a threat. I needed him to let us go.

"You're a waste of space, Immie," he said at last. "What did I ever see in you? Look at you. You're pitiful. Now, Ruby, she's smart. And Naomi, she's hot. But you? I felt sorry for you. I only proposed to you to stop you from crying. Couldn't stand the wailing. I needed someone to look after Alistair for me—otherwise I'd have got rid of you years ago."

He bent over and took my chin in his hand. He tilted my face upward so he was looking directly at me. His blue eyes were icy, his pupils enlarged and glaring.

"No one would miss you if you were gone," he hissed. "You're middle-aged and on the shelf. Has anyone even looked twice at you since I left? No? Your own mother hates you. Even Alistair would be better off without you."

His opinion didn't matter. Shouldn't matter. And yet.

I'd muttered my insecurities across the pillows back in the days when he said he'd never hurt me, and he used them as ammunition. The fear of being so unlovable that not even my own mother could love me. The fear of losing Alistair, the only thing in my life worth keeping.

Phillip knew what kept me awake at night and he made my nightmares come alive.

He smiled as tears escaped my eyes. Phillip let go of me but stayed bent over with his smug face two inches from mine. I raised my chin, swallowed back the tears, and spat in his face.

He reeled backward, then hit me across my face with the back of his hand. I fell onto the bed and laughed out loud. Mocking him and his pathetic attempt to control me.

"Is that all you've got?" I shouted.

Phillip gave no indication that he'd heard me. He simply went to leave.

I scrambled off the bed and stumbled over Naomi's outstretched leg. Phillip kept walking.

I got to the foot of the stairs as he switched off the light and plunged us into darkness.

"Wait! Phillip, wait. You can't just leave us," I shouted.

"Sweet dreams," he said.

He was illuminated momentarily as he went through the door. A scrabble of dogs was at his knee.

I heard him say, "Down! Get down!" before the bolt slid across the door and the key turned in the lock.

And then there was nothing, except Ruby's gentle sobbing in the impenetrable darkness, and the fear in my chest that Phillip was going after my son.

CHAPTER 18

10 days before the funeral

"Naomi?"

She was blinking at me, dazed but conscious. The bruising was already starting to bloom at her neck. Ruby had helped me untie the scarf around my wrists with her free hand and her teeth. Putting our personal issues aside, we would have to work together to get out of here.

Ruby was trying to pull her wrist out of the handcuffs, but there was no way it was going to slide out. She was grunting to herself in frustration, and occasionally shouting in the direction of the closed cellar door, "Pip! I know you can hear me!"

I helped Naomi up. Her ankle was chained to her wrist, so she had to kneel rather than sit.

I skated my tongue around my mouth and felt it snag on the jagged edge of a broken tooth. I tried swallowing, but I tasted metal and my throat was too dry to let anything down without a fight. I opened my mouth, poked the insides of my cheek with my tongue, and wriggled my jaw. It clicked and shot pain into my temple like a whip.

I couldn't breathe through my nose, but taking in air through my mouth began a wave of nausea that threatened to drench me. I turned suddenly, bent double, and vomited on the floor.

"What the—"

Naomi turned away as the warm contents of my stomach hit the floor beside her. I closed my eyes thinking the word "sorry" over and over again.

Sorry.

Sorry.

Sorry.

I hoped she could hear me, even though I couldn't speak. I was sweating and shivering, unable to move because of the pain, yet unable to stay put. I had to find Alistair before Phillip did.

Naomi struggled to maneuver her foot in front of her and passed the cuffs under her and to the front.

I groaned and wiped my chin. I pressed my lips together and held my breath until the pain became bearable. I was stiff, sore, and my head was threatening to split every time I moved. But I had to get free.

I steadied my breathing. Listened. Footsteps above my head. At least Phillip was still in the house and we knew where he was.

Naomi's white top was ripped and there was dried black blood on her lips. I touched her shoulder and she flinched before crossing her free hand across her body and placing it on top of mine, giving it a squeeze.

Such a good idea to lock him up and yet so idiotic. I thought it would subdue him, show him who was boss—and, in a way, I suppose it had. It wasn't me.

Ruby was on the floor leaning against the radiator, a sad, bitter smile on her face.

She had made me pity Phillip, believe that I was the one being cruel. She had made me doubt what I knew to be true. Her I-see-the-best-in-everyone attitude didn't make her better than me; it just made her more gullible. I shook my head at her and looked away. Looked around. Looked up. Down. Looking for a way.

I stood up quickly, desperate to find a way out. My head was swimming.

"Are you all right?" asked Ruby.

The darkness was spreading like ink on a pristine white table-cloth. The floor swayed and dropped from underneath me. I gripped the wall. It was the only thing stopping me from falling.

Danger was breathing down my neck. I could hear it like a gentle tide over a pebbled beach. I could smell it and it caught in the back of my throat. I tried to cough, but the cough turned into a choke. I couldn't breathe. Nothing. I pulled at my jumper, trying to let the oxygen in. There was no air in the room. I was suffocating. I pushed at the walls, hoping for a loose brick or a covered window, even though I knew there to be none.

I blinked to clear my vision, but the figures before me blurred and danced away as I tried to make sense of them. The room was full of darkness and low ceilings. Pain in my nose, in my ribs, in my stomach. I bent over the unmade bed and groaned. The sickness was coming and I didn't want it. It would stop me from getting what little air there was in the room.

Ruby said, "Imogen? Sit down. Can you take some deep breaths for me? Nice and slowly. Listen to my voice. *In*, two, three, four, *out*, two, three, four, *in*, two, three, four . . ."

I tried to do as she said but could only grab at the air in short gasps. I had to get out and I had to get to Alistair before Phillip did. He would take him away because he knew it was the only way to hurt me.

I could have let myself go, given in to the panic and despair, but I knew if I was going to get out of here I had to keep my mind clear and get the others to help me.

Naomi's eyes skated between curious and fearful. I tried to speak, but my mouth was dry and my tongue stuck to the roof of my mouth. My head throbbed and I coughed to check that I could still make a sound. My entire face hurt. As I mentally traveled down the length of my body, I found that every inch of me ached to some degree. I had little control over my mind. Simple words were difficult to grasp. All I knew was I had to get out.

"Phillip's still here," I said. "Which means he's not worked out where Alistair is yet."

Despite the pain, I shook my head to reset it. On and off. But I was struggling to think clearly or form a plan. There was a series of images and feelings, but they were out of order, a dropped deck of cards waiting to be shuffled.

"Listen," I said quietly. "I'm sorry about this. It's my fault that we've ended up down here, that he . . . hurt you both. I never thought he'd go this far. If I hadn't . . ."

"It's not just you." Naomi was mumbling through swollen lips that she was doing her best not to move. "I bought into that crap about the cancer."

"You weren't to know," I said. "Why would you suspect him of lying about it?"

"You did," she replied.

And yet I'd let myself be convinced.

Ruby coughed. "If anyone should say sorry, it's me. I didn't believe what you were telling me upstairs. I—I—er, I've never seen him react like this. Not physically. He has a temper—I know that much—but I've never . . . He only raised his hand to me once, and it was more of a push than a hit. But I've seen how he likes to punish people who've hurt him. I blame his parents, of course. His mother was a piece of work. That woman knew how to hold a grudge."

I wanted to shake her for blaming anyone but Phillip, but in her own way, I knew she was trying to make amends.

"He adored his mum," I said.

"She has a lot to answer for," Ruby continued. "The woman breast-fed him until he was five. Used to tell him he was better than everyone else. Cleverer, better-looking . . . but she never put store in kindness or helping others the way that other mothers would. It hit him hard when she died. He proposed to me just afterward. It wasn't lost on me that he was replacing her with *me*, an older woman. But I did so love him. And don't get me started on his dad . . . Never met him, of course—he died when Pip was young. What was he? Ten or eleven, maybe? There were always rumors that he wasn't Pip's real dad and that's why he was so harsh on him. I've always tried to bear that in mind, you know? When he's behaving badly, I try and take into account that his childhood wasn't all it should have been and he was never given the tools the rest of us were. But still . . . he's not the only one who had it tough." She sighed. "Perhaps I've excused too much. Maybe I *am* like his mother after all."

I closed my eyes as Ruby spoke. Her voice was low and smooth, with a melodic lilt toward the end of each sentence as if, way back, she'd spent time in Wales.

I was back on my feet checking the camping equipment, the discarded clothes, the boxes of things with no homes. There had to be something I could use on Phillip when he came back.

"It's all right sitting here now, covered with blood, saying he's a bad person, but why did neither of you warn me or something?" Naomi asked.

"I don't know," I said. "I suppose I suspected that it was just *me*. Something between Phillip and me that was toxic. That maybe I provoked it? And what would I have said anyway? That he was mean to me and called me names? It wasn't until I saw the way you reacted when I spilled my tea that I began to suspect that he was abusing you too. I wondered about saying something at the time, but you didn't make it easy for me."

"You don't seem the type to hold your tongue," she said.

"You know as well as I do that not every victim of domestic abuse is timid and quiet. For every abuser who looks like butter wouldn't melt, there's a woman with a smile painted on her face. God forbid the neighbors should find out."

Naomi nodded.

"He never abused me," said Ruby. "He was no saint but . . ."

Perhaps she was telling the truth, but I suspected she just wasn't ready to admit it to herself.

"Do you hate me?" Naomi asked me.

I stopped searching through boxes. I didn't know what I'd expected to find, but it wasn't there. "Why would I hate you?"

"Me and Phil."

I considered her question. Two weeks earlier I would have said yes without missing a beat, but now I had to reconsider my feelings.

"I used to. I knew that he had affairs, but you were the one he couldn't walk away from, I suppose. If I stop and think about it, I was jealous. Which is ridiculous because I wanted shot of him. Him leaving *me* was . . . humiliating. It made me look like I was the one to blame. And the fact that he left me for a younger woman made me look undesirable too. Old. God, if I couldn't even keep a man like Phillip . . ."

"That's not what other people think," said Naomi.

"Well, it's how I felt at the time. No one knows about the years of abuse that have led to that point or that you're actually better off without him. And then when he says it's your fault because you've had depression . . ."

Naomi nodded.

"The things he said I'd done—they were half right. There was just enough truth in them to sound plausible. I couldn't argue with the fact that I'd had serious depression after I lost the baby. But that wasn't the reason that our marriage broke down."

I picked up a fractured leg from the broken table. It was light, probably wouldn't do much damage.

Naomi said, "I didn't know you'd lost a baby."

I stopped studying the wood and stared at Naomi.

No. Why would she know? It wasn't something I would have told her, but wouldn't Phillip have mentioned it? Of course not. It didn't mean anything to him.

"Yes," I said quietly. "At twenty weeks. There was a car accident."

I looked over at Ruby, but she had her eyes closed.

"That's hard," Naomi said. "I was pregnant once. Had an abortion, though. Some days I regret it, some days I don't. I know it's not the same, but it were hard. Really hard, and that were *my* choice. Can't imagine how difficult it must've been for you. Shit."

I coughed to clear my discomfort rather than my throat.

"Your baby—" I began. "Was it Phillip's?"

"No. It were when I was with a foster family. You know, the posh teenage son. They kicked me out soon after. No. Phil had a vasectomy, didn't he?"

I was still digesting the fact that her foster brother had gotten her pregnant, so it took a moment to react to the news that Phillip had had a vasectomy.

"Vasectomy?"

"I know what you're going to say. People have vasectomy reversals all the time, but neither of us were that hung up on having kids so . . ."

"Actually, I was going to ask when. It seems like an oddly selfless act. I would have thought he'd rather you got your tubes tied or something."

"Wasn't it when you were pregnant with Alistair?"

I shook my head. "No. Another lie."

"He told me he knew he wouldn't want any more kids so had the snip before Alistair were born. Wait. Does that mean he could've got me pregnant?"

I put my fingers to my temples, closed my eyes, and swayed slightly. "Actually, Naomi, there's a chance that he might have been telling the truth for once."

I remembered him going to the doctors with a "swelling." I was worried for him. He said it was a cyst and it could be taken out at the doctor's office. Just a day case, he'd said. I'd offered to go with him, but I was eight months pregnant and huge with discomfort. Phillip was a little tender afterward and I'd looked after him as well as I could.

After I'd had Alistair, two things happened. One, I experienced love like I had never known possible. Holding that sweet baby in my arms was a moment so close to perfection that I never wanted it to end. Two, I felt my biological clock speeding up. No time like the present, I'd said. I refused the midwife's recommendation to go on the pill. My family wasn't yet complete and Phillip had agreed. Hadn't he?

We tried and we tried but each month I had to cope with disappointment. I shouldered the heavy burden of failure while he shrugged his shoulders and said, "Not my fault." I'd badgered him for sex. I peed on sticks, I kept charts for my ovulation, and I took my temperature daily. I called him at work and said, "Now. Come home now. It's time," and he went along with it. Of course he did.

"God, I didn't think I could hate him any more than I already do," I said.

"You and me both."

"The things I put up with. I was so desperate for another baby that I slept with him even though I knew he was going with other women. You should have seen some of the tramps he—Oh, no offense."

"None taken, until you said 'no offense.'"

"Sorry."

I pulled the air into my chest. My heart was beginning to hammer again, but I slowed my breathing and put my cool hand across my hot forehead.

I looked over at Ruby. Her smile was beginning to worry me. Her eyes were glazed and she looked like she was bordering on mania. She was shaking her head, over and over, as if she couldn't take in what she was hearing.

There was a bang at the top of the cellar steps, the sound of a key in the lock.

I hid the table leg behind my back and picked up Ruby's scarf, balling it behind my back, pretending I was still tied up. Phillip came down the stairs lightly, spring stepped, smug, with my mobile phone in his hand.

"How are we, ladies?"

"Pip," said Ruby. "You're not thinking straight. You're ill. It's—"

He interrupted her. "Weren't you listening? There is no cancer."

Ruby was shaking her head. She was struggling to come to terms with what was happening. I felt sorry for her in that moment. At least when people treated me badly and lied to me, I was half expecting it. Ruby had spent so long believing the best of people that, now that she'd applied the brakes, she was skidding out of control.

"No, I know. But this isn't like y—" Ruby looked at me and I saw her realization that Phillip *was* like this, to me at least.

"This behavior isn't normal, Pip. You need some help. Let me help you. Whatever you do, don't make things worse."

Phillip stepped past her, ignoring her pleas. "Imogen," he said, leaning against the wall at the bottom of the step. I slowly took both ends of the scarf in my hands, imagining tying them around his neck.

"You need to come up with a better pass code for your phone. Alistair's birthday? Really?" He shook his head. "You make this too easy for me. But the job's done. I've sent a text to your mother saying she's not invited to Sunday lunch tomorrow because of your stomach bug. I hope you don't mind, but I went into quite graphic detail. And the other one to Rachel."

My skin tightened at the mention of her name. Had he guessed that Alistair was with her?

"I've asked her to tell work that you won't be in on Monday. Same stomach bug, obviously. Have I missed anyone?

"And as for you two," he said, looking from Naomi to Ruby. "There's no one, is there? No friends, no work in your case, Nay.

And, well, you, Ruby—you're the boss, aren't you? No one's going to begrudge you taking a day or two off work. And the great thing about this is that even if someone did miss you, they wouldn't think to look here for you, would they?"

"You can't keep us down here forever. Think about what you're doing," I said.

"Just treating you the same way as you did me. Do unto others . . . Isn't that the saying? Can't have you getting to Alistair before me."

"You won't get away with this," Naomi said. "There's no covering this up."

The phone in his hand buzzed. He glanced at it casually. His eyes widened and he smiled.

"Well, would you looky here? Heard back from Rachel wanting to know if that means she should keep Alistair for the whole weekend."

"Don't, Phillip," I warned.

"Don't what?" he answered.

He looked down at me with a smirk.

"So he's not with a school friend, then? Well played, Imogen. I didn't know you had it in you."

He wasn't close enough for me to be able to get the scarf around his neck or attack him with the table leg. Without Naomi free to back me up, there was no way I could overpower him. My only hope was to reason with him.

"Wait. I can explain," I said.

"I'd better go get him. Any message?"

"Wait! She won't give him to you. She knows what you're like. Let me come with you."

"Fair point. And one I'm grateful to you for raising. I'd better text her back."

His eyes were on the screen and he spoke out loud as his thumb and forefinger picked out the letters.

"'No, thanks, Rach.' You do call her Rach, don't you? I want this to sound genuine. 'No, thanks, Rach. Phil on way 2 yours 2 pick him up.'"

I shifted across the bed toward him. My fingers groped for the piece of wood. I needed to get closer.

"Don't do this."

He continued tapping the screen. "'He'll be with u in 10 mins. Have Alistair ready. Kiss. Kiss.' There. Done." He looked me straight in the eye. "Oh, and stay where you are. I know that you've untied yourself. You really don't want me to go on a road trip with our son in a foul mood, would you? You wouldn't want me to lose my temper with him."

"Don't you dare take him! I will go to the police and I *will* track you down."

He held my gaze for a moment longer before laughing.

"Where was that spirit when we were together? I'm going to take some credit for giving you a backbone at last. No need to thank me. It's been a pleasure."

He turned and ran up the stairs two at a time. I scrambled after him. By the time I'd reached the bottom, he'd already shut the door. Halfway up, I heard the key turn in the lock. He was in a rush and didn't bother sliding the bolt across the door. Why would he? The door was locked and no one knew where we were. At the top of the stairs, I threw myself into the door, turning the handle even though I knew it wouldn't budge.

"Phillip!" I shouted. "Don't you dare touch my son! Let me out!"

There was silence.

"Phillip!"

I kicked the door and threw my shoulder into it. Though it buckled with the effort, it wouldn't open. I tried looking through the keyhole, but the key was still in the lock and I couldn't see anything. At least, I comforted myself, if someone did come into the house, they'd be able to unlock the door. The fact that he hadn't taken the key with him was our first stroke of luck.

I pulled my hand back and unleashed as much force as I could against the door. It bowed but didn't give. Again. Again. I kicked at it with my heels; I threw my shoulder into it. My body screamed out in agony but I wouldn't give up.

"Shit!"

Naomi hopped to the bottom of the steps, balancing on one leg with her free hand against the wall to steady herself.

"What can I do?" Naomi asked.

Ruby was pulling at the radiator, but it had managed to contain Phillip, so it was unlikely to budge.

"Can you get up the stairs?"

"I can try." Naomi started up the steps.

Naomi got halfway up, grunting with exertion, then turned and sat down, changing tactics and pushing herself up one step at a time.

"*Help!*" I cried. "Help!" I knew no one would hear us. How could they? It was one of the reasons that it had been such a good place to keep Phillip locked up in the first place.

Naomi and I swapped places and she began hitting at the lock with the heel of her hand. I was about to tell her that it was pointless, that this door was as strong as any door had a right to be, when we heard the clatter of the key falling from the lock on the other side of the door. We looked at each other.

"What was that?" she asked, though her eyes were wide with hope. Hoping that it was what she thought it was.

I put the side of my face on the floor but I couldn't see anything.
"Turn the light off!"

Naomi struggled upright and flipped the switch. A thin blade of
light cut the door from the floor and, in the middle of the shaft, lay a
long, narrow metal key.

"Yes!" My fingers couldn't fit under the door. The gap was too
narrow and the key too far away. I got to my feet, put the light back
on, and ran back down the stairs.

"We need something thin and curved to slide under the door to
hook the key under. Can you see anything, Ruby?"

I cast about, but there was nothing but blankets, pillows, dust,
and gloom.

"There has to be something."

The key was tantalizingly close and I had to get to it.

"Thin and curved," Ruby muttered, looking about her.

I watched Naomi try to squeeze her fingers under the door, but
there was no way they'd fit. The key, so close, and yet useless unless
we could get our hands on it.

I wondered how far Phillip had got by now. Was he at Rachel's
yet? Would his bruised face give her enough of an indication that not
everything was as it seemed? I had to pray that she wouldn't let him
take my son.

I sat on the end of the bed, my head in my hands. *Think.*

Phillip was one step ahead of me and wouldn't stop until he got
what he wanted. But I would find a way to stop him. I had to.

Think.

He'd had things his own way for far too long. Ruby, Naomi, and
I had let him get away with too much because his displeasure was
too hard to bear.

Think.

Even his mother had indulged him for too long, breast-feeding him until he was five.

I leaped to my feet.

"Yes!" I shouted.

"What?" asked Naomi.

Ruby was looking at me hopefully. "Imogen?"

I took my jumper off. It had gone crisp with the drying blood and it scraped my cheek.

"I can't reach . . . My ribs hurt. Ruby, can you help?" I crouched down by her side.

"What *are* you doing?" Ruby was leaning away from me.

"Unhook me."

Ruby undid my bra and I slid it off my shoulders. With my back to her, I pulled my jumper back on, feeling vulnerable as the rough material grazed my chest.

I bit the material at the front of the bra between the pale blue cups. The bow came off easily between my teeth and I spat it to one side and then bit at the bra again. My jaw ached but I continued to bite and tug at the delicate material until a small hole began to appear.

"Wait. Here it comes."

I pushed at the metal and it poked at the thinning fabric. As I pushed again, though my fingers slipped, the wire broke the surface. I took the end of it in my teeth and the underwire from my bra slid out.

"Thin and curved," I said.

I ran up the stairs and pushed Naomi to one side.

"Please, please, please," I murmured.

I pushed the underwire under the door while keeping hold of one end. At first it moved the key to one side but failed to bring it any closer. I took a deep breath to steady myself. The gap at the bottom of the door was so narrow it was difficult to see anything other than a shadow.

I tried again, felt the wire touch something heavy, but it didn't move. I readjusted my grip on the wire and pulled a little. The key moved slowly at first, then slid with ease. As the end of the key became visible under the door, I let go of the wire and pulled at it.

The circular head of the key was thicker than the body and it got stuck, but I shook, wriggled, and pulled on it until I worked it free. In my haste, I fumbled to get it into the lock. I shouted with exasperation and took a deep breath.

This time the key slid into the lock and it opened. We burst free, the door slamming backward against the wall. I crawled into the hallway and lay on the cool tiles.

The sweet, pure air smelled like the beach after a cloudburst. The late-afternoon light had never been so beautiful. I took in as much air as my lungs would let me until my chest ached and I was light-headed. I had no time to gather my thoughts. I ran into the kitchen and out again. Searching. Panicking.

"The keys. The keys. I don't know where he's put the—"

I spotted them on the shelf in the hallway and ran back to unlock Naomi. She groaned with pleasure as the cuffs sprang open first on her wrist, then on her ankle.

"Do Ruby," I said, and left the other key with her. The back door was open and there was no sign of Phillip, my phone, or—I checked the driveway—my car.

"Naomi, I need your car. Where are your keys?"

"In my jacket. I'll come with you. Have you called Rachel?" she asked urgently.

"He's taken my phone."

"Use mine," she called.

"I can't remember the number. Zero-seven-eight-eight—No, zero-seven-seven . . . Shit. I need to get to her house. It's only ten minutes away."

"Does Phil know where she lives?"

"I don't know. I don't think so, but it wouldn't take him long to find out from the police database."

Ruby appeared as we flung open the front door.

"Call the police," I said. "Tell them what's happened—"

"But," Naomi cut in, "he'll tell them we locked him up."

"This is about my son! You can blame it all on me. I don't care!"

Ruby was looking about her, dazed. "The dogs. Where are the dogs? Don't tell me he's done it again!"

It hadn't occurred to me before, but the dogs hadn't made a sound since Phillip had escaped the cellar. They were long gone.

"I don't know. Ruby, we've got to go. Just call the police!"

We ran out of the house—shoeless, covered in blood, and desperately hoping that we weren't too late.

CHAPTER 19

10 days before the funeral

"I've found a mobile number, but it's a work one."

I was in the passenger seat of Naomi's car searching the Internet for Rachel's details.

"Call it!" Naomi said.

A car sounded its horn as Naomi passed it on the inside lane and pushed in front. Lights flashed in the rearview mirror and she pushed the accelerator as far down as it would go. The engine was slow to respond.

"Straight to voice mail. She'll have it switched off."

"Leave a message," Naomi said.

I listened to Rachel's voice in my ear. *"Hello, you've reached Rachel Scott. Sorry I can't take your call right now . . ."*

I was picturing her unable to answer her phone because she was handing Alistair over to Phillip, packing him off with a cheery wave. The high-pitched beep of the voice mail brought me to my senses.

"Rachel, hi—it's me, Imogen. Phillip's on his way to get Alistair.

You mustn't let him take him. Do whatever you have to do. Call the police. Just—just don't let him take him. Please! Call me back on this number when you get this message." I looked at Naomi. "Number," I said to her.

I repeated her number, digit by digit, into the phone and then said, "We're on our way to your house now. We'll be with you in five minutes. Call me back."

There were brake lights ahead of us reaching into the distance like a landing strip.

"Take this turn," I said.

I looked at the clock; it was almost four. Rachel and Alistair were probably on their way back from the movies. Rachel would be speeding slightly to get back in time to meet Phillip, thinking she was doing me a favor. Alistair would be excited to see his dad.

Naomi swerved off the highway and onto the off-ramp. The traffic was just as bad leading up to the roundabout and I swore as we joined the end of the queue staring at the red light, willing it to change.

Naomi put her hand on my arm. "It's okay," she said. "We'll get to him. I'm not being funny, but there's no way Phil wants to take Alistair away. He wouldn't know what to do with him."

"You don't get it," I snapped. "If he really wanted to spend time with him, I wouldn't be so scared. Right now, his hate for me is stronger than his love for Alistair. Something's changed. Look at what he did to us in the cellar. He's crossed a line and it's anyone's guess what he's going to do now. We've all underestimated him and I can't make that mistake again. He knows the worst thing that could happen to me is to lose my son."

The light changed but the cars ahead of us seemed slow to respond. They trickled onto the roundabout. As we approached the

light, it changed to amber. As if reading my mind, Naomi acceler-
ated and turned a hard left. I caught a glimpse of red light as we
passed.

We sped through the country lanes. I gripped onto my seat but
didn't ask her to slow down. We turned in to Arnold Crescent, smacking the curb hard and causing us to leave our seats for an instant.

I scanned the vehicles parked in the neighborhood lot, whipping
my head from side to side. My car wasn't here. Neither was Phillip.
Perhaps he'd already left; perhaps he hadn't found her address yet.
For the first time in my life, I was thankful I'd left the car with an
empty tank. Hopefully the car had run out of petrol and left him
stranded.

The street was stiff with middle-class respectability. Trimmed,
neat houses and glinting cars sat on either side of the tree-lined road.

"Here. This one on the right." I pointed to the house and undid
my seat belt as Naomi pulled up outside Rachel's at a rush, bumping
the car onto the sidewalk. I ran up the steps and struck at the door.

"Rach? Rachel!"

I looked through the letter box into the empty hallway.

"Alistair!"

I went over to the window and looked in. There was nothing out
of the ordinary. No signs of a scuffle. No signs of life. Naomi ran up
behind me.

"Anything?"

I looked about me wildly. I shook my head.

"Nothing."

A sudden sound behind us, a crack, had me spinning around. I
was on edge, expecting an attack at any moment. I instinctively
ducked, but it was only Naomi's car rolling backward into a shiny
black Corsa.

I straightened up and exhaled. If Phillip was nearby, he must have heard the sound.

A door opened next door and a small, irate man ran out.

"Hi," I said, stepping in front of him. "Have you seen Rachel?"

"That's my car!"

"I need to find Rachel," I said.

Naomi went out into the road and looked up and down it while the neighbor went to assess the damage to his car. He put his hands on his bald head and walked around the vehicle.

"We've only had it three weeks," he said.

"Sorry, but this is important. Rachel has my son."

I yanked on his arm, pulling him round to face me.

"Do you know where she is or not?" I was angry and I was desperate, and couldn't care less about his car.

He arched away from me in shock and then saw my face for the first time.

"Are you okay?" he asked. "Your face!"

I touched my nose instinctively, knew it was misshapen, bloodied, and probably broken. I watched as his wide eyes traveled to Naomi and widened even more. She looked even worse than I did. One of her eyes was half closed—I was surprised she'd been able to see well enough to drive. Seeing the horror on the small man's face made me see us through his eyes. It was the stuff of nightmares. Bruised faces, ripped clothes, bare feet. We looked like we'd been pulled from a car wreck.

"The man who hurt us is coming here for Rachel and my son."

His eyes snapped back to mine.

"There was a man here not fifteen minutes ago. It wasn't—"

"Did he see Rachel?"

"He had bruises too, but he said that—"

"What about Rachel?" Naomi was almost shouting at him.

"No. I spoke to her around lunchtime, and she said she was on her way to the pictures. She's not back yet."

Relief nearly knocked me off my feet and I steadied myself against the cool black railings.

"What did you tell the man?" I asked.

"Same as I've told you. Are you sure you're okay? Do you think you should be getting yourself to the hospital?" He winced as he looked at my nose.

"Do you know where he went?"

"To the nearest cinema, I assume. He didn't seem to be in a huge rush. Said she must have forgotten their meeting."

I looked at Naomi, unsure what to do next but feeling I couldn't just sit by and wait for something to happen. Rachel should have been home by now. Where were they?

"I need you to keep an eye out for Rachel coming home," I said to the neighbor. "*Really* watch the front of the house. It's important that she doesn't speak to that man who came earlier. Tell her to call Imogen straightaway, and call the police if you see that man again."

He puffed out his chest with a sense of importance.

"Well, yes, of course."

I motioned to Naomi to get in the car but shook my head as she reached the driver's side door.

"I'll drive," I said.

"What about my car?" the man said.

I glared at him and he shrank away from me. Naomi had left the keys in the ignition and the engine started the first time. I put the car in first gear and had to press the accelerator hard to get the car to bump forward.

I continued slowly up the road, accelerator hard to the floor, leg straining with the effort. The car picked up and lurched forward, gathering speed over the crest of the hill and down the other side, around the crescent and back onto the busy thoroughfare.

"At least we know that Phillip hasn't got him yet. Rachel must have got the text about Phillip coming to pick Alistair up. I'm worried that she's already sent him a message thinking he's me arranging a different time or place. The house, maybe? Perhaps she thinks she's doing me a favor by bringing him home?"

"Ruby will deal with it if she does."

"You think? She's always quick to side with Phillip."

"Not this time," said Naomi. "She'll be scared. She's probably already got the police there by now."

"Call my home number and see if she's heard anything."

I gave Naomi the number and she keyed it in.

"Battery's running low," she said.

"Shit."

I turned the car and started heading toward the house. Praying all the while that I could get to Alistair before Phillip did.

"Ruby, it's Naomi. . . . No, he wasn't there. I guess that means they've not turned up there either? . . . No. Sit tight—we'll look for them as soon as we've found Alistair, okay? . . . I know, I know. But they're chipped, right, so as soon as someone finds them . . . That's right. See? It'll be okay. We'll be back in"—she looked at me as she said—"ten minutes?" I nodded and she said into the phone, "Yeah, ten minutes."

She started to take the phone away from her ear and then changed her mind. "Oh, wait, Ruby? Ruby?" She looked at the screen but she'd already lost her. "I was going to ask her what the police said, but she was freaking out about the dogs. Do we need to get our stories straight before we get home and start talking to the police?"

"Tell them the truth. It's okay. As long as I get Alistair back, I don't care what the police think."

"You will get him back. Phil ain't got him yet. He still thinks we're locked up. He don't even know that we're looking for him."

She was right. Phillip wouldn't expect us to be looking for Alistair yet. He was in no rush. I came to a halt at a three-way intersection and waited for a break in the traffic. I was looking at every car as it drove past to see if it was Rachel or Phillip.

Where are you, Rachel?

Naomi's mobile rang.

"What shall I do?" she said.

"Answer it!"

"Hello?"

She listened. I kept glancing over at her.

"Who is it?" I hissed.

"Oh, hi, yeah. No, I'm with her now—she's driving."

"Who is it? Pass me the phone!" I reached for the phone, but she elbowed me away and transferred the phone to her other hand.

"We'll be right there."

She hung up the phone and turned to me.

"That was your mum. Guess who's just turned up at her house?"

CHAPTER 20

10 days before the funeral

I kissed Alistair all over his face and hair and then again, over and over.

"You left some kisses at home," I said, and kissed him again.

"Mummy?"

"Yes?"

"What happened to your face?"

"I fell over a cat in the garden. I was carrying a cup of tea so didn't have my hands free and just . . . *splat!* Broke the fall with my nose."

"What cat was it?"

"Big, fluffy ginger one."

"Did you hurt it?"

"No, but when I catch it, I'll . . ." And I chased him about the room, tickling his sides and his tummy. I caught him and breathed him in.

"I love you *so*, so much," I said.

"Love you most. Did Nomey fall over a cat too?"

I looked at her half-closed eye and the bruising on her cheek.

"No, Naomi tripped down the stairs. Would you believe she fell over her own feet?"

He skipped away, saying, "Silly Nomey."

We were at Bill the gardener's house. We couldn't be sure that Phillip wasn't going to turn up at Mother's. Couldn't be sure he wasn't there already.

Rachel and Naomi were eyeing each other warily, while Mother reached out a hand to me and snatched it back again before she could make contact. She opened her mouth and then shut it before unfamiliar words came out. Her eyes darted from me to the closed door where Alistair sat watching television. Bill was making hot chocolates with the ease of a man at home in his surroundings. Whipped cream from a can. I shook my head when he offered marshmallows, but he put them on anyway and said, "You need feeding up, love."

Now wasn't the time to question Mother about their relationship, but I liked seeing how comfortable they were in each other's company.

"Spain?" Mother said, picking up on our earlier conversation now that Alistair was out of earshot.

"You've seen what he's capable of. It's the only way to stop Phillip getting his hands on Alistair. Rachel offered to take him away. The Easter holidays are about to start, so no one's going to ask any questions. I could book a resort, but it would be better if they could stay with Aunty Margaret. Please, Mother, go with them. You said yourself you were considering going there to recuperate."

What I didn't say was that it also had the added bonus of getting everyone I cared about out of the country, where I knew Phillip couldn't follow. I wouldn't put it past him to take out his anger on any or all of them.

"Of course. But I don't see why you aren't coming as well. If everything is as bad as you say it is . . . And what's to stop him coming out to Spain?"

"He won't expect me to let Alistair far from my side," I said. "He'll be looking for Alistair wherever I am. And besides, Naomi has Phillip's passport."

Naomi had been planning to leave Phillip for months, but seeing as he had stopped her working, she hadn't the means. The women's refuge had advised that it would be easier for her if she could take a passport and birth certificate with her when she fled. She'd taken his too so that he wouldn't find his and realize what she'd done. This way, she hoped, he'd think they'd put them somewhere "safe."

"How bad was it?" I asked Naomi.

"I dunno. Not too bad, I suppose. There's always someone who's got it worse, i'nt there? I thought about tellin' someone or going to the police or whatever, but I never thought they'd believe me. I've been in trouble with the police before. You know, small stuff. Forgery, fraud . . . Got a suspended sentence."

"Does Phillip know?"

"'Course he does. It was something else he could use to control me. And then, failing that, he'd use his fists. I mean, he never left bruises or did anything in front of anyone who could back me up. Besides, it's only painful for as long as it hurts, right? I'd just think, 'This time next week it won't hurt anymore.' It was the stuff he said, you know? The threats . . . And, I suppose, after a while, he had me believing that it were my fault. And you start to wonder, don't you?

Whether you could have done summat to stop it. And where could I have gone anyway?"

I wished I could have told her that I would have helped, but I couldn't lie to her. I'd misjudged her and wouldn't have been the first person to come to her aid.

"He didn't hit me," I said. "He pushed me down the stairs and, you know, did that stuff with pressure points. There was one incident where he slammed me into a wall and I ended up with a black eye, but he never left a mark after that. The knuckle behind the ear was one of his favorites ways to subdue. He liked to bring his work home. But mostly it was the things that Phillip said and how he treated me that hurt the worst. I guess I had it easier than you."

"If you believe that, you're dumber than you look," she said.

I'd told her that she should leave now, while she could, and was relieved when she refused to leave me to face Phillip on my own. After seeing with her own eyes that Alistair was safe, she drove to get his passport from our home.

Rachel hitched herself up onto the kitchen counter and Mother didn't even roll her eyes.

"How did you know that text wasn't from me?" I asked her.

"Two things. First, it would take more than a tummy bug for you to put Alistair in Phillip's care. He'd be safer in a lion enclosure. In fact, even if the text had been from you, I'd assume you'd lost your mental faculties and I'd have staged an intervention anyway. But the thing that sealed it for me—" She turned to Bill and took the proffered hot chocolate. "Thanks, Bill. It was the fact that you used text speak. A number two instead of the word 'to'? And the letter 'u' instead of the word? That's when I knew you'd been abducted by aliens."

I leaned over and kissed her cheek.

"You're a wonderful woman, Rachel Scott."

"I've often thought so. When I got to your mum's, I checked my messages, and as well as the one from you, Clive from next door called and said people had been looking for me all day and a madwoman had crashed into his car and driven off. I reckoned that was you and suggested to your mum we went somewhere else just in case Phillip was on his way."

"May I have a word, Imogen?" Mother asked.

I followed Mother into the conservatory.

"Yes?"

"Should I be worried?"

"No, you're completely safe."

"Not about me. You! I don't like the idea of leaving you behind."

I nodded. "He's coming for Alistair," I said. "And he's going to make me pay. But all I care about right now is getting you and Alistair to safety. Once you're out of the country, I'll have nothing to lose."

"For goodness' sake." She sighed, her exasperation shining through. "What good will it do Alistair if you're hurt . . . or worse?"

"I don't plan on being hurt. I'll get him away from Alistair, but I won't run from him. But if . . . if anything does happen to me—"

"Nonsense. I won't have you talking like this!" snapped Mother.

"If anything *does* happen to me, you'll take care of him, won't you?"

Instead of facing a future without Alistair, I was contemplating the fact that Alistair might be facing a future without me.

"Come with us, Imogen." Her voice was softer now. "I was there, remember—I saw the way he treated you. You forget I was on the sidelines watching throughout your entire marriage."

"I don't remember you offering any help at the time," I said without bitterness.

"What could I possibly have said? You've never listened to me. I warned Phillip off on more than one occasion, but he told me to keep my nose out. Said that he would tell you things that I didn't want you to know."

"Like what?"

Mother brushed invisible fibers off her sleeve.

"Do we have to do this now?" she said with a sour look on her face.

"I can't think of a better time. I need to know everything that Phillip could use against me."

"Imogen, it's complicated."

"So simplify it."

Mother walked to the window and folded her arms. It was gloomy outside and the lamp was on in the corner. I could see her face reflected in the glass.

"It's your father."

"What about him?"

"I drove him to it."

She waited for me to speak, and when I didn't, she took a deep breath before continuing.

"We'd had problems when you were little, the place we were before. There was a girl who went missing. It was a huge misunderstanding. She lived five doors up the road from us and your father offered her a lift home. It wasn't like he forced her in the car or snatched her off the street or anything, but to hear the news on the radio—well, it was like he was a pervert."

"What happened?" I asked. It was the first I'd heard about this and I was fearful of how the story might end.

"He took her to the park. It was nothing really. Her aunt was meant to pick her up, but she was running late. When the girl wasn't where she said she'd be, well, the aunt panicked and called the police. Some of the children described the car they saw her getting into. They said it was a brown Cortina like your father's.

"The police found them at the park eating ice cream. The girl said he'd tried to kiss her, which was absolute rubbish. He only received a caution, but people called him names and we had a brick through the front window. Well, after that we had no choice but to move. Your father lost his job. I lost friends. They said they didn't believe a word of what the papers said, but they wondered. How could they not? I did, and I was his wife. What kind of person takes a young girl he hardly knows to the park? He was never the cleverest, your father.

"You were small at the time. Four years old. We thought it was better to start again, so we moved from Kent to Derbyshire."

Another day, in another life, I would have been shocked at the news. But on the day that my ex had attacked me and tried to abduct our son . . . I only felt numb. It had the feel of a story about it. A tale being told that had all the right elements of a page-turner but nothing to do with me. I pictured my dad, smiling, affectionate, and I couldn't believe that anyone would have considered him capable of such a thing. I was about to say that to Mother, to brush it away as irrelevant, but she was biting her lips and her eyes looked pained.

"There's more, isn't there?" I asked.

"The day that he died, he was messing around with you and those girls from across the road. I got so mad with him. I told him that I would not have a repeat of what had happened in Kent. He was as angry as I was. He saw it as betrayal, and I suppose it was. He was a fragile man. I knew I'd hurt him by bringing it up again. I was worried that the rumors would follow us and I suppose I was worried that maybe . . . that maybe . . . well, you know, that there was some truth to it. I thought he should be careful how it looked to the neighbors. I told him he wasn't welcome in my bed that night. I thought he'd sleep on the settee but instead he went to the garage and—"

She stopped speaking and put two fingers to her lips to stop them from quivering. We both knew what happened next.

"The last words I'd said to him," she whispered. "They were so unkind."

I went to her and held out my arms. She hesitated for a moment and then sank into them. I was taller than she was and rested my cheek on the top of her head. She felt small and brittle, like the memory of my father. It seemed absurd that people could accuse him of any wrongdoing, but then I had always idolized him. He'd been perfect in my eyes.

"Don't torment yourself," I said. "It takes more than one argument for someone to take their own life. You can't blame yourself for what happened."

"To this day I don't know whether it was because of that argument or because there was some truth to my accusations. Or perhaps it had nothing to do with any of it. I just wish we'd talked."

When I became old enough to think of such things, I'd come to the conclusion that my father had committed suicide because of depression in a time when men didn't talk about their emotions. Nothing Mother had told me changed any of that.

She shuddered against my chest as if she were crying, but she made no sound.

"What's this got to do with Phillip? Did he know?" I asked gently.

She laughed bitterly. "Of course he knew. He did background checks on you before he proposed. I saw how he was controlling you. I always said he was no good for you. I tried to warn him off, but he said I should keep my nose out and that it wouldn't take much to reopen old cases of abuse and join the dots to your father."

"You should have told me."

"And broken your heart? You adored Phillip, but you idolized your father. He was the one who left us, but *I* was the one you despised. He never did anything wrong; I wouldn't have that man sullying his memory. It was all that you had left."

"But there was no evidence, surely? Otherwise they'd have arrested him."

"Of course not. But that husband of yours made it sound like all he needed to do was to place your father in certain places at certain times and, well, he wouldn't be around to deny it, would he?"

She stood back, her moment of weakness over, and wiped under her eyes. I sat down on the arm of the chair. Phillip had known about the accusations against my father and yet he hadn't mentioned a thing. I would have thought it was the perfect information for him to attack me with. He must have been waiting for a special occasion. Either that, or the information was more important as a way to control Mother than as a stick to beat me with.

She looked at a picture on the wall. It was a watercolor of the Lake District. She went to it and straightened it—though, to my eye, it was straight enough.

"Mother?"

"Can we stop talking about this, please?"

"Get your bag," I said. "The sooner we get to the airport, the better. And then, once I know you're safe, I'm going to come back and deal with Phillip. He won't get away with this."

CHAPTER 21

10 days before the funeral

Naomi met us in the departure hall, carrying a small bag of clothes for Alistair and his passport. There'd been no sign of Phillip at the house, and as far as she could tell, she hadn't been followed. Ruby said she'd call if he turned up.

We swerved around shorts-wearing holidaymakers dragging suitcases and looking vacantly at the departures board. Alistair and I hadn't been on holiday since Phillip left. I was disappointed that I wouldn't be with him to see his eyes light up when the airplane took to the skies or to hold his hand as he ran across the beach. But then I remembered that this wasn't a normal holiday.

I was wearing a mixture of Mother's and Bill's clothes so that attention wouldn't be drawn to my bloodied clothing. I'd wiped my face and tied my hair back, and tentatively applied powder to my bruises. Naomi had changed her ripped top, and she had her long red hair over her face so that the worst of her injuries were hidden from view.

Rachel said she was looking forward to reequipping her wardrobe. She acted as if it were a wonderful adventure, but her scared eyes gave her away. Her passport was always in her bag, ready for last-minute getaways and romantic weekends. A mad dash out of the country to flee a friend's unstable ex wasn't quite in the same league.

Naomi hung back, looking over her shoulder for any sign of Phillip. I held Alistair's hand tightly.

"Isn't this exciting?" I said.

Mustn't cry. Mustn't cry. Mustn't cry.

"Mummy? You said I was going to holiday club with Jacob."

If he could see through my false smile, he didn't show it.

"I know, sweetie, but then Rachel suggested that you all go on a special holiday to Aunty Margaret's. She's got her own swimming pool."

This seemed to please him, and I hauled him onto my hip. He was getting heavy, and I didn't know how much longer I was going to be able to lift him.

There was a slight delay at the barriers as Mother had difficulty working out how to scan her boarding pass. I made the most of the gifted seconds and told Alistair how much I loved him. He wriggled out of my grasp and Rachel squeezed my hand.

"Don't worry," she said. "I'll look after him. You look after you."

I kept my voice low so Alistair wouldn't hear. "Rach, I'm scared."

"Then come with us. I'll pay for your flight." Her words were urgent and eager but I shook my head.

I hugged her. "You're a good friend. Thank you. But I have to do this now or he'll always be a threat."

And then Mother was through the barrier, and it was Alistair's turn. I gave him the briefest of kisses on his head, the tightest of hugs, and then he was beyond the barrier where I couldn't touch him. And neither could Phillip.

They vanished around the corner, and I stood there for a moment longer, expecting, hoping even, that Alistair would dash back to me, refuse to go without me. But he didn't, and Naomi and I were jostled to one side by a steady stream of travelers.

"What now?" Naomi asked.

"We go home and wait for Phillip to come to us."

We didn't want to alert him to the fact that Alistair was out of the country. As long as he was still looking for him, he wouldn't look far from where I was. For my plan to work, Phillip had to believe that we were still in the cellar and he had to be arrogant enough to return to the house. And if there was one thing Phillip wasn't short of, it was arrogance.

He was a danger to us and, if he could get to him, to Alistair. He wasn't going to skulk away quietly with his tail between his legs. We could all go back to living our lives as usual, but we would be looking over our shoulders. And I couldn't be with Alistair again until Phillip was no longer a problem.

"But what if he's already there? Waiting for us?" she asked.

"We'd have heard from Ruby if he'd turned up. Besides, he'll still be searching for Rachel and Alistair. He won't want to come back empty-handed until he knows he has no other choice."

And by that time, we'd be ready for him.

I was desperate to shower the stench of Phillip off me. I ran the water as hot as it would go and scrubbed at my body. I could have spent hours in there but I didn't have time for such a luxury.

Ruby and Naomi took turns in the bathroom. We made sure that there was always one of us at the bedroom window keeping watch. The sun was slipping away but the streetlights hadn't come on yet. There were already shadows for Phillip to hide in.

While Ruby was in the bathroom, Naomi stood at my shoulder.

"I didn't tell her what I was doing," she said.

"Hmm?"

"When I came back for the passport, I didn't tell Ruby. I just said I was picking up some clothes for Alistair. Said he'd stay with Rachel for a bit longer."

Without taking my eyes off the rose-gold street, I said, "You don't trust her."

"Don't trust anyone, duck. The way I see it, she's the weak link. She'll blab as soon as he raises his voice. The less she knows, the better."

Ruby was withdrawn. Her face was pinched and her hands trembled. It wasn't like her to be so quiet. She wanted us to go and look for her dogs, but when I told her she had to stay put in case Phillip saw her, she didn't argue. She hadn't called the police because, she said, it had slipped her mind. I doubted that. Even with what she'd seen him do, she wasn't ready to give Phillip up yet. Still, it suited us to keep the police out of it for now, at least.

The police couldn't help us. For one thing, they would wonder why we'd left it so long to report it. For another, the main reason for calling them—Alistair's safety—had already been dealt with. To involve them now would mean having to let them know where he was, and Phillip would be likely to hear about it.

And finally, there was the same reason as always. The one that had stopped Naomi and me from picking up the phone countless times. Phillip *was* the police.

From bitter experience, I knew that they would be inclined to believe him over us. Me: the bitter ex who had a history of depression, who had a vengeful vendetta against Saint Phillip. It was all too easy to see how he would spin it. And Naomi, who knew better than to trust the police—she'd been in trouble before, had a mark against her name; who would believe her over him? And then there was Ruby, who just so happened to turn up just as her ex had been locked in the cellar. It was a coincidence that was unlikely to be believed.

We were on our own.

"We wait for Phillip to come to us," I said to Ruby. "By now, he'll know that Rachel isn't at home and that she's not going to hand Alistair over. There's been too much of a delay. He'll know it's not just cinema trip or a visit to Pizza Express. He's going to be pissed off. Where else is he going to go? He'll watch her house for a while, maybe go to Mother's, but in the end he'll come here. He'll come here to look at us, gloat, remind himself of how powerful he is. That's what men like him do."

"What if you're wrong?" asked Ruby. "What if he isn't going to do any of those things? What if he plans to leave us in the cellar? What if he's come to his senses and is on his way to let us out? He could have calmed down, he could've—"

"I don't know who you're trying to convince," I snapped. "Open your eyes, Ruby. He tried to kill Naomi. You got off lightly, but you saw what he did to us and what he's like when he's angry. Stop making excuses for him."

I explained how we would wait for him to check on us in the cellar and then lock the door. I told her that she would be free to leave after that, but until we had Phillip where we wanted, she was to stay.

We made the house look just as it did when he left, put the keys to the handcuffs back on the table, put Naomi's mobile back where we'd found it. We opened the back door and locked the door to the cellar, leaving the key in the outside of the lock just as it was before.

I could picture his smug face as he unlocked the door. I imagined his feet on the cellar steps, expecting to see us when he rounded the corner, and then the confusion when the door behind him slammed and locked. Only when he was back where he'd started would I be able to breathe freely again and put phase two of our plan into action.

Phillip, so proud of the power of the law, would find himself suffocated by it. If he didn't agree to our demands, I would get a restraining order against him. I might not have enough evidence to get charges brought against him, but I was confident that I had enough for a restraining order. And if he broke the order to stay away from me, he would be arrested—and Phillip would rather die than let that happen.

Ruby sat by an upstairs window close enough to the glass to be able to see the street and far enough away to be hidden by the shadows. She would see anyone approaching the front of the house. Naomi took up position behind the door in the living room. She wanted to be the one to lock him in. I pulled together some food, to keep our strength up.

I had no appetite, but the only thing I'd eaten had been ejected from my stomach in the cellar. I'd not seen the other two eat all day. I opened the drawer for the big knife, my favorite one with the thick silver handle. It wasn't there. I glanced about, hoping to see it on the table, but I couldn't see it. I opened the dishwasher, but apart from two mugs and a bowl it was empty. I was about to ask the others whether they'd seen it anywhere when there was a hiss from upstairs; Ruby's voice was urgent and low. I pushed myself against the kitchen wall, out of view from the hallway, wondering whether I had time to hide and glancing at the door to see if he was coming in the front or the back.

There were furtive sounds at the front of the house, but, as yet, no key in the lock. I risked a quick glance down the hallway. A shape moved beyond the door. Crouched, half hidden. I was breathing heavily, ready to creep out the back door if he came in the front.

The letter box opened and I saw gloved fingers groping at the air. The fingers disappeared but the flap stayed open. I held my breath as the hand appeared again and dropped something rectangular onto the mat. I jumped as the letter box snapped shut and the figure moved away from the doorstep. It was a leaflet for the local Chinese takeaway.

We picked at the food and then sat in relative silence: Ruby upstairs, Naomi down, and I moving silently between the two. We jumped each time a car went by or we heard voices in the street. Naomi went to get a drink and I looked at my newly shaped face in the large mirror above the fireplace. My nose was swollen and my eyes were puffy. They were the color of stormy skies.

The phone rang. One in the kitchen and one upstairs on the landing. It sounded too loud. I felt nervous, wondering who it was and why they had chosen this moment to call me, thinking of all the things it could be.

The ringing stopped abruptly and I relaxed. Let them think that no one was in. But then I heard a voice say, "Hello?"

I rushed from the room to stop Naomi, to tell her to hang up, but it was too late.

The light from the open fridge door showed Naomi's face was rigid with . . . what? Fear? Anger?

"Naomi?"

She jolted when she heard me and dropped the phone. She reached out for a chair to steady herself. It scraped across the terra-cotta floor, like an orchestra warming up for a performance, and then toppled with a clatter.

"Sorry," she whispered. "I wasn't thinking—I—"

I picked up the phone, which had spun across the floor and come to a stop by the dishwasher.

"Hello?" I said.

Silence.

I tried again. "Hello?"

My heart was pounding so loudly that I couldn't hear the person on the other end of the line.

A familiar voice slithered into my ear.

"Look who made it out of the cellar. Aren't you a clever girl?"

CHAPTER 22

7 years, 19 weeks, and 5 days before the funeral

Imogen was putting the finishing touches to dinner when she heard the front door slam. She'd had to cook in stages. So much for morning sickness only lasting for the first three months.

Phillip was over an hour late and she was close to bursting with her news. She'd been waiting for him in a cocoon of excitement all afternoon, watching as her stomach hiccupped and shook. It was doing it again. A family of eels somersaulting in her stomach.

She was wearing a summer dress and a thin cardigan even though winter was waiting in the wings. She was hot all of the time and she didn't own many clothes that stretched around her expanding stomach. This little bundle was a furnace in her belly. At least she looked pregnant now, rather than like the consumer of too much chocolate.

She bounded into the hallway ready to throw her arms around him. He was already on the stairs and all she saw was his hand sliding up the banister.

"You're home," she said.

"Nice detective work, Sherlock."

Imogen's smile slipped a little. He was in a bad mood, like so many days of late. She listened as his heavy feet drummed into the bathroom. She waited a moment, heard the shower start to run, and then disappeared into the kitchen to cook the spaghetti. She lifted the lid on the Bolognese sauce and nearly gagged at the smell. Baby appeared to be a vegetarian.

She'd used a splash of red wine in the orange Le Creuset pan but hadn't let a sip of alcohol pass her lips since the day the blue line had appeared on the magic wand in the bathroom.

She poured some of the wine into a large glass when she heard Phillip exit the bathroom, and arranged herself at the table. It was like a 1950s advert for a good wife. *Take fifteen minutes to prepare yourself and put a fresh ribbon in your hair. Be a little gay, as your husband will have spent the day with work-weary people.* There was no ribbon, though there was a little gaiety and a genuine willingness to not throw up at the dinner table.

She had pictures from today's scan and she knew the sex of the baby. Phillip would be over the moon. It was what he'd been wanting all along, and she couldn't wait to share it with him. Today, for the first time, she had seen her stomach move with heels and knees and was confident that he would be able to feel it. *Her.*

Phillip was wearing his robe with nothing on underneath. The message was clear. He was done for the day. He took the wine from her fiercely and, in doing so, slopped some over the terra-cotta floor.

He sniffed at the air. "What's that?"

Imogen jumped up and grabbed a tea towel to wipe up the spillage, finding it difficult to bend around her growing belly.

"In the pan?" she asked as Phillip lifted the heavy lid. "Spag Bol."

"You said we were having chili."

"Changed my mind. I didn't fancy the spice. That's okay, isn't it?"

Phillip clanged the pan lid down heavily, leaving it at an angle, steam escaping from the crescent gap.

"I was looking forward to chili." His voice wasn't accusing, not even annoyed. It just . . . was.

"I can do a chili this weekend if you like?" Imogen asked, throwing the cloth on the side and reaching up on tiptoes behind him to reach over his shoulder and kiss his cheek. She snaked her arms about his waist and laid her cheek on his back.

"I've been looking forward to that all day and you just change your mind? I suppose this is to do with your bloody pregnancy hormones and the baby, is it?"

"The baby's been kicking a lot today. Here, give me your hand— I think you'll be able to feel it."

Imogen stepped back from him and pulled back her cardigan to expose her bump. Phillip turned around to look at her. He seemed hurt, like she'd missed something important.

"What?" she asked.

"Jesus, Immie, you're not the first pregnant woman in the world."

"Hey," she said softly, "don't be like that. I know that I've been preoccupied with the baby but I've got some good news. I had the scan today."

She steepled her hands together in front of her face. She would have clapped and jumped on the spot, but Phillip's face was darkening.

She reached out to him, but he turned away and looked at the pan again.

"I've had a hell of a day. The things I've—" He threw his head back and blinked at the ceiling. "God, I'm tired. Can we just not talk about this now? I'm going to watch a film."

He took the wine bottle and added more liquid to the glass even though it was still more than half full.

"Don't you want to know about the baby?" Imogen was getting impatient with him. This wasn't how she'd imagined the evening playing out.

He held up his hand as he began to walk away. Imogen clenched her fists.

"Wait! Everyone else had someone with them today. All the other women were with their partners. Do you know how it felt to be sitting there on my own? The least you can do is pretend to be interested in your own baby!"

Her voice rang round the kitchen. She knew she should stop, but the anger in her had awoken now. "I'm sick of this, Phillip. You say I shouldn't be preoccupied with the baby, but what about *you?* Perhaps if you weren't at work all the time—"

"That's enough!" he shouted, and took two long paces toward her until their faces were inches apart. He slammed his glass down on the kitchen table without looking. The stem broke and tilted contents over the table.

"That's enough," he said again, quieter this time. "Enough."

Imogen held her breath, as startled by her own outburst as by his.

She instinctively wrapped her arms around her stomach. It wasn't like her to argue with Phillip, nor was it like him to be so dismissive of the baby.

Phillip sighed. "I'll be downstairs watching a film. Don't wait up." He turned, picked up the wine bottle, and stalked down into the cellar, his sanctuary where she wasn't allowed to go. The only place he could get some "bloody peace."

The outburst echoed in Imogen's chest. She was panting as if she had run up stairs. She started picking up sharp polygons of glass among the sticky liquid. She sucked in air through her teeth as a piece of glass slipped over her fingers, causing them to split in a wide red grin. Tears blurred her vision, though they were nothing to do with the pain from the cut. She took the pans off the heat and finished cleaning up the mess with a cloth. The smell of the wine mixed with cleaning fluid was overpowering, and her face hovered over the sink for a moment waiting for nausea to pass.

Perhaps Phillip had forgotten she was at the hospital today for her ultrasound. She was bursting to tell him that all was well with the baby and that the baby was a girl. A daughter. A sweet pink bundle. They were going to be parents to a girl. Phillip had told her that he wanted a girl more than anything. A child who would adore him and admire him. He would be so proud when she told him. But she'd leave him to calm down a little first. She sat. She stood. She couldn't settle. The news would burst from her if she didn't tell someone.

Imogen closed the kitchen door and dialed Mother's number, a smile already on her face as she listened to the ringing.

"Yes?"

"Mother, it's me."

"Oh, Imogen. I thought you were someone else. I'm expecting a call from the boiler people. It's on the ruddy blink again. Can you get off the line? They might be trying to get through at this moment."

"Oh. Well, it's just a quick call. I was at the hospital today, for my scan."

"Lovely, dear. Can you tell me about it tomorrow?"

"Sure. Yes. Tomorrow."

Imogen placed the receiver back in its cradle. She refused to be brought low. She was bursting with the desire to tell someone, anyone. It was all she could do not to run into the street and tell the first person she saw. She went to the cellar door and could see a film flashing around the dark room.

"Honey? Phillip? I'm sorry about dinner. Okay? You're so right. I wasn't thinking. I'm happy to get you something else. Let me make it up to you. I could go down the chippy?"

He grunted, and she took that to mean yes.

"Okay, then. I won't be long. I'll get haddock, yeah? And mushy peas?"

"Battered sausage," he said.

"Righty-ho. I shan't be long."

He grunted again and she shut the door on him. Since she was making this gesture, perhaps he would come out of his sanctuary and talk with her while they ate. She was determined to get this evening back on track.

Imogen was as glad of his cinema room as Phillip was. He wasn't a bad man, but sometimes the weight of the world got to him. As a policeman, he dealt with death, rape, and assault on an almost daily basis. It was too much to expect him to leave it all at the station. He said that he was surrounded by people who lied to him and attempted to mislead him. It made it difficult for him to trust anyone.

Imogen's winter coat no longer fit her, so she took Phillip's from the coat stand. It smelled of his aftershave, musky and woody, and made her smile. She took his scarf too, but only because it was soft, not because she needed the warmth. She slid her arms into his sleeves and imagined that she was wrapping his arms around her as she closed the door behind her.

Outside, in the dark street, she saw her next-door neighbor with the hood of his car up.

"Hi, Roger."

"Antifreeze," he said, raising the bottle in his hand. "There's a frost coming."

"Yes, the temperature has dropped today, hasn't it?"

"Not long now," he said, pointing at her belly.

"Four more months yet," she said, rubbing the bump. "I'll be the size of a whale by the end. I was at the hospital today, actually, finding out about the sex of the baby."

"Jane was too. Ingrown toenails. Gone septic, they have."

"Oh. Sounds painful." She paused, wondering about how she could get the conversation back to the topic of the baby, but decided against it.

"Well, I suppose I'd better get on," she said.

It was pleasurable to be in the cool evening air watching people scurry into their houses, their breath clouding the cold air before their faces. Cyclists blinked past her with only their eyes poking out of balaclavas and scarves. Ice crystals glistened like diamonds on the sidewalk and lit her way to the high street. The journey that used to take her five minutes on foot now took twice as long. Her hips and her back ached. She'd stiffened up from sitting in the hospital waiting room for so long.

As she stopped at the crossing, Imogen could see that the queue for the chip shop was snaking out the door. A man in a donkey jacket was stamping his feet against the cold, looking to all the world like he was doing an ancient war dance. A car slowed to let her cross and she waved it onward with an apology, turning instead to walk along the sidewalk and away from the lights. She would come back in ten minutes when the queue had gone down. She was anxious with the desire to see the shimmering sky diamonds. The village lights masked the sky's clarity. Beyond the edge of the town, they would be waiting for her in the cloudless black.

She harbored a childish dream that her dad looked down on her from the sky, part guardian angel, part heavenly body. The thought had her quickening her step away from the cars and the people. She wanted a quiet moment alone with him to tell him her news. He'd listen. He always did.

The road signs proclaimed that the national speed limit applied on the unlit road, though cars were accelerating far before the sign was upon them. Apart from the occasional car passing too closely to the narrow sidewalk, Imogen felt remarkably serene. Not even Phillip's foul temper and the broken wineglass could shake her contentment. She looked at the night sky and sent her mind forward to when she would have a baby in her arms and she would show it the stars. She would promise her the moon if that was what she wanted. She had never felt so happy. Significant. Useful.

Throughout her life, she had been an "add-on." Someone who was only invited to parties as a "plus one." Always the second name on the Christmas cards and the last person on someone's mind when they wanted to call a friend. She hadn't kept in touch with any friends from school and she'd dropped out of university after the first term.

It was easier to start afresh and to keep people at arm's length, because when people knew you, they wanted to know *all* of you; they felt they had the right to pry. To some, she said her parents lived a peaceful life in Norfolk. To others, she said they had died days apart after a long and happy marriage. But to Phillip she had told the truth, through tears and reddened cheeks. Her father's suicide was a constant reminder that, as a child, she wasn't good enough to make him stay and face another day. Her head, and her therapist, told her that wasn't the case, but there were still days when she believed it.

She had begun to think that she could create something fresh and new and pure with a family of her own and protect it from the past, becoming the nucleus of happiness and safety for a child or two. And now that she was growing life within her, she had never felt so powerful. She was capable of so much. This baby was giving her a second chance to live the childhood that had been denied to her. She'd hardly remembered what it was like to have both parents at her side. When she lost her father, she'd lost her mother too—mentally, at least. This baby would wipe the slate clean. This baby would show her what it was like to love for love's sake and not as a means to an end. This baby gave her hope.

As she wandered into the night, the hedgerows took on a pungent aroma of earthy foliage and the bitter brown scent of turning leaves. Imogen always found autumn to be the saddest of times. She felt an unqualified sorrow for the brown and limp leaves, wondering if they knew they were reaching the end of their lives, and one strong gust of wind would end it completely. Even the ripening of black currants made her sad for the end of summer days and late-evening barbecues.

There were no cars now. A light and delicate quiet fell past her ears. She didn't know how long she had been walking, but she knew that if she was too long Phillip would be angry. Or, rather, *angrier*. She should have turned back, but her feet kept on moving. Her hips ached from sitting down most of the day. The baby wasn't big yet, but it managed to lie in such a way that it caused her immense discomfort, and the walk was loosening her joints. The cool night air was a balm on her hot skin.

She had expected Phillip to want a boy to play football with, attend matches with, teach the ways of the world to. It made her think about her own father. It was no myth that girls had a special bond with their fathers, but if Phillip were to ever let their daughter down, like her own father had, then it was likely to do irreparable damage. No, she had wanted a boy. A resilient, hard-wearing boy that she could teach to respect women and show his softer side and to know that true strength came from the heart, not the hand. But now that she knew that the life inside her was a girl, she couldn't imagine anything else.

She's been thinking about names. She favored old-fashioned belowstairs ones like Daisy, Alice, and Iris. Phillip liked the classics like Charlotte, Rebecca, and Elizabeth. They'd know her name when they laid eyes on her.

A car sped past her too close and she was buffeted by the force. She really should turn back. She looked over her shoulder, surprised to see how far behind her the town was now. She slowed her pace and took one last look at the night sky, imagining her father's face becoming visible through the dot-to-dot sky.

Daddy? she thought. *You're going to have a granddaughter.*

For a moment, the road was empty. A sense of unbelievable calm settled over her. She thought she heard an owl hoot, smelled frost on the air. She placed her hands over her belly, and as if the baby felt her there, it gave her a nudge and somersaulted. It wasn't an altogether enjoyable feeling, but neither was it unpleasant.

She turned away from the open road and set her sights on the orange streetlights that fringed the village. She heard a car on the road behind her, going too fast in too low a gear. Its headlights were on full beam and they cast Imogen as a shadow across the narrow sidewalk, kinking at the knee and bending at the hedge. She heard the change in tone as the car changed gear but the engine was still laboring as it neared her. She walked slowly, in no hurry to face Phillip's bad mood, wanting to hold on to the vestiges of contentment.

The engine sound was rising. *Boy racers,* she thought to herself. She began to turn, intending to shake her head at the driver as he sped past, but the car veered wildly toward her. The front end of the car lurched upward as it climbed the deep step and hit her side on. The lights scorched her eyes and made green imprints on her vision.

It's true what they said about time slowing down when your life was being torn from you, though she didn't see her life flash before her eyes. She saw a young girl with red hair, smiling, skipping, and then fading as her future was wiped away. Iris. She looked like an Iris.

Imogen's feet left the ground and she arced through the air. The car lights were beneath her now. She soared through the purple night, closer to the stars than she had ever been.

She had time to think, *Look after her for me, Daddy,* before she blacked out. And then there was nothing. Only darkness, inside and out.

CHAPTER 23

10 days before the funeral

I put the phone back, letting my hand linger on the smooth black arch of the handset. The game had changed.

Phillip had been almost playful on the phone, asking how we'd done it. He wanted to know who'd let us out of the cinema room. There was genuine interest in his voice, but I wasn't about to tell him our secrets. Through terse laughter, he said he had ways of finding out.

"I know every little thing you do. A little bird whispers in my ear," he said.

I didn't rise to it. I knew he wanted me to think the worst of Naomi and Ruby, and to doubt whose side they were on. The truth was, I didn't need any encouragement to distrust those around me, but I was as sure as I could be that this was another one of his games. If either Naomi or Ruby was working with him, he wouldn't be so keen to alert me to the fact.

"Why don't you come on over?" I asked. "It'll be like old times.

You can sleep in the cellar and we'll go back to plan A. We've got a lot to chat about, you and me."

"Oh, don't worry. I'm not far away. I'm always watching you."

"So what are you waiting for?"

"The grand finale," he said, then hung up.

I slammed the back door. There would be no luring him into the cellar now. He was back in control and we were back to waiting to see what he was going to do next. There was no point hiding in the shadows and waiting for him now. We turned the lights back on and sat in front of the fire. Ruby was in the armchair and Naomi and I sat on the floor with our backs against the sofa. If he was watching, let him see that we weren't scared.

"If I hadn't answered the phone, he would've thought we were still in the cellar. I'm such an idiot." Naomi was being hard on herself.

"It was always a long shot," I said. "In some ways nothing has changed, except he has the freedom to do something unexpected. Some things stay the same. We have to gather enough evidence against him to get a restraining order. We can do that with or without him in the cellar. If either of you want to leave now, I won't stop you."

Naomi patted my arm like I was a deluded elderly relative. "You don't honestly think I'm going back home to let him lay into me again? Safety in numbers, duck. I'm going nowhere until we know he can't hurt us."

"What about you, Ruby?"

"Yes. Yes, I might. If someone has taken the dogs to a vet's, they'll have found they're chipped and be calling my home. I should probably get going while the weather's good."

I nodded. "Stay safe, though, yeah? I don't think he'll go after you—he's most angry with me. And if he does contact you, don't tell him where Alistair is."

"I don't *know* where Alistair is," she said. "Where is he, by the way?"

Naomi deflected the question by turning to me and saying, "Just me and you, then."

I watched the flames dance in the hearth and wondered what Phillip would do next. He'd already hurt us physically, and Alistair was safe from his reach for now. But Phillip didn't know that.

I'd already called Chris Miller, the DC whose wife had had an affair with Phillip; he'd agreed to see me on Monday morning. I hoped I could count on him to help me build a case for a restraining order.

I was sure Phillip's desire for custody of Alistair was at best a passing whim and at worst an attempt at revenge. In a fair fight, a court would rule in my favor, but Phillip didn't play fair. If I was to get the upper hand, I needed to stay one step ahead of him. His reputation was spotless, his service record exemplary. If I could put the slightest question in people's minds as to his suitability as a father, then he would have no power over me.

As I leaned back against the sofa and stretched my arms above my head, my ribs popped gently and my back cracked.

Thud.

We snapped our heads toward the window. The sound was loud and close by. The shutters were closed, so I couldn't immediately see what had caused the noise.

I leaped to my feet and crossed steadily to the window. I listened. Nothing. I pushed the slats open, peering one eye, then two. There were two cars on the driveway, Ruby's and Naomi's. At first I couldn't see what was wrong, what might have caused the sound. Naomi pulled the shutters open further.

"Shit, Ruby! Your car," she said.

On the hood of her car was a brick. Her windscreen was a concave of spiderwebs where a solid sheet of glass should have been. The streetlights were dim but the light over the front porch cast a spotlight onto the damage.

"Childish," I muttered. I thought Ruby was still in the room with us until I heard the front door open. "Ruby! Don't go out there."

I went after her, cautiously, knowing that Phillip wasn't far away. Naomi peered over hedges for signs of Phillip but saw nothing. I hadn't expected Phillip to carry out childish acts of vandalism. I was flustered and skittish. It unnerved me that he was still close by.

Ruby sniffed back tears. I put my arm loosely around her shoulders, still looking all about me. I could feel his eyes on us.

"Hey," I said. "It's just a car. We can get that fixed on Monday morning."

She stroked the roof of the car gently at first and then slammed the heel of her hand down on it.

"Why would he do this to me?" she cried. "I've only ever tried to help him."

Before I could answer her, Naomi said, "You seen this?"

Under the wiper blades there was a white piece of paper. She slid it from beneath the blade and I saw it was ripped from the back of an envelope. I'd been too intent on watching out for Phillip to notice it before. In a hand we all recognized—though it was bolder and messier than usual—it said, *Bitches get what's coming to them.*

There was no sign of Phillip, but his presence hung heavily in the air. I was glad of the note. At least now Ruby couldn't convince herself that this was the random act of a bored delinquent. This was Phillip's way of telling us it wasn't over yet.

The curtains at Mary's house twitched, dropped, and swayed to stillness.

"Go inside," I said to Naomi and Ruby. "I'll be back in a minute."

"No," said Ruby. "We should stick together."

"Fine, but wait here." I ran across the road and knocked on Mary's door.

"Mary? Do you have a minute?"

The door opened quickly.

"Shh! He's asleep!" She motioned up the stairs behind her.

I didn't know if she meant the shift-working boyfriend or one of her children.

"Did you see what happened?" I asked.

"It wasn't me who did it."

"I know. I wondered whether you'd seen anything."

"Saw a bloke hanging around on his phone about ten minutes ago."

"Did you see who it was?" I asked.

She looked away, uncertain. "It's dark," she said. "I couldn't say for sure."

I lowered my voice. "There's a note in his handwriting. You wouldn't be getting anyone into trouble by confirming what we already know."

She nodded just slightly.

"So it was him? Phillip?"

She nodded again.

"And if I went to the police, you'd be able to confirm that, yeah?"

Mary looked at the floor and ran her tongue over her lips.

She nodded. "Okay."

I waited for her to look up so that she could see the sincerity in my eyes. "Thank you, Mary. I appreciate it."

I started back down her driveway and then stopped. "Did you see where he went?"

"Sorry. No."

I jogged back over the road. Naomi and Ruby were waiting for me by the car.

"Did she see anything?" Ruby asked.

"Not the actual brick throwing, but yeah, she saw Phillip."

I looked back at the damage the brick had done. The red paint-work on the car hood was scratched where the brick had bounced onto it. The color underneath was darker. Around the windscreen the paint had bubbled with rust. I touched it and a chunk as big as a fifty-pence piece flaked in my fingers. The darker paint was obvious underneath.

"Have you had this car resprayed, Ruby?"

"What? Yes. And I suppose I can do it again, but it's such a pain and—well, it's hardly the point, is it?"

"What color was it before?" I asked.

My heart was beating faster now than when we'd heard the brick hitting glass.

"It was blue. Why does that matter? I'll just have the red touched up. No need to do the whole thing."

Ruby used to drive a blue car. If she realized the significance of what she'd just said, she didn't show it. My mind worked slowly, but I pictured Ruby behind the wheel of the car that had hit me, imagined Phillip finding out and Ruby promising to do anything for him if he didn't report her. Surely not even Phillip would cover for the person who'd killed our unborn child.

CHAPTER 24

10 days before the funeral

Naomi took photos of the car, the brick, and the letter. I noted the date and time in the back of my planner along with Mary's name under the column marked "witness." I watched Ruby move around muttering about her dogs and her car, but all I could do was question if she could really have been so jealous of me that she would have driven straight at me.

I rubbed my eyes. If I were to outthink Phillip, I couldn't get distracted. Still, I looked at Ruby with a wariness that wasn't there before. I poured us all a glass of wine and we took it into the yard under a starless sky. I locked the back gate and deadlocked the front door. Naomi sat next to Ruby on the bench while she smoked her cigarette. Naomi talked of her childhood and how she'd always dreamed of finding her mum. She wanted to meet her just one time. To see if they looked alike, to ask who her dad was, to see whether they had the same habits.

She knew it shouldn't matter, but she wanted to see someone

who was related to her. Just once. Her grandparents refused to talk about her mum and she never even asked whether they had any theories about her dad. It was as though her parents had never existed. If she didn't know better, she'd think that Nan had found her under a gooseberry bush.

I nodded, though I was only half listening. Ruby sympathized. She was without family too. Her parents had died when she was young. They were elderly and she had been a surprise baby when her mother was fifty-two. By the time she was twenty, both of her parents had passed away, followed the next year by her only sister, who'd taken off to Thailand for a diving holiday and was never seen again. Her death was ruled accidental and the diving company shown to have no liability.

"It's funny, isn't it?" I said.

Naomi snorted.

"Which bit?" she asked. "The bit where he slapped cuffs on Ruby, kicked you in the face, or the bit where he tried to strangle me to death?" She took the pack of cigarettes out of her pocket and lit another one.

"I mean the three of us being here. Look at us! We're completely different. Phillip would never have thought in a million years that we would be here together. I'm still legally married to him and we share a child, so I can't get him out of my life. You, Naomi, are his girlfriend—"

"Not anymore, I'm not," she said.

"Still . . . the one that confuses me is you, Ruby. Why do you still hang around Phillip? You're free to go and never see him again, and yet here you are. What does he have over you?"

I watched her falter and squirm. I wondered whether I could ever forgive her if she confessed to driving the car that night.

"Nothing," she said with a nervous laugh. "He has nothing over me. We have history, we've seen each other through dark times, that's all. We've been there for each other when no one else was." She scratched her chin. "But going back to your point . . ."

No, I thought, *you're steering me away from it.*

". . . we are rather different, aren't we? The way we look, our ages, our personalities. He doesn't really have a type."

"And I thought I were the dumb one," Naomi said.

"You're not . . ." Ruby began.

"Obviously! I mean, me without a dad and my mum sodding off when I were one day old. I know Imogen's mum's still about, but her dad died when she were young, right? Ruby, you had no family when you met Phil either, did yuh? I'm going out on a limb here but what's the betting that you weren't the type to have a gang of mates you could call on either? He's got a type all right."

She took a deep drag on her cigarette.

"He saw us coming. Singled us out, didn't he? He goes for women who have nowhere to go and no one to turn to. He preys on vulnerable girls."

"I take offense at being called vulnerable," said Ruby.

"I take offense at being called a *girl*," I said.

We sat in silence, all of us searching for a reason why that wasn't true and coming up empty-handed and empty-hearted. Realizing what, perhaps, we had always known in our hearts: that Phillip's relationships with us had been driven by a love for himself and a desire for control.

"Do you really think he would be that calculating?" Ruby asked.

Naomi scoffed. "You don't?"

She was right, of course. I'd not had many friends growing up. I was inoffensive enough so that no one picked on me and insignificant enough so that no one invited me to parties. I was one of those girls who sat one row back in class, quietly listening and getting on with things. Taking on board everything that was going on around her but never quite being part of it. Rachel was the closest thing I had to a friend, and I didn't even know if she had dreams for her future or nightmares about her past.

"For what it's worth," said Ruby, "I don't think that means he didn't love us, in his own way. It says more about him not loving himself enough—"

"Chuffin' 'eck, Ruby! I've never met a man who loves himself more. You can stuff your psychobabble. There's no one he loves more than number one."

"I'd love to disagree with you," she said. "But perhaps you're right."

The silence was brittle. Our easy conversation from earlier was stunted.

"Sorry," Naomi said. "Sorry. Shouldn't've said that. In a way, it's nice that you still try and see the best in him. But I've had enough of that crap."

Naomi swiveled in her seat to face Ruby. "Can I ask you something? What was he like when *you* were married to him?"

Ruby looked surprised by the question. "I don't know. I suppose it wasn't so bad. I tried my best to protect him, but the smallest things—a perceived slight, me taking too long at the shops, or smiling at another man—was enough to send him into a tailspin. I got tired of mothering him, though. I don't know whether it was the age difference or because he'd never had to look after himself.

"He only physically hurt me once. He hated my work colleagues, and when I wouldn't give up my job he tried to get me sacked. We had a huge row about it. I still don't know whether he meant to hurt me, but we were in the kitchen. He went to slam the door in my face, but my fingers were in the doorjamb. Broke every one of them across the tips. I would have forgiven him straightaway if he'd apologized, but he tried to tell me it was my fault for goading him. The next day I moved into a hotel and then from there went to Africa."

"You did what?" Naomi seemed impressed.

"I was angrier back then. I went to work for UNICEF, and it was five years before I saw Pip again."

"Good on you, duck."

"I don't know." Ruby looked at her hands. "I felt quite guilty. Pip said he'd have counseling, take time off work. He told me he wanted to work things out. I wonder whether I should have given him a second chance. I loved my time in Africa. I'd finally found my calling, and I really thought that the time alone would do Pip good. I tried to persuade him to come out and join me, but he never was one for foreign countries. When he wrote to me, he sounded like a broken man. His letters showed he'd done a lot of thinking, a lot of growing up. I fell in love with him all over again. And of course, I'd changed by then too. I'd learned to forgive.

"We'd been together for thirteen years, and even though I hadn't seen him for almost half of that time, I still wore my wedding ring and used my married name. I came back to give our marriage another chance, but by that time he had already met you, Imogen— which was something he'd neglected to mention in his letters."

"Sorry," I muttered. "You must have been furious." I was thinking about the accident again.

"Goodness, no. When you've seen what I've seen in Africa and the atrocities that people manage to forgive each other for, I could never be angry over him finding love when I hadn't been there to give it to him. We shouldn't be apologizing to each other, darling. We were all spun a line by Pip and we took the bait. He caused this hurt. Now that I think about it, I was wrong about Pip's type, though. I know what he saw in us. We're all bloody fabulous."

"I'll drink to that," said Naomi.

"Me too."

We raised our glasses into the air and drank deeply. My head was spinning and it wasn't the wine.

"What now?" Naomi asked.

As if waiting for its cue, the doorbell shrilled from within the house. Curious rather than fearful, we went inside. A man who threw bricks through windows was unlikely to have the courtesy to ring the bell.

Naomi said she'd get it, but we both went with her to the door. She had her hand on the lock and waited for me to nod before she opened it a crack. A tall young man stood on the other side of the doorstep. He had a blue baseball cap perched on top of a mass of curls and he was sliding two pizza boxes out of a red bag.

"What's this?" asked Naomi.

The delivery boy looked at the boxes, then back at Naomi like it should be obvious. She opened the door a little wider.

"Pizza?" he said, though he wasn't sounding sure of himself.

"We've not ordered anything."

He looked at the paper attached to the uppermost box and then leaned backward to look at the number by the side of the door, and then slowly back to the paper.

"Number twenty-eight?" he said.

"Yes," I answered.

"Rochester?"

227

"Yes," all three of us said in unison.

He looked back to the paper like he was trying to work out a particularly tricky math equation.

"This is your pizza," he said finally.

"We've not ordered any bloody pizza."

"Number twenty-eight?" he asked again.

"Yes," repeated Naomi, "twenty-eight, and yes, it's Rochester, but we've not ordered any pizza."

"It says here you have," he said. He was young and his voice was quavering. I started to feel sorry for him. It wasn't in his job description to deliver threats to suspicious women. Because that's surely what it was: a threat. Phillip letting us know that he could get to us whenever he wanted.

"Silly me," said Ruby, pushing to the front with purse in hand. "I forgot I'd ordered it. How much do we owe you?"

Naomi shook her head and disappeared into the kitchen. I watched the street. It had to be Phillip. He was watching us. Laughing at us. He was there. I could feel him. We eyed the pizzas warily as if Phillip himself had sneaked into the house.

"I don't get it. Why send pizza?" I asked.

"Who cares?" Naomi said. "He's trying to mess with our heads, but the joke's on him because we got to eat, right? And I'm not eating any more of that bloody hummus. You've got nothing else in the house 'cept tins of palm hearts and jars of chutney."

I took a slice of cheese and tomato and went to the window. I'd switched all the lights off in the front room so I could open the shutters and look out onto the night. The street was empty. The sun had long since deserted its post, leaving a night watchman moon as lookout. *What's going through your mind, Phillip?*

A blue van pulled up outside the house, blocking the end of the drive. A man in overalls began to walk toward the house.

"Ruby? Nay? We've got company."

I put the crust of my pizza on the window ledge and headed into the hallway. This time I was the one who answered the door, with Ruby and Naomi standing behind. The smiling man pointed at his jacket at the prominently placed gas company logo. He pulled a lanyard out of his overalls to show me his picture and his name in bold capitals.

"Gas board, love. Reports of a gas leak. That right?"

"No, not from us. Perhaps one of the neighbors?" I went to close the door.

"Hold on." He looked at the black device in his hand and checked something before asking, "You didn't call the emergency number?"

"No, sorry."

"Rochester?"

"Yes, that's me, but I'm afraid I didn't make the call. There's been some . . . nuisance calls. An ex."

I almost smiled. Phillip was playing into my hands. He was hoping to scare us, but instead he was proving himself worthy of a restraining order.

"And you've not noticed the small of gas?"

"No, sorry."

He laughed. "God, don't apologize, love. And your ex is doing this, you think? What a prat!"

"I know. He's quite special. I don't suppose you could note it down on your device thing, in case this escalates? It probably won't, but you know . . ."

"I can try, but I don't know whether anyone'll look at it. It'll be on record if you need to refer to it. You definitely don't have a problem that you know of, then? Just to be sure, before I get home for me tea?"

"I'm certain that we haven't noticed a gas leak."

I watched him walk back to his van. I was sure Phillip's eyes were on me, watching every move, listening to every word. I didn't want him to think I was scared, so I stood there for five defiant minutes, breathing in the night air, glaring at shadows, and pretending I wasn't scared by his petty games. If he wanted to remind us that he was out there somewhere, it was working a treat. I couldn't settle. Waiting.

Waiting.

Giving him enough rope to hang himself.

I closed the door and Naomi said, "What the hell's he playing at?"

I made a note of the time and date and wrote the name I'd seen on the gas man's identity card. With Mary to back up my story about the brick and the note about nuisance calls to the gas board, I was getting closer to a restraining order.

"Can I borrow your phone?" I asked Naomi. "Phillip's still got mine."

I scrolled through Naomi's contacts until I found Phillip's number and then I sent him a text.

Is that all you've got?

CHAPTER 25

10 days before the funeral

was happy for Phillip to keep sending a stream of unsuspecting people to my door. It all added to the case I was putting together to prove that he was harassing me. It would be nice to think that I would be able to get Phillip arrested, but until I spoke to DC Chris Miller, I wasn't sure I had enough on him.

Nine o'clock. Ten o'clock. Ruby was sniffling and I didn't even try to comfort her. It was mainly the dogs, she said, but also, how could Phillip be doing this to us, to *her*? And then she would cry again, pulling tissue after tissue out of the box like a magician pulling a string of flags from his sleeve.

There was something at the back of my mind, a faint buzz like a bee was trapped in my brain. I shook my head and it quieted for a while.

A car beeped outside. Close by. Three sharp hits of the horn. Ruby stopped crying, Naomi stood up, and I grinned. The more pranks he pulled now, the better my case was going to look. Another longer beep sounded and Naomi went to the window.

"Don't know what this one is," said Naomi. "I hope it's Chinese. I could murder a spring roll."

The man stayed in the car and we stayed at the window. After five minutes, he pulled himself out of the car, hitched up his trousers, and waddled up the drive. Ruby and Naomi went to meet him while I stayed at the window watching. I scanned the shadows, looking for Phillip.

"Taxi," the man said.

"Sorry, you've got the wrong house. We've not ordered one." Ruby was polite and warm. The taxi driver said nothing, simply sighed and wobbled away without discussion. I wondered how many hours of people's lives would be wasted on Phillip and his schemes, but it was another incident to add to my growing list.

I couldn't work out what Phillip was playing at. We were unsettled and confused, but his childish antics were more annoying than terrifying. Ruby was on her feet, bustling about, plumping up cushions, and straightening rugs.

"I wouldn't take too much notice of it. It's just the equivalent of him ringing the doorbell and running away. He's a big kid. Ignore it."

"That's it," I said. "I've had enough. I'm not answering any more calls or doors. I'm going to bed. I'm locking the doors and shutters and am going to try my best to get some sleep."

We made our drinks for the night. Brandy for Naomi, water for me, and chamomile tea for Ruby. Naomi had her last smoke of the day and left her lighter and cigarettes by the back door for a quick nicotine fix in the morning.

We checked that the doors were locked. Windows too. He wasn't getting in tonight. Bolts, chains, chairs under doorknobs. Tonight we would sleep. Tomorrow we would compile more evidence against him. I pocketed my mobile and switched off the lights.

I followed the others up the stairs and paused at the top to look at the messages on my phone. I looked down the stairs and then back at my phone.

"Naomi," I said urgently. "Naomi!"

"What?"

She came over to where I stood. I held out my mobile.

"What?" she said. "What am I looking at?"

"The phone."

My hand began to shake. My chest was being crushed. I sucked air into my lungs, feeling like they were shutting down.

I watched as it dawned on her. Her eyes met mine.

"But you didn't have your phone," she said quietly.

I shook my head. My breath was coming quickly. Phillip had taken it when we were in the cellar.

Ruby craned her neck around the bedroom doorway.

"What is it?" she asked.

"Imogen's phone's turned up," said Naomi.

Ruby ducked into the bedroom and called out, "I didn't know you lost it."

"I probably didn't. I thought I had, but perhaps it was here all along," I said weakly.

She called back, "Mind if I use your bathroom, darling?"

"Help yourself."

"Yeah, I bet that's it," Naomi said loudly. "God, you had me scared for a minute then."

She put her hand over her heart and rolled her eyes—playing too hard at being fine—and handed my phone back to me.

We were both thinking the same thing. My phone hadn't been here earlier. We were certain that Phillip had taken it, so how had it found its way back into the house?

Naomi took my arm and pulled me into the spare room, where we could keep an eye on my bedroom door.

"Are you thinking what I'm thinking?" she asked. "There's another possibility, isn't there? Who was here all day while we were tracking down Alistair and going to the airport? Ruby's the only one who could have let him in. She was the only one he didn't hit when he locked us up. She's the one who's always sticking up for him. And the dogs? He's probably taken them somewhere for her. If he'd just let them free, someone would have spotted them by now. I don't buy the act."

"You think he's been back to the house while we were out?"

"Makes sense," Naomi said.

"But her car . . ." I began. For everything I'd suspected Ruby of over the years, I still hoped that I was wrong. If she'd lied about Phillip, what else had she lied about?

"Like you said, it's just a car. Easier to fix than a broken nose."

"All this time, she's been listening to us and reporting back to him. She's more devious than I gave her credit for."

I thought back to the car accident and the blue car that conveniently disappeared.

I lowered my voice. "Don't say anything yet. We could use this to our advantage."

CHAPTER 26

9 days before the funeral

I didn't want to believe that Ruby was helping Phillip, but now that the idea was in my head, it was difficult to shake. I had images of her letting him into the house in the middle of the night. Of waking to find him standing over me with a knife. The knife that was missing from the kitchen. Did she have it? Should I be more worried about *her* attacking me in the night?

We lay in semidarkness. Ruby was by my side, in bed with me. Naomi was on a doubled-up duvet on the floor. I let them think I was fearful and wouldn't be able to sleep on my own knowing that Phillip was out there somewhere, when the reality was I wouldn't let them out of my sight. I wouldn't have either of them slipping away and letting Phillip in. I doubted Naomi would be helping him, but mere hours ago I would have said the same about Ruby.

Naomi and Ruby fell asleep a little after one a.m. Hearing the breathing of other people in the room, the rustle of bedsheets, was both a comfort and a distraction. Naomi's breathing was quick and heavy, suggestive of active dreams and a troubled mind. Ruby slept on her back and snored. I felt my eyes closing of their own accord and blinked them open suddenly. I pinched the inside of my thigh. I wouldn't let myself fall asleep tonight.

I'd thought we were becoming friends, and now, thanks to Phillip, I was keeping them at arm's length again. It was as I'd always suspected: I could only rely on myself. I looked at Ruby, wondering whether she was plotting to bring my family down. If Naomi and I were right, then the sooner I sent Ruby back home to Brighton, where she could no longer spy on me, the better. But if Naomi was bluffing and *she* was the one betraying me . . . No, there was no way she would help him after he had tried to kill her. If it was anyone, it was Ruby. Kind, compassionate Ruby. I wanted to cry with frustration at my own stupidity. This was what happened when you trusted someone. Phillip was still outsmarting me, still making us all dance to his tune.

I wondered what their plan was and why Ruby would help him at my expense. I'd never been unkind to her, but wasn't welcoming either. I would never have expected her capable of subterfuge, which showed what a terrible judge of character I was. My mind kept going back to the accident. Had she been responsible? If she was, then surely Phillip would know. Was this what he held over her? Was this why she was doing his bidding?

As I looked at her slack face in the darkness, I tried to picture her playing happy families with Phillip and my son. Had she planned to take my son as her own? I'd always known she'd wanted a child, but she bloody well couldn't have mine.

I hadn't spoken about Spain in front of her, so I was as sure as I could be that she hadn't told Phillip where Alistair was. Even if she had, he couldn't have got a replacement passport yet. And I'd personally watched Bill burn Phillip's old one in the fire pit in his backyard.

It occurred to me that this could be the reason she was still here. Listening, waiting to find out where we'd hidden Alistair. And the brick through the window was just an excuse so that she had to stay. Those two were cleverer than I'd given them credit for.

I'd checked online; even if Phillip paid to get a passport processed in twenty-four hours, the earliest appointment he could get would be Tuesday. I had until then to build a case against him. If Ruby was feeding information to Phillip, then I'd make sure she had the wrong information. I'd send him to the ends of the country, perhaps even abroad. I could start dropping hints about Alistair enjoying French food, and how nice the weather was in the South of France. I needed Phillip to leave us alone. I had a meeting with Chris Miller on Monday morning where I would see what kind of a case we had against Phillip. I would have to tell him the whole story, which would mean admitting to locking him up in the first place.

A shaft of orange light fell across the bed, growing occasionally brighter as infrequent cars sped down the road. Since the accident, I had feared cars at night. I rarely drove in the dark and never walked anywhere after dark. I slid out of bed and went to look out the window. The street below was still.

A door opened somewhere and I heard the familiar rattle of milk bottles being put on the step ready for dawn and the milkman. I wondered who would be awake so late. None of the neighbors looked like they outstayed the ten o'clock news. Sensible families, not hiding out from psychotic husbands, slumbered sweetly under the covers. And somewhere, my sweet boy Alistair was sleeping under a warmer sky than this. The pain of being separated from him hit me like a blow to the guts. When I thought of him, I ached. He was so precious to me—so perfect—I could scarcely believe he was mine. It was miraculous that someone like me, damaged and weak, could have created something so stunningly flawless. Being separated from him was worth it if it restored our future. I had to be strong for a few days more if I was to make it safe for him to come back to me.

A sound, like the click of a light switch, had me snapping my head round. The lights in the bedroom were still off, and neither Naomi nor Ruby had moved. I looked out the window again, half expecting to see a shadowy figure running from the house, but everything was silent and all houses surrounding me were in darkness. I cocked my head, but there was no sound. I perched on the end of the bed and alternately scrunched and relaxed my toes, waiting for something else, a sound to confirm my fears or to tell me that it was something perfectly and easily explainable.

I thought I heard a door shut, and I concentrated to feel whether anything seemed out of place. How much was real and how much was my mind playing tricks on me? My heart was pounding too loudly for me to pick out the sounds that didn't belong there. I tiptoed to the door. Everything was the same, just as I hoped it would be. There was only emptiness, stillness, and paranoia.

I told myself to get a grip. He couldn't get in the house unless one of us opened the door for him, and no one had left the room. I closed the door a little too firmly and a gust of air ruffled my hair. Something was on the breeze, an unfamiliar scent; it was dry and scratchy at my throat. I opened the door once more and inhaled deeply but couldn't grab hold of the scent that had slipped past me a moment before.

"What is it?" mumbled Naomi from behind me in the darkness.

"I don't know. Maybe nothing. Can you smell anything?"

She sniffed the air audibly. I heard the rustle of sheets as she sat up.

"What am I smelling for?"

"I don't know. I thought I . . ." I couldn't smell it now and was unsure whether I was imagining things. I was tired, had had little sleep all week. My weak mind was playing tricks on me. But still . . .

Naomi came to my side, dressed in a long T-shirt, and looked out onto the landing. The glare had us squinting and blinking.

"Can't smell anything, can't see anything," she said.

Ruby muttered something unintelligible in her sleep.

"No," I said. "You're right. It's probably nothing."

Naomi yawned.

"Still, I'm just going to check downstairs," I said. "Otherwise I'll never settle."

"I'll come with you," she said.

We looked over the banister, but there was no sign of light or life. I hoped my imagination was getting the better of me. We started our way downstairs and I asked, "Can you smell gas?"

Naomi shook her head.

"You're only thinking that because of the fella from the gas board earlier."

"Maybe," I said.

The front door was still locked and bolted, and there were no signs of an open window. There was something in the air, a scent that wasn't quite there but just on the outskirts of my senses.

"I'm sure I can smell something," I said.

"It's probably outside," Naomi said.

The smell hit me again and I put the back of my hand over my mouth.

"Shit!" I said. "It *is* gas!" I dashed into the kitchen. "Don't switch on the lights," I shouted.

The gas range was hissing to itself from the two front burners. I switched it off and the whispering—which I hadn't even realized was in my ears—stopped. I pulled at the back door to open it, groped in the dark for where the keys should be. My fingers groped at the handle and found the hole where the key should be. But the key wasn't there.

"The keys! Where are they?"

I held my breath against the smell of gas. I fumbled with the kitchen window and flung it open, taking in big gulps of fresh air. The security light blinked on overhead and brought the length of the backyard to life.

I opened the drawer where I kept the spare keys, but they were gone.

"Naomi, he's in the house. I know he is."

"Don't be daft," she said, though her voice lacked the conviction of her words. "One of us banged into it or something. Either that or Ruby—"

"She's not moved all night and the keys are missing!"

Neither of us had an answer.

Something behind Naomi caught my eye. Indistinct and unfamiliar.

"What?" she said.

I raised my hand to silence her and gently pushed her to one side.

From the light spilling from the hallway, I could just make out the word *BITCH* in twelve-inch letters on the kitchen wall.

CHAPTER 27

9 days before the funeral

I groped my way around the kitchen until I found the handle of the knife drawer. I picked the largest knife in there—not the largest one I had, since either Phillip or Ruby had that one—and held it out in front of me.

"What are you doing?" whispered Naomi.

"He's in here, Naomi. He's in the house."

"But the doors are locked," she said.

I looked at the wall, covered in script from knee level to fingertip high.

"He's been here all along."

The brick through the window had been the perfect distraction. The endless stream of people coming to the door giving him the opportunity to get settled, hide somewhere, and wait. And he had been listening to every word.

I pictured him lingering round corners, laughing at us. Hearing our hopes and fears. Using them to get at us. Phillip Rochester was still pulling our strings and controlling the game.

"We can get out the window," whispered Naomi.

I shook my head. I wasn't running from him again. I tiptoed into the hallway and checked that the cellar was still locked. It was.

"Imogen! What're you doing?" hissed Naomi.

"He's here somewhere."

"That's why we need to get out of the house," she said urgently.

"No."

I could still smell the tangy scent of gas in the air, but I could breathe freely now. My jaw ached and I realized I was clenching my teeth together. I was as alert as I was angry. *Come out, come out, wherever you are.*

Naomi pulled at the back of my top and I glanced over my shoulder at her.

"I don't want to do this," she said.

Neither did I.

Phillip had been in my house all evening. Hearing every word, watching every movement. His presence was everywhere—in corners, behind doors—and I didn't know how I'd missed it.

Always one step ahead.

I put my finger on the kitchen light switch, nervous about switching it on, too many movies making me think the whole house would explode because of the gas. But I needed to see what lurked in the corners.

The light grew above me and showed the kitchen as it had always been. Cluttered with paintings and notes from school and shopping bags that needed recycling and wilting pots of herbs on the windowsill. But the wall. The wall was covered.

Thick black letters gone over again and again and again. The boldest words were at eye level, the rest written thinly at full stretch. In red, the word "DIE" was the bull's-eye that everything else radiated from. I reeled in shock. I could understand that he wanted to hurt me, but why would he want me to die? There was still a piece of the puzzle missing. His behavior and violence had escalated to a point that didn't correspond with what I'd done. This was Phillip, a law-bending, controlling, narcissistic man, but not a killer.

Footsteps overhead. A door opened. Closed. A steady, even-paced stride trying not to make a noise but hitting every creaking floorboard. Naomi and I looked at each other; then she looked wildly around the room for a weapon. She settled on a bread knife and nodded to me.

The steps were quieter on the stairs. A dry hand on the banister brushing skin against chipped paint. They took three steps and then stopped. We listened and they listened. The steps began again. Sounds were amplified, came to me on the back of the hiss of air in my ears. They were getting closer. Bare feet landed on the floor tiles at the base of the stairs and *slap-slapped* cautiously, slowly toward us.

Naomi was at my shoulder. I could feel her shaking behind me, the air around her reverberating. I held the knife outstretched and took long sideways steps so that I was out of view of the hallway. Naomi stepped with me.

I held the knife tightly, imagining Phillip's face. Would I stab him? Would I hold a knife against his jugular and get him back into the cellar? Would he attack me first? And if I killed him in self-defense, would anyone blame me?

I waited. I was neither hot nor cold, could feel no pain, no sensations other than a pulsing of adrenaline through my body giving me energy to attack.

A hand snaked around the doorframe—I adjusted my grip on the knife—followed cautiously by a head of gray-brown curls.

"Shit, Ruby! You scared us!" hissed Naomi.

Ruby reared back and recovered herself, speaking in the same hushed voice as Naomi had.

"What are you doing? I woke up and you were gone."

I sank into myself. The tension that had been holding me up suddenly drained, and I lowered the knife.

Ruby stepped warily away from me, her eyes on the knife.

"What's going on?" she asked.

"Do you expect me to believe that you don't know?" I turned from her in disgust.

Her face was worried, but I didn't know it well enough to know whether it was genuine. She couldn't take her eyes off the blade in my hand, and I placed it on the table to let her know it wasn't intended for her.

"Can I smell gas?" she asked.

"Gas burners were on," said Naomi. "Who did it? Were it you or him?"

"What do you—"

"It can't have been her," I said. "It had only just been switched on and she hasn't left the bedroom all night."

The black letters caught Ruby's eye and she stepped closer to look at the wall.

"What's this?" Her finger reached out to touch the writing as if to check whether it was real. She traced the word "DIE" with her index finger. "Why would Pip . . . ?"

I kept my voice low as I spoke, not knowing if Phillip could hear us. "We know he's here and we know you've been helping him. Tell us what you know."

"But it doesn't make any sense," she said, without taking her eyes off the wall. "He said he only wanted to . . ." Her voice trailed off.

"What, Ruby? What?" I whispered. "Ruby, have you seen Phillip since we got out of the cellar?"

She shook her head vigorously but didn't meet my eye.

"No, but . . ."

"But?"

"There was a phone pushed through the letter box. It rang and Pip's name flashed up. I gave him a right earful, told him to turn himself in to the police if he knew what was good for him. He was sorry, so sorry. He was crying on the phone and asking me to help him. He said he'd never ask for anything from me again. He said you'd been trying to keep him from his son. He said there were other things too, the amount of stress he was under—there was something going on at work and he said he snapped. He couldn't take it anymore.

"I was to persuade you not to press charges. He knew he'd done wrong and said he had nothing to live for anymore. I was worried he might hurt himself if he thought I'd turned against him too.

"He asked me to unlock the back door, and when he created a diversion outside, get you both out front so he could creep in and work out for himself where you'd sent Alistair."

"The car," I said.

"Yes, but I didn't know that's what he was going to do. That's when I realized Pip was angry with me too. I left your phone where you could find it. I didn't want him contacting me again."

It was hard to know if she was telling the truth, but she seemed genuine. But then, hadn't I thought that earlier too?

"Where is he now, Ruby?"

"I honestly don't know. I had a peek around earlier and couldn't find him. I assumed he'd already left. But this—" She gestured to the wall.

I picked up the knife again and, without a word, moved quietly along the hallway. The door to the cellar was still locked. The living room was empty, spaces behind sofas, the door, under tables—there was no sign that Phillip had been in here. There was no other graffiti, no disorder, no menace. There was nowhere he could hide.

I thought of him upstairs, close to where we were sleeping, or trying to, and I shuddered. I pointed my finger up the stairs; Ruby and Naomi nodded. I went first. Eight heartbeats to every step.

I put the knife in my other hand and wiped my palm on my shorts. Nerves were making me perspire. I craned my neck to peer up onto the landing. There were five doors, two of them closed, the bathroom door open with the light still on. I could see that it was empty. The other open doors were Alistair's room and my bedroom.

The first door was Mother's rosebud room. I looked at Naomi and hesitated. Perhaps she was right. Would it really be so wrong to run from the house now? To leave Phillip behind and never come back?

Before I could explore this thought, there was a sound from downstairs. I moved away from the bedroom door toward the noise. It sounded like running water. A splatter. A steady stream.

I frowned and looked down the stairs into the hallway below. Liquid was dashing the tiled floor. I struggled to make sense of it. I put my hand on the banister and eased myself down two steps—toe first, then softly placed heel. There was water in the hallway, but I had no idea where it was coming from. It reflected the overhead lights and shone golden, turning gilt everything it touched, like Midas.

There was a sweet familiar smell that I couldn't place. It reminded me of cars, of traffic jams, of setting out on holiday at predawn o'clock. I tried to swallow but the scent lay cloying on my tongue. Thick. I couldn't smell the gas anymore, but this felt like an add-on, an escalation of the same. My heart tremored and I clenched until my nails dug into the palms of my hands. My mouth was dry and my throat started to prickle. I wanted to cough but didn't want to make a sound. I still couldn't be sure where Phillip was or if he was acting alone. I swallowed deeply.

I should have known that Phillip would have more up his sleeve than pizza deliveries, bricks through car windows, and childish games of hide-and-seek. It was stupid of me to think that I had the upper hand just because I'd managed to get Alistair safely away from him. Phillip would make me pay. He always had.

The slick by the front door was spreading, slowly and thickly, finding channels in the tiles and diving down them. I took another step. Feet diagonally across steps, firm-footed yet still cautious.

"What is it?" asked Ruby.

I started. I'd almost forgotten Naomi and Ruby were there. It was difficult to believe that this was anything but a personal attack, Phillip coming for me, and me alone.

"Shhhh!" My finger went to my lips like I was berating a child. *Phillip*, I mouthed.

I took two more steps. I was halfway down the stairs now, exposed, too far from safety, too close to Phillip. The front door was still locked and closed, but there was a dark tube sticking through the letter box. Clear liquid was flowing into a rippling puddle that jumped, then smoothed out with every glug. He wasn't in the house after all. He was outside, watching and listening, laughing as we searched for him.

Naomi joined me on the stairs, her hand brushing against the cold wall.

"What are you doing?" I hissed.

Naomi gestured to the door and raised her eyebrows. She spoke quietly so that only I could hear. "What does it look like I'm doing? I'm going to open the door and ask him what the fuck he's playing at."

"Wait!"

I grabbed her arm. I had a sense of being in immediate danger. The smell was making my breath catch in my throat and I swallowed hard. Naomi shook me off and started banging down the stairs.

"Oi!" she called.

The letter box shut suddenly. Naomi turned back to me with a look that said *See?* as if all that was needed was to threaten to confront him and he would go away.

"Wait, Naomi. Wait! It's petrol!"

The letter box was opening again. A teardrop of flame hovered in the air long enough for me to think I could catch it, could save us all. I ran toward it, taking the steps two at a time, shoving Naomi to the wall. She looked at me openmouthed as gravity took hold of the match and pulled it to the ground.

CHAPTER 28

9 days before the funeral

The flame spread with a deep *hush* and covered the hallway floor. I jumped back with one hand on the wall and one on the wooden railing. My immediate response was to retrace our steps. Naomi stumbled and crawled up the stairs on the tips of her fingers and toes. Already I could feel the heat from the flames, though they were still only inches high. They tickled the baseboard and I could see the paint beginning to blister. I thought, *This is how I'm going to die.*

Statistics scrolled through my mind about how more deaths come from smoke inhalation than from the flames themselves. I couldn't fight smoke any more than I could fight Phillip. Neither could be contained. It was an uncontrollable haze that seeped into your pores, your lungs, and choked you from the inside out.

It would be reported as a tragedy, of course, and Phillip would be interviewed by the local rag as the grieving partner. And he would get everything he wanted—rid of us all, custody of his son, sympathy and revenge.

I started to sway on my feet. Panic causing me to stop breathing. The flames were roaring in my ears, stopping me from hearing my thoughts. Not again and not now.

There was a split second where I could have given in to the inevitability of the panic attack. A streak of resignation ran through me like a seam of gold. But then I pictured Alistair's face. I couldn't let him be brought up in Phillip's care—or lack of. The thought of my child cowering beneath his covers, crying, hurt, was enough to snap me to my senses. I ran back up the last few stairs and into the bathroom.

"Ruby," I called. "Wet the towels in the bathroom. Go!"

I turned on the taps and threw the towels in the bath.

Ruby didn't move. She had her hand over her mouth and was leaning against the wall. The flames reflected in her eyes. She had shut down, gone somewhere else—somewhere of no use to me.

Naomi pushed past with an "I'll do it!" and ran to the bedroom.

With sodden towels, I ran to the bottom of the stairs, hesitated, then dropped the largest towel over the stretch of tile by my feet. It folded over at one corner and didn't get the coverage I had hoped for. I threw the other one away from me so it landed by the door. They hissed. I stepped onto them and stamped over the wet material. Smoke was rising from the damp towels and I could feel the heat on the bottom of my feet, as if stepping on hot springs. I coughed and held my forearm over my mouth.

Naomi passed me and threw more towels on the floor. The flames were stroking the doorframe, encompassing it as if burning all around it yet not touching the actual wood. It moved quicker than I would have thought possible. The cheap fibers were melting and blackening instead of taking to blaze. I stepped over the first towel and picked it up to beat the doorframe. Naomi was running back up the stairs for more items to soak.

Ruby had stumbled up behind me. She was making strange sounds in the back of her throat, as if her mouth were too tightly clamped to let words out.

"Ruby, call nine-nine-nine."

The flames squatted and lost some of their potency, if only we could keep on top of them. I began to cough, a rough retch from the base of my stomach clearing nothing and only having me pull the tainted air deeper into my lungs, which started the hacking all over again. The air was thick with smoke. My eyes were watering and it was hard to see where I should be directing my efforts.

"Ruby!" I spluttered. "The phone!"

She seemed to snap to. Hopping over the towels, she pulled her dress up as if paddling in the sea.

"And then come back with wet tea towels," I shouted. "If this . . . gets out of hand—the window. Get out that way."

Naomi thundered down the stairs with a dripping blanket in her hands.

"What? Jump right into his arms? No, thanks."

I took my yellow coat off the peg by the door and started smacking at the flames on the doorframe. Even though they were dying down, the air was thick. I pulled the neckline of my top over my mouth and blinked against the stinging. I took shallow breaths, fighting against inhaling the smoke again.

"Ruby?" I shouted. "Have you called them?"

There was no answer.

The fire was spluttering, dying. The towels smoldered. Naomi pulled them into a pile showing blackened tiles beneath and bubbled paint on the back of the front door.

"D'ya think we've got it all?"

"Yeah. Think so."

"Lucky you got tiles. I'd've been screwed." Naomi slumped against the wall and wiped her hair back off her face and laughed bitterly.

I hurried into the kitchen, where it was cooler. The back door was open and the keys were in the lock. Old keys with a bejeweled cat on the key ring—ones I'd not used in years. I faltered momentarily, began to speak and thought better of it. One thing at a time. I began running water into the washing-up bowl and, as it was filling, immersed the tea towels in the cool liquid. I kept my eye on the back door, glad of the breeze and the fresh air but feeling betrayed and fearful. Ruby had the spare key and had used it to save herself. How many times would I be betrayed before I realized that I couldn't trust anyone?

Leaving the water running, I ran back into the hallway and dropped the tea towels in the entrance to the living room. I motioned to Naomi to follow me and we went into the kitchen.

"Ruby's gone," I said.

"What?"

"The door's open."

"She had the keys?" Naomi put her head in her hands; I thought she was going to cry, but when her face came back up again, it was twisted with rage.

"I knew it. Bloody knew it. Didn't I say? I knew she was helping him. They were in it all along—she knew he were going to set fire to the place. I tell you, she had me fooled." Naomi shook her head and swore under her breath.

I switched off the running tap and lifted the full bowl of water. In the doorway of the hall I splashed it over the floor.

"What you going to do now?" Naomi asked.

"Call the police. He won't stop until we're dead. The only hope we've got is that they can catch Phillip for setting the fire. I think we can prove it's attempted murder."

"Not gonna happen. He'll get off with it like he always does. Ruby'll give him an alibi, and he'll go free. We should go after him ourselves. He can't get away wi' what he's done to us. And neither should she. Double-crossing bitch."

I couldn't take my eyes off the door. I wanted to rush out into the open but was scared of what I might find.

As if reading my mind, Naomi said, "He's long gone. And he's taken her with him. They deserve each other."

She held out her hand and dragged me outside.

"Come on, this air's no good for you. More people die of smoke inhalation than fire. I bet you didn't—" The security light snapped on as we fell into the damp night air. "Christ!"

I spun around so quickly, I fell against the wall. At the edge of the light's reach was a pale-faced and haggard Phillip.

CHAPTER 29

9 days before the funeral

Phillip had a bitter look on his face and his mouth was curled into a sneer. His hands were down by his sides, clenched into knuckle-whitening fists. He lurched forward, taking small reticent steps.

Moths flitted around him, having a dogfight in and out of the halo of gold from the security light. A tentative cough behind him had him half turn, but he was pushed forward again. Ruby stepped into the light.

I reached behind me but couldn't remember where I'd left the knife. It had been in my hand, and then I'd noticed the fire, and nothing else mattered. I was defenseless.

Naomi said nothing. She was mesmerized by the sight of Phillip and Ruby. Neither of us could comprehend what this meant or why they were still here. I started to back away, wondering where my phone was, whether I could scream for help.

Ruby's right hand was raised in line with her eye, holding something I couldn't see. In her left was a red container with a black spout. The kind you get from the garage when your car has run out of petrol two miles down the road. I should have filled up my car when I'd had the chance, because Phillip having to refuel had worked against me. The breakdown that I'd hoped for had nearly resulted in my death.

You bastard.

The hair on one side of Phillip's head was wet, plastered to his face. His collar was stained dark and his top clung to him, showing the outline of his arm muscles. He reeked of petrol.

"Move," Ruby said to him, and splashed the liquid at his back. She skirted him as if he were a dangerous animal.

There was something off about the way she was talking to him. Ruby wasn't helping Phillip anymore.

"Ruby? What's going on?" I asked.

"You won't do it," Phillip said to Ruby, as if I hadn't spoken. His voice was tight and his entire body taut with malice. I realized then that the item in Ruby's right hand was the lighter Naomi had left on the window ledge.

"I trusted you," Ruby said to Phillip. Her voice was barely more than a whisper. Her thumb clicked the lighter and, though it failed to light, Phillip flinched.

Ruby's face had changed. Gone were the crinkling eyes and the soft lips. Her face seemed more angular in the shadows. Her eyes were glaring and dark. She stood with her feet apart, sturdy and strong, and kept flicking her head as if disagreeing with voices in her head.

"Ruby?" I asked again.

Naomi had stepped away from us all. She could make a dash for it now and get help. I gave her a small nod. *Do it.* But she shook her head, captivated by the scene playing out in front of us.

255

"I'm sorry," Ruby said, but I couldn't tell if she was talking to me or to Phillip.

Phillip looked at her with disgust and curled his lip at her.

"He—he made me think . . . I thought that you were plotting to take his son away from him. And the house. He told me that you wouldn't be happy until you'd destroyed him. It didn't sound fair. I swear I was only trying to do the right thing."

She didn't take her eyes off Phillip. Fairness was important to Ruby. Loyalty more so. Her loyalty had been thrown back in her face. Phillip had been wrong to drag her into his scheme and then leave her to die.

"He tried to kill us all," she said. "Me! Me who'd helped him. I never expected . . ." Her voice broke.

"Get in!" said Naomi, punching the air. "I'll get the cuffs."

She ran into the house and I heard her pull open the door to the cellar and switch the light on.

"Wait! I don't understand," I said. I'd been fooled too many times and I wouldn't let it happen again.

I stepped backward until the back of my ankles found the door-step. I slumped down onto it. My legs didn't have the strength to hold me up. I was shaking. I watched the scene in front of me as if it were happening to someone else. The energy drained out of me and I was light-headed. It was almost too much to process. Phillip had tried to kill us and now he was back, but this time we held the power.

Phillip glared at me as Ruby pushed him into the kitchen. The stench of the petrol caused me to gag as he passed me by. Ruby was muttering something in his ear, but I couldn't hear anything above my hammering heart.

I pulled myself back up to watch as Naomi reappeared and cuffed his hands together. Ruby stood by him with the lighter and a faint smile on her face. Satisfied, Naomi stepped back and picked up the knife from where I'd dropped it when I was running to get water.

"Go on," she said to Phillip. "Give me a reason to use this."

"I'm not going back down there," he said.

"Your choice. But I reckon it's better than the alternative." She tilted her head at Ruby. Phillip took a couple of steps toward the cellar.

"Ruby," said Phillip, imploring, "you know I never meant to hurt you. It all got out of hand. You're better than this. Better than *them*. Put the lighter away."

In response, Ruby gave the lighter a shake and lit it. Phillip winced and then tried to laugh it off, like he wasn't worried.

"You're not thinking straight," he said. He shook his head and went through the cellar door like he was doing it out of choice, not because he was being forced.

I slid down the wall until I was sitting on the step. I stared into the garden. The overgrown lawn, the discarded toys, everything so normal and yet nothing was. I sat so still that the security light clicked off. A rectangle of light fell from the back door out into the night, my hunched shadow at its base.

I could hear the faint murmuring of voices from the cellar. They were clipped and harsh. Ruby's soft spot for Phillip had hardened. It took a lot to lose Ruby's trust, and Phillip had broken it with a finality that could have been fatal.

I heard Ruby and Naomi come out of the cellar and bolt the door behind them. They joined me in the garden and the light clicked on again.

"I truly am so very sorry," Ruby said. "You'd think I'd have learned my lesson by now."

There were pale lines down her face where her tears had washed away the smoke residue.

Naomi pulled over two wooden garden chairs, and they sat down. Naomi put her hand out for Ruby to drop the lighter into the palm of her hand. She took her cigarettes from her pocket and lit up. Sucking deeply and blowing away the smoke through the side of her mouth.

"Where did you find the keys to open the door?" I asked. My throat was scratchy and my voice was weak.

I wasn't angry, just curious. From now on, I wanted to know everything.

"Phillip told me on the phone where you kept the spare keys," she said.

I noticed that she was calling him Phillip now. Gone was the endearing and familiar nickname Pip. On her lips it sounded like an angry parent using his full name in order to chastise, to show just how much trouble he was in.

"Go on," I said.

"He didn't think you trusted me. I had the spare set in case I needed them to unlock the door for him to sneak in while we were looking at the car. Not that I knew that's what he was going to do, of course. I hadn't got around to putting the keys back—you barely left me alone for a minute—so I still had them in my pocket when he set fire to the house."

"And what?" said Naomi. "You thought, 'I know, I'll go and threaten to set fire to the bastard'? Was that it?" Naomi sucked on her cigarette, the orange glow from the tip like a beacon in the dark. She was going to take some convincing. Ruby had let both of us down.

"I don't know. I was furious. I would have taken the knife if I'd seen it, but the lighter was just there. I didn't expect him still to be there, really. I thought he would have run. I didn't have a plan. I just

258

wanted to confront him. Picking up your lighter was a pointless thing to do at the time. I had some stupid idea I could use it as a weapon, but when I got outside I thought, 'You silly woman, how's that meant to scare him?' and I almost threw it away. And when I got around the side of the house, he was crouched down, watching, with the petrol can behind him. His face . . . You should have seen his face. He was smiling."

Her voice cracked and she began to cry. Naomi put her arm around her shoulders.

"I picked up the petrol can," she continued, swallowing back her sobs, "and looked at the lighter and it all came together. That was that, really."

"He can't have thought you would go through with it, though," Naomi said.

"Oh, but that's the thing," said Ruby. "I would've done."

I looked up to the sky. It was much like it had been on the night that I had the car accident, warmer perhaps but just as endless. I believed Ruby. Despite what she had done earlier, I didn't believe that even a loyalty like Ruby's would stand the test of attempted murder. I nearly asked her about the night of the accident, but I'd had all the betrayal I could stand for one night.

"We can't let him go again," I said.

The other two nodded.

"But we can't keep him locked up indefinitely."

Naomi shrugged like she'd heard worse ideas and said, "Then what the hell are we going to do with him?"

CHAPTER 30

5 years, 5 months, and 1 day before the funeral

Naomi got a buzz from arguing. It was something she excelled at. Half a dozen therapists had told her she was sick. Anger issues, they called it. Anger issues? She didn't have any issues with being angry. And if any of them were in the same situation as her, they'd be angry too. Sitting in a hospital. On her own. Knocked up. Who wouldn't be angry?

There was a feeling inside of her, when she raised her voice, like the bubbling of a stream. Her arms became an extension of her anger, lightning rods for the fury, which would burn her from the inside out if she didn't let it free. If she couldn't find someone to argue with—and sometimes the goody-goodies refused to—then she would re-create that feeling by pulling a sharp blade over the pale part of her arm. She had learned quickly that if she shouted and screamed they would fold themselves small and back away, but if she cut herself they would send her someplace new. She would rather be sent away before they got bored of her. If you jumped before you were pushed, you at least had a chance of a decent landing.

She'd been moved to a new home. If it didn't work out there, she'd pack her things and leave. She was old enough to look after herself now. She'd give it until Christmas. Maybe a bit longer, because who wants to be on the streets in winter?

Naomi had been thrown in children's homes and stuck with foster families. She'd discovered there were two types of foster families: ones where their kids were grown up, flown the nest, Mum and Dad had a heap of "goodliness" going to waste, and they truly thought they could help. As if sitting down and watching *Doctor Who* on a Sunday night with a "decent" family was enough to turn a wayward child into a straight-A student.

The other ones were in it for the money. Naomi liked to make sure this type earned it the hard way. Most of the time they didn't even need the cash. One family she stayed with lived on a farm in the Peak District, but there were no pigs or sheep, just a barn full of Range Rovers and Mercedes. They had two sons at private school and Daddy had his own business while Mummy stayed at home and polished her pearls or whatever the hell she did.

"This is your room. You have your own bathroom and a television."

Patricia said *baaaaathroom* like she was one of the missing sheep, but she was just playing posh. Naomi could hear it in her voice and was sure that she said "mi duck" and "ey up" like the rest of them.

Naomi could tell, from the moment she clapped eyes on her, that the lady of the manor didn't think much of Little Orphan Annie. Patricia's upturned nose cranked up another notch and her thin lips fought to meet over her buckteeth as her eyes rolled up and down the skin and bones in ripped jeans.

"I hardly think you need to come out of your room at all, Naomi."

And she rarely did, apart from the Easter holidays when she slid into bed with the precious youngest son.

Naomi tried not to think about Nana and Gramps. She missed them in the moments when she forgot to be angry. They had kept her and loved her after her flighty mother, Helen, had taken to wing without a backward glance. She had wanted to have Naomi aborted—not that Naomi had a name at that point, but she'd concealed the pregnancy for so long that it was becoming impossible to face. Nana thought Helen would change her mind when she held the squirming bundle, but, true to her word, Helen left the next morning on the back of a motorbike and never returned.

Gramps was so angry that he took all the photos of Helen and burned them. Nana was only allowed to mention her in whispers over the washing line. When Nana died, Naomi had felt a buzz of excitement beneath the heartache. It was like electrical wires overhead: you might not notice it if you weren't listening really hard. She hated herself for the twitching dimples in her cheeks, but she couldn't help but think that now, finally, she would meet her mum. Everyone came back for funerals, didn't they?

There were women of about the right age in the church—one even held her eye and gave her a small smile—but none of them were *her*. And Gramps shouted so loudly when Naomi asked about her mum that she didn't dare ask again.

Nana died when Naomi was nine, and then it was down to Gramps to look after her. He said he didn't know anything about girls but he knew how to light a fire, and grow pumpkins bigger than yer head, and whistle like a bird, and Naomi couldn't care less that he couldn't braid her hair.

One day Gramps took ill and Naomi nursed him as well as an eleven-year-old could. The bustling busybody from the post office came out to drop off a parcel and Naomi said to her, "There's summat up with 'im. He won't get outa bed."

Hilda Grayson told her not to worry, but by that night Naomi was in foster care and Gramps had tubes up his nose. Three weeks later Naomi was back in the same church, front row again, with people she hardly knew passing her tissues. Again there was no sign of her mum, and with no one willing to take her in, she found herself "in the system," surrounded by people who had never heard of Gramps. No one could tell her stories the way he used to. No one knew how she liked her toast cut into triangles. It was as if Nana and Gramps had never existed and Naomi ceased to exist too. Old Naomi, the Naomi who was loved and cared for, was long gone, buried in the ground between Nana and Gramps. She was reborn into a life where she had to fend for herself.

"I've got a mum. She don't know where I am. As soon as I tell her, she'll come git me. I won't be here for long. You'll see."

The social worker helped for a while. Helen's name was on Naomi's birth certificate, but there was no one of that name on the electoral roll, marriage licenses, nor, thankfully, a death certificate.

After two homes and three foster families, Naomi's ideas of her birth mother had soured. She could imagine her saying, "I wanted you to have the life I could never give you blah blah blah," when in fact she wanted the life that having a baby could never give *her*. Having a baby was a buzzkill and that was exactly what Naomi thought when she fell pregnant with the posh fella's child. He gave her enough money to make her go through with the abortion and keep her mouth shut. She'd have done it for free. She had no other choice.

The other girls in the waiting room looked ashamed. One

woman was older and kept saying, "But I just can't cope. I got another six at home." She wouldn't stop mithering and making them all feel uncomfortable. Naomi just wanted it over and done with.

Shown through to their own pristine beds, they were each given a gown and told to strip. Naomi lay on the bed as they slid a catheter into the back of her hand. For the anesthetic, they said. Naomi tried to read, but the words kept shifting about the page. A nurse told her that they would like to fit a coil while they were in there. Save this kind of thing from happening again.

"Won't happen. I'm never having sex again," Naomi told her. But the nurse looked at her like she'd seen her type before and they always did.

"They'll be up to get you in a minute," she said. "You're first on the list."

She drew the curtains around Naomi's bed. Naomi lay on her back and the tears fell from her eyes like they would never stop. She wanted her mum. A woman she had never met, a woman who had discarded her as easily as a chip packet. With the start of a life in her belly, she had never felt more like a child.

It was the most traumatizing thing that Naomi had ever had to do, but she had no home, no job, no family. She couldn't have this child, only for it to be taken into care and become easy prey for another foster father or friend of the family.

She dried her tears. She had to toughen up. Despite her anguish, she was sure she was doing the right thing. For her own mother to have her, then desert her, was the act of a selfish person. Naomi had grown up knowing she'd been abandoned and unwanted. How could she inflict that on another? It was time to stop the cycle. She wouldn't pass on her unlovable genes.

CHAPTER 31

9 days before the funeral

I walked through the rain, hood down on my coat, umbrella at home. I wanted to be wet and cold, to be anything other than scared of what might have been. My flip-flops paddled beneath my jeans. I'd forgotten to change them for something more suitable. I'd been desperate to get out of the house; it was a wonder I'd remembered a coat. All thoughts were preoccupied with Phillip right now.

He'd spent the morning shouting at us. Mostly he was reiterating what he had written on the wall, but every now and again he let something slip. He was desperate to get out in the next forty-eight hours but wouldn't, or couldn't, tell us why. He clammed up when we probed.

He tried to get us on our own and whispered lies about the other two. Promising us the world if only we let him out.

We stopped seeing him alone. Stopped seeing him altogether.

We gave him bottles of water and a pack of biscuits. Told him to help himself. I was meeting Chris Miller in the morning and until then I just had to keep Phillip out of my head.

My feet slipped around and squelched against the rubber, slapping at the shallow puddles and the bubbling pavement. It was one of those showers that looked inconsequential but soaked you through in minutes. It was light, soft rain, cooling but not cold. Refreshing me and washing away Phillip's stench.

Until I was surrounded by people, I hadn't realized how much I enjoyed my own company. We were temporarily safe, and for the first time in two days we felt able to let each other be alone without fear of retribution from Phillip. I felt free and lost at the same time. I could keep walking or I could be home in ten minutes, and no one would bat an eyelid. With Alistair so far away, I had lost my schedule and my purpose. It felt like I was wearing someone else's clothes and they were rough and heavy on my shoulders.

I hadn't told the others where I was going, only that I *had* to go. Now that Phillip was back under my roof, there was no more talk of either of them leaving, and I needed some space to breathe.

My safe space, the place of silence and calm, was calling to me. I slipped through the gap in the hedge to the spot where I came to talk to Iris. There was a small bench that I had placed there, under the outstretched arm of an oak tree, and I sat on it now. The field sloped down and away into a valley. Ahead of me were sparse and thin trees angled over a shallow stream. They were beautiful on a summer's day, but in the rain they were raggedy and lachrymose. Sheep huddled in the far corner, and in the distance lines of blue and red appeared as cars sped by on the bypass but were far enough away that the sound of engines was buffered by the rain. The patter of the rain on the ground rolled over me like a meditation CD in a spa, a place where women padded about beneath fluffy robes drinking freshly squeezed juices in between glasses of prosecco.

The rain dripped off the branches overhead and struck the ground, popping like bubble gum. I shook wet hair out of my eyes and huddled in my cocoon, shivered against the damp. If I'd had the energy, I would have cried.

I buried my head in my hands and dug my elbows into my knees.

The games Phillip played drove me insane. There was always something to hold over me. So much I didn't understand.

He wasn't one to shy away from low blows and base comments. Everything he did was calculated to hurt. He would never change, and I could have laughed at myself for ever thinking that he would. My biggest problem—*our* biggest problem—was what to do with him now that he was ours. We would start with a restraining order, but we needed more. We needed to make sure that he could never hurt us again.

He'd made our lives a nightmare in ways we were only just coming to realize. Things we had blamed ourselves for, problems we thought we could have avoided, were all down to him. He had isolated us, stopped us from making friends, but he hadn't realized that, by doing so, he would create a commonality between us—a bond that not even he could break. I was lucky to be able to count Rachel as a friend, but neither Ruby nor Naomi had mentioned anyone they could count on.

I could have sat in the rain until the night smothered me and I still don't think answers would have come. Usually, it would ease my mind to sit on Iris's bench, but today I couldn't feel my way.

There was too much going on in my mind. I couldn't shy away

from the thought that Ruby—the woman who'd turned on Phillip last night and had given us the upper hand—was responsible for the accident that killed my unborn child. Forgiveness was a gift to those who gave it as much as it was for those who received it, but I was struggling to be that kind.

Only Rachel understood why I came here. Anyone else would find it morbid. They could be forgiven for thinking of this as the place where I lost my baby. But I viewed it as honoring the last time that we were together. I remembered telling her about the stars and my dreams for her future. A good memory. A strong memory. That last walk I felt so happy to be pregnant. Just because of what came next didn't stop that from being a happy time. I never got to push her in her stroller or carry her in my arms, but I got to carry her in my body, and that was as good as it was going to get.

Rain funneled into rivulets that set off down the hill. I couldn't tell whether it was heavier or just sounded that way as it tried to find its way through the canopy above me.

I needed a drink. My ribs hurt as I stood up. If anything, they hurt more now than when Phillip had first attacked me. It was a reminder, in case I needed it, of Phillip's need to control everything around him, to have the last word and come out victorious.

The rain had become more persistent since I'd been sitting on the bench. The wind had picked up and was throwing needles sideways into my face and uncovered hands. I pulled my hood up, folded my arms around myself, and walked back to the sidewalk. My feet slipped on the mud and I was pleased to feel pavement under my flip-flops once more. The traffic was slow and light. Windscreen wipers swiped at the rain like giant metronomes.

I put my head down against the rain and walked quickly. A car, driving too close to the curb, hit a pothole, throwing dirty rainwater over my jeans. I gave out an involuntary shriek and turned away too late.

I turned to glare at the car, considering showing the driver my middle finger until I saw that the car had stopped and was reversing toward me. I almost ran but held my ground; it was about time people started apologizing for the way they treated me.

The window slid down and a man's face appeared. "Christ, I'm so sorry, Imogen. Would you let me give you a lift? Please? It's the least I can do. I feel just terrible."

It took a moment for me to recognize him out of context, and to place him where I'd last seen him—the school gate. He pushed his glasses up the bridge of his nose and I realized it was Ethan's dad.

"Tristan?"

"I didn't see the pothole. Here. Get in."

He opened the passenger door for me and I scrambled inside the warmth without even wondering if it was a good idea. I was making his plush seat wet, but seeing as the fault was his, I didn't care.

"God, I'm sorry," he said. "I thought it was you and I was trying to get close to see if it was. Didn't mean for that to happen at all. Where are you off to?"

"Don't worry. I was wet already. I was just out for a walk to clear my head."

I took my hood down and smoothed back my hair before turning to him and smiling. His hand was on the gear stick, about to put it in first and drive away.

"Christ! What the hell happened to your face?"

I considered the usual explanations of "tripped over the cat" or "walked into a door," but I was beyond covering up for other people as if their actions reflected badly on me. I wasn't to blame for what they did.

"This?" I pointed to my nose and my now blackened eyes. "That's nothing—you should have seen the other guy." I laughed, but Tristan didn't.

"Imogen?"

"I'm okay. It was my ex and—believe it or not—this isn't even the worst thing he's done in the last twenty-four hours. Can we go somewhere? Not home—I don't want to go there just yet."

He drove for five minutes, not saying much except, "Talk if you want to. But if you'd rather not . . . Whatever you need, Imogen. Whatever you need."

He pulled onto a drive in a new development. Golden-bricked houses with gleaming white window frames and navy blue doors. It was still a building site at the end of the road as the houses multiplied over fields and wasteland, creating dwellings for future lives and loves.

By the time I had untangled my coat from the seat belt, Tristan had opened the door for me. I let him take my hand to pull me out of the low car and into his house.

"You're shivering," he said.

At the front door I kicked off my flip-flops and wiped my bare, wet feet on the doormat. The carpet was plush and cream. I melted into it and stood looking at my dirty toes. There was a shoe rack and a low table with a telephone. Old-fashioned with a circular dial. Tristan took my sodden coat without a word and hung it from a stag's-head hook on the wall.

"Come through," he said.

The open space at the back of the house was a kitchen-diner. This was obviously where most of the living took place. The wall by the fridge was one large blackboard of drawings and doodles and notes of *Love you, Daddy* and reminders for *shampoo, milk, bread.*

There were beanbags and sofas in deep moss green and purple. A retro record player stretched across the back wall, a haphazard stack of vinyl showing that it was more than an ornament. A breakfast bar was teamed with tall dark-wood stools. On the top was a folded-back newspaper, a French press with an inch of murky brown liquid, and a mug that awarded the drinker the accolade of *World's Best Dad*.

Tristan draped a blanket over my shoulders and rubbed my arms.

"You warming up?" He was looking at my face, taking in my bruising. He quickly dropped his gaze. It pained him to look at me. I knew I looked a sorry state, but I was too tired to be embarrassed.

"Drink?" he asked as he straightened his arm to present the sofa to me. I nodded, pulled the blanket around me, and fell into the sofa, which sagged more than I expected and shot my knees higher than my hips. There was a skylight above me in the sloping roof, letting in the light but no prying eyes. There were no curtains, only sky. I rested my head backward and gazed up at the glass. The rain had stopped. In patches, there was a silver clarity. A brightening that promised the sun was still there if only I could stretch that far.

I listened to Tristan move about the kitchen and watched birds dart through my field of vision and out again. Swooping, playing, rapturous in the ceasing of the rain. I smiled slowly and let my eyelids close. Just for a minute.

I must have dozed off because I opened my eyes to find Tristan's hand on my shoulder. "Imogen?"

"Hmm?"

"I've run you a bath. You're still wet through and cold. There's clean towels and clothes in there. The best I can do, I'm afraid. Let me show you where it is."

I was led upstairs into the only bathroom. A basket in the corner was full of bath toys. A shark, a duck, a submarine, a mermaid. On the end of the bath a purple candle in a glass jar was pulsing gently. The bathroom smelled slightly of bleach, but the lavender from the candle was doing its best to compete. I dipped a toe and the water scalded. I stepped in and felt like my skin might blister with the heat. I didn't mind. I was ready to shed this layer of skin, to be born afresh. Renewed.

I sat in the water and it burned my thighs. I wrapped my arms around the back of my legs until I got used to the heat and began to feel it penetrate my skin. I lay back in the water. And back. I slid down until my hair was submerged. I was shut off from the world. I closed my eyes and let myself drift away.

I kept picturing the flames. In my fear-fed recollections, they now leaped higher and hotter. I could hear Phillip's laughter, though in truth he hadn't made a sound. I imagined and I wondered. I pictured us sleeping when he lit the fire, which would have, in turn, ignited the gas. I saw our bodies in black bags being wheeled out of the front door on gurneys. I pictured Alistair without a mother.

I don't know how long I lay there, letting my imagination run free, but my skin had wrinkled and the water was cold by the time I sat up and let the water fall from my hair. I considered adding more hot water but had already outstayed my welcome. I hardly knew this man and yet I was naked in his bathroom. It was stretching our school gate acquaintance to the limit.

The clothes he'd left for me were a pair of his tracksuit bottoms, a T-shirt, a pair of socks, and a sweatshirt. I put my underwear back on. It was damp and felt dirty next to my skin. His clothes smelled of a foreign washing powder, perfumed. The T-shirt was soft and the sweatshirt heavy. I looked at myself in the mirror. My hair hung limply around my shoulders. I began to wipe away mascara from beneath my eyes before I remembered I wasn't wearing any makeup and the black smudges were bruises. I dried my hair as well as I could with the towel and tamed it with my fingers.

As I opened the bathroom door, I heard footsteps going down the stairs. I went to join Tristan and found a cup of tea and two slices of cheese on toast on a green plate on the counter.

"Thought you might be hungry. My culinary skills don't stretch very far, I'm afraid. This is what you might call my signature dish."

I sat on the stool and my vision began to blur. I fought the tears. Blinked hard and said, "Thanks, for . . . all of this. The bath, the clothes, food. It's . . . I can't tell you how much I appreciate it."

My voice wavered and I took a sip of tea rather than continue to give way to my emotions.

"No problem. I know it's none of my business, but you should go to the police. He can't be allowed to get away with it."

I shook my head.

"I know if I was any kind of man I'd offer to march over to his house and punch his lights out, but he'd most likely knock me on my arse."

I laughed. I couldn't imagine Tristan hitting anyone with those soft, elegant hands.

"No, honestly," I said. "I'm dealing with the Phillip situation. He won't get away with it. I needed to get away for a couple of hours to work out what I was going to do. I'm a lot clearer now. Thanks."

"Is he . . . Is Alistair with him?"

"God no. Alistair's with my mum. No, I won't let Alistair be alone with Phillip ever again. But, you know, it's complicated."

Tristan nodded.

"Eat up," he said.

He took a triangle of the toast off my plate and ate it. I did the same. I couldn't put my finger on what I was feeling, but it was the most relaxed I'd been in days.

"Can I ask you something?" I said.

"Sure."

"What do you think about forgiveness?"

He shook his head and looked alarmed. "Sorry, but no. This isn't one of those times. You need to go to the police."

"I'm not talking about Phillip, actually. I have a feeling that someone did something really bad to me a few years back. If I'm wrong and I accuse her of it, it could make things awkward when I could do with her on my side at the moment. And if I'm right, I'm not sure what good it would do. I've always wanted to know who was responsible, but the thought that I might be close to getting my answer . . . well, it's not as satisfying as I thought it would be."

He chased crumbs around the plate with his finger.

"I don't know what to tell you," he said. "The only situation I can compare it to was when my wife left me. I'm sure you've heard the rumors."

I looked away and concentrated on my cup. I doubted there was anyone at the school who hadn't gossiped about him.

"I'm not happy with how our relationship ended. I thought we would be together for the rest of our lives, you know? The hardest thing was that she wasn't sorry for what she put me and the kids through, but as soon as I made up my mind to let it go, I was free.

"I couldn't be happy with someone else if I was still angry with Sally. It's the easiest thing in the world to hold a grudge, but it takes a strong person to forgive. You need to love yourself and believe that you deserve better. A wound doesn't heal if you keep poking it. And if that sounds straight out of a self-help book, it's because it is. I read hundreds of the things when she left me."

He laughed gently and held my gaze.

"I'm not sure if that helps?" he said.

"More than you could know." I slid my hand across the counter between us. Tristan reached for it and rubbed his thumb in circular motions over the back of my hand.

I asked him to drop me home, and though he hesitated, he agreed. At the end of the drive, he asked if he could give me a call sometime.

"I'd like that," I said.

"Great." He started reaching across me to get his mobile out of the glove compartment. I stopped him by placing my hand on his wrist.

"But not just yet."

"Okay. Sure. No—" He was flustered. "You're obviously going through a lot right now, so why don't I give you my number and you can call me when things have settled down?"

"Thanks."

"But"—he looked out the window rather than at me—"this doesn't have to be a date thing. I would like to be able to be there for you even without that, you know? For emergency baths and cheese on toast?"

"Thanks," I said again, and smiled as he handed me his business card.

I slipped from the car and was gratified that he waited until I had unlocked the door before he drove away with a wave.

Naomi came running down from upstairs.

"Oh, thank God. We were worried." She threw her arms around me and I hugged her back, touched by her concern.

Ruby was all hands-on-hips disapproval in the hallway.

"We had no idea where you were. Anything could have happened to you. Would it have hurt you to call?"

"Sorry, I didn't think that you'd be . . ."

I was touched. It was a long time since anyone other than my son had cared. I apologized for having scared them.

"Are you wearing different clothes than the ones you went out in?" asked Naomi.

"Long story," I said.

"Ruby's bought wine," she said. "Enough to last through a long story, I reckon."

I looked at Ruby. She looked tired and worn. It was time to move on from the past. We had more important things to do. We couldn't turn on each other now.

CHAPTER 32

8 days before the funeral

Monday started with an argument. I called work to excuse myself for the morning meeting and to say I would need a few days off. I had meetings with the solicitor and Chris Miller this morning. Besides, I couldn't pretend that the world was carrying on as normal when Phillip was in my house.

It started with my boss referring to me as "we."

"We've been distracted lately, haven't *we*?"

And ended with me telling him that *we'd* had enough of being told what to do and gave examples of where *we* could stuff his job.

Everything was changing.

It had to.

Phillip had stopped shouting and threatening. He had another ace up his sleeve, he said. The final act, he called it. We told each other he was bluffing and worked hard to find examples of when Phillip had overstepped the mark at work. Anything that could be called illegal.

DC Chris Miller agreed to meet me at ten thirty in the Pitchfork café on the high street. It was a glorious day, blue skies without end and enough of a breeze to take the sting out of the sun. I stopped by the bank, filed the papers with my solicitor, and still thought I had enough time to collect my thoughts before he arrived, but he was already there, sitting at the corner table with his back to the wall. I would have to pick up my thoughts as I stumbled over them.

He held a small coffee that looked like doll's china in his over-large hand. Chocolate-brown crumbs peppered a white napkin and the crease at the side of his mouth.

He stood as I approached, his smile shrinking to a pucker and a wince. I touched the side of my nose. I kept forgetting about the bruising until I saw the shock on the faces of others. He knocked the table as he came out from behind it and gave me a squeeze. We laughed a little, nervously.

"How've you been keeping?" he asked.

"Really well, thank you. And you?"

"Same. Can I get you a drink?"

"Please. Latte."

I settled down on the creaky wooden seat and waited. There was a plant pot filled with uneven white and brown sugar lumps. I pretended to busy myself with the contents of my bag and checked my phone messages, though I knew there wouldn't be any.

I brushed imaginary crumbs from the wooden table, sat back, then sat forward again and rested my folded arms on the table.

I jumped as a heavy hand touched my shoulder.

"Did you want a cake with your coffee?"

"Oh. No, thanks."

Chris turned back to the counter. "That's everything, thanks."

He came back to the table, pushing his wallet into his back pocket before sitting down.

"She'll bring it over."

"Right."

"Am I meant to be ignoring the black eyes?"

"For now."

"Check. Black eyes, broken nose, first time you've called in two years. These are normal things that are not to be brought up. Got it."

I smiled. I'd always liked Chris. He was one of the few people I knew who could see through Phillip. They'd been partners in the early days of their careers. They'd been a handful back then. "Work hard, play hard," they used to say. I couldn't vouch for how hard they worked, but more than once I'd had to pour the pair of them into the back of my car when alcohol had stolen the strength from their legs.

"Do you ever hear from Julia?" I asked.

He bristled. The pain was still too raw to be a casual topic of conversation. It was unfair of me, but I wanted him to remember why he hated Phillip.

A young girl with elaborate tattoos creeping out the bottom of her sleeves stopped by our table. She placed my latte in front of me and another coffee and a blueberry muffin in front of Chris. Wordlessly, she took away Chris's spent crockery.

"Not had any breakfast," he said, explaining the cake. He'd put on weight since I'd last seen him and I didn't think it was because of lack of breakfast.

I sipped my coffee and watched him drop large brown lumps of sugar into his cup.

"No. Me and Julia don't have reason for our paths to cross anymore. I think she's working over in Nottingham now."

"Right. I'm sorry about . . . you know, all of that."

"Not your fault. I'm not sure it was even *her* fault, but there we go. Water under the bridge, eh?"

"Seeing anyone?"

"Married to the job," he said, and winked.

He was a lovely man, and he didn't deserve to have Phillip swan in and destroy his marriage on a whim.

It was starting to get busy in the Pitchfork. People stumbling in, pushing sunglasses onto their heads with one hand and juggling bags in the other. It was still too early for lunch, but those late-morning coffees might spread, languish, and turn into an early lunch in the pools of sunlight that gathered over the tables.

"As lovely as this is," he said, "and, believe me, it is lovely—I think you might have ulterior motives for calling me."

"Yeah."

"Phil," he said.

"Yeah."

"What's he done this time? Or do I already know the answer to that?" He pointed a corner of his muffin at my nose.

"That's not why I called."

"Did you report it?"

"Chris . . ."

"Sorry. Ignoring it. Check."

"I know this is wildly inappropriate, but I could do with some advice. As you've guessed, things are *difficult* with Phillip right now. I have considered going to the police—I'm *still* considering it—but I've always been put off before because there's been . . ." I struggled to find words that wouldn't offend Chris.

"I suppose you might say there are certain individuals on the force who prioritize looking after their own instead of investigating domestic incidents. I've always thought—and been told actually—that any complaint I make wouldn't be taken that seriously."

"We're not all like that," Chris said with a frown deeply etched between his brows.

"I know. And I'm not saying you are. I'm just saying that Phillip is persuasive and I'm scared that if I—" I paused and let out a sad laugh. "Actually, I'm just scared."

"What are we talking about here? Has this happened before? What complaints might you make?" asked Chris gently.

I shook my head. This was harder than I'd expected.

"I need to know I'll be taken seriously and that Phillip will either be locked up where he can't touch me and Alistair or he'll be given a restraining order. There's others too. His ex-wife and his girlfriend. They'd need protection. Before I take this any further, I need to know that I've got a better-than-good chance of making this stick—otherwise I'll have to find another way to deal with him."

"I can't tell you whether you'd have a case unless you tell me what he's done. And even then, I can't guarantee that he'd be convicted of anything. You know that. But the force isn't like it used to be. They take domestic abuse very seriously. That *is* what we're talking about, right?"

"Mostly. But there are other things too. Arson, false imprisonment, car theft, criminal damage . . . And that's just the last forty-eight hours."

Chris looked at me like he couldn't be sure I was serious. I smiled at him and shook my head. I wasn't ready to tell him the details.

"Well," he said, "you can't just get a restraining order off the shelf. You need to report things as they happen. Even if the police don't act on it immediately, there'll be a record and over time it might build up to something concrete. Reporting it once might be enough to stop him from doing it again."

I shook my head. "No, that won't do. It needs to be something immediate to stop him retaliating."

"You might be better talking to a solicitor. It's not my area of expertise, but as long as you've not done anything in response to his threats . . . There was a woman I knew, got into an almighty slanging match with her other half. You should've seen the text messages. When it came down to it, the police couldn't distinguish between the offender and the victim and she couldn't get a—" He stopped talking when he saw the look on my face. I shifted in my uncomfortable seat.

"Should I take it that there has been a certain amount of retaliation?"

"Yes, but nothing compared to what he's done to us."

"Might it border on criminal conduct?"

I pursed my lips and gave a noncommittal shrug.

"Look, I don't want to know what you've done. I do know that whatever you've done might be for a good reason, but I'm just saying it muddies the water a bit. Your best bet is to go after a criminal conviction."

"Ha!" I couldn't help but shake my head at him. He must have known how futile it was to try to pin anything on Phillip.

We sat with our thoughts and our coffee. The café was filling up around us. The noisier it got, the more remote I felt.

"Hear me out," he said after a while. "If Phil has committed a crime, you need to press charges. I know it's difficult, but if you don't, you'll regret it. He shouldn't be allowed to get away with the things he's done. He should pay."

"You've not seen his violent side, Chris."

"But you have, and that should be enough. If you're worried about reprisals, then the police will consider that and offer protection."

"And if it doesn't stick, Chris? What then? Who'll protect me when he gets the charges thrown out? I've got my son to think about."

Chris looked at each person in the café one by one, checking whether anyone was listening, seeing whether he knew any of them. He leaned over the table, pretending to search for a brown sugar lump.

"I shouldn't tell you this," said Chris. "But I have reason to suspect you'd get a warm reception should you choose to press charges against Phil."

His guarded response had me checking over my shoulder too.

"Chris? Has something happened?" I asked.

He inhaled deeply and screwed up his face, as if what he was about to tell me was distasteful. I looked at him, but he didn't speak for a moment. He was staring into my eyes, searching for something, looking for a sign that he could trust me. I took a breath of my own, teetering between wary and curious.

Chris pushed his plate to one side and placed his hands flat on the table in front of him.

"Please. Tell me," I said. "He had an affair with your wife and he has systematically abused me for years. If you've got something to say that could help me—well, he hardly deserves your loyalty. So please, tell me what it is."

He carried on looking at his hands, but he was nodding slowly as if he knew what he had to do and was working up the courage to do it. He took one more look around the café.

"You didn't hear it from me," he said. "But . . . it'll be public information soon enough anyway. From what I hear, he's pretty confident that he'll be cleared of any wrongdoing. But whether or not— Christ, I'm really not meant to talk about it."

"Chris, tell me what's going on." I was desperate to hear what he had to say. I moved my chair as close to the table as possible and fixed my gaze on him. "Chris."

When he spoke, his words came out at a rush like a burst water main.

"He's being investigated for gross misconduct by the IPCC. The hearing is tomorrow afternoon and he's been telling everyone it's a witch hunt. Political correctness gone wrong. He's got a list as long as your arm of people willing to give him a glowing character reference. I don't think they can make it stick."

"What?"

"He's been suspended."

"Hold up. That's why he's not been in work?"

Of course. It made perfect sense. I'd not considered that this could be the reason for his secrets, for his anger. With Phillip's job came status. It meant as much to him as his reputation. The fact that anyone could question his conduct, when he had given everything he had to the force, would be enough to tip him over the edge.

"Why's he being investigated? What's he done?" I was eager for news.

"There was a sexual assault," Chris continued. "Years back. I mean, seven, eight years ago now. Phil interviewed the suspect and took his word for it that it was consensual. He was a flyer, this fella. Money, flash suit. He was clean-cut, white, and entitled. His argument was that he had offers of sex every day and he didn't need to force a woman to sleep with him. The girl says Phil told her in no

uncertain terms that no one would believe her version of events—
that her sexual history would be brought up in court and she was no
angel. She says she was harassed into dropping the charges. She also
says—" Chris took a deep breath, as if fighting to get the words out
against his better judgment.

"Phil told her that as she was black and the accused was white,
the case wouldn't go in her favor."

I gasped in incredulity that even someone like Phillip would
think that was acceptable. My mouth was still agape when Chris
started talking again.

"Look, as much as it pains me to be fair to him, he had a point.
Some juries are still biased, but back then it was even worse. Sexual
assault cases are difficult to prove. The women are pulled apart on
the stand. Pictures of them posing in skimpy clothes are taken from
Facebook and splashed all over the media. This guy, the accused—
he had more money than her, his lawyer would have had a field day.
It's not nice, but unless these cases have a really strong evidential
base, we can't always guarantee it'll get to court. She'd gone back to
his flat voluntarily, and she didn't report it until a week later, when it
was difficult to get evidence. There's a good chance CPS would have
chucked it out, but still, it wasn't Phil's call to make. The fella in
question went on to sexually assault other women."

"Shit."

"I don't know if we'll ever know how many, but he was sentenced
a couple of months back for the sexual assault of two women. That
first woman from years ago saw it in the paper and recognized the
guy. She went straight to her local nick and lodged a complaint. If
procedure had been followed, those women might have been spared
their ordeal. If there's been these three that we know about, there
could be more who are too scared to come forward."

Chris sighed and looked out the café window.

I had no words.

I'd always known that Phillip bent the rules to suit himself, but I had never considered other victims of his behavior. I slumped back in my seat, numb, wondering about the ripples that stemmed from Phillip's prejudices and arrogance. I'd always thought his manipulative behavior to be solely aimed at me, and anyone else who was stupid enough to love him, but I had believed him to be a good detective. Until now I hadn't considered that Phillip hurt strangers who deserved his protection too.

Chris went on. "There was an internal investigation and they agreed to take formal disciplinary proceedings against him. He's disputed the findings, of course, and has a hearing tomorrow where he can present his arguments and mitigating circumstances. If he fails to sway them, then it's an instant dismissal."

"Tomorrow?" I pictured him sitting in my cellar, chained by his ankle, and wondered whether the court would get to see him defend his honor.

"Is he . . . I don't know how you'd know, but has he shown any remorse for those women?"

Chris snorted unhappily. "Not that I've seen. I've read the report he's put to the panel. It's all about him being victimized and being made a scapegoat. He talks a lot about things that were going on in his personal life at that time too and how it might have clouded his judgment for a while. No mention of the *actual* victims, though."

He opened his mouth and then shut it quickly.

"What?" I asked. "You were going to say something else?" I leaned forward. He was starting to look irritated. Talking about Phillip and the things he had done was causing Chris to grind his teeth.

"This is all confidential. No disciplinary action can be taken before the full investigation has run its course. I . . . I could almost accept that he made a mistake with this one woman—no one's perfect—but people are coming out of the woodwork, questioning some of the decisions he's made in the past. Some are saying that he's used his position to threaten or to get favors. There's some talk that he's set people up for crimes they hadn't committed.

"If you were to approach the force with your own grievances, I would expect them to be sympathetic, if you know what I mean. There's a small group of people who would be very happy if they could get as much information as possible before tomorrow's hearing."

"Would it give them enough time? What with taking statements?"

"They might have to postpone the hearing for a day or so, but just knowing that the allegations had been made could be enough to get the decision in our favor. And if you stressed that you were worried about your safety, they might keep him locked up until the case has been decided. Of course, he has to turn up first, and no one's heard from him for a couple of days."

I looked away quickly before Chris could read anything on my face.

"What would happen if he didn't turn up?" I asked as casually as I dared.

"Dunno. Found guilty of misconduct and sacked, I guess. I mean, if he's not there to put up a defense, then there's no one to argue against the accusations."

"But he won't actually be arrested?"

"Doubt the CPS will think there's a case to answer. Not based on what we already have, anyway. If other things come to light . . . well, who knows."

287

It was tempting to keep him locked up until after the hearing. He'd be ruined, but we still wouldn't be free.

"What about his colleagues, though? Aren't they standing by him?" I asked, conscious of the only time I'd called the police and they had sided with Phillip, not me.

"No one's saying much in case they're implicated in anything. Phil's allowed to have a colleague with him for these meetings and hearings, but no one will do it. He's had to get someone from the union instead, but I don't know how much of his crap they believe."

He drained his coffee, licked his finger, and picked up stray crumbs from his muffin.

"If anyone asks, you didn't hear it from me," he said.

"Of course."

"Good. That's what that journalist said as well." He grinned.

I smiled. "Chris, what have you done?"

My legs were tingling. I placed my hands on my thighs to see if the reverberation was real. It took me a moment to realize that it was excitement. Thrill. The walls were coming down.

"Oh, I don't know. I might have given her copies of the reports and promised her a full transcript of tomorrow's hearing. She's already interviewed the three victims—she reported on the attacks originally—and she's very keen to do a follow-up."

This was going to be a big story. These women were willing to be named and photographed, to talk of their ordeals. They were braver women than me. They weren't victims.

Phillip would be identified, probably pictured, and held accountable. He would have nowhere to hide. His golf buddies and casual acquaintances who had all talked so highly of him in the past would find out what he was really like. He would be exposed. I should have been pleased. There would be nothing more ruinous for him than the loss of his job and status. But it didn't make me or my son any safer.

I still had to present myself to the police station and make a statement. And I would have to explain why he was locked in my cellar in the first place.

"And you think they might take me seriously if I was to go to the police?" I asked with trepidation.

"I reckon," he said. "They'd be bloody stupid not to."

CHAPTER 33

8 days before the funeral

"Let me go," Phillip said.

It was an order from someone who was in no position to make demands and, as such, it fell flat.

Ruby and Naomi decided that I should be the one to talk to Phillip. Ruby was so hurt by his betrayal that she couldn't stand to look at him. She was sorry she'd ever trusted him. Her insistence on seeing the best in him had nearly got us killed.

Naomi didn't want to see Phillip because she thought she might just throttle him. Whenever we spoke of him, which was often, she would fly into a rage. I left the cellar door open so that Naomi and Ruby could choose to listen to the conversation between Phillip and me if they wanted, though I wouldn't be saying anything that we hadn't already agreed.

Since my conversation with Chris, I'd pieced together every bit of information I could about Phillip's behavior. Ruby and Naomi were eager to give names and dates that could incriminate Phillip.

We'd drawn a timeline and plotted his cycles of abuse, instances of betrayal. It might not be what the court wanted to hear, but it made us feel better.

He and Ruby used to have interesting pillow talks, and she knew of cases he had "helped" in order to make sure the right person went down for the crime. He'd been proud of his initiative. And now Ruby was proud of her memory. I felt sure that these stories would match with some of the complaints against Phillip. Ruby said she didn't care if she got in trouble for not sharing this information sooner. She said there was a bigger picture to focus on. With so much time passed and so little evidence, it was unlikely that these recollections on their own could bring Phillip down, but taken with everything else it all made for a compelling case.

"We already tried letting you go," I said to him as I took a seat opposite him. "You didn't seem very grateful. Imagine if you'd just left us alone rather than come back for revenge? You wouldn't be sitting here with me and you wouldn't have a couple of exes sitting upstairs waiting for an excuse to smother you with a pillow. You had a choice. Forgiveness or revenge. You chose the wrong path and now here we are at the same crossroads. Forgiveness or revenge. What shall I choose? I wonder."

"If you don't let me go right now, I will make you suffer!" he shouted. The last word of his sentence seemed to ring around the corners and in my ears. *Suffer, suffer, suffer.*

He pulled at his cuffs, but the radiator stayed firm.

"So," I said, ignoring his outburst, "I know that you're being investigated for gross misconduct."

He blinked his eyes slowly. He was trying to keep his features neutral, but I could see through him. He was ruffled.

"You should've said something," I said.

He folded his arms across his chest and clenched his jaw.

"Things might have turned out differently if you'd just been honest with us. It was you lying about being in work that led me to tell Naomi, which led to her confronting you, which led to you assaulting and lying to her. What a mess you've made."

He crossed and uncrossed his legs. He was uncomfortable, wondering how much I knew and what I was going to do about it.

"The hearing's tomorrow, isn't it? It would be a shame if you couldn't attend. 'Mitigating circumstances,' is it? Isn't that what you told them? That there were mitigating circumstances?" I could feel my anger rising.

He didn't respond, but there was a slight shift in body language. His shoulders were tense and the muscles in his neck were twitching.

"Seriously, Phillip? You're using the death of our child as *mitigating circumstances*? How *dare* you use her as an excuse to get you out of trouble? You were a bastard long before the accident." I stood up and paced the small room.

"You're going to lose your job. No notice and no pay. I'm beginning to understand why you wanted me out of the house. You're worried about money, aren't you? The repayments on The Barn are costing you a fortune. So what was it? You were going to leave Naomi to pay the mortgage on her own and move in here instead? And here was me thinking that you had another woman. I should have known that no one else would be stupid enough to have you."

"I'm waiting," he said.

"For what?" I answered.

"The demands, the clauses in the divorce, or whatever. You want the house? Fine. You've got the house. Bring me a pen and I'll sign your papers. I'll make a deal with you. I want to get out of here and you want me gone, yeah? Let's call it quits. I'll go away and leave you be. Just unlock the bloody cuffs and we'll say no more about it. But leave it much longer and the deal's off."

"You'll have to try harder than that," I said. "The house is already mine, or at least it soon will be."

"What have you done?"

"That friend of Rachel's—you know, the Mickey Mouse solicitor—well, she helped with the paperwork. Naomi really is very good at your signature, isn't she? The mortgage company is drawing up the deeds in my name. Your signature will still be required, but I'm sure Naomi will help with that. It's not uncommon with divorces for couples to sign over property rather than sell it or go through the courts.

"Talking of houses, she's been looking at the paperwork for The Barn. It dawned on her that it's only in her name, isn't it? A little plan you cooked up together so that I couldn't get my hands on any of it when we divorced. We think that's why you panicked when Naomi said she was leaving you. Are we right? Is that when you came up with the idea of saying you had cancer? To court sympathy and buy time to sort out the paperwork? Stop me if any of this is wrong. It's clever, Phillip, but not clever enough."

I could tell that this had hit home. He unfolded his arms and sat up. He was worried now. I could see that he was wondering what else we could possibly want from him.

"Let me go and I'll make it worth your while."

"You don't have anything I want," I said. "Oh, yes, and you've paid for the repairs to Ruby's car. The least you can do after putting a brick through her window. And did you honestly criticize me for using our son's birthday as my PIN number for my phone when you use your own birth date for your cash card? Lax, Phillip, lax. But totally within character for a narcissist."

Phillip was clenching and unclenching his fists, and I could hear his breathing coming quicker. He was starting to fidget, to squirm.

I'd said everything I wanted to say to him. I was enjoying the feeling of power and reveling in the prospect of Phillip getting what he deserved. I turned my back on him and began walking up the stairs. My legs were tired, my body aching, my head bowed against the effort of propelling myself up the steps, but I felt satisfied.

I could see Naomi's shadow at the top of the stairs. She and Ruby had been listening to every word. She smiled at me as I neared the top. There was a look of happy determination on her face. The air at the top of the cellar steps was warmer, thicker. Naomi and Ruby were standing in the hallway, arms linked. We were finally in control of the situation.

"I can tell you everything," Phillip shouted from beneath me.

I shook my head. He was getting desperate and I didn't want to hear anything more from him.

"I've told you," I called back, "you're in no position to make a deal."

Before I could close the door, Phillip said, "Really? Don't you want to know who killed your baby?"

CHAPTER 34

8 days before the funeral

"What makes you think I care anymore?" I called, though the voice didn't sound like my own.

"Oh, I know *everything.*"

I hesitated at the top of the cellar steps. I wanted to confront him, to shake him, and tell him that he couldn't say things like that. Scream that he couldn't use what hurt me most to manipulate situations to suit him. I knew I had to walk away before he got into my mind. I was starting to make peace with what had happened, but there was still that part of me that wanted to know for certain. I couldn't look at Ruby. I feared what I might see on her face.

Naomi put her hand on my arm and shook her head. Her eyes were saying, *Don't rise to it.* But I couldn't pretend that he hadn't said anything.

He had my attention.

I stiffly descended the steps. He arched one eyebrow at me. He knew he had me now.

Hook.

Line.

Sinker.

I studied his face for an essence of truth, but I wasn't sure I'd recognize it in him anymore. Had he always known? Was it Ruby? Or was it someone else entirely? A stranger perhaps? I could bear if it was an accident. Could he have found out only recently? Or, more likely, could he be lying to save his own skin?

"You almost had me there," I said. "But then I remembered that you're a liar. Whatever you tell me now, I won't believe."

"Oh, you'd know. I think you've always known. Let me go, and get the confirmation you've always wanted."

I glanced up the stairs to where Ruby and Naomi stood. Ruby was biting the side of her thumb and Naomi had her arms folded.

Before I'd begun to suspect Ruby, I thought the person responsible would eventually bow under the weight of their guilt and have to tell someone. Had they wondered what had happened to the woman they'd hit? Did they regret fleeing the scene? I'd told Phillip that I wanted to look the driver in the eye and ask why. Were they drunk? Had they lost control of the car? Had a cat run out into the road? I needed to know.

And here was Phillip telling me he had all the answers. When he was about to lose everything, he pulled an ace out of his sleeve.

"You *must* be desperate," I said.

I folded my arms with hands tightly under armpits and leaned on the wall, fooling no one with my feigned nonchalance.

He laughed. "Perhaps I *am* in a position to make deals after all."

"This is low, even for you. If I let you go, you'll tell me a story that I'll have no way of verifying. All that will have changed is that you'll be free to go to your hearing and try to clear your name while

I sit around wondering if you're going to try and take revenge on us again."

And, I thought, *I'll never be able to look Ruby in the eye again.*

"No," I said. "No. I won't let you do this to me. I won't let you use the death of our daughter as a bargaining chip. I would rather go to my grave not knowing what really happened that night than give you the upper hand."

As soon as I said it, I knew that I was right. Even if he was telling the truth, it wouldn't change a thing. It wouldn't bring Iris back.

He looked past me to the stairs.

"Ruby?" he shouted. "Naomi? I know you're listening up there. You may as well come down."

There was a short delay while they decided whether to respond to Phillip's call, and then they joined us in the cellar. I moved away from the foot of the stairs to let them into the small room.

"You're summat special, you are," Naomi said. "You can't go lying about somethin' like that. You're sick."

"I'm not lying to her. And I'm not lying when I say this either. I need to get out of here. You know that I've got a hearing I need to be at tomorrow. I have kept things from all of you over the years . . ."

Ruby scoffed and looked away, refusing to meet his gaze. She looked heavy with discomfort.

"It's up to you, ladies. Whichever of you lets me go will get the answer to a question that's been bugging you for years."

"It's quite a coincidence," I said, "that you just happen to have a nugget for each of us, isn't it?"

He looked at Ruby. It was a soft look, one of sad resignation. Perhaps he did care about her after all.

"Ruby," he said.

She didn't look at him.

"Ruby? That night, after the party. I know you've always wanted to know what happened to the dog. If you let me go, I will tell you exactly what happened to Rufus."

She looked up, despite herself. Shook her head quickly and gave him a tight-lipped smile.

"Oh, Pip. You think I've been sulking over that for the last twenty years? I know you were responsible. Whether you simply opened the door or buried him in the garden, it makes no difference to me. I forgave you a long time ago. I accepted that you were sick. My only mistake was to think that you'd changed."

Phillip frowned. "Then what do you want from me?"

"Nothing. I used to feel responsible for you. You relied on me so heavily after your mum died, and I felt guilty for leaving you when I did. You used to tell me how Imogen used emotional blackmail to make you stay with her, that she tricked you into having a child. Otherwise you'd have left years ago. I've lost track of the times you've told me you wished we'd never split up. I've waited in the wings for years for my chance to make it up to you, but now I see how stupid I've been. Good-bye, Phillip."

She spun around and began to climb the stairs.

"Ruby, wait!" Phillip shouted.

I steadied myself against the cool wall and watched her back disappear up the stairs.

"Don't have the charm you thought you did, eh?" said Naomi. "You got something for me, then? This should be good. Hold on. Wait for me to get comfy—I love a good fairy tale." She slid down the wall until she was sitting on the floor. "Right. I'm ready. Go on. Once upon a time . . ."

Phillip narrowed his eyes. For a moment, I thought he was reconsidering offering her a deal. "You've always wanted to know where your mum was, yeah?"

The smile fell from Naomi's face. Her expression was thunderous. She looked at him like she might fly at him at any moment.

"What of it?" she spat.

"I know where she is."

"Bollocks."

"Her name is Helen."

"You could have got that off my birth certificate. That don't mean anything."

"Born 8 June 1979," he continued. "Married twice. The last records show her as Helen Beresford."

Naomi scrambled back to her feet and looked at me and Ruby. I reached out and put my arm around her.

"Ignore him. We've got a name now," I said to her. "We'll find her on our own."

"Wouldn't be so sure of that," said Phillip. "She's been in a bit of trouble with the police. The apple doesn't fall far from the tree. She's got several aliases."

"Well, that's handy for you, isn't it?" I said. "If that's true, how did you manage to track her down?"

"I didn't," he said. "She tracked me. Well, Naomi, actually. She wrote to Naomi, and I opened the letter. Surely that's not too hard to believe? So how about it, ladies? It's a onetime offer. Whoever gets me out of here by nine o'clock tomorrow morning will get the news they've always wanted. It's up to you to decide whose need is greatest. Yours, Imogen, for wanting to look the person in the eye who killed your baby? Or yours, Naomi. So you can look into the eyes of the woman who gave you up. But remember, the clock's ticking."

CHAPTER 35

1 year, 3 months, and 5 days before the funeral

Phil folded the letter back into the envelope and tapped it against his knuckles. It was a shame, but there was only one thing for it. Couldn't be helped.

He spun it into the fire, where it curled at the edges and flared brightly before shrinking and crumbling away as if it had never been there at all. And as far as Naomi was concerned, it hadn't.

The flames jumped, squatted, and danced about the hearth. It wasn't cold enough for a fire, but the glow was for soothing his mind, not his body. Sparks were like waves. You could watch them, no matter what the weather, and feel your worries shrink into insignificance. Fire and water didn't care for your strengths or your weaknesses. They were the reminder that some things were bigger than you were.

Phil had always loved to watch things burn. Letters. Pictures. Evidence.

The cleansing effect of the flames and the eradication of things that shouldn't be. As a kid he'd sit by and watch buildings and warehouses color the skies orange and spit sparks like fireflies among the stars. And then the firemen would come and do their best to master the beast. He wasn't a vandal. It wasn't arson when it was art.

Phil always opened Naomi's mail. Why shouldn't he? If she objected, it was because she had something to hide. But this particular letter had been different. The handwriting was small and deep. Someone had taken great care over addressing the envelope. It wasn't Naomi's birthday, nor was it Christmas. It was obviously not a bill, nor nuisance junk mail from some company. It was personal. Intriguing. Dangerous.

Of course, the claims in the letter might have been preposterous. Anyone could have made them without a shred of evidence to back them up. Phil wouldn't have been doing his job as a boyfriend or a police officer if he hadn't investigated further. So, in a way, he was protecting Naomi.

The woman who wrote the letter lived over two hundred miles away, so he'd had to call in favors from another force. No one was more surprised than he was when it all checked out. Right age, right name, but, unfortunately, completely wrong for Naomi.

The note said she'd been looking for Naomi for six years. Wondering, crying, lighting a candle on her birthday, telling her brother and sisters about her. Six years. What about the other years? What was she doing for over a decade before that? Not wondering where her firstborn was, that was for sure. Not imagining the childhood years she'd spent with her grandparents or the teenage years she'd spent in care. She could dress it up however she liked, but she had abandoned Naomi and it had been left to him to pick up the pieces.

She said her name was Helen. It checked out on Naomi's birth certificate. The father's name was noticeably absent. Helen was settled now and would do anything to be reunited with her daughter.

Well, she would, wouldn't she? It was safe to crawl out of the wood-work now that Naomi didn't need anything from her anymore.

Naomi wasn't the only one she'd had taken from her. To read her letter, you'd think this woman was blameless. Life had put her in a bad position, dealt her a terrible hand. She couldn't help the past but, as God was her witness, she was ready to make amends—if Naomi would let her.

Initially Phil had considered taking the credit for this woman's reappearance. It would be the best gift that he could ever give Naomi.

Ta-daaa, I've found your long-lost mother.

Naomi would be forever in his debt. He would have done what no one else could. She'd be grateful at first—of that, there could be no doubt—but what if the woman turned out to be a money grabber or a sponger? Or, worse, what if she lived up to Naomi's expecta-tions?

He was all Naomi had in the world. Until now. He had to consider his options because, after all, it didn't just affect Naomi. Bringing someone else into the fold would mean turning his life up-side down too.

Phil had uncovered the basic facts. She'd changed her surname on more than one occasion, so it wasn't a surprise that Naomi had hit dead end after dead end when searching for her. Married, divorced, married again. In some cases, the surname had changed without there being a marriage certificate to back it up. These types were al-ways the same. Always running from something or someone.

He'd had a couple of the lads from the local force go check her out for him. She had a skeletal figure, a hard face, and more tattoos than brains. She was living alone and claiming benefits. He thought of his own mother. Why couldn't more women be like her? His mother had been a hard worker, not prone to womanly vapors or emotional outbursts. She was as strong as any man and twice as clever. If Naomi's mum had been halfway like Mam, he would have made up the spare room himself. But she wasn't, and the rational decision was to sever all ties with this woman as quickly as possible. He'd already left it too long and he was worried it was giving the woman hope.

He took a pen and paper from the sideboard.

Dear Mrs. Beresford,

Sorry to write with disappointing news, but I'm afraid you've made a mistake. I am not the Naomi that you are looking for. My parents are alive and well, so I am quite certain that I am not your daughter. Please do not contact me again, as it has upset my mother greatly. Wishing you the best of luck with your ongoing search.

Yours sincerely,
Naomi

CHAPTER 36

8 days before the funeral

"This doesn't have to change a thing," Naomi said.

"I want him gone." I couldn't settle.

I paced the living room, walking into the blackened and blistered hallway to look at the cellar door and then back to Ruby and Naomi.

Ruby was standing by the window with her eyes glazed over, and Naomi was lying on her back smoking. I'd given up asking her to go outside. It was a small problem compared to everything else we were dealing with and, besides, the whole house still smelled of smoke from Saturday night's fire.

"Look, we have a plan. And I've not heard anything to make us change that. We take all the information we've collected and go to the police station with photos, dates, and times. It's obvious we can't trust Phillip. He will always seek to manipulate and control. That's what men like him do."

"He'll tell 'em we locked him up," Naomi said, knocking ash into a disused coffee cup.

"And we'll tell them that it was self-defense after he tried to kill us. The evidence is all there if they care to look. And as for the first time I locked him in the cellar . . . well, it's his word against mine."

"Ours," said Ruby. "I'll back you up. I'll tell the police I had dinner with him on Friday, as planned, so he couldn't have been here."

"Yeah," Naomi chimed in. "I can vouch for that, and then we came round here to see you, what with Ruby not having seen you for so long, and Phil overpowered us and locked us in the cellar. Lucky we escaped. Rachel's neighbor can vouch for timings of us getting out and the state of our faces. And the fact that you sent Alistair out of the country backs up how scared we were of him."

"That's right," said Ruby, picking up the story. "We all stayed together on Saturday night, knowing what a foul mood he was in, and woke up to find graffiti on the walls, the gas on, and then he poured petrol through the letter box. As far as we know, he scarpered and we thanked our lucky stars that we were alive. It's not like we're stretching the truth very far, darling."

"I couldn't ask you to lie for me," I said.

"You didn't," Naomi said. "We offered. In fact, why don't we go to the police now before any of us cave? I got to tell you, it's bloody tempting to find out where me mum is, so let's go give our statements now before I change my mind."

"No. I don't want them to find him locked in my cellar. If we let him go in the morning, he'll go straight to the hearing and I can clear out the cellar as if he's never been in there. Right now, there's nothing more important to him than clearing his name."

I watched the soft clouds blow by the window. They were in a hurry.

"He must know we've got something planned," said Naomi. "Perhaps if we tell him one of us is going to cave in tomorrow he'll accept the fact that he has to stay put for a bit longer."

We sat in silence for a moment, wondering how much he knew and what we could get away with.

"It's not a bad idea," I said eventually. "He doesn't know that we were planning to let him go in the morning anyway. I think that we should at least get something else out of this. Naomi, you need the information more than I do. We'll get him to tell you where to find your mum. The only thing we need to work out is how we can un-chain him safely without having a repeat of what happened last time."

Ruby looked at me sideways. Was it my imagination, or did she look relieved?

"Thanks, but I don't know. Perhaps it should be you. It must be eating you up not knowing."

Naomi was trying to show how much she didn't care about her mum, but she was transparent. She cared very much. I hadn't known her for long and yet I knew how much she wanted to connect with her mother. The knowledge that she would give that up for me was a warm glow in my chest.

"That bike lock has a combination code, right?" said Naomi.

I nodded.

"How about we hide a phone down there close enough for him to reach but not in plain sight. I reckon we take him some clean clothes, wrap the phone in a shirt or something. And then we get out of the house, leaving the doors unlocked, and call him. Tell him that we'll text him the combination code if he tells us . . . you know . . . whatever."

I looked up at her. It might work.

The three of us had spent only a few days together, yet it felt so much longer. We had reluctantly agreed we wouldn't contact each other for a while. We didn't want the police to think that we were plotting to bring Phillip down. As we'd had little contact in the past, it was unlikely the police would think this was part of a master plan. Though they were bound to be suspicious, we could honestly say that until a few days ago we hardly knew each other and it was only Phillip's actions in the cellar that made us confess to each other how much we had lost because of him.

As far as anyone else was concerned, we were nothing more than three ex-partners of the same man who couldn't stand each other but had all suffered at his hands. Circumstances had thrown us together, but if anyone asked, they weren't enough to keep us there.

"Taxi's here," Ruby said. She sounded glad to be leaving.

She embraced Naomi and me at the same time. It was an awkward tangle of arms that gave me a mouthful of her hair and crushed Naomi's elbow into my breast.

"Be wary of him," she said. "And if the dogs turn up . . . ?"

"Don't worry," I said. "We'll call you straightaway."

Ruby climbed up into the passenger side of the taxi and sat watching us for a long minute. Suddenly I didn't want her to leave. I felt tears come to my eyes. We had shared something life-changing, something that we might never speak of again.

Naomi linked her arm through mine as the taxi disappeared into the hazy afternoon, and neither of us mentioned the tears falling down our faces.

CHAPTER 37

8 days before the funeral

There was no guarantee that Phillip would deliver on his end of the promise. But that didn't matter. All that mattered was that he believed he was getting one over on us. Our time spent with Phillip hadn't been entirely wasted. We'd learned about duplicity from the best.

I took a cup of tea into the garden. It was a golden evening with far-reaching wisps of cloud. I settled into the tree swing and swayed gently. Perhaps I should have been worried about what tomorrow would bring, but it felt like a fresh start for all of us. Whatever happened to Phillip now would be up to the courts to decide. We were finally standing against him and he would never have the same kind of power over us again. The three of us had survived the worst he had to throw at us and we'd found that there were others who'd suffered more than us because of Phillip's nature. Women who had suffered worse abuse, and it was as important to get justice for them as it was for us.

Ruby was finally able to move on from Phillip. She could stop feeling responsible for him and let herself love another person—not only her dogs. Naomi was on the cusp of a new life. If Phillip delivered what he'd promised, she would meet her mother for the first time. And she knew now that, though it might be twenty years later than she would have liked, her mum wanted to be with her.

Naomi came out into the yard dragging a case behind her and with her jacket slung over her arm.

"What's this?" I asked.

"I'm off," she said.

I placed my cup on the ground and got up.

"Why? What's happened?"

"Nothing." She smiled at me. "You've been dead good to me, and you didn't need to be. If anyone deserves answers, it's you. I'm not going to be the one to let him go. If my mum is trying to find me, then she's out there somewhere and there'll be a record of her. She's not going to be in hiding, is she? Never underestimate the power of social media for tracking people down. Of course, he could have been talking bollocks all along, in which case me letting him go wouldn't change anything anyway."

"But . . . you're leaving? You don't have to go," I said.

"I do. I'm not going to give you the chance to change my mind. Besides, we're only guessing he's going to go straight to the tribunal in the morning. He might go back home, and I want to get there first and get my things out. I want to get photos of the broken table and the blood on the carpet too, to show the police fella tomorrow. What was his name? Chris, was it?"

I nodded.

"But where will you go?" I asked, with my hand on her arm to stop her from leaving.

She shrugged. "Anywhere I like. I've got his credit card, so for tonight, at least, it'll be a fancy hotel. I'll check in from time to time so I know when it's safe to come back. Now come 'ere and give me a hug."

I held her tightly. She dropped her bags and returned the hug. I didn't want to let her go but my tears wouldn't make her stay.

"Get out of here," I said with a smile.

"You'll call me, yeah? If there's a problem tonight or any night?"

I nodded. She leaned toward me again and gave me another squeeze. I watched as she disappeared through the gate and I stood and listened as she started her car and drove off.

And then I was alone with him.

I walked inside. The house was quiet without Ruby and Naomi in it. I opened the front door and looked out. I don't know what I was hoping to see. But, whatever it was, it wasn't there. It struck me that I was without a car. I didn't know what Phillip had done with it. I would have to rethink how I was going to get to the police station tomorrow.

I locked the door and walked from room to room. The house was a mess. Empty cups. Discarded socks. A book facedown with its spine bent. The ghosts of a normal life.

I wiped the table, I loaded the dishwasher, I even put in a load of laundry, and when I'd run out of anything else to do I sat at the table and allowed myself to remember.

The morning after the accident played in my head as if I were viewing it through the fog. It loomed without a specific size or face. It was an undisclosed mass that blocked out the sun and stopped me forging onward.

The accident had nearly killed me. My pelvis had been crushed, my right leg broken, and two ribs had pierced my lung. Lucky to be alive, they had said, but I didn't agree. When I awoke inside the pristine white walls, the first thing I knew was not where I was or what had happened, but that my baby was gone and the pain was more than the morphine could ever touch.

A thin tube held my hand to a drip that was *tip-tapping* above my head. Another tube ran beneath the covers into a bottle to collect urine. A pale blue gown was over my front but wasn't tied at my back and I didn't care. The foot of the bed was at an angle to match that of the head and I looked away as they injected something into the tube affixed to the back of my hand—apparently to help keep blood clots at bay. Like I cared.

Phillip hadn't left my side for forty-eight hours. We clung to each other under the umbrella of the "there-theres" and the "one days."

I'd lain in that field for five hours. A late-night reveler on his way home, stopping to pee in the hedge, had spotted my shoe hanging on a low branch. When he looked closer, he saw the other shoe still attached to my foot. Thinking he had found a dead body, he called for help. The nurses said I owed him my life, but I couldn't find it within myself to be thankful.

He visited me in the hospital, a bunch of supermarket flowers in the crook of his arm. They made quite a fuss of him. Phillip shook his hand and the doctors slapped him on the back.

"Right place at the right time," he said, but I couldn't look at him.

He left. They all did eventually. Shift change, lunch times, their lives going on around me as I lay immobile. Silently suffering. Time ticking by, taking me further away from *her*. They say time's a great healer. They lie.

CHAPTER 38

7 days before the funeral

The night had passed into the hour before morning, when secrets unfolded and lies were covered up. Birds were beginning their songs of freedom and joy at the sight of the lightening skies. I sat at the kitchen table drinking coffee. It was strange how calm I felt.

I refilled my coffee cup, made Phillip one too, and then went down into the cellar to wake him. Like a fearful child, he'd slept with the light on.

I stood over him. Most people looked angelic when they slept. Fluttering eyelashes on smooth cheeks giving an air of serenity and purity—but not Phillip. His face was chiseled from granite, with a lifetime of disapproval etched between his brows. It wouldn't have been out of place between the gargoyles and stone sprites that adorned the squat church where we wed. It had been months since I'd studied that face. Strong nose. Full lips. Square chin. To those who didn't know, he looked like a savior, my knight in shining armor. But I'd seen his eyes when the mask slipped and I knew the devil lived in his soul.

I watched him wake slowly. He jolted when he saw me and forced his eyes wide. He sat up, yawned, and took the mug from me.

"No milk?" he asked.

"Haven't been shopping."

I placed the folded-up clothes, with mobile phone in the trouser leg, on the back of the sofa.

"You want to know, then?" he asked with a gradual smile. "I knew you would."

I took a deep breath and considered him. His skin was sallow; a few days out of the sun was all it took for him to lose that healthy outdoor look that was part of his charm. His teeth were yellowing and I could see every line on his face. I'd mistakenly thought his tired face and thinning frame had been because of cancer, but it had been the stress of being suspended. I should have known.

He sat on the edge of the bed and I stood out of his reach.

He bent down to the handcuffs and looked at me. "Come on, then. I'm going to need the key."

"Not yet."

"I can't tell you the whole story until you let me go, Imogen. We had a deal."

"Later."

"Imogen?" His voice was dripping with menace now. A warning.

"Don't worry," I said. "I'm letting you go, but not yet."

I had no more pain in my nose and my ribs had stopped aching. I felt strong, invincible. I felt more myself than I had ever felt. I had stopped wondering what other people thought of me and now only cared what I thought of me. As long as I could look myself in the mirror and say honestly that I had done my best for me and my son, then I would be happy. The door to my future was wide open and I couldn't wait to pass through it and close the door to my past.

I balanced one foot on the bottom step and looked over my shoulder at him. I tried to fix him in my mind. He was flesh and bone like anyone else, but his heart was empty. I felt absolutely nothing for him. Not even pity. He was solely responsible for the position he was in and he would get what he deserved.

CHAPTER 39

7 days before the funeral

walked out the front door under the early-dawn skies and ambled along the road, past the blackened windows and stationary cars. For most people, the day hadn't yet started. For me, it was still the tail end of yesterday.

A lone cat stalked me for half a mile before jumping over a wall and disappearing down an alleyway. I missed its company as I walked the last few yards on my own. The streetlights clicked off suddenly, announcing the arrival of morning. I hadn't noticed them until they weren't there.

I turned sideways to slip through the gap in the fence, but my clothes caught on the bushes that had thrown out long grasping branches as rain had turned to sun had turned to rain over the past week. I slipped my bag off my shoulder. It was heavy with essentials—clothes, passport, book, phone.

I settled onto Iris's bench as the early-morning traffic began pulsating behind me every ten seconds or so. Workers eager to be the first to their desks. The keenest, the hardest working, the ones re-plete with self-importance impressing no one but themselves.

I took my phone from my bag and dialed Phillip's number.

It rang and rang, and I began to panic, thinking I'd left it on si-lent or that I'd placed it where he couldn't reach, but then the ring-ing stopped suddenly.

"Imogen," he said.

I breathed in. Breathed out. Breathed in and spoke.

"Surprised?" I asked.

"Not really. You've always been weak. Should have known you'd be hiding from me."

I was tempted to leave him locked, remind him who had the power, but it was even more appealing to set him free to face the disciplinary panel so I could clear away the evidence that he'd ever been there. Tomorrow it would be all over the papers; Chris had seen to that. Today it would be all over social media; Naomi had promised that.

"Are you going to tell me?" I asked.

"Are you going to set me free?"

"I'm going to tell you the combination lock. Once that's open, you'll be able to leave the cellar. The key to the cuffs is on the shelf in the hallway."

"I'm not telling you anything until you give me that code."

"I wouldn't expect anything less from you," I said. "It's eighty-five thirteen."

I heard him grunt with the exertion of bending over and fid-dling with the lock. "So it is. Got to tell you I'm surprised. I've been trying all kinds of combinations of birthdays and anniversaries but I would never have expected you to use the number thirteen."

"You don't know me as well as you think you do," I said.

"Really? Then how did I know that you would be the one who'd give in? I knew you couldn't resist."

I could hear him walking up the stairs. There was less of an echo to his words now that he was at the top.

I tried to envisage my life without Phillip, but couldn't grasp the shape of it. There was no blueprint for freedom; it was formless, endless, and it alarmed as much as it excited. Soon, everyone would know what Phillip was capable of and his reputation would be just where it should be.

"Well, well, well," he said into the phone. "And the keys are just where you said they'd be. You're desperate for this information, aren't you? No more playing games. Now, where should I start?"

"I don't want to hear what you have to say, Phillip."

It would have been easy enough to sit and listen, to let him tell me something between a truth and a lie, but I realized that it would make no difference.

"Nothing you say will bring her back to me. Nothing you can say can undo the past. I thought I wanted to know, but now it's come to it, I don't think I could bear it. It's done. *We're* done."

"We're not done until I say we're done. I thought you wanted to hear the truth?" His voice was harsh in my ear.

"I do," I said. "But I'll never get it by listening to you."

I hung up on Phillip and immediately scrolled through for Tristan's number.

I felt lighter than I'd ever felt. Free. Tranquil.

I sent a text to Tristan, hoping to catch him before he set off for work. I told him my car was out of commission and he was right, my ex shouldn't be allowed to get away with what he'd done. Was there any chance he could drive me to the police station later this morning? Get a coffee afterward? His response came almost immediately.

I'd love to.

I switched off the phone in case Phillip tried to call me back.

I wasn't deluding myself. I knew that the chances of a healthy relationship coming from all of this were slimmer than remote, but it was nice—comforting—to think that somewhere out there was a person who liked me enough to want to spend time with me.

I thought of Naomi and Ruby—women I had despised this time last week. I should have known they were nothing like the picture I had painted of them. Should've known better than to believe anything Phillip had told me. I had grown fond of them. More than fond. Ruby had a big heart, even if her loyalties had been misplaced.

And Naomi. Vulnerable, damaged, and yet stronger than the rest of us put together. I could see now that I had been jealous of her confidence and her easy life, not knowing that it was only a sugar-spun shell.

I closed my eyes and felt the day settle around me. The traffic was heavier now, the intermittent rush of cars replaced by a steady buzz. Birds shouted to each other from treetop to treetop. A swish overhead from the bowing of the branches. A rustle to my side of wind-ruffled leaves. Minutes passed easily and I reveled in the new-world smells that I'd barely noticed before. The air was tangy with the promise of more rain. I thought of the passport nestled in my bag. Once I'd finished at the police station, I was getting on the next plane to Spain to see my son.

"So, what now?"

"Jesus!" I jerked and knocked my phone to the ground. I scrabbled to my feet and turned to face him.

Phillip.

"How did you—" I began. My arms were outstretched, warning him to keep his distance.

Phillip's slow smile and raised eyebrow uncovered his pleasure at having found me. His hands were behind his back. Solid stance like an army major. Superior.

"You think I don't know that this is where you come? You think this is your *secret* place? You have no secrets from me, Imogen."

"What do you want?"

My heart was beating out of my chest. I hadn't expected him to come here. This was my place, somewhere I should have felt safe. He was between me and the gap in the hedge. I was trapped. This wasn't how it was meant to happen. He should have been heading home to shower and shave, to get ready to put his case at the hearing. He shouldn't be here. He shouldn't be looking at me like he wanted to kill me.

I thought about shouting for help, but no one would hear over the sound of the traffic. My phone was out of reach, and Naomi and Ruby were long gone. No one knew where I was.

"To talk," he said. "C'mon. Like old times."

"We don't have anything to talk about. You really should leave."

"Should I?" His eyes shone with malice. He jutted his chin out and looked past me, something on the horizon catching his eye and making him smile. He looked down at his toes and pushed himself up onto the balls of his feet and back onto his heels. I glanced where he was looking and almost missed the lightning movement of his hands as he whipped something out from behind his back. A knife.

"You left before we could talk, Imogen."

He gripped the kitchen knife in his hand, the tip slightly raised and splitting the reflection of the weak sun. I'd misjudged him. Revenge meant more to him than reputation.

I had just enough time to think *So that's where the knife is* before he lunged at me.

I staggered backward and Phillip laughed. I couldn't outrun him, couldn't beat him in a fight.

The traffic was insistent now, but the people in the cars couldn't see me, hear me, or help me. I edged around the side of the bench, using it as a shield.

"Phillip, remember last time you tried to get revenge on me? It didn't turn out so good for you. Don't make the same mistake again."

"Mistake? No, Imogen, it's not me who makes mistakes, is it?"

I licked my lips, considering whether I could dash past him to the road, whether I'd be better off running across the field, but my darting eyes gave me away.

"Don't even think about running," he said. "You'll never get away from me."

There was something in the way he said "never" that made me think he was talking about more than today.

"Phillip, please. What about the hearing? You said you needed to clear your name. This isn't going to help."

I was starting to panic. If he didn't care about his job or his reputation, he had nothing to lose.

"That was the plan, but then you hung up on me. Rude, Imogen, rude. You do disappoint me. But then, you always have. Come, sit down."

He pointed with the knife at the bench. I did as he asked, buying time, slowly lowering myself onto the bench without taking my eyes from the blade. He sat heavily by my side and I recoiled from him. Phillip grabbed my right hand in his left and held tight when I tried to wrestle it from his grip. He pressed the tip of the blade into the fleshy inner part of my arm and smiled when I winced, but I wouldn't cry out. When he took it away again, there was the fleeting imprint of a crimson bird in flight before my blood distorted the image.

"Set me up nicely, haven't you?" he said, pushing my arm away from him in disgust.

"You brought it on yourself."

He laughed. A volley of nasal coughs.

"You hung up before I could tell you the truth about your little accident."

I dipped my head but kept my eyes fixed on the knife in his hand. He was waving it up and down like he was assessing its weight.

"You've still got time to get to the hearing," I said. "Surely this can wait."

"Not so quick. Not so quick. Somewhere else you've got to be?"

"No," I said. "Nowhere."

My eyes traveled from the knife to his face. He was looking over the horizon again, in the direction of our house. Eyes narrowing to keep the thoughts from spilling out. The skin under his chin quivered. It was slack and gray and belonged to a man much older than him.

"I know who was driving the car that night," he said.

"So go to the police," I said. "There's nothing I can do about it now, is there?"

"But you want to know, don't you? You've always wondered why it happened to you. Were they drunk? Was it an accident? Would you recognize them? Were they aware of what they'd done? Remember, I understand you, Imogen. There isn't a thought in your head that I don't know about."

"Tell me or don't tell me," I said. "I don't really care." I tried to sound casual, but it was true. I really didn't want to know.

He sucked in a sharp breath over his teeth. "You know I hate it when you lie to me. You're going to make me angry, Imogen. Don't do that."

The side of his little finger touched my leg. I could feel his icy skin through the denim. I flinched away from him, but he grabbed my thigh. His fingers dug into my flesh and I tensed as he leaned toward me.

"Where's Alistair?" he asked.

"I'll never tell you."

He put his arm around my shoulder and clamped me to him. He raised the knife to my face. I tried to lean away, but his hand pushed my head into his shoulder and brought the blade to my eye. I blinked and felt my eyelashes graze the sharp edge.

"Where's my son?" he asked.

"Where you won't find him."

He stood and pulled me up with him. He grabbed my hand, and with his hand clenched around my thumb he started to bend it back. I yelped with pain. There was no longer any point in pretending it didn't hurt. He was an expert in disabling people, in causing the maximum pain for the slightest of effort. I had police training to thank for that. My knees started to buckle as I bent away from the force.

He shoved me with such strength that I fell to the ground. I rolled as I hit the ground and spun away from him. I grabbed at a thin branch on the ground and brandished it in front of me. He laughed loudly, throwing his head back.

"Don't make me laugh," he said. "Never played rock, paper, scissors? Knife beats twig any day."

He put his head to one side like he was considering something. I noticed he was glancing behind me, over the horizon again.

"What are you looking at?" I asked.

He rolled his shoulders like he was releasing tension and smiled at me, ignoring the question.

"So, what now?" he asked. "You throw me to the dogs and then carry on with your life? Happily ever after? Do you think I don't know that you three witches are planning something? You're in cloud-cuckoo-land if you think I'm going to let that happen."

"I don't have any plans. I guess I'm just hoping that we both get what we deserve."

"You will," he said. I moved to my right and Phillip moved with me. We were facing off four feet away from each other. He could have the knife at my neck in seconds.

He was letting the knife drop slightly, his mind preoccupied. I adjusted my grip on the branch.

"Don't you have any regrets?" I asked.

"Oh, plenty. I shouldn't have married you. Should never have divorced Ruby. But otherwise can't say I'd do anything differently. You?"

"I don't know. I can't say I wish I hadn't met you. Because without you I wouldn't have Alistair. I feel like everything was necessary to lead us to this moment. Don't you? Even losing the baby. Everything. It was all . . . I guess it had to happen." I took a deep breath. "You know it was here that Iris died, don't you? That's why I come here."

"For God's sake, Imogen. She never existed."

"She did to me."

Phillip scratched the back of his head with the knife still in his hand. The wind played with the branches of the trees that lined the field. It ruffled my hair and blew the past away. Phillip wasn't someone to be feared; he was only a man. A weak, damaged, and empty man. I blinked and took a deep breath.

I no longer felt afraid. He had tracked me down to tell me about the accident because I didn't want to know. He hated that. It was

Phillip who was desperate, not me. He was impatient to regain control, for a vestige of the power he used to have over me. His weakness for control was making him reckless.

I stood straight and took a step closer to the hedge.

"You don't want to hurt me," I said.

"Don't I?"

"Phillip, you can still walk away from this. If you don't, you'll only make it worse for yourself."

I took another half step along the fence. He was looking away from me. Again, the horizon. Again, in the direction of our house. He turned to me suddenly.

"I hope you've enjoyed playing your little game, thinking that you had any authority over me, because you're nothing now. You're mine. You do what I say, when I say it."

Now his attention had flipped back to me. I could feel his anger start to build again. Specks of rain dotted my face and I wiped my hair out of my eyes. Phillip's grip tightened on the knife and his eyes grew hard. I took another couple of steps. Closer to him but also closer to the gap in the hedge. If I could get there without him stopping me . . .

"I was there," he said.

He held my gaze, a malevolent look on his face.

"Where?"

"I was there. *Here.*"

He gestured with his knife to the bench and my discarded bag. "I saw it all."

"I don't believe you," I said, without conviction, wondering what kind of reaction he was hoping to get from me.

"Yes, you do."

"Don't do this." I readjusted my grip on the tree branch and straightened up. The wind was gusting about us and throwing the rain like spears into my cheeks. Could he have seen Ruby mow me down and done nothing about it? . . . My mind was racing but getting nowhere.

"I left you at home."

"I followed you. In the car."

Phillip's sneer slipped from his face. He lowered the blade. It was me and him now. No games.

"What are you saying?"

"Haven't you worked it out yet? I was driving the car that hit you."

I didn't want to believe it was true. It was hard enough to contemplate Ruby driving the car, but to believe that my own husband could have been responsible was more than I could take.

"Don't," I muttered. "Just. Don't."

"All this time, Immie, and you never wondered? Never questioned why we'd got a different car by the time you came out of the hospital? Never wondered why no one had ever been caught? Come on. Not even you could be that blind. Could you? But then you've always been one to ignore the signs if they don't suit."

"Stop it." I wanted to shut his mouth for him in that moment. I never wanted to hear his voice again. The wind was loud in the trees. I concentrated on the rustling instead of Phillip's words.

"You'd stormed off . . ." Phillip said.

"No. No. Don't—" I clenched my free hand, causing my nails to dig into my palms. I didn't want to hear what he had to say.

"You were halfway along Long Eggington Road when I saw you. On your way to God knows where."

"The queue at the chip shop was too long. I was—God, no. I refuse to get into this with you, Phillip."

I took another step. I was level with him now. Next time he glanced away at the horizon I would make a run for it.

"Stop it, Phillip."

"Stop what? The truth? Your face, though," he said. "I thought you'd seen me. You seemed to look me straight in the eye as I hit you."

The wind died down. Cars were suddenly absent from the road. It could have been only me and Phillip in the world at that moment. Birds paused in their flight and gave up their morning call. His face showed no remorse. He pushed his free hand into his pocket. Casual. Like he hadn't been the person to shatter my life.

"But you . . . you were upset too," I said.

"Of course I was. I hadn't set out with the intention of running you down. It nearly broke my heart what you made me do."

Being let down by Phillip wasn't a new sensation for me, but this betrayal was spectacular. How could I have been so blind? He wasn't protecting Ruby; he was protecting himself. We had a new car by the time I came out of the hospital, and I had been stupid enough to think he was being considerate.

A car sped by and noise flooded back into the world again. A dozen birds scattered from the trees and flecked the sky. A distant siren wailed, low and long. I was very conscious of my own shallow breaths and the quickening of my heart. There was the familiar feeling of a vise around my head and the world narrowing around me.

I would not pass out.

I would not hide.

I stood as tall as it was possible and pushed back my shoulders.

"Is this a game to you?"

"Oh, it's a game all right. The endgame. It's the final card up my sleeve." He took a step toward me and I stood my ground. Let him come. He looked to the horizon again, smiling, and I launched myself at his face.

"You killed our baby!" I pulled back the branch, intending to hit him with it, but it was too long and unwieldy. Phillip grabbed it and wrenched it out of my hand.

I scratched at his eyes and he crossed his hands in front of his face, too busy protecting himself to use the knife. He pushed me away and staggered backward, losing balance and falling. The knife skittered along the grass and I ran to pick it up.

"You killed her!" I swiveled and kicked him in the stomach. Eight years of pain. Eight years that I could have had with our daughter and he'd taken it away from me. Every one of those years gave me a strength I didn't know I possessed. As Phillip bent over with the pain of the kick, I bent low and charged at him. My shoulder caught him on the chest as he began to straighten. His eyes flew wide as he launched through the air, his feet leaving the ground.

He grunted as he hit the dirt and squeezed his lips together like he had tasted something unpleasant.

"Her death was collateral damage. It was you I wanted to punish," he said.

I walked round in a circle, pulling at my hair. I couldn't believe it, and yet I could. I turned to look at him and doubled over, feeling that I might vomit, or scream, or both. My face was hot and I had spittle on my chin. I fell to all fours. The rain was falling heavier now and my clothes were sticking to me.

"Christ, Phillip. Why would you do that?"

"You wouldn't understand," he said quietly. "I'd had a bad day. Had to break it to some kids that their parents had died. You were full of 'baby' this and 'baby' that. I wanted to come home to a nice meal and a supportive wife. I needed you, and you just walked off into the night. When you took so long, I drove by the chip shop but you weren't there. I found you a mile away like you hadn't a care in the world."

I looked at the knife in my hand and then looked at his throat. Wondered about ending it for good. Ending *him.*

"You did this because you felt sorry for yourself? You're pathetic. Thank God I'm not like you," I said.

"More's the pity."

"No, Phillip. It would be so easy to hurt you right now, but I have a future ahead of me. I still have my son. I have friends. I have family. What the hell do you have? Nothing. *Nothing.* And it's all your own doing."

I struggled to get back to my feet. Phillip was sitting up with one arm across his stomach. His face was twisted in a snarl.

"You don't scare me, Phillip. You're a weak, useless man and you will die alone. You can't control anyone anymore. You have no power. All of your secrets are out. Everyone will know what you are like. Ruby and Naomi will be giving their statements right now. Mother has already spoken to one of your colleagues about your threats about my father."

"What threats?" He wheezed. "She jumped to the conclusion. I didn't put the thought in her mind."

"Was there even any truth to it?" I asked.

"Maybe. Maybe not. I can't vouch for what he was thinking when he took that girl." Phillip pushed himself into a crouching position, wincing at the pain.

"Couldn't find anything to link him with any other cases. He might've topped himself because of thoughts he was having, or because he couldn't stand being accused, or to get away from the constant bloody nagging. How the hell would I know? But your mother believed the worst of him. What does that tell you about *her*, eh?"

Phillip had caused so much hurt, but he would only affect me from now on if I let him.

"Your carefully built reputation is unraveling, Phillip. I'll try and keep Alistair from seeing the news, but when he's old enough to know the truth, it'll all be there for him to see. He'll know what kind of a man his dad really is."

I picked up my bag and slung it across my chest. I still had the knife in my hand. I felt liberated by the truth. No matter what he did to me now, he couldn't win. Phillip stood up slowly, eyes full of hate.

"And here's something else you should know," I said. "I forgive you."

"I don't want your forgiveness," he said with his eyes on the knife.

"I don't care. I forgive you because that's the kind of person *I* am. Not because of the person *you* are. I won't be someone who holds grudges, someone who lets the past hold her back. Not anymore."

Something in the air caused me to sniff. There was the unmistakable smell of smoke. The siren was louder and had changed pitch. Rolling black clouds were hanging low on the horizon in the distance. It was my house. And it was on fire.

"You haven't. For God's sake, Phillip! That's what you've been looking for? What do you think you've achieved?"

I drew my arm back with the knife in it and threw it as far as I could beyond the trees.

I gave him a slow clap. "Well done, you. You've managed to get rid of any evidence you were ever locked up in there. Saved me a job."

I raised my hand in resignation. "We're done."

I kept my eyes on him as I turned and moved quickly toward the gap in the hedge. I tripped over the rutted earth but somehow stayed upright. I fell into the bushes and felt sharp twigs tear the flesh on my hands in my haste to be away from him. There was a car coming, but I stumbled into the road before I registered its approach. Its horn blared at me as I reached the other side. Phillip was close on my heels. I could hear him grunting.

My mind was whirling. Looking wildly at the cars, I wondered about flagging one down, asking for help, but then it struck me that I didn't have to run anymore. There was nothing to run from. The sirens were getting louder. Called, no doubt, by a well-meaning neighbor to attend my burning house.

I turned to face Phillip. He was opposite me, watching the traffic, waiting for a gap. Standing just where I had been when he had mown me down that night eight years ago. The rain ceased abruptly like a tap had been turned off. Clouds skittered away, taking the drizzle elsewhere.

The early-morning school run had added to the steady stream of commuter cars moving by us at speed. Phillip was balanced on his front foot ready to dart through the traffic and chase me down. I watched him with an intensity that made him look back at me. He was panting from the exertion of his brief run. I had nothing to fear from this man.

I had done enough running. Across the road, Phillip straightened up and squared his shoulders. I could feel the push of the cars as the displaced air lifted my coat and my hair.

He looked at me and I felt the force of his hate like a solid iron bar. Neither of us moved and we barely blinked. I gently shook my head and gave a slow smile.

It's over.

I looked away. I didn't fear him. I began to walk and didn't turn when he called my name.

"Imogen! Don't you dare walk away from me. Look at me!" he shouted.

I walked in the direction of the house, where Tristan would pick me up to take me to the police station. I'd be safe there with the firemen and the kindly neighbors. I pushed my hands into my pockets like I didn't have a care in the world. And, for that split second, I didn't.

The screech of tires. The blare of horns. I faltered in my step and, despite myself, turned.

A car was turning sideways, another was mounting the curb closest to me. Phillip's face was suspended too far above the ground. A gust of wind pushed hair over my eyes and I swept it aside, stunned at the scene in front of me. The smell of burning rubber mixed with the smoke-heavy air. There was a pause, a vacuum where sound was lost and feelings couldn't travel. I was watching a macabre drama played out by a familiar actor. A contorted face overplaying his part.

I could see everything in that moment. The fire engine turning the air red and blue rounding the corner; the black four-by-fours and neighborhoods with family homes; the old white van with the faded lettering on its side, showing a dialing code no longer in use; the line of geese making a victory sign overhead. And Phillip.

He was hanging midair, limbs flung outward, comical almost. *Look at me,* he'd shouted.

And I did.

The sound of crushing metal and the thud of body on bumper refocused the act and everything sped up before me. Phillip was thrown up and backward. He dangled in the air for a long moment, his mouth gaping but his eyes clenched. His head snapped back and he fell from sight. Someone screamed.

I collapsed as he dropped, feeling our ties sever. My view of Phillip was blocked as cars swerved and crashed into one another in confusion and panic. The fire engine, which was pelting with purpose toward a fire that couldn't be stopped, began to brake too late. The car that had mounted the curb stopped inches from my face.

I crawled on my hands and knees, looking between wheels and running feet. The fire engine smacked into the back of a heavy vehicle and set the dominoes falling. I heard car after car shunt toward where I'd seen Phillip drop. I could see his legs. His left leg moved, bent, then straightened. And then the last domino, the old white van, was propelled forward by the momentum. It bumped over Phillip's torso.

His legs twitched.

Once.

Twice.

And then they were still.

Phillip Rochester turned to stone before my eyes. He was gone and I was free. I lay my cheek on the cold hard ground and rolled onto my back. In the sky above me, a rainbow bloomed. *Iris.*

I closed my eyes and let gravity claim me as its own.

CHAPTER 40

43 days after Phillip's funeral

I expect to cry, give way to the emotions I've kept bottled up for years, but as the curtains close around the silk-lined coffin, all I feel is lost. The strings have been cut. I'm no longer dancing to anyone else's tune.

Naomi squeezes my hand and I squeeze back. I know I'm being watched. I should dab at my eyes, sniff loudly, lower my head, but I've been looking at the floor for far too long. I'm done with apologizing for who I am. I sit up a little straighter on the pew and tuck my hair behind my ear.

It's a new vicar. A woman. Her eyes crinkle at the sides even when she isn't smiling. She nods at me. It's time to leave. Or go to pieces. I stand and hear a collective sigh behind me as everyone realizes I am going to keep my composure. Creaking chairs and bones tell me they are moving en masse in a somber, respectful procession at my back.

On one side of me, Naomi, and on the other, Rachel. I catch

Rachel's eye and she winks, then stands back to face the congregation, one arm outstretched as if she is my protector. I slip out the side door and look up to the sky. So blue, so fresh, already too warm to be wearing a black pantsuit.

There are floral tributes on the table despite me making it clear I'd rather people made donations to the Stroke Association. People like to be seen, judged, and declared good. Decent. All the while, wanting to be noticed. Saying they loved her most, knew her best, would be the ones to remember her fondest. They were welcome to that title. My flowers were simple, red and white. Not because she liked red, but because *I* did. The card said, simply, *Mother, We loved each other the only way we knew how. I wish we'd had more time to make it right. Imogen x*

After Phillip died, we tried to break down walls, build bridges, but we weren't architects and our foundations were weak at best. I had only just come to terms with the fact that Mother could never be who I wanted her to be, and by expecting more of her than she was able to give, I would always be disappointed. If she could love me for who I was, then surely I could love her for who she was too. We agreed that neither of us was perfect but we loved each other and that had to count for something.

There are people milling around the courtyard who I think I recognize. I knew so little about Mother's life, and she mine, that I don't know which are genuine friends and which have come for the free buffet at the Joiner's Arms. I nod and thank people for coming, agree that Mother would have been pleased at the turnout and, yes, it was lovely weather for it, wasn't it?

Bill is shaking hands and cracking jokes. He seems happy to have a day out. I get the impression that Mother's wasn't the only garden he tended.

Tristan is here somewhere. I saw him when I arrived. He looks handsome in his dark suit and thin black tie. Black looks good on him but, then, everything does. I spot him now by the entrance. He's been cornered by Aunt Margaret. He notices me looking and smiles at me in a way that makes my heart flutter. We'd agreed to take things slow, though I was wondering about quickening the pace.

The black car that had followed the hearse has gone. Naomi is on her mobile and signals to Rachel, who links her arm through mine and escorts me around the corner to where the sun is at its brightest.

"Won't they think it's rude if I leave so early?" I ask.

Rachel raises an eyebrow and reminds me, "You don't care what they think."

We walk up the narrow road and I step up onto the neatly mown grass as a yellow camper van swerves wildly around the corner. Gingham curtains sway as the van stops by our side.

"Sorry I'm late," says Ruby through the open window. "Alistair was in desperate need of ice cream."

Alistair leans over the back of the white leather-look seat and proudly holds his cone aloft. Old Tom makes a game attempt to lick his ice cream and Alistair laughs. All three of the dogs were reunited with Ruby not long after Phillip's death. The other two were found locally, but Old Tom walked his tired legs all the way back to Ruby's home in Brighton.

Alistair had lost two people he'd loved in the space of two months. I'd readied myself for the nightmares, the attachment issues, the neediness, but he'd taken it in his stride, astounding me with his resilience. I let him sleep in my bed—though that was more for me than for him—and I clung to him as if he was my anchor, when I should have been his.

I lean over and kiss his forehead.

"You okay, buster?"

He nods. "You look pretty, Mummy."

"Are we ready or what?" asks Naomi.

I take my jacket off and slide into the front of the van.

"She's a beauty, Roobs," I say, looking appreciatively around her recent purchase.

Naomi slides the side door open and gets in next to Alistair.

"You sure you don't want to come with us?" I ask Rachel.

"No offense, but some of us still aren't ready to let our leg hair grow and join a commune."

I laugh and so does Alistair, though he doesn't know what he's laughing at.

"We'll only be gone a week or so," I say.

"And I'll keep an eye on everything here. Besides, I've got a weekend away with Chris Miller."

"I didn't think you did relationships."

"I didn't think I did policemen either. Goes to show."

She pauses like she's weighing up whether she should say what's on her mind. This is so out of character that I feel the fingertip of fear on my spine.

"What is it?"

"Just . . . enjoy yourselves, yeah? But . . . but not too much. I want you to come back. And if you find your dream location or whatever for this wine bar of yours—"

"I never said I was looking for a wine bar."

"You can thank me for the idea later. Anyway, make sure there's enough room for me 'cause you don't get rid of me that easily, you know?"

"I know."

I smile.

We hug awkwardly through the open window.

"I'll call you," I say.

"I'll probably be too busy to answer, but sure, whatever makes you feel better."

We drive away and I watch Rachel return to the dark puddle of mourners. Behind me, I hear Naomi unzip a bag.

"I got you a gift," she says.

She hands me a heavy blue cylinder.

"What's this?"

"Wrong question, duck. You should be asking *who* is this?"

"No, it isn't. Is it? What's he doing here?"

"I'm sick of him being under my kitchen sink. Gives me the heebie-jeebies thinking of 'im lurkin' in my kitchen."

I glance at Alistair, who's engrossed in his iPad. Building blocks in alternate worlds. A universe away.

"What do you plan on doing with . . . *it*?"

"Thought we could dump it somewhere," Naomi says.

"Where? I don't know. I feel odd about it. Like perhaps we should wait?"

"You know, darlings," says Ruby, "you can put ashes in fireworks or make them into jewelry, or even tattoos?"

"Why on earth would we want to . . ." I begin, but my voice trails off as I look at the urn. I lift him up and he's heavier than I expected.

The coroner ruled the whole episode as accidental death, even though the driver of the car said there was no doubt in his mind that Phillip had stepped into the road on purpose. Witnesses said they'd been begging the council for years to do something about that stretch of road. In fact, they wouldn't be surprised if he'd tripped over the wobbly curbstone that hadn't been replaced since that accident where a woman lost her baby. Such a shame. One minute you're out for a nice morning walk and the next . . . *Bam!*

"The important thing," says Ruby, "is not to get too hung up on it. We should respectfully dispose of his remains. Not for *his* sake, but for ours."

"Yeah, but there's no reason why we can't have a bit of fun doing it, though, eh?" says Naomi. "I don't want to do it on me own. I'm not being funny or anything, but it's something we should do together, symbolic like. You know, he brought us together. Us being, well, *friends*—he'd hate it. But, you know, I sort of like it. It's the closest thing I've ever had to a family. Talking of which—" She pauses and takes a deep breath. "I'm meeting Helen when we get back."

"Oh, darling," says Ruby, craning to look in the rearview mirror at Naomi. "That's wonderful news."

"Yeah," Naomi continues, "she sounded lovely on the phone. A bit dippy but, you know, nice. I don't know what to call her, though. Do I call her Mum? I mean, it's not like she's been a mother to me, but it don't seem right calling her Helen neither."

"Why don't you decide when you meet her?" I say. "You could ask her how she feels about it. God, Nay, I'm so excited for you."

I settle back into the seat, carefully cradling the urn, scared I'll spill some of Phillip on the pristine interior of Ruby's new camper van.

I put my hand upon Ruby's on the gear stick.

"Thanks for this. I think that we might live to regret going on a road trip together, but still . . ."

"I bet you we'll get on like a house on fire," Naomi says.

There's silence for a moment as the three of us are brought to mind of being locked in a burning house. I can feel the heat prickle the hairs on my arms and my breath catches in my chest, but it's only the heat of the sun. I start to laugh. Quietly at first; then Naomi and then Ruby join in with such vigor that Ruby has to pull the van over to the side of the road.

Ruby wipes the tears from her eyes, but they keep coming with every laugh. Just the sight of her makes me double up and struggle to regain composure. A bird lands on the lip of the plastic waste bin by my open window and appears to look at us quizzically. Three madwomen.

"How the hell are we still sane?" I ask.

"We're not," Naomi says. "But, sane or not, we're stronger for it. We know what we're capable of, and, more than ever, we know what we want. Am I right?"

I nod yes, and Ruby puts the van in first gear. We cheer as she flicks on the indicator.

"Wait," I say.

I look at the urn. I lift it up.

"What *is* this?" I ask.

"You know who it is," says Naomi.

"Not who. *What.* It isn't him anymore, and yet he's still a burden. A heavy weight, both physically and metaphorically, taking up room in our minds as we wonder what to do with him. This feels momentous. Like I'm starting again, reborn. I know that sounds cheesy but . . . there's no one telling me I can't do what I want, that I'm no good. I don't want to start this new chapter with . . . *this* thing still in it. Would you mind if . . . ?"

I glance at the bin. Ruby puts her hand on my arm and gently squeezes.

"It's fine by me, darling. Naomi?"

"You know me—I'd've chucked him in the bin yonks ago."

"So I should . . ."

"Do it," says Naomi.

"Go on," says Ruby.

I look down at my hand. Though I've lost enough weight to take it off, the thin wedding band is still there. It gives the illusion of having separated my finger from my hand. A part of my body that still belongs to Phillip Rochester. I slip it off with ease and roll it between my thumb and forefinger. It weighs almost nothing. Inconsequential. And I wonder why I've attached such significance to it all these years. In an instant I throw the ring and the urn into the bin. At the dull thud, flies take to the air, disturbed from their heat-induced stupor.

I raise my right hand by Ruby's side. Both Ruby and Naomi grasp it and cheer. I look at them. These newfound friends who know me better than I know myself, who are each a part of me and I a part of them. Brought together in hardship but with nothing but respect for each other. I know that we will be friends for life.

Naomi lets go of my hand and throws both arms around me from behind.

"Can we get out of here before I start sobbing?" she says. And again we laugh as Ruby presses the accelerator and we leave the past behind us in a cloud of dust.

ACKNOWLEDGMENTS

I must begin by thanking my agent, Imogen Pelham at Marjacq Scripts. She believed in me when I didn't dare to believe in myself. I had no idea how many people would be involved in bringing my debut to life, so I'd like to extend a huge thank-you to everyone at my publishers. Special thanks to Danielle Perez at Berkley, for taking the women of *The Exes' Revenge* to her heart and making their voices heard, and to Jade Chandler at Harvill Secker, whose patience and insight I'll be forever grateful for.

I have such gratitude for Curtis Brown Creative. Especially my course tutor, Lisa O'Donnell, and my talented course-mates Jane, Anjana, Andrew, Steven, Yvonne, Osman, Amanda, Johan, Cate, Deborah, Helen, Phil, Nik, and David, whose critique and encouragement has been invaluable. The next round is on me.

York Festival of Writing gave me a life-changing opportunity when they shortlisted me for Friday Night Live, and I can't thank them enough. It also led me to the women who would become my writing group: Roz Watkins, Fran Dorricott, Sophie Snell, and Louise Trevatt. They are a talented bunch of writers I'm proud to call friends.

The Derby Book Festival and, in particular, Jenny, Sian, Liz, and Theresa deserve a special mention. It has been an honor to be involved in the festival since its inception in 2015. Their continuing support means the world to me.

Thanks also to Alex Davis, the first person not related to me to read the full manuscript. He gave me support, guidance, and encouragement, which I treasure.

Thank you to my friends, too many to mention by name, who have encouraged me to write for many years before this book was even an idea. I am indebted to each and every one of those who played a part in keeping me sane, whether offering critique of my work, making me laugh, or topping up my wineglass when empty. I couldn't have done this without them.

Finally, and most enthusiastically, I have to give thanks to my family and acknowledge the part they played in breathing life into this book. My sons, Alex and Danny, are my greatest cheerleaders and never complain when I shut myself away to work. They are possibly more excited than I at the prospect of this book being read by complete strangers, and I love them without end. My mum, Julie, provided food and child care in times of desperation and has never knowingly passed up an opportunity to tell people about this book!

And last, my husband, James. He deserves a page all to himself. His unwavering support, when I considered giving up writing altogether, is the only reason this book exists. In a world blighted by Phillips, he is my knight in shining armor.